VIRAGO
MODERN CLASSICS
618

Mary Renault

Mary Renault (1905–1983) was best known for her historical novels set in Ancient Greece with their vivid fictional portrayals of Theseus, Socrates, Plato and Alexander the Great.

Born in London in 1905 and educated at the University of Oxford, she trained as a nurse at Oxford's Radcliffe Infirmary where she met her lifelong partner, fellow nurse Julie Mullard. Her first novel, *Purposes of Love*, was published in 1939. In 1948, after her novel *Return to Night* won an MGM prize worth £150,000, she and Mullard emigrated to South Africa.

It was in South Africa that Renault was able to write forthrightly about homosexual relationships for the first time – in her last contemporary novel, *The Charioteer*, published in 1953, and then in her first historical novel, *The Last of the Wine* (1956), the story of two young Athenians who study under Socrates and fight against Sparta. Both these books had male protagonists, as did all her later works that included homosexual themes. Her sympathetic treatment of love between   hip.

RETURN
TO NIGHT

Mary Renault

virago

To R.R.W.

VIRAGO

This edition published by Virago Press in 2014
First published in Great Britain by Longmans in 1947

Copyright © Mary Renault 1947
Introduction copyright © Sarah Dunant 2014

Lines from Walter de la Mare's 'The Journey' from *The Listeners*, published by
Messrs Constable & Co reproduced by kind permission of the Literary Trustees of
Walter de la Mare and The Society of Authors as their representative.

A CIP catalogue record for this book
is available from the British Library.

ISBN 978-1-84408-953-6

Typeset in Goudy by M Rules
Printed and bound in Great Britain by
Clays Ltd, St Ives plc

Papers used by Virago are from well-managed forests
and other responsible sources.

MIX
Paper from
responsible sources
FSC® C104740

Virago Press
An imprint of
Little, Brown Book Group
100 Victoria Embankment
London EC4Y 0DY

An Hachette UK Company
www.hachette.co.uk

www.virago.co.uk

INTRODUCTION

At a white-tiled table a young girl was sitting, sucking a bullseye and sewing a shroud ... She was nineteen, pretty, undersized and Welsh; hideously dressed in striped cotton, a square-bibbed apron that reached her high collar, black shoes and stockings and a stiff white cap.

... the child who presently would wear the shroud was lying with a pinched, waxy face, breathing jerkily through a half-open mouth. An apparatus of glass and rubber tubing was running salt and water into her veins to eke out the exhausted blood. It was all that could now be done ... The little nurse stitched doggedly away ... She had made plenty of shrouds; the first few had made her feel creepy, but they were just like the rest of the mending and darning now.

Mary Renault was in her early thirties when her first novel, *Purposes of Love*, was published. That quiet but dramatic opening was also a mischievous one. Neither the young nurse nor the child would make it past page two. Instead, the story is thrown down a staircase, along with a heap of soiled laundry, into the hands of Vivian, a trainee nurse, whose experience both of hospital life and an intense relationship with Mic, an assistant pathologist, make up the core of the book. So far, so hospital romance conventional. But it isn't long before a fellow female nurse seduces Vivian and we discover that Mic has had an affair with her brother. By anyone's lights, such a book, coming out in 1939, marked the arrival of a bold new voice.

For those who, like me, grew up gorging themselves on Mary Renault's historical stories of ancient Greece, it may come as a surprise that for the first twenty years of her career she wrote only contemporary novels. For others more attuned to the homosexual subculture that the Greek novels explored, or having read *The Charioteer*, published in the 1950s, it will be less a revelation to learn that even as a fledging popular novelist she was interested in issues of sexuality and sexual orientation, writing with a directness that made some people, including an early reviewer of *Purposes of Love*, wonder if the author's name might be a mask for a man.

In fact, Mary Renault *was* a pseudonym, but not one designed to protect her gender. She was born Eileen Mary Challans, the first daughter of a middle-class doctor, in 1905 in London's East End. Her early memories show an intelligent, strong-willed child with an independent streak, no doubt exacerbated by her ringside seat on an unhappy marriage. 'I can never remember a time ... when they seemed to me to even like each other,' she wrote later in life to a friend. Though her fiction often takes the knife to frustrated, resentful mothers – both classical and contemporary – she could also be understanding. In her third novel, *The Friendly Young Ladies* (the euphemistic title refers to two women in a sexual relationship), she dramatises elements of her own childhood, but not without sympathy for the wife who, though she is intrusive and manipulative, is also clearly unloved.

Mary's escape from her parents came through education: at

the insistence of her university-educated godmother, Aunt Bertha, she was sent to boarding school in Bristol and then went on to St Hugh's College, Oxford, subsidised by her aunt, as her parents considered the expense wasted on a daughter. An early love for history and literature would colour her whole life, allowing her later to meet the challenge of immersion in Greek history. She became involved in theatre, another passion that was to persist, but in other ways Oxford University in the 1920s was a conservative establishment, especially for the few women who went there, and there was no hint from her friendships with both men and women of the more radical way her life was to develop.

Her first attempt at serious writing came in 1928, when, during her last term at Oxford, she began work on a novel set in medieval England. J. R. R. Tolkien was perhaps an influence, as Mary had attended his lectures and clearly admired him. She was later to destroy the manuscript, dismissing the story as 'knights bashing about in some never-never land', but she was still working on it at twenty-eight when, looking for a way to support herself independently from her parents, she started to train as a nurse at the Radcliffe Infirmary.

It was to be another defining experience. Nursing was extremely hard work, but it offered the burgeoning writer a richness of experience that would have been well nigh impossible for a woman of her class elsewhere at that time. While others were marrying and starting families, she was deep in the business of life and death, meeting people from all backgrounds. It also gave her first-hand knowledge of the human body, both in its wonder and its fragility. All her fiction would drink deeply from these experiences. When she turns her hand to Greek myth and history she will confidently inhabit its overwhelming masculinity, celebrating athletic, erotic male beauty side by side with the heroism and agonies of battles and death. Meanwhile, the dramas of medicine and illness would permeate all her early novels.

Purposes of Love, not surprisingly, draws heavily on the training she has just come through; even the novel's title is taken from the prayer that the nurses recited every morning. Peopled by a beautifully observed cast of minor characters ('Sister Verdun was a little fretted woman with an anxious bun, entering with a sense of grievance into middle age'), it plunges the reader into the gruelling physicality of hospital life, contrasting the drama of sickness and injury with relentless rules and routine. Near the end of the book we sit with a nurse in night vigil over the mangled body of a dying, but conscious, young man. The scene is rich with the authenticity of detail, but it is clever as well as upsetting, since we know the man much better than the nurse does, which makes her mix of professional care and natural compassion even more affecting. The novel was an impressive debut, and became a bestseller, attracting fine reviews both sides of the Atlantic.

Kind are Her Answers was published the following year. Mary was under considerable pressure to write it quickly, as both publishers, especially Morrow in America, wanted it delivered before the outbreak of hostilities. In the end, it came out the week of the evacuation of Dunkirk, in 1940, which meant that it was largely critically ignored. Perhaps for Renault's long-term reputation that was no bad thing as *Kind are Her Answers* is a much more conventional love story. It has its moments, though. Kit Anderson is a doctor locked in an unhappy marriage, who meets the woman with whom he will have an affair on a night visit to her seriously ill aunt. For a modern audience, the sexual passion is the most convincing part of the story. Their hungry young bodies make a painful contrast with the old woman's ageing, fading one and the adrenaline of risk and proximity of death adds to their abandon; during his unofficial night visits they must keep their voices down when they make love in case they are heard.

Return to Night (1947), which won Mary the MGM prize, a whopping £150,000, is a doctor–patient romance, though it cunningly inverts the stereotype by putting a woman, Hilary, in the white coat. The book opens with a riding accident and the time-bomb of internal bleeding inside the brain, which Hilary must diagnose in order to save a handsome young man's life. Renault had done a stint working on head injuries and the drama of the diagnosis and the tussle of wills between the complacent matron and the woman doctor is expertly played out.

In her fifth novel *North Face* (1949) nursing becomes character rather than plot. Inside a love story between two guests in a Yorkshire boarding house after the war, Renault uses two women in their thirties as a kind of spatting Greek chorus, ruminating on the morality (or not) of the affair. Already very much professional spinsters, one is a desiccated prissy academic, while the other is a blowzy, more down-to-earth professional nurse. Though the satire is at the expense of them both (at times they are more entertaining than the rather laboured love story), the nurse at least feels in touch with life. If Mary Renault had ever considered academia, this is surely her verdict on the choice she made.

But nursing did more than fire her fiction. It also changed her life. It was while training at the Radcliffe, living inside a set of rules to rival the most oppressive girls' boarding school, that Mary met twenty-two-year-old Julie Mullard. The coming together of their fictional equivalents after an evening tea party in one of the nurse's rooms is one of many perfectly realised scenes in *Purposes of Love*. Mary Renault and Julie Mullard were to be a couple until Mary's death. In England they mostly lived apart, often working in different hospitals, snatching precious weeks in holiday cottages or visiting each other under the radar of the rules. Then, in 1948, helped by the money Mary had won for *Return to Night*, they moved to South Africa.

Despite the fact that they would live openly and happily together for the next thirty-five years, neither would refer to herself as lesbian, nor talk publicly about their relationship (though elements of it are there to be read in Mary's fiction: the character of Vivian is clearly a mix of both of them, even down to the dramatisation of the short affair that Julie had with a hospital surgeon soon after they met). Some of their reticence can be explained by Renault's own personality: private and contained, with success she became more so. Some of it was no doubt a throwback to the difficult moral climate in which they began their relationship; the only contemporary public example of lesbian culture had been Radclyffe Hall's provocative *Well of Loneliness* and both of them found it 'self-pitying'. But it was more nuanced than that.

In 1982, a year before her death, Renault was the subject of a BBC film directed by the late writer and poet David Sweetman, who later went on to write a biography of her. I was a good friend of David's at the time and, like many gay men I knew, he was eloquent about the place Renault's novels had played in his life. When he asked her about the sexuality in her work, she had this to say: 'I think a lot of people are intermediately sexed. It's like something shading from white to black with a lot of grey in the middle.'

The words describe perfectly much of the shifting sexual territory Renault fictionalised in her first five novels. For the sharp-eyed, *The Friendly Young Ladies*, published in 1944, is a portrait of a sexual relationship between Leo(nora), writer of

x

cowboy novels – Mary herself loved cowboy fiction – and Helen, a lovely and talented nurse who has the odd dalliance with men. We meet them first through the eyes of Leo's young sister, who runs away from home to stay with them. Suffused with Mills & Boon sensibility, she sees only what she wants to see; Leo's tomboy manner and clothes, the shared bedroom and the domestic familiarity are all taken at platonic face value. A young doctor, full of his own psychological insights, is equally blinkered, trying his hand with both women (and being turned down more because of his personality than his gender). It makes for playful story-telling as it divides not only Renault's characters, but presumably also her readership. In the end, this cosy set-up is broken apart by the rugged American writer Joe, who has a night of passion with Leo that results in what feels like a conventional but unconvincing happy ending.

Interestingly, in 1982, when, on the recommendation of Angela Carter, Virago reissued the novel, Mary herself wanted to alter the ending. In a letter to the publisher, written barely a year before her death, she said: 'You will see I have marked a cut of several pages near the end, and will I am sure agree that this was a thoroughly mushy conclusion ... far better leave Leo's choice in the air with the presumption that she stays with Helen. The ending I gave it looks now like a bow to convention, which it wasn't, but it was certainly an error of judgement.' A compromise was reached, and instead of changing the text she wrote a new afterword, which is reproduced again now.

The same criticism of an imposed happy ending might also be levelled against *Return to Night*, where the heroine doctor falls in love with Julian, the young male patient she saves. Breathtakingly beautiful, emotionally quixotic and under the thumb of a domineering mother, Julian yearns to be an actor and a halo of sexual ambivalence hovers over him throughout the novel.

Hilary meanwhile, eleven years older, in a man's job with what could be a man's name, finds herself cast as half lover, half mother. As they head towards the happily-ever-after of marriage you can't help thinking that they would both benefit from more wriggle-room to experiment.

Mary Renault was eventually to find that wider sexual and imaginative freedom in her Greek novels, but not before one last, extraordinary, contemporary book. Freed from the grey British skies of post-war austerity and culture, in 1951 she wrote *The Charioteer*, an explicit portrait of homosexuality during the war. Its rich backdrop is drawn from her experience nursing soldiers in a hospital partly staffed by conscientious objectors, and it tells the story of Laurie, an intelligent, introspective young man, who comes to understand his sexuality through a platonic but profound encounter with Ralph, an older prefect at his public school. Injured at Dunkirk, he goes on day release from hospital and is introduced into a homosexual subculture, in which Ralph, now a naval officer, is a player. The hot-house atmosphere of this hidden society is brilliantly, though not always flatteringly, observed (Renault had had experience of such a world in her early years in South Africa).

Laurie's continued self-analysis and his struggle as to how to live as a gay man, dramatised as a choice between his love for Ralph, who he learns had saved him at Dunkirk, and the growing connection with a young conscientious objector working at the hospital and yet to realise his own homosexuality, make up the rest of the book.

Reading *The Charioteer* now is to be blown away by its intensity and bravery. In 1953, when it came out in Britain, it was a cultural thunderbolt (in America it took another six years to find a publisher); reviews were overwhelmingly positive and Mary received scores of letters from appreciative readers. By then, though, she had moved on and was submerged in two years of research for her next book, which was to be something altogether different.

From the opening sentence of the *The Last of the Wine* (1956), ancient Greece and the male voices through which she enters it burn off the page with an immediacy and power that will characterise all her historical fiction. Homosexual love, sacrifice, companionship and heroism abound in a culture which accepts, encourages and celebrates sexual diversity. At nearly fifty, Mary Renault had at last found her world.

Sarah Dunant, 2014

Morn like a thousand shining spears
Terrible in the East appears.
O hide me, leaves of lovely gloom,
Where the young Dreams like lilies bloom!

What is this music that I lose
Now, in a world of fading clues?
What wonders from beyond the sea
And wild Arabian fragrances?

In vain I turn me back to where
Stars made a palace of the air.
In vain I hide my face away
From the too bright invading Day.

That which is come requires of me
My utter truth and mystery.
Return, you dreams, return to Night:
My lover is the armèd Light.

LAURENCE BINYON

I

The cocks were crowing in the cool glassy darkness before the dawn. Their cry, thinned by long silent distances, crept faintly through the early chill; ghostly, menacing, full of danger and of promise. From its grey tower half-way up the hill-side, the clock of a village church struck five.

Hilary pulled off her white coat, saw that it was splashed with blood, and tossed it into a corner of the floor. On second thoughts, she stirred it with her foot till the bloodstain came uppermost. This, she hoped, might indicate to someone that she did not want to see it again on her next call.

The little changing-room had a high Gothic window, almost filling one of the walls, for the place had been adapted from one of the huge impracticable rectories of the 1860s. Hilary flung up the sash and leaned out into the soft cold Cotswold air. It smelt of dewy grass, of arbutus, and of pine. The heaviness of interrupted sleep had been cleared from her brain by concentration, urgency, and a strong cup of the night sister's tea. She continued, for a few moments, to think about the lacerated arm she had just been suturing, and to speculate on its chances of getting back full mobility; then tossed it all away, like the white coat, into a dim background consciousness of a sound job done. The hills were growing black against the eastern skyline. Birds began to chitter, and then, on a note of happy and hesitant surprise, to sing.

Below her the garden, which the Cottage Hospital's lack of funds had preserved unspoiled in a tangled peace, sloped away downhill, bushes and trees emerging in faint intimations of shape from the thinning night. Under the window where Hilary stood, another window, lit more brightly, sent a pale yellow pathway streaming across the grass of the half-tended lawn. It belonged to the duty-room, where, in the last of the lull before the scramble of the morning work began, the night nurses were drowsing over their tea. Carried by the silence, their low voices threw upward, now and again, an audible word or phrase.

'... in Dr Dent's time ... bit sharp sometimes, but ever such fun. ... Well, in a way ... have to get used to it. But *you* know ... seems dead-alive somehow ... Now you *know* what I mean, don't be ... always get that with women doctors ... no, I know they can't, but ...'

Hilary pulled in her head from the window and unhooked, mechanically, her tweed driving-coat from behind the door. She shrugged into it and stood still for a minute, her well-kept sensible hands pushed into her deep pockets, standing back a little in her crêpe-soled shoes. The shoes, her suit and overcoat, had the casual rightness which age stamps upon good clothes; her face, with its unstressed breeding, impatience, and humour, had a kind of allied quality, which promised to become more marked before so very long. She was thirty-four, and, because she had set out in a hurry and without regard for appearances, looked a few years older.

The voices sank to a sleepy blur, and died away in a yawn.

Hilary smiled to herself, and got out her cigarette-case and lighter. She became conscious of the slight hollowness and sinking which nicotine induces when combined with fatigue and an empty stomach, but continued, obstinately, to smoke and to smile. She recalled to mind, for supplement, a few broad jokes with which she and her fellow students, confident in their numbers, their enthusiasm, and their youth, had decorated this familiar theme. But the jokes needed someone to cap them; or perhaps it was the wrong hour of the morning.

Even here, she thought. For the last thirty years, to my certain knowledge, and since the place was opened to the best of my belief, the casualty work here has been done by crusted, dyed-in-the-wool GPs. When they get a middling good general surgeon you might imagine that someone, one solitary human soul, would remark on some kind of impalpable difference. Well, what did I expect? She remembered at this point another hospital story, a simple but unprintable classic about a woman surgeon and a saw. Even in solitude and at five in the morning it made her grin faintly. She shut the window, and went downstairs in search of her car.

She found it without the help of her torch, for the darkness had yielded to a grey glimmering twilight. A small, keen wind was stirring; she felt cold, and thought with dejection of the two hours, an interval too short for sleep, but far too long before breakfast, which stretched ahead. She lived in two rooms of a house which, though friendly, was not her own, and had the usual female taboo against invading someone else's kitchen even in time of need. Reflecting that such occasional inconveniences were more than balanced by daily comfort and freedom from domestic fuss, she was about to push in the starting-button when she noticed a foreign object on the seat. It turned out to be a thermos flask in a canvas bag. She uncorked it; the

3

incense of good, strong coffee rose from the narrow neck like a benevolent djinn.

Hilary drank it, slowly and luxuriously. Her estimate of human nature, and more particularly of her own sex, went up as the coffee went down. However many nights, she wondered, has Mrs Clare been doing this, and quietly removing it in the morning? My last night-call was a week ago. After all, I'm only a glorified lodger. The telephone probably disturbs her, too.

There was a thick rug in the back of the car. Deciding that she might as well wait, now, till there was light enough to drive by, she wrapped it round herself and curled up comfortably, sideways on the seat. The outer and the inner warmth made her body drowsy, while the action of the coffee kept her thoughts stirring. It would be pleasant, she thought, to watch the dawn come up over the valley; a very good reason for staying out here instead of sitting in an arm-chair in the night sister's office, by a warm fire. Quite good enough. She recalled the politeness of the night sister, the politeness of other night sisters in her house-surgeon days; the cups of coffee (always with saucers); the conversation, so well-intentioned, only so very slightly strained; the sudden warming and loosening of the atmosphere when one of the men strolled in to dawdle after a late party or an emergency call. All these things she had accepted impersonally, having no wish to expend useful energy in battle with biological or social laws, or with the tradition of centuries. She had, perhaps, dismissed them with too much haste, like dust swept into a corner or under the edge of a carpet, which any disturbance of the room stirs up again. Since she had broken with David they had become irritatingly noticeable.

Angrily she twitched at her mind, to disengage it from the too-smooth channel into which it still slipped so easily; but this morning it all seemed distant and unreal and hardly worth an effort, so after all she let it run.

She had met him three months after her finals, when she had still scarcely got over her pleasure and self-satisfaction at having been offered a house-appointment in her own hospital, the only woman kept on. David, who had qualified elsewhere only six months before her, had arrived trailing some kind of hearsay reputation for promise, which he lost no time in confirming. It had flattered her when he sought her advice, in preference to anyone else's, about local etiquette and procedure and the fads of the more difficult powers, such as the housemen's butler, the matron, and the registrar. (Now, in drowsy and indifferent retrospect, she reflected that he must of course have counted on this reaction, and at the same time gained among the men a reputation for natural acumen, thus killing two birds with one stone.) Having found his feet, he had been less in evidence for a while; but later on there had been an outstandingly good leaving-party, at which his approach had suddenly become much more personal. Within a few more weeks they were lovers.

The affair had gone on for more than a year. They had had nearly everything – community of interest, physical compatibility, good spirits, and the same jokes. The compound of affection and zest which these elements produced they had accepted – for they prided themselves on being realists – as an intelligent manifestation of love. Through the accident of their circumstances, the streak of emulation in them had seemed as natural as all the rest; they did not examine its quality in themselves, or in one another, or recognise the implication of David's careless confidence in his own erratic brilliance, Hilary's dogged determination to succeed in a field where successful women were challengingly few. Their enjoyment of life, and Hilary's reserve, made them serious only in abstract discussion, flippant in speaking of their own ambitions, and apt to take conversational colour from one another.

Their work happened never to overlap. Hilary was house-surgeon on the neuro-surgical firm, which was thought to be an enviable chance; David proceeded from paediatrics to gynaecology with conscientious efficiency and a boredom which he concealed perfectly from his successive chiefs. Looking back with the fairness of perspective she found herself admitting that the knowledge of being half a step ahead of him had added something to her fondness on more occasions than one.

It had been Sanderson, the neuro-surgeon, who had told her, before it got about, that Ossian Bradford would soon be looking for a new second assistant. It was the best appointment in the hospital which anyone without a Fellowship could hope to expect; Bradford was a chest surgeon, a bold and successful innovator, who would undoubtedly lead his branch in a few years, and to have worked with him was already something of a hall-mark. Sanderson was his personal friend. Hilary knew that he had liked her work; and the significance with which he had spoken had conveyed something stronger than a hint.

She said nothing about it to anyone: partly because she wanted to surprise David, partly from a superstition that premature brag would spoil her luck, partly because it meant too much. Another reason, and the strongest, she had not recognised; she could not tolerate the thought of admitting to him that she had tried for it and failed. Theirs was the kind of relationship in which people pride themselves on a certain toughness; and, because for her it was also the first, she had never asked herself whether she was following her own instincts or David's lead. It could scarcely be said of him that he had a horror of sentimentality; he regarded it rather as a

6

remote kind of mental slum, of which one had vaguely heard, as a dweller in Mayfair might hear of West Ham. Her training and surroundings had made her ready to accept these values without a struggle, and without asking herself whether her definition of sentimentality was becoming more wholesale than her temperament had meant it to be.

It was just a month later that David strolled into her room and said, 'Hallo, poppet. Did I once hear you say you'd bought Ossie's book?'

'Yes,' said Hilary. She picked it up from the table – she had spent all her spare time on it for weeks – and shook out her notes from between its pages. 'What do you want to look up?'

David helped himself to a cigarette.

'What I really want to do, if you can spare it for a couple of days, is to read the darn thing. He's just offered me Creighton's job, so I feel it may be expected.' He bent his stooping aquiline head over the pages; he had the knack of reading, not line by line, but in blocks and paragraphs at a time. 'If you're using it for anything,' he added, 'I dare say I could run over it to-night.'

Hilary said quite naturally, 'Keep it as long as you like, I've done with it. Nice work, David.' Realisation filtered in gradually, and was not complete till she had finished speaking. 'Very nice work.'

'Hard work,' said David, 'is what it looks too much like to me. However, like breaking the ice on the Serpentine, it's a thing to have done, I suppose.' She knew he was not posing; if this had not fallen at his feet he would have been sure of its equivalent elsewhere.

Peering at a diagram he went on indifferently, 'I hope a couple of years will about see me shot of surgery, and getting on with something. A century from now, of course, surgeons will be almost period survivals. All this glamour surrounding the theatre is just a temporary breakdown in proportion. Atavistic, really. The physician, the biologist, and the chemist will be where they always belonged, and tucked away somewhere in decent obscurity, like the mortuary, will be a sordid little hole, still known by courtesy as the theatre, in which a seedy breakdown gang will slice up the few failures in the minimum of publicity. "Old So-and-so's getting past it. Don't say I told you, but two of his cases have gone to the theatre in less than six months." That's how it will be ... What's the name of that Swede who does the fancy pneumonectomies, doesn't seem to be here.'

'I can't remember,' said Hilary. She had little concentration to spare from the sudden, inescapable knowledge that she had never loved him; that, at the moment, to keep from hating him was exacting from her her last reserves of decency and control.

She would have done better to have kept this intimation in sight; but, imperfectly knowing herself (she had always been busy) she had dismissed it with shame as the temporary effect of disappointment and shock. So the internal pressure had risen without vent; and the decisive quarrel, when it came, had sprung from a trifle, a bathetic business about some slides which neither had remembered to put away and which had, in consequence, been broken; a squalid bickering, not leaving even the satisfaction of a large gesture behind.

'It's typical of a man,' Hilary had brought forth, to her own shocked surprise, from the boiling within her, 'to crash through to every objective by plain selfishness, and take for granted it's just superior ability.'

David had learned early the art of keeping his temper, not out of charity, but because he had recognised its usefulness. He looked at her with his eyebrows raised, paused for effect, and spoke. 'I'm sorry,' he said. 'I always supposed you were competent to hold your own as a human entity, without having resort to the squalling apologetics of feminism. You make me feel rather at a loss.'

It had been as if a nerve in her had been touched with something red-hot. The rest of the conversation had not signified. From that moment they were finished.

They had avoided a crisis on major issues; both would have felt it to be embarrassing and melodramatic. They had behaved with restraint and with what had seemed, at the time, to be economy of emotion. Their friends had no opening for gossip, only for occasional surmise. It had never become impossible to invite both of them to the same party. If they met in the group at the head of the main corridor, where the housemen loitered at ten o'clock waiting to pick up their chiefs, they had spread no awkwardness around them. Hilary had approved of this, as she had believed she approved of their undemonstrativeness while they were still together. She was not analytical of herself. There had never been much time.

Her intellect and abilities were another thing. These she had studied with the attention she gave to other tools of her calling. She examined her failure, and drew, impartially, as she believed, the unpalatable conclusions. Determination, industry, good organisation of a good second-class brain, had done their best for her. She was now at the level where they had to be set against the male powers of intellectual and imaginative endurance, the male reserve of stamina for a mental sprint; and she recognised the difference, fully, for the first time. It shocked her with a sense of fundamental injustice. Her relationship with David, which might have resolved everything, had lacked the single essential ingredient; but she did not reflect on this. She merely left the hospital.

In a kind of spite against herself and life, she had thrown herself away on this country practice in a small Cotswold market town. It carried a fair-sized panel, a sprinkling of private patients in the neighbourhood, and, one week in a rota of three, emergencies at the Cottage Hospital. By the time she had been there three months, she found herself counting the days to the third week, which sometimes passed without any emergency at all. The cut tendon had been the most interesting event since her arrival.

Her body muffled in the thick plaid rug, her brain spinning these thoughts into a confused web, she drowsed with half-closed eyes till a thrush, made unconcerned by her long stillness, whistled with startling suddenness in a bush a yard or so from her ear. She looked up to find that the sun had risen; its great pale disc, cool and chaste in the white mists, hung already over the valley, and, on the hill-tops, light and shadow were beginning to separate into golds and blues. The birds had ceased their experimental tuning-up, and begun their concert-pieces. The grass glittered, and in the arbutus-bush from which the thrush had sung, a fine radiating cobweb was defined in crystal beads. The sky was already coloured above her head.

Hilary stretched herself out of the rug, and, after half an hour's sheltered inactivity, at once shivered with cold. It became suddenly obvious to her that the only possible time-filler was a walk. She let in the clutch; the noise of the accelerating engine seemed shattering in the stillness. She imagined the night sister raising her eyebrows at it, and, with the instant reaction of her kind to unconformity, remarking irritably, 'Is that Dr Mansell going *now*? Whatever has *she* been doing here all this time?'

The car twisted downhill, between hedges in which the scent of the may was still quenched by dew and the chill of dawn; dropped into shadow in the valley, and climbed again. She turned off from her homeward road, and, slowing to an easy twenty, began to meander over the hills, looking about for a place to park.

She found it at a white, five-barred gate into a larch-wood, whose trees, thinly spaced, let in the sun. The breeze dandled their tender green tassels. The gate gave on to a ride, evidently private land; but it was too early to feel very serious about trespassing, and, having had a country childhood, she could judge that the place was not heavily preserved. If she did meet a keeper she knew how to talk to him. She opened the gate, closing it conscientiously behind her.

The grass of the ride had the extreme velvety fineness which generations of rabbits create about their ancestral homes. It was a good morning for them; their sentinel ears pointed her approach, their white scuts bounced before her, and their jaunty young, losing their heads, took the longest way across the track before popping down into the green. Between padded mats of needles under the larches, bluebells lay in cloudy lakes and streams. Exercise was already making her warm; her self-questionings seemed morbidities of the night, needing no answer but morning. She swung on, through patches of strengthening sunshine, feeling simple, self-sufficient, and free.

The ride gave out in a clearing, stubbled with cut bracken; through the rusty stalks the hard new shoots were uncurling in fantastic crooks and croziers and little fans, mixed with sparse hardy bluebells, deeper coloured than the lush ones under the trees. The sky, growing to full day, had reached the same shade, and the sun was beginning to have heat in its brightness. Hilary let herself down on to a heap of old bracken, and sighed with animal content. Her tweeds melted into the landscape like the protective colouring of a partridge or a hare; she felt, like one of them, comfortably and inconspicuously at home. The warmth, after her broken night, began to make her healthily sleepy. She shut her eyes.

It might have been after five minutes, or thirty-five, that she opened them again with a start. Among the light rustlings and cracklings of small life in the undergrowth, a new noise, rhythmic and strong, was growing louder, the thud over turf of a cantering horse. It came from the ride she had left, facing her now across the clearing. She did not disturb herself about it; she was too drowsy and at ease for embarrassment or exertion. Besides, the wood was too dense behind her for anyone to ride that way, and, sunk in her form of bracken, it was unlikely that she would be seen. The hoof-beats slowed to a walk; a stick cracked sharply and quite near. In a dim curiosity to know whose solitude she was sharing, she raised herself a little on one arm.

They came out into the lake of sunlight in the clearing, a big light dun, and a rider sitting loosely and at ease. Hilary stared, forgetting her trespass and the apologies she might need to improvise. She felt a little detached from reality. The light, the setting, the hour, seemed a theatrical extravagance, exaggerating, needlessly, what was already excessive, the most spectacularly beautiful human creature she had ever seen. Because her habit of mind had made her hostile to excess, she thought irritably, It's ridiculous. It's like an illustration to something.

He had not seen her; both he and the horse were tall, and he was looking the wrong way. If he came nearer she would find that distance had been playing tricks. When he passed near enough for her to hear the creak of leather she still did not quite believe in him, though her eyesight was excellent and the air brilliantly clear. His boots and breeches, which were old and good, were topped off with a blue cotton shirt open at the neck; a carelessness natural to the hour, but transformed by the wearer to something traditional, the basic costume of equestrian romance. He was slender, but strongly boned. His hair was so black that the brightening sun did not touch it with brown; his face had the hard, faintly hollow planes in which art seems to have lost interest between the fourteenth century and the twentieth, unless life ceased for seven centuries to reproduce them; the lines which invite not paint or marble, but stone or bronze. But sculpture would have missed the contrast of a fair skin and grey eyes with the blue-black hair, the slanted brows, and lashes which were emphatic even from that distance away. His grace in the saddle, flexible and erect, was something separable from good horsemanship, as if it would have cost him a deliberate effort to make any movement which was ugly or out of line. His head was up – he and the horse were getting their breath – and this chance pose gave him a look of medieval challenge and adventure which went with all the rest. It was fantastic that anyone unself-conscious and alone could look so faultlessly arranged.

He seemed quite unaware of himself, and happy. His long mouth had the rare mingling of sweetness and arrogance, which can last only for a few years while youth holds them in suspension; for he was very young, perhaps twenty or so, per-haps not out of his 'teens. It was hard to say; his beauty was of that mind-arresting kind which silences other questions. Now his face reflected only movement and the morning. Two mag-pies, scared up from the edge of the wood, flew suddenly out against the trees. He lit with a flash of pleasure as vivid as their flight, then touched his horse with his knee, and trotted away into an open aisle of the larches. The fallen needles muffled the sound, so that he seemed to vanish like a legend, leaving, as with all transitory splendours untempered by the common touch, the sadness of mortality in his wake.

Hilary sat up and brushed bits of bracken smartly from her tweeds. With amused impatience she dusted off also the impression from her mind. She naturally distrusted, and felt ill at ease with, physical perfection in either sex; not from envy – for she seldom troubled to improve on her own moderate good looks – but because she found it a confusing irrelevance, camouflaging the personality which interested her more. Within her own observation the principal function of beauty had been to make a fool of intelligence; in one or two instances, a tragic fool; she heartily approved Shaw's legendary postcard to Isadora Duncan. The way to enjoy it was like this, impersonally, at a distance, for what it was worth; and she felt grateful for the absence of introductions, which had doubtless preserved her from hearty, illusion-shattering banalities about the clemency of the morning and the prospects of golf.

These reflections, with a few remembered illustrations, carried her back to her car. As she drove home the air was still sweet and cool, but the early magic had dispersed; it was not sunrise, but day, and already there was white dust on the road. Her mind began to travel on to the day's work, and the glimpse in the larch-wood only remained there as an incidental part of the pleasures of early rising, like dew and young rabbits, which in general cause one to say, 'Why don't I do this more often?' while knowing that one will not. She wondered what there was for breakfast, hoped that in any case there would be a good deal of it, and reminded herself to say something nice about the coffee to Mrs Clare.

2

Hilary sat at the cottage table, holding a little glass pipette like a fountain-pen filler, and gazing down into a cardboard shoe-box. In the box was cotton-wool, lined with a clean handkerchief of her own, and, embedded in the handkerchief, a tiny waxen face, no bigger than the palm of her hand. The face was full of an ancient ennui; the eyes were closed, showing infinitesimal reddish lashes; the mouth was shut too, in remote obstinacy, passively resisting the pipette which Hilary was trying stealthily to introduce to it. With her finger-tip she drew down the lower jaw, revealing a cavity much the size of the moon on a thumb-nail. A few drops of brandy and water trickled in. The mouth sketched a grimace of languid, but definite, resentment, and out of it came a cry, thinner than the mew of a new-born kitten. Moving out from under the handkerchief in undirected protest, a hand, perfect and slender like an adult's in miniature, closed round one of Hilary's fingers, scarcely making the span, and let go again in fastidious distaste.

From the bed against the wall a dim voice said, 'Was that her crying?'

'Yes,' said Hilary cheerfully. 'And about time, too.'

'I couldn't hardly hear it.'

'Give her time. She's not much over three pounds, by the look of her.'

'Will I rear her, Doctor?'

'I hope so. But not here, you know. She'll need everything rather special. Nurse has gone to ring for the ambulance to take both of you to hospital.'

'Oh, dear, oh, Doctor. Whatever will my husband say?'

'Your husband has been very sensible about it. He wants to do what's best for both of you.' Or if he doesn't, she added to herself, recalling with some satisfaction their recent interview, he can be learning.

'And what's to become of the children, that's what I can't see, and Mother with her leg bad again.'

'We'll fix something. You've just got to concentrate on this one now. Would you like to see her?'

The woman on the bed gave a harassed sigh; but her head craned a little over the worn sheet. Hilary carried the shoe-box over and tilted it. 'We musn't uncover any more of her. They feel the cold.'

Between the folds of the handkerchief the tiny unmoving mask in the box lay with closed mouth and eyes, withdrawn and refusing. It had nothing to say to the life that had been thrust on it seven weeks too soon. Its arms and legs were folded in its pre-natal posture; its whole grain of being seemed bent on affirming that the unpleasant fact of birth had not happened, or, if it had, could be decently ignored. Its composure made Hilary's efforts towards its survival feel gauche and intrusive.

The mother's face puckered, and a tear slipped down her cheek.

'The little love,' she whispered. 'You do what's best, Doctor. Anything so's I don't lose her, bless her heart.'

16

Hilary put down the box on the table and went over to the window, in which tall geraniums excluded half the small available light and air. Looking out, she reflected that Mrs Kemp had three small children already, one of them 'backward', and a husband who did little for her beyond ensuring that events like this were frequent and regular. She had tried to stop this one, as Hilary knew, by every means short of the criminal, and now ... How on earth, she wondered, does Nature manage to pull this trick?

The rattle of a parked cycle sounded outside; the district nurse, panting a little, for she was elderly and stout, came up the path and into the room.

'The ambulance will be along in a few minutes, Doctor. It was Matron herself I spoke to.' She had a fat gossipy voice, which professional etiquette tinged unnaturally with primness. 'She was ever so pleased to know you were here, because she was just going to ring you. Would you be able to come straightaway, she said, because there's an urgent casualty just come in, a head injury, she said, and the patient's unconscious.'

'Thank you, Nurse. I'll go along now, if my instruments are boiled.' Hilary stood up briskly, shocked next moment by her own feelings of pleasure and excitement. In the days when she had worked for Sanderson this would have been simply a typical moment in a packed unremitting routine. Grumbling mechanically, she would have picked up the internal telephone – any scalp lacerations, any bleeding from the nose or ears, any response to painful stimuli? She almost turned to ask the district nurse these questions, but, sourly amused, stopped herself in time.

Her instruments were ready. On her way out through the kitchen she stopped for a few parting admonitions to the husband, by way of striking while the iron was hot. He glowered at her in sullen resentment – exactly, Hilary thought, as if *I* were responsible. By this time he has probably convinced himself that I am. Really, these men.

The Cottage Hospital was in a flutter, with the Matron and Sister in violent circulation; Hilary, who liked smooth-running machinery, felt her irritability increased. The Matron was competent enough in her sphere, but the rare advent of something both acute and complex was apt to go to her head. Probably, Hilary thought, it gets under my skin because I'm going the same way. In reaction, she affected an easy social manner, which put the Matron on her dignity and produced a certain amount of simmering-down.

It emerged that the history of the patient's injury was unknown, for he had been found lying in the road and had not since recovered consciousness. She gathered that signs of gross damage to the brain were so far absent. 'Nurse Jones,' the Matron added, 'has just finished undressing him.'

Hilary stopped herself from saying, 'Well, I hope she hasn't been rolling him about.' Since her rustication she had trained herself out of many exigencies; but Nurse Jones, a plump, china-eyed blonde, still seemed to her less intelligent than any citizen at large had a right to be. This opinion she had concealed less perfectly than she imagined; with the result that in her presence Nurse Jones was shaken out of what simple wit she had. Hilary knew this; found it shaming and infuriating; and began every fresh encounter with good intentions.

The Matron led her to a small single-bedded ward on the ground floor, one generally reserved for the dying. The door stood open, a screen across it inside. Nurse Jones came out of it, a large enamel bowl of soapy water in her hands. Seeing Hilary and the Matron, she pulled up sharply, and the water slopped over the edge of the bowl.

'I don't think,' said Hilary with studied reasonableness, 'that I should have bathed him just yet, Matron. Is there much shock?'

The Matron, who had not ordered a bath but had forgotten to be explicit, said, 'Nurse, you should have known better than to have bathed this patient. I left that to your common sense. Don't you realise that cases like this are very shocked?'

With the bowl wobbling in her hands Nurse Jones began to stammer, 'I didn't do much, Matron. I thought, as I was admitting him ... in case his feet were dirty or anything, you know. But he was quite clean. I didn't do much. I'll just go and get him a bed-gown.'

'You should have had it ready, Nurse, before you prepared to bath him.'

'Yes, Matron. I ...'

'Well, get it now.'

'Yes, Matron.'

'That will be all right for the moment,' Hilary said. 'I shall want him stripped to go over his reflexes.' Seeing the Sister bearing down urgently upon them she added, thankfully, 'Don't let me keep you if you're busy, Matron, I'll come and talk him over with you when I've had a look.'

Nurse Jones had set down her bowl. Eager to restore her status with a display of zeal, she darted ahead of Hilary into the room, and flung back the bath-blanket which lay loosely on the bed. Hilary, following her, noted with speechless exasperation the open window, and the long motionless form of the patient lying in its draught, exposed down to the loins.

With slow, careful control Hilary said, 'I meant undressed, Nurse, not stark naked. Shall we have that window shut? And then perhaps you'll bring a couple of hot-water bottles.'

Nurse Jones flushed – her fair skin made the process

painfully conspicuous – and hurried away. Hilary stood for a moment tapping one foot on the floor, filled with irrational and conflicting sensations of satisfaction and guilt. They coalesced into a general irritation. She turned sharply towards the bed; took hold of the blanket to twitch it upward; and stood still, with its fold suspended in her hand.

Lying flat and straight on the cotton sheet, in a marmoreal peace, was the young rider of the larch-wood. A narrow first-aid bandage, covering a cut on his forehead, bound his dark hair like a fillet; his head was turned a little to the left, as if in sleep. As if in sleep, one arm lay on his breast, the other slackly at his side. His body was as strictly cut and as faultless as his face. The black iron bed on which he lay seemed odd and incongruous; he looked like the flower of Sparta brought back from Thermopylae on a shield.

For a few moments the normal processes of professional routine in Hilary's mind were wholly arrested. Her reaction was purely human and aesthetic. She felt, not compassion, for there was no suffering to awake it, but a sense of cosmic tragedy and a kind of awe. Drawing up the blanket, she looked again at the quiet face. On one of the cheekbones the skin had been grazed, and picric dabbed on the place; it jolted her mental mechanisms; the wheels began to go round again. She felt the skin temperature, and noted signs of a fractured collarbone. On the same side, the right, the palm of his hand was scraped. She flicked back her cuff from her wrist-watch and took his pulse.

It was slow, but not to the point of danger; and the wound on his head, when she examined it, proved to be superficial and without sign of deeper injury below. Naturally there would have to be an X-ray; a portable, he had better not be moved. She proceeded to pick up a fold of chest-muscle, and, twisting it expertly, noted in relief a faint flinching, indicative of some response to pain. The leg and foot reflexes were normal. Just as she had ascertained this, Nurse Jones reappeared with two hot-water bottles, looking like a schoolgirl who, sent on an errand to the headmistress's study, has hoped against hope to find it empty. To her own surprise Hilary smiled at her and explained the salient points of the case in simple terms. In her haste to be off before the weather took a turn for the worse, Nurse Jones nearly upset the screen; but Hilary never noticed it.

The Matron presented a problem. She was a competent and practical person; but her notions on the treatment of head injuries were archaic, and the powder of instruction would have to be mixed with liberal coatings of jam. It proved unexpectedly easy, for other preoccupations were keeping her dignity in check.

'That's very interesting, Dr Mansell. I'm afraid my nurses get a bit behind with some of the new methods here; it will be good experience for them. Now with regard to his condition; you think his relatives ought to be here?'

Hilary considered. The question was a strictly technical one.

'I don't see any need, if you can get at them easily. These cases do queer things, but we ought to get some warning of any deterioration. They'll only be a nuisance to you, camping about; and if he starts recovering consciousness, that's just when we'll have to keep them away. I should leave it, provided they know his condition and can get here in reasonable time if they're sent for.'

'That's just what I thought you'd say, Dr Mansell. I was wondering, if he's a stranger about here, how soon the police would be able to trace them.'

'Do you mean,' said Hilary, startled, 'that you don't know who he is?'

'Only the surname. That was on his underwear. Of course, when he comes round . . .'

'He may come round with complete aphasia. Or, of course, just possibly never.' She listened to her own voice, hard and incisive, and thought, Do I always talk like this?

'Where was he picked up?' she asked. 'Surely someone knew him there?'

'He was found by some people motoring from Birmingham. Of all the silly things, they didn't 'phone for the ambulance, just bundled him into their car and brought him here because they'd noticed the sign driving by. You'd think, with a head injury, anyone would have more sense.'

Hilary had no such expectations of the lay intelligence. She further suspected that these rash Samaritans had been responsible for the accident, which would explain their leaning to informality. No one, of course, would have taken their number. She said, absently:

'What about his horse?'

The Matron was impressed.

'Why, Dr Mansell, you're quite a detective, aren't you? I did mean to have told you he was picked up in riding things, but it quite slipped my memory.'

'Oh, well,' said Hilary casually, 'the injuries were typical.' She found herself, for some reason (conceit, she supposed, at this tribute to her deductive powers) unwilling to explain. 'You've been through his pockets, of course?'

'Yes; I've got everything on my desk, to go over it, but really it doesn't tell you much. Do come in, Doctor, and take a cup of tea with me – I see the maid's just bringing it in – and then perhaps you can do some more of your detecting.'

Hilary laughed politely.

On the Matron's desk, looking slightly sacrilegeous against

its daily polish and the geometrical symmetry of its equipment, a heap of oddments strewed the speckless sheet of the blotter. Hilary turned them over. Seventeen-shillings-odd in loose silver; a key-ring without a name-tag; a crushed postage stamp; part of an electric plug; a twist of fuse-wire; matches; a silver cigarette-case, empty, with the initials J.R.F. in one corner; an ancient square of wrapped toffee; and a dirty scrap of paper of the sort which, drifting into the corner of a pocket, lies there till it is reduced to debris. The little handful suddenly struck her as rather moving. She said, curtly, 'Not much help,' and unfolded the paper, which had been used as a spill and burned at one end. Through the creases and rubbings she managed to decipher, 'Dear Julian, I shan't be in Hall to-night, so if by any chance ...' The other side of the paper was blank, and there was no date; but she knew the college crest, having been at Oxford herself.

'That ought to do,' she said. 'It's the vac, but someone will be there. A first-year man, I should think; he can't be more than twenty.'

The Matron, to whom the crest conveyed nothing, and who lacked the happy self-effacement of a Watson, waited aloofly.

'There can't be two J.R.F.'s in one college, I suppose.'

With some self-satisfaction the Matron said, 'If you remember, Doctor, we have the surname. From the underwear. It was at the top of his chart, but perhaps you overlooked it. Fleming was the name.'

'Julian Fleming,' said Hilary, and laughed. 'No, really ...'

'I beg your pardon?'

A little annoyed with herself, Hilary said, 'I only meant that by all the laws of human compensation he ought to be called Henry Pratt, or something of that sort, don't you think?'

'You mean he reminds you of someone called Pratt?'

23

'Yes,' said Hilary desperately. 'I expect that's it.'

The trunk call was through before they had finished tea. After listening nostalgically, over the wire, to the muted noises of an Oxford street, she learned that Mr Fleming had gone down in the previous year. In spite of this – which put her guesswork some three years out – the porter sounded, when he heard her business, quite personally upset. He gave the address as Larch Hill, near Lynchwyck, Gloucestershire, and begged that she would convey to Mr Fleming his best wishes. As soon as she had disengaged the line the telephone rang again; she left it for the nurses, and went back to the Matron's room with her news.

The Matron in the meantime had decided that she herself ought to have taken the call, and had to be thawed out with pains. Just as the operation could be said to have succeeded, and the milk was going into the second cups of tea, there was a knock at the door.

'I'm so sorry to disturb you, Matron. But I thought you'd like to know that the mother of the new patient, Fleming, has just rung up. She says his horse has come home without him, and she thought this would be the best place to inquire. She seems very much upset. What would you like me to say to her?'

'I'll speak to her myself, Sister.' The Matron rose with conscious poise. At the door she turned, with a geniality under which prickles were faintly discernible. 'Well, fancy, Dr Mansell; after all that clever detecting of yours. What a waste, wasn't it?'

Hilary suppressed an offer to pay for the call to Oxford, and smiled nicely. Left alone, she experienced an odd sense of flatness. Helpless, nameless, and defenceless, he had given her a feeling of proprietorship which, when she noticed it, struck her as singularly silly. He hardly looked the kind of property to be lying about unclaimed for long. She had better look him over again, and make good her escape, leaving the Matron – who would enjoy it – to cope with the swarm of loving relations, fiancées, and candidates on the waiting-list with whom, of course, the place would presently teem.

Meeting the Sister in the hall, she said, 'How is he now? Any sign of consciousness yet?'

'He did seem to be coming round for a minute. He was sick. But now he's gone off again.'

The Matron, who disliked to miss anything, had suspended her journey to the telephone. Hilary turned to her quickly.

'Oh, Matron. I think you could be reassuring to the family, within reason. But if anyone comes round, I don't want them let in to see him on any account. He's just at the stage when fuss and excitement will do him a lot of harm. Relatives are usually disastrous to cases like this.'

She opened the door of the little room, and went in.

Almost total darkness greeted her. For a moment bewildered, she then recalled hearing, at a lecture, that this treatment had obtained at some remote pre-Cushing era of the past. She groped her way towards the window.

Her hand was on the blind-cord when she was arrested by a sound behind her; a smothered, labouring breath which, perhaps because of the gloom, gave the impression not only of struggle but of acute fear. As she turned to listen again, a voice which was no more than a whisper said, 'No.'

Hilary twitched the blind; it shot upward, letting in a clear evening glow of reflected sun. His eyes were open, and turned, it seemed, in her direction, though it might only have been towards the light. They were wide and fixed; before, she had pulled back the lids to examine the pupils, but she seemed to be seeing them now for the first time. Their Celtic grey was

25

startling against his black lashes and brows. Whether he saw her at all it was impossible to say. His face was set in a stiff mask of suffering, but the eyes and forehead were not contracted as if physical pain had been behind them. She thought that he must be experiencing some kind of hallucination; but the sight of his distress conquered her professional instinct to observe more. She sat down on the edge of the bed, and, finding his good hand under the blanket, took it firmly in both her own.

'It's all right,' she said, leaning over him. 'Everything's all right. There's nothing there.'

He drew in a long, gasping breath; she saw the iris of the eyes contract, trying to focus, then relax into blindness again. His fingers, at first loose and unresponsive, closed round hers and tightened, slowly, into a crushing grip. She could feel the bones of her hand grinding together, and began seriously to wonder if he would succeed in fracturing one of them. Too much interested to be fully conscious of the pain, she sat watching his face. The fixed stare was leaving it (the hard clearness of the bone-structure, followed so closely by the flesh, made the least loosening of the muscles clearly evident) and his breathing was easier. Presently his grip on her hand became something that could be comfortably tolerated. She was about to withdraw herself – for his disrupted thought would, no doubt, already have forgotten its former images – when she saw that he was trying to speak. He parted his lips twice, and, defeated by the effort of organisation, closed them again.

At last he said, with difficulty, 'Where are you?'

'Here. Can't you see me now?'

'Yes.' But his eyes were looking through and beyond her. She had known people before (but they had been children) who would not admit that they could not see.

'I've opened the window,' she said. 'Look, it's light.'

He narrowed his eyes for a moment as if aware that some endeavour was expected of him; then he closed them, and tightened his hand a little on hers. She saw that his face was damp with sweat, and wiped it with the towel that hung on the locker. He turned towards her, and appeared to sleep.

Time was passing, and she had a good deal to do; but she thought she would stay a little longer. In this twilight phase, which might be short, observation might be interesting, and there was no trained observer to take her place; it would be Nurse Jones, as likely as not. His face had lost the look of sculptured impersonality it had had when his unconsciousness had been complete, and had now a kind of forlorn peace, like an exhausted child's. They had dressed him in faded flannel pyjamas, rebandaged his head, and slung up his arm to fix his collar-bone. He looked very neat and clean and young.

A spasm crossed his eyes and forehead, so sudden and sharp that the pain seemed to move visibly over them. She thought that to slacken the bandage might help, and unpinned the end. He reached up a hand in fumbling resistance; she put it firmly aside.

'What the hell are you playing at,' he muttered, 'mucking about?' And, more irritably, when she continued, 'Don't shift that, you fool, I'm on in two minutes.'

Her attention elsewhere, she said, 'I'll only loosen it; it's too tight.'

'What's the idea? I always do myself. If he wants it done straight he can put in someone else. I tell you—'

'Sh-sh. It's all right. Quiet now.' She had finished, and laid her hand restrainingly on his forehead.

His face relaxed. 'It's you,' he said; and then, with the

exaggerated feeling of delirium, 'I'm very, very sorry. Terribly sorry. Stay with me now. I lost you. I'm very sorry. Let me stay here. I'll hold you, can I? Don't go away.'

His hand wandered over the counterpane. She put hers into it; he groped at her sleeve and tried to drag himself towards her. She supported his head quickly, laid him down again, and to quiet him sat with his hand clasped in hers. Someone had turned on a radio for the patients' tea-hour. It was Purcell; far too loud; in a minute she must see about it. He went on murmuring, under his breath. She could only hear a word here and there. 'It's all right now. Don't let me fall,' and something that sounded like, 'The pool's low to-day.' Then, after a longer pause which gave her time to disapprove again of the radio, in quite a different voice and so strong that it startled her, 'Art thou afeared? Be not afeared, the isle is full of noises, sounds, and sweet airs, that give delight and hurt not. Sometimes . . . sometimes . . . ' To her own surprise – she had not known that she remembered it – she said gently, 'And I awake, and cry to sleep again.' He smiled, shut his eyes, and lay still. But, just as she was making up her mind to go, he opened them again. She knew at once, by the accommodation of the pupils, that now they were linked with the brain. He was looking, with trustful incurious acceptance, into her face.

She became cautious; if he was becoming rational, he must be left in quiet. Getting out her note-book, she framed quickly the routine questions which would tell her what she had to know.

'How are you feeling now?'

'Fine.' She saw, while he was speaking, the pain move across his brows.

'What else do you feel?'

'A bit sick. It doesn't matter.'

'Tell me your name.'

'Julian.' He sounded dimly surprised. She made an entry.

'Yes? Julian what?'

'Oh, sorry. Julian ... Richard ... Fleming.' He gave it the blank obedience of a lesson.

'Do you know where you are?'

'Not really.' He moved his head, flinched, and shut his eyes. 'It doesn't matter.'

'It's a hospital. But don't worry, you're doing quite well. Do you know why you're here?'

He looked at her appealingly. She could see that he was in pain, and thought, Of course he wonders why I'm badgering him with stupid questions. One takes things so much for granted. He has speaking eyes, as they say.

'I shan't have to bother you much more. In a moment I'll leave you in peace.'

'No, please.' His hand, which she had relinquished for the note-book, stirred under the clothes. 'I'm sorry, please don't go.'

His voice had sharpened painfully. She said, 'Don't move, it will hurt you. I'm not going yet.'

'I'm so sorry,' he said again.

'Do you know why you're in hospital?'

'I took a toss,' he said slowly, 'I suppose.'

'Do you remember it?'

'No.'

'Now don't worry. Take your time. Just try and tell me the last thing you remember.'

'Do you live here?'

'Yes,' she said soothingly. 'I live quite near. Do you remember starting out from home?'

'I said I'd be back for tea.' She checked his movement, and settled his head.

'Where did you go?'

'The usual way.'

'Yes?'

'Down the bridle-path ... and – and out on the Lynchwyck road.'

'And then?'

'There's a gate lower down.'

'Did you open it?'

'I heard a car coming.'

'And then?'

He shut his eyes. 'I don't know. You came then.'

Hilary wrote: 'Period of amnesia uncertain. No witnesses. Replies suggest clear recollection to within few seconds of accident. Period of unconsciousness, no history, evidence vague, ?40 to 60 mins.'

She looked up from the note-book; he was enjoying the relief of silence, with closed eyes. It seemed cruel to disturb him again; but it might be important, later on, to have assessed any mental impairment now.

'I've nearly finished. Tell me where you live?'

He gave her, with gentle weariness, the correct address.

'How many brothers and sisters have you?'

He drew his brows together. He was, she saw, growing irritable. This did not surprise her; his evident attempt to conceal it did. She repeated the question.

'Not any. Just the two of us.'

'You and ... ?'

'My head aches rather.'

'I know. I'm going to give you something for it. Do you know who I am?'

'Yes, of course.' For a moment he seemed about to smile.

This would not do. To test his alertness she took the

stethoscope out of the pocket of her white coat and hung it by the ear-pieces round her neck.

'Tell me,' she repeated with patient clear insistence, 'who you think I am.'

He lifted his dark lashes. A kind of reproach was mixed, in the look he gave her, with a confidence which changed, presently, to bewildered effort.

'Why, you ... you're ...' It was plain that his own doubt both distressed and shocked him. Strain was the last thing she wanted. She said, 'I'm a doctor.'

He turned his face away on the pillow, like a refusing child who will not hear.

'Don't worry. I'm not going to ask you any more questions. You can go to sleep now.'

He had still the look of someone seeking for a known word which remains absurdly elusive. Presently, however, something more urgent took its place. He was getting to the stage when people begin to think of sending messages. Very likely, she thought, he's just remembered his girl; sometimes it happens that way. It suddenly occurred to her that she had had a long day and was feeling tired.

'Yes?' she said encouragingly.

'Look out. I'm going to be sick.'

'Here.' She caught up the enamel bowl from the locker and steadied his head. Movement and disturbance made things worse, and he was very sick indeed. She took his weight on her shoulder, protected his injured arm, and felt under her hand the loose, boyish softness of his black hair. When he had finished, and she had put the bowl out of the way, he made no attempt to move; probably he was exhausted. She put her arm behind him and settled him back on the pillow again.

He said, confidingly, 'How good you always are.'

'Now keep quiet, or it will start again.'

'Yes, I will, I've been sick twice already. You have to get properly tight once, to see. It's a bit overrated, I think. The only thing I ...'

'Sh-sh. Go to sleep.' He was getting to the excitable stage, which must not be allowed to develop. Picking up the case-sheet, she wrote him up for an intramuscular injection of luminal.

'You can have one more pillow, now.' She got it from the other side of the room and fixed it correctly under his shoulder. It seemed that he had composed himself for sleep; but when she stood up, he caught at her sleeve.

'You're not going away?'

'Not far. Talking's bad for you, so soon.'

'Stay with me. I won't talk.'

'Another time. You're going to sleep now. I've ordered you an injection; you'll feel better when you've had it.'

'I don't want to go to sleep.' His eyes had opened, widely, and fixed themselves imploringly on her face.

'All right,' she said, humouring him. 'You needn't till you feel like it. But you simply must rest.'

'I'd rather go back with you.' His fingers had clenched themselves on the white drill. 'I called, and she wouldn't answer. She went away.'

Good heavens, thought Hilary, where *does* this place get its nurses? 'Don't worry, I'll see that doesn't happen again.'

'It was bound to happen. If I'd known you were there ...'

He must be sat with all night, she thought, and no bones about it. I'll see the Matron. Or the next thing anyone knows, he'll be getting out of bed.

'That's all over now. It was only a bad dream. But I'll stay a little if you'll promise to be good.'

He murmured, hazily, 'Like we were before,' and turned over on his side.

She decided to ring for the luminal and give it herself, so as not to disturb him. Long before it had had time to act he had fallen asleep.

She remained a few minutes longer, looking down at him and wondering what, in a normal state, he was really like. By the standards of her experience he had behaved with commendable restraint; patients with this degree of concussion had, as a rule, few inhibitions. They wept, they shouted, they were explicit about the unmentionable. He must have a nice, innocent little subconscious, she thought.

His hand had loosened in hers; she slid her fingers gently away and tucked in the bedclothes behind his back. As she bent over him he murmured, 'Good night, dear.'

She did not answer; he had spoken almost in his sleep. When she looked back at the door his head was half buried in the pillow, but she could see the last trace of a smile fading from his face into a dreamless calm.

3

'... and you will make it quite clear to the night staff, won't you, Matron, that I want to be called if there's any sign whatever of raised intracranial pressure? Hourly temperature, of course, half-hourly pulse and respiration. If his pulse falls below sixty or his respirations below sixteen, or if his temperature starts to climb, and most particularly if he becomes drowsy and hard to rouse ...'

The Matron assented at intervals, with growing resentment. She had read all these instructions on the case-sheet and was already convinced that she had known it all beforehand. Well, it would be Dr Dundas's take-in in three days. 'Yes, Dr Mansell, Night Sister is quite accustomed to acute work.' (And so am I, young woman; I was learning it when you were wetting your nappies on a rubber sheet.)

The unspoken part of the responses was not lost on Hilary, whom experience had made receptive. She smiled and said, 'Of course, Matron, I know. You mustn't mind me; head cases happen to be rather a bee in my bonnet. Night Sister's so considerate, I know she hates to give one an unnecessary call. But this case happens to be rather interesting, so she needn't mind.'

The Matron acknowledged this tacit apology with a gracious inclination; and, to show it was accepted, vouchsafed a little small-talk as they moved towards the front door. But it had already been opened. The maid stood beside it, hesitating, the presence of the Matron having caused her to fluff her lines. The visitor advanced past her towards them.

Hilary knew at once who she was. The correct tweeds, halfway between sporting and urban; the discreetly toning cashmere jumper with the permissible small pearls; powder, but no lipstick; fading fair hair becomingly, but not fashionably, dressed, under the inevitable Henry Heath; the tense concealment of emotion before the maid. Hilary recognised the breeding, but not the resemblance she had half expected to see; and, used to tracing the permanent set of faces through the temporary disguises of sickness or grief, received also a general impression of graciousness, a little conscious perhaps, but real. A deeper level of her mind was aware also of those avoidances and taboos which are taken for granted by women who observe them, and sensed instantly by women who have cast them off; of that natural self-repression which manifests itself, through sorrow or trouble, in a faint defensive hostility.

'How do you do? You are the Matron, I think, who spoke to me just now on the telephone. I am Mrs Fleming. May I see my son?'

The Matron embarked on the routine of reassurance, sympathy, and exposition. She received few private patients, and her lowered self-confidence made her a little pompous and genteel. Hilary stood ready for her turn; and was aware that her presence was being felt as an unexplained intrusion. If she had been a man her function would have been instantly apparent; she had ceased to think about such things, but, under the skin, continued to feel them.

The Matron was saying, 'But I'm sure you'd like to talk to Dr Mansell, who's in charge of the case.'

'Yes, indeed. I should like to see him immediately. Is he with my son now?'

'This is Dr Mansell.'

'Oh. I'm afraid I didn't . . . How do you do?'

Her dismay was badly evident. To Hilary it seemed that she had barely attempted its concealment. She fought her own resentment, as she always did; finding it, in this stale situation, strangely fresh and strong. Ashamed of herself, she took particular pains; was simple and clear without the air of talking-down, hopeful and confident without dishonesty about risks. She followed it up with a friendly smile.

Mrs Fleming replied with one which was purely social and perfunctory. She had relaxed neither her strain nor her reserve.

'I see. Thank you. May I go to him now?'

'I think perhaps it wouldn't be very wise to-day. To-morrow, or perhaps the day after, for a few minutes, would be a safe promise, I think. It's just in these early stages that absolute quiet is so essential. It does seem unkind, I know; but we've proved over and over again that it's much the best.' As she spoke she was feeling behind her, not the Cottage Hospital, but the prestige and authority of her own.

Mrs Fleming's face altered. It took on the look which every doctor and nurse knows well; the look of someone confronted with a soulless and impersonal organisation, whose members have lost touch with the humanities and require to have them explained in words of one syllable.

'Dr Mansell, please let me see my son. I can assure you I shan't fuss or excite him. I know how one should behave in a sick-room; and besides, I understand him far too well.'

Hilary had, when she knew it to be essential, a long reserve of patience, which at other times she did not always trouble to employ. She employed it now. She explained, gently and with detail. At the end she saw that she had made no headway at all.

'Yes, I quite understand that of course he must be kept quiet, since you say he has concussion. Even we lay people realise that, you know. But you see, that's the very reason why I must be there. My son and I have been a great deal together; we're accustomed to one another's companionship. When he was ill at school I put up at a hotel close by and spent every day with him. The first thing he'll look for, when he recovers consciousness, will be to see me in the room. Unfortunately, he's rather highly strung. If he misses me he'll be terribly worried. You don't want that to happen; you said so yourself.'

She waited, with confidence, the effect of her words. To Hilary, whose grounding in neuro-surgery had been sound, they were in fact conclusive; she abandoned any fleeting thought she had had of giving way. Her feet felt familiar ground. She became inflexibly courteous and calm.

'We should certainly want to avoid that; but I don't think there's any fear now that it will arise. Your son recovered consciousness nearly an hour ago. He's quite passive and lethargic, and content to take everything as it comes, unless he's stimulated in any way; then he gets pain and sickness and so on. That's quite usual. It's vital that he should simply vegetate till he's past that stage. I'm sure you understand.'

'If he's conscious,' said Mrs Fleming sharply, 'I'm sure he must have asked for me.' Her voice and her eyes added, all too plainly, that she suspected Hilary of being ready to conceal it.

'Hardly yet. He doesn't even remember how he came here. He's had an injection now to make him sleep. Don't you think, if he were roused and the effects were bad, as they would be, it

37

would only distress you? Please believe I know how you feel – I've had relatives ill myself, you know – but I'm afraid I must say no visitors, for to-day.'

'In that case,' said Mrs Fleming, 'I must defer to your judgement, of course.' Her face looked closed. Hilary moved with her towards the door.

They paused on the threshold. Hilary had felt her thinking as they walked. She waited.

'There's just one thing that perhaps we should discuss now. Dr Lowe – you know him, I dare say – is our family doctor. He will be looking after Julian when he's well enough to come home. It wouldn't be fair, busy as you must be, to expect you to drive out for such a distance. I don't know the etiquette in such things; but I imagine you would like to have him here quite soon, and discuss the case with him. A second opinion, it's called, isn't it?'

There was a pause. Hilary held on to herself, coldly and rigidly. The motive was so palpable that she felt contempt for her own sensations. But the half-healed wounds in her self-esteem, scratched raw, made no response to reason. Their protest was the only part of her own emotions that she recognised. She was pleased by the certainty that her face expressed nothing at all.

'Certainly, if you wish.' She recalled Dr Lowe, who had practised in the neighbourhood for some thirty years; a large, kindly man, radiating fresh air and those homely clichés which the patient can repeat, afterwards, with pride to his friends, or the relatives with reverence over the port at the funeral. 'I'll ring up Dr Lowe,' she said, 'and arrange for a consultation. Good afternoon.'

She walked back into the hall. Her cigarettes were in her pocket; she lit one, and saw the flame of the lighter quiver from the shaking of her hand. It was something, she thought, that the Matron had not waited; how sorry she would have been to know what she had missed. From some recess of memory a voice came back to her, casual and cool, the voice of David. 'You women have an extraordinary delusion that you should reason with the layman. You over-explain. It never works.'

In her car she grappled seriously with herself. Probably, she thought, this will turn out a perfectly straightforward case, who'd recover without any trouble in his own home, with Sarah Gamp to nurse him. Why am I making an event of it, getting my hackles up, behaving as if this average silly woman had raised some major issue in my career? It wouldn't take David long to tell me. The shrillness of an inferiority complex. When he wakes he'll be almost normal, and delighted, no doubt, to see Lowe walk in at the door. I shall be well out of a tiresome business. I'll put the call through to-morrow; the old boy will have turned in with his feet in the fender by now.

It was late when she got back, having taken in two or three visits on the way. The sun had gone in; her tension had slackened into flatness; she felt chilled and tired. It cheered her to see firelight through the windows of the square hall where, in the evenings, she often sat with Mrs Clare. Hilary found her the ideal hostess, landlady, or what you will. She was placid and effortlessly efficient; friendly, but never obtruding; her reserves were profound – in all this while Hilary had not discovered what it was her husband did abroad – but they had the effect of laziness rather than of strain. Her opinions, which were intelligent, and her gossip, which was tolerant and amusing, were given with a gentle air of commonplace. She was about Hilary's age; her soft contours and smooth dark hair knotted at the nape gave her a look of ripeness which was a

39

matter of poise rather than of shape. In the minor crises of life Hilary never failed to find her extremely soothing; she hoped she would be in to-night.

Fatigue making her a little clumsy, she opened the front door with a noisy carelessness which was unlike her, and slapped down her bag and gloves on the table outside the door. As she went through into the hall, the stiffness of driving made her step heavy and long. The lights were not on yet, but the fire was bright in the big stone fireplace, and it was by this that she saw Mrs Clare. She was on her knees on the rug, with the fire-tongs in her hand; her head and body were turned, in a moment of swift arrested movement, towards the door from which the sounds had come. Her face was clear in the glow of the flames she had been stirring; lit with a brilliant, incredulous, transforming joy. Hilary paused, suddenly awkward; but next moment Mrs Clare had seen and recognised her. The unfamiliar face returned, quietly, to familiarity, like the smooth dwindling of a lamp when a steady hand has turned the key. It was then that Hilary recalled hearing her say once, in her low, peaceful voice, 'Sometimes he gets back to England at short notice and just appears. He cables if he can. I never really know.'

There seemed nothing to say, but Mrs Clare, as was her way, seemed to require nothing. She said that Hilary had come in at just the right moment, for she had been about to make tea. This was her pleasant habit at unexpected hours. Hilary said it was just what she had been longing for – which, she discovered, was true – and went up to take off her things. It was not till she was alone in her own comfortable, well-ordered room that the twilight closed round her like loneliness made visible.

4

The premature baby was dead. It had breathed, imperceptibly, through half the night in its oxygen tent, looking, through the transparent cover, like a wax doll in a glass case, an antique doll from a stiff, well-behaved Victorian nursery. In the small hours its heart had failed, and it had died without a movement or a sigh of protest, with no sign at all except a faint blue shadow on the skin. They had not called Hilary; there had been nothing that could be done. They opened the little white cotton parcel for her to see it before she signed the death certificate. The handful inside looked relaxed, as if in the relief of a creature which has returned, after a brief encounter with some hostile element, to its instinctive state.

Hilary went up to the women's ward and spent a few minutes with the mother. They talked softly, because the beds of the other women were not far away. Like her child, the mother did not protest. She received Hilary's consolations meekly, seeming even a little apologetic for having indulged so long the impertinent folly of hope. Hilary took, for a moment, her thin, rough hand, and felt ashamed of the strength and vitality of her own as if she had offered some insulting ostentation.

The mother pressed it, timidly and politely. As Hilary moved from the bed she was already closing her eyes; she had been waiting, one would have said, to do so, and the checking of such discourtesy had been for some minutes her chief concern.

Hilary went slowly downstairs. Habit made her able to shift such things quickly from the surface of her mind, to confine them in protective formulae. Beneath the surface they still worked inward, colouring her mood. She had only one more patient here to see; the Fleming boy. She formed the words clearly in her mind, as she had formed the phrases about the state of the baby's heart. (They had had it christened in time, its name was Greta Marlene, written in neat print on a label tied round the cotton parcel with tape.) The Fleming boy; the head injury. The X-rays were ready in the Matron's office, empty just now; holding them to the light she saw a faint something which might have been a fine frontal crack. At all events, nothing gross. She had better take one more look at him, before putting in the call to Dr Lowe. And that, she thought, will be that. She crossed the hall to the single ward, and went in.

Nurse Jones, she found, was engaged in giving the patient his midday drink. She had fixed him up quite correctly, high enough to swallow, but not high enough to disturb him, and was holding a feeding-cup of Benger's, taken from a neat little tray with a clean traycloth. She was, Hilary reflected, a conscientious girl. She had not heard the door open, and was coaxing prettily; for all the world, Hilary thought, like a nurse in a film.

'Now *come* along, Mr Fleming. Just a teeny drop. You won't pick up, you know, if you don't take your dinner, now will you?' She poised the feeding-cup with an engaging smile.

The Fleming boy seemed inattentive to all this. He was

looking past Nurse Jones and across the room towards the door. Hilary smiled at him, and opened her mouth to speak; but checked in her forward step, because his face had undergone no change at all. At this moment Nurse Jones popped the spout of the feeding-cup into his mouth; he muttered something blurred and indistinguishable, and moved his head away, so that part of the liquid spilled. Nurse Jones said, 'Now, please, Mr Fleming,' and mopped his chin with the diet-cloth. He was still looking at the opposite wall.

Hilary shut the door sharply behind her and went up to the bed.

Nurse Jones put down the feeding-cup on its tray, and straightened herself with politeness and some difficulty in disposing of her hands. She looked modestly self-satisfied; supported by the clean traycloth, perhaps. With timid cheerfulness she ventured, 'He's being rather *naughty*, Dr Mansell, I'm afraid, over his diet. But he took his breakfast ever so nicely, didn't you, Mr Fleming.'

Hilary leaned across the bed and took hold of his sound shoulder, sinking her fingers deeply into the flesh.

'Julian, how are you?'

She spoke loudly and clearly, almost into his ear. His face was stupid and slack; the loosened jaw took from it even the vacant beauty of a mask.

'Julian.'

His eyes focused for a moment; dimly and fleetingly the look of personality returned. 'I'm – allri'. Good night,' he said, indistinctly and laboriously, and shut his eyes.

Hilary turned round. Nurse Jones was regarding her with wide-eyed curiosity, in which was beginning to intrude the first shadow of a doubt.

'How long,' said Hilary levelly, 'has he been like this?'

'Well, really, till just now he hasn't been difficult at all. He took his Bovril at ten with hardly any trouble, and since then he's been sleeping every time I've been in to him. I just woke him up for his dinner. I think really he's a bit sleepy still.'

'A bit sleepy!' Hilary felt her voice rising, and forced it down. 'I want his pulse-chart, please.'

Nurse Jones fished it out, with a clatter, from the box that hung on the foot of the bed. The last entry was for ten o'clock.

She took the wrist which lay inertly on the counterpane. His pulse was a bare fifty; his respirations about twelve to the minute, against a normal of twenty. The chart had said sixty-two and sixteen.

'This pulse,' she said slowly and carefully, 'has been falling steadily since eight this morning. Why hasn't the chart been kept up?'

Over Nurse Jones's candid face spread a look of relief and virtuous rehabilitation. 'Sister said two-hourly would be enough to-day, as he was so well. It isn't quite twelve; I was just going to do it.'

'All right, Nurse. I see. Another time, always report if a head injury gets drowsy. Where can I find Matron?'

'I'm afraid she's serving dinners now, Dr Mansell.' Nurse Jones spoke with apology, but with a finality she might have used for stating that the Matron was at Communion and had gone up to the altar rails.

'Never mind. Get this ready, will you, and give it straight away.' She wrote on the chart. 'Nothing more by mouth, he may not be swallowing.' She crossed the hall and picked up the telephone.

'Give me trunks, please.'

The inevitable delays followed. She knew them in advance, and, drawing savagely at her cigarette, wondered at herself for finding them suddenly insupportable. The delay at the exchange, a prosperous voice crossing the line with a deal in hardware; the delay at the internal switchboard when she was through; the delay in the ward – dinners were being served there also – the inevitable announcement that Mr Sanderson was operating, the search for the houseman. At last the jar of the picked-up receiver, and a brisk time-pressed voice she knew.

'Mr Sanderson's house-surgeon speaking.'

'Oh, George, is that you? Hilary Mansell here ... Yes, of course, where else would I be? ... Like a duck to water, I told you I should, and what about you? ... No? Congratulations, George, well, we could all see it coming. Listen, how are you off for beds? ... Yes, I know, but I've got to have one ... I don't care if they're parked in a queue on the stairs. This is a sub-dural. Acute ... Yes, every indication, I'll give you the history in a minute. How soon will the theatre be free? ... Ye-es, I suppose so, just, if it's no longer. He's been getting drowsy since ten this morning, the fools didn't tell me ... Yes, but that's about all you can say. Do you want to take anything down for the chief? I'll be coming in with him myself ... All right – ready? Man, aged twenty-three, thrown while riding about 3 p.m. yesterday ...'

When she had finished, found the Matron, informed and calmed her, she came back to the telephone again. Now, for the first time, she hesitated, and found herself tracing vague flourishes round the number she had written down. The Matron, who had been with her, was just disappearing.

'Oh, Matron, before you go – has his mother been to inquire after him to-day?'

'She rang up this morning.' The Matron had been a good nurse, and the instincts remained with her, mixed with the

45

corrupting infiltrations of prestige and power. They had conquered, just now, the urge to find a scapegoat, or a flaw in Hilary's instructions of yesterday. 'Yes, Sister brought me the message. I didn't commit myself to any improvement, I'm glad to say. Comfortable, I think I said, and condition much the same. That would have been at about nine-thirty, she was coming in this afternoon ... If only I hadn't spent so long over those dressings this morning. Once the nurses see you do anything slipshod they get so slack themselves you've got no check on them ...'

'Don't worry about it, Matron.' Hilary warmed to her; would she herself, she wondered, have hauled down her flag with so much grace? 'They do sometimes slip by in the first stages, we had a few cases in as advanced as this, and there was still just time ... I hope the mother's at home.'

'Yes, poor thing. Poor woman. If she doesn't see him alive again ...'

There was no reproach in her voice; but Hilary guessed that, left to herself, she would have let Mrs Fleming in yesterday, and was remembering it.

'I know,' she said. 'It seemed best at the time. Spilt milk, you know.'

'Perhaps she could go with the ambulance, if we kept it just—'

'No,' said Hilary. 'The ambulance can't wait.' She took the receiver down.

The bell at the other end seemed to ring for a long time. Hilary imagined the sound filling a sunny morning-room, and, out in the garden perhaps, a woman turning and crossing the lawn, in gardening gloves and an old, good hat; she would certainly wear a hat in the garden ... The receiver clicked at the other end.

46

It was Mrs Fleming. Hilary announced herself, and came to the point quickly. She had learned to distrust too much preparation, which, its purpose apparent from the first, only sensitised the mind for the coming blow. When she had finished there was a silence. It lasted a second or so; to Hilary the tension seemed endless. Then an even, held-in voice, from which the distortion of the wire took away any faint trace of betraying expression.

'And Dr Lowe? What does Dr Lowe say?'

Hilary gripped the edge of the telephone-table. She was beyond personal affront. It seemed merely another trip-line set by malignant circumstance, like the Sister's stupidity and the ignorance of Nurse Jones. At any moment the ambulance would be here. All she could take seriously was that it might have to wait while she wasted time on a maddening side-issue.

'I had intended asking him to come over this afternoon. But in view of this development I haven't felt justified in risking the delay. I'm afraid it's absolutely essential that your son should see a neuro-surgeon – a brain specialist – immediately, and go where there are facilities for—'

'Then Dr Lowe hasn't seen him at all?'

The accusation in the thin voice was unmistakable. Oh, God, thought Hilary desperately, does the woman need a trephine herself to get a fact inside her skull?

'Mrs Fleming, I'm sorry. I've the highest possible opinion of Dr Lowe. But I'm afraid I must make it clear that this condition is very urgent; one of the most urgent in surgery. If we wait here for a consultation it may be impossible for Mr Sanderson to operate in time.'

Another pause: this time so long that Hilary began to wonder whether the woman at the other end had fainted. She found that her mind had no room for a second anxiety, a second compassion. She would feel them, and remorse for her own callousness, hereafter. Now she thought only about the delay, and listened for wheels in the drive.

At last, slowly and a little jerkily, 'Very well, Dr Mansell. When will the surgeon be here? I should like to see him.'

'I'm afraid it would be useless for Mr Sanderson to come here, even supposing he could get away. He couldn't do anything without his own theatre and his own staff. In view of the urgency, I've sent already for the ambulance to take your son to the Clyde Summers Hospital, where his department is.'

There was a sharp indrawn sound; it came over like a friction against the wire.

'To take him away? Away from here? But that hospital's in ... it's almost the other side of England. At a moment's notice like this. It gives me no time to make any decision, to ...'

Why, thought Hilary desperately, can't I say as I've said a score of times, 'My dear, I know how you feel, but you must trust me?' They always have. But I don't know how she feels; and she'll never trust me. There's no time now for anything but the truth.

'I'm sorry to have to tell you this. But without an immediate operation I don't think your son has any hope of living through the day. There's bleeding going on somewhere inside the skull. Until it's found and stopped the pressure on the brain will go on increasing. That means that sooner or later, the vital functions, such as breathing, will stop. I should expect that to happen within twelve hours, at most.' (In her own mind she had given it six.) 'You understand?'

'Yes. Yes, I understand.' The voice suddenly changed, it grew febrile and desperate; and yet, it seemed to Hilary, the fear and distrust below it remained the same. 'I'll come just as

48

I am. I'll get a coat and come straight over, so that I can go with you. I can be there in just over half an hour.'

'I'm terribly sorry.' (Was that the bell of the ambulance, far along the road? She could see herself as this woman must be seeing her, a callous automaton. As if the image possessed her, she struggled to feel, and could feel nothing.) 'I do so wish we could. But the ambulance is due any moment now. That half-hour might mean everything. A car will get you there almost as soon. Sooner, perhaps.'

'I see,' said the thin voice. Through the open window Hilary heard the ambulance drive in, and stop with the engine running. 'Very well, Dr Mansell. You leave me no choice. I find it hard to believe that things couldn't have been managed differently.' Hilary waited; but there was no more. The receiver clicked at the other end.

Hilary went into the hall, where the men from the ambulance were bringing in their stretcher. As she went in with them, to supervise the lifting, she thought, If he dies, as he well may, and if this woman has local influence, as no doubt she has, I can put my practice up for sale. The sooner the better. But the thought was as unreal to her as a dinner engagement for next week. She could only see the still face on the cotton pillow, darkened and shadowed, since yesterday, with a faint growth of beard that made it look, curiously, more boyish than before; and the unseeing eyes which, as she watched, closed again heavily as if sleep were pressing them down. When the stretcher had been settled on its racks, and she sat down beside him to feel his pulse again, his fingers closed vaguely on hers. It would be as well to know, she said to herself, when the reflex was obliterated. She sat still and took the pulse with her other hand.

5

The theatre sister was new this year. She shot at Hilary, over her mask, a glance of hurried curiosity as she made a last round of inspection, kicking the pedal of the diathermy into the right place for the assistant's foot and pushing back a trolley which was a little near. The surgeon's rubber-topped stool was too high, and her hands were already sterile; she beckoned a nurse to twist it lower.

The anaesthetic-room was still empty. Reaching from the familiar places the mask, cap, and student's gown, Hilary almost expected to see Sanderson's head lean out of the men's changing-room and say, 'You'd better scrub up, I think, Miss Mansell. Collett's tapping a ventricle downstairs.' Familiar smells of warm ether and Dettol wafted in from the ante-room door. A bitter nostalgia filled her. She forgot, for a moment, why she was here, and felt only that she had been a fool to come. She had been reconciled and dulled; she had almost forgotten.

The other door, the door behind her, opened, and the trolley came in.

He lay quite still under the thick scarlet blanket, his face composed as it had been in his first unconsciousness. She stood watching him, while the ward nurse who had brought him picked up the band of the blood-pressure gauge and bared his arm to fasten it on. His lips parted in a long, slow, shallow breath. She realised that during all the previous interval he had not breathed at all. About four to the minute, she thought.

'Excuse me a moment, Nurse.' She picked up part of his biceps muscle and gave it a sharp, vicious twist. His face, immobile in another pause of breathing, was wholly passive; she might as well have been using her strength on a fold of the blanket. The nurse said, 'He did respond, very faintly, in the ward. I had to do it pretty hard then.' Hilary nodded, and held up the arm for her to fix the strap.

The porter came in, wheeling in front of him a little trolley with soap and brushes and razors on a tray, and knocked on the door of the changing-room.

'How much do you want taken off, sir?'

Sanderson came out, in the kit he wore under his theatre gown; a sleeveless shirt and blue jeans under a clear oilskin apron. He had a fine carriage and physique, and this bleak costume displayed it well. He nodded to Hilary (they had talked already) and looked down at the trolley.

'His pulse, Nurse?'

'Forty-six, sir. And respirations three.'

Sanderson said to the porter, 'Half head. Frontal. And be quick.'

The porter slid a rubber sheet under the quiet head as the nurse lifted it. Whistling faintly between his teeth he picked up a pair of clippers from the tray and nibbled them in a broad arc. A deep soft swathe of black hair slid down on to the mackintosh; the balance and composition of the face were instantly changed. Sanderson looked again, said thoughtfully, 'I think we can keep the flap clear of the forehead,' and went on into the theatre. The porter, clipping away, remarked, 'S'right. Shame to spoil 'im for the girls,' and winked at the nurse, who, conscious of Hilary's presence, ignored him. Hilary picked up the stethoscope and took the blood-pressure.

Sanderson had the reputation of being able to turn an osteoplastic flap quicker than anyone in two continents. This time, having nothing else to do, Hilary watched the clock. The lid of bone was lifted in just seventeen-and-a-half minutes. As far as she knew it was a record. As she stood under the great frosted window, out of the track of those who had work to do, she fell back into the old impersonality. There was, indeed, nothing personal to see. The shape on the table was only a coffin-like oblong, a stand placed across the chest supporting a long green drape so that not even a human outline was recognisable below. All the varied activity in the room was focused on a six-inch oval; already even the bone-flap, with its fringe of artery-forceps, had been swathed with sterile gauze. There was only one reminder of the incidental presence under the green cloth; the anaesthetist on his low stool, the stethoscope in his ears connected to something unseen, making at intervals a tiny point on the chart beside him. This vigil over the hidden life was his only function. Nature had done his work for him; he could have added nothing, except death.

The theatre had an oppressive, greenhouse heat; with no activity to stir her, and drowsy from the ether fumes still hanging after the last case, Hilary felt drugged and suspended in time. Over Sanderson's shoulder she stared with fixed eyes into the neat red oval between the towels, seeing scarcely the hands that made tiny precise movements about it; only the fingers, the direction of the slender forceps and the long glass irrigator, with which the assistant washed their orbit clear.

Once something went awry, and she heard Sanderson swallow a word. He never permitted himself to swear in the presence of women, and it delighted him when occasion served to get the place clear of them. Hilary smiled into her mask and thought, Well, in any case the Sister's there ... Hallo. He's got it.

The thin steel had found its objective. Finely, delicately, it was removing the blood-clot it had been seeking. Hilary watched, single-minded; in her mind a tactile imagination reproduced the movements and stored them against a future which she had forgotten was already the past.

Her trance was interrupted. A voice spoke, curiously out of key with the tone of the proceedings; bewildered, angry, blurred as if with drink or sleep.

'For Christ's sake, let go of my head.'

There passed through the theatre an unseen flash, an inaudible breath. The sister took a quick, motiveless step forward; the anaesthetist, his eyes moving in something that was not quite a smile, reached up his hand into the green catafalque. Sanderson and the assistant met one another's eyes in a quick inexpressive glance. Hilary was entirely still. With such economies they acknowledged the passing incident of a homemade resurrection. A man who, in all but the last failing mechanisms of the body, had been two hours dead, abused them from his pall. So far, so good. The forceps began their quiet precise movements again. The anaesthetist peered under the drape and remarked conversationally, 'Don't worry, we shan't be long now.' A resentful grunt answered him.

'Diathermy,' said Sanderson. A faint electrical fizzing began and ended.

The hidden voice said, with a tipsy kind of violence, 'Take this bloody sheet off my face. Damn you, I can't see.'

At the far end of the table the green twill was stirred by the movement of a foot below. The anaesthetist looked towards Hilary and jerked his head.

She came forward, and, stooping, slid her hand under the cloth. It found another hand, gripping exploringly at the edge of the table, seeking a leverage. A strained leather strap creaked.

'Let me get up. I can't—'

'Keep still,' said Hilary. 'It's all right. The doctor's dressing your head.'

There was a pause, filled with the renewed buzz of the diathermy. Then, 'Is that you?'

'Yes. Keep quiet now. We've nearly finished.'

'Sorry. I was asleep.' She heard him grumble under his breath, 'They didn't have to tie me down.'

Sanderson's deep voice said, with apocalyptic finality, 'I want you perfectly still, please.' Stillness followed; the impertinent *revenant* seemed impressed. The operation proceeded.

Hilary kept her station, confident of more trouble; for though the tissue-layer they were working on was insensitive to pain, as a rule the irritation of the almost exposed brain would find vent in a rambling petulance and a breakdown, more or less complete, in the normal controls. But he only asked later, quite meekly, for a drink, and thanked her when she guided it to him under the drape. When it came to suturing the scalp, which really hurt him, he began to swear in a helpless, schoolboy way, but seemed to remember himself when she held his hand.

When it was over, and they lifted him from the table to the bed which had been wheeled up ready from the ward, he glanced for a moment wonderingly about the theatre, but seemed at once to slip into acquiescence. Hilary, deflecting the hand with which he was trying to explore the bandages, walked beside the bed towards the door, a couple of half-remembered lines tagging in her mind.

At the raising of Lazarus, someone said,
'What was it like, in the dark with the dead?'

She had wondered the first time; then, dulled by custom or preoccupation, had forgotten to wonder till now, when it seemed freshly and urgently important to know.

She must hurry, she thought presently, stripping off her gown, if she was to catch the last good train of the day. But she felt suddenly small, motiveless, and lonely, and was glad to spend ten minutes wise-cracking with the theatre porter, an old friend who could not in any case have been ignored. Then Collett, the assistant, came back from seeing the case down into the ward, and was anxious to show her his new laboratory.

She was taking leave of him, in the corridor outside the ward, when she felt the unmistakable sense of being stared at from behind. Turning, she saw Sanderson, standing with his back to them and talking to Mrs Fleming. It was her eyes that Hilary's met. Sanderson followed their direction, turned and smiled; then stepped back a little, like someone giving a cue.

Mrs Fleming came forward, Sanderson following with his slow, measured pace. Hilary felt a chilling discomfort, a cause-less feeling like guilt, making her want to escape as if from an accuser. She waited, doing something socially inoffensive with her face.

'Dr Mansell, Mr Sanderson has just been telling me that if you had not acted so promptly in sending Julian here, he – we should have lost him. I want to say how grateful I am for everything you've done.'

'You must thank Mr Sanderson; the diagnosis wouldn't have

been much use without him.' Hilary smiled, and took the outstretched, perfectly gloved hand. It felt brittle and, even as it grasped, aloof, as if its gesture had been imposed on it over a secret resistance of its own. She looked into the light-grey eyes, and it occurred to her for the first time that Mrs Fleming had been beautiful, and possessed, in skin and feature, the materials of beauty still. Not the form was lacking, but its acceptance and adventure and inward light.

'I shall be staying here, of course, for the present. Later on, I hope perhaps you will be able to spare an evening for dinner with me.'

Hilary expressed happy anticipation. Curiosity, interest, and a habit of facing uncomfortable things, kept her gaze straight and direct on the face that smiled at her; and suddenly, like a strained surface cracking, the smile wavered, the grey eyes looked aside. But in them Hilary had seen the look of someone placed, by cruel luck, under obligation to an enemy.

As she turned away she found that she felt no resentment and no surprise. Her mind sought parallels where it had experience; what she had done, she thought, was to confute a specialist in the field of her own speciality, a specialist without the redeeming loyalty to truth. About any other thing, perhaps, this woman would have forgiven anyone who had put her in the wrong. This she would never forgive. Coolly reasonable, Hilary accepted the fact, knowing that she should have felt more than acceptance, some compassion, some gentleness. She could not feel them, because in her world the specialist who would not absorb new truth was out, finished, scarcely worth the notice of contempt. Pursuing the truth, one simply moved on. The sister of the ward was passing; Hilary seized the moment for escape.

'Oh, Sister, may I just take a look at my patient before I go?'

'Of course, Miss Mansell. I'll show you where we've put him.'

The glass porthole in the side-ward door was open; Hilary paused a moment and looked in. They had tidied the bed and settled him more comfortably in the pillows; a nurse was giving him iced water to drink. She was young and neat-handed and trim, with a warm prettiness that triumphed over her ugly Victorian uniform. Her face was a little above his eye-level (he was preoccupied with his drink, in any case) and, thus secure, she was regarding him with undisguised, tender admiration.

The door was ajar. As Hilary put her hand on the knob to open it she heard the chink of the cup on its saucer, and then his voice, placid and friendly, as she remembered it in the strangely removed distance of yesterday.

'Thank you. That was good. Is my mother anywhere about?'

Hilary took her hand from the doorknob. The sister looked at her inquiringly, ready to go in and see what was causing the delay.

'He looks very comfortable, Sister. I think I won't disturb him after all.' She closed the door softly and went out into the light, cool evening to catch her train.

6

May turned to June. Influenza and measles died down; road accidents doubled. People discussed whether they should go abroad this summer; decided that nothing would come to a head about Czechoslovakia yet, and went. Hilary, who suspected that next summer decisions would go the other way, put in a locum and spent more than she could afford on a holiday to Scandinavia. She saw the Stockholm town hall, a number of fiords, and four hospitals which, when she planned the trip, she had had no intention at all of visiting. At one of them she got an invitation to spend the last seven days camping *à deux*: it came, blossoming out of an acquaintanceship half an hour old, from a cheerful young Viking with wide blue eyes and a sense of humour like sweet champagne. She spent three hours of the ensuing night wondering why on earth she had refused.

In sulky clouded weather she got back travel-weary and dispirited by the general and personal shape of things to come. As always, Lisa Clare's welcome was soothing and reviving; but Hilary thought that the recent heat must have tried her. Her eyelids looked blue and transparent in the clear pallor of her oval face, and she had a kind of lassitude which seemed, curiously, to have left her vitality undimmed. Perhaps she enjoyed hot weather, Hilary thought; there was a kind of still glow under her fine-drawn look. She had just come back, she said, from town.

Since she seldom went there, Hilary thought it an odd season to choose; but, having a horror of inquisitiveness, merely remarked that she expected it had been pretty warm.

'I suppose it was.' Evidently she was making an effort to remember. 'I didn't go out much.' After a pause in which she seemed to have closed the subject, she added, 'My husband had a week in England. He couldn't leave town, he had too much to do. We stayed – somewhere in Lancaster Gate. I've forgotten the name already. We've stayed in so many places.'

Not for the first time Hilary stayed herself from a leading question. She liked Lisa too much, by now, to risk even so negative a rebuff as one of her tacit withdrawals would give. It was too bad, she said, that he couldn't have managed Gloucestershire before the summer got stale.

'He meant to. But he had to start for the Sudetenland a week sooner than he'd planned. Things seemed to be moving rather fast.'

Hilary's speculations were suddenly illuminated.

'How stupid I am. Why didn't it occur to me before that he was Rupert Clare?'

Lisa smiled briefly. It was as if for a moment she allowed the hidden glow to reach the surface, and then gathered it quickly within herself again.

Hilary had always admired Rupert Clare's journalism, to the extent of changing her daily paper when he had transferred himself to another; she trusted his integrity to a degree which made her distrust any journal he fell out with. She told Lisa so, with sincerity and warmth. Lisa said, as usual, very little; but though she changed the conversation almost at once to the subject of tea, Hilary had a pleasant feeling that the quiet progress of their friendship had advanced a little.

It was over the tea that Lisa said, 'How tiresome of Pound's not to send your new suit-case till after you'd gone. Were you short? I could have lent you one.'

Hilary, who had ordered nothing, went up to investigate as soon as the meal was over. The package was behind the door, where she had overlooked it. Stripping off layers of board and shaving, she found, preciously guarded in a fine canvas jacket, a dressing-case of pale pigskin, with H. M. stamped in gilt across the corner. Inside, it was fitted with everything imaginable in cream enamel and gold. It was the kind of thing which might have been possessed by a film star with exceptionally good taste. An envelope was stuck inside one of the dove-grey silk bands in the tray. She opened it.

Dear Dr Mansell,
    I hope this very inadequate token of gratitude from my son and myself will be in time to go with you on your well-deserved holiday this year.
    Sincerely yours,
    ELAINE FLEMING.

Hilary sat back, squatting on her heels, staring at the elegance which only its perfect design redeemed from ostentation. She was shocked by her own feelings of sinking embarrassment and outrage. Flowers, a book, some pleasant trifle for her room, anything like that she would have welcomed as a peace-offering and in relief. But this was horrible. There must, she thought helplessly, be some way of returning it without the appearance of studied insult. She recalled the stamped initials; the writing-case inside the lid, she saw, carried them too.

The letter was still in her hand. She looked at the date. It had lain here, unacknowledged, for eleven days.

A light leisured step was crossing the landing. Hilary swung round on her heels.

'Do come in here a moment. I don't know what to do.'

Lisa Clare came in, a point of rest amid the disordered rubbish of packing on the floor. She looked down at the case, and lifted her eyebrows in cool humorous admiration.

'Good heavens. Is it yours?'

'Not if I can help it.'

'What a pity. Think of packing it up again.'

'It's stamped all over with my initials,' said Hilary desperately. 'What does one do?'

Stroking appreciatively a cream enamel powder-jar, Lisa said, 'Why worry? He must have known he was taking a gamble on it. Leave it till to-morrow, and do whatever you feel.'

'I wish it were so simple,' said Hilary lightly. As she spoke she wondered why Lisa's use of the masculine pronoun had made her feel so raw. He was little more than a boy, he was probably still away somewhere convalescing; what more natural than that his mother should write? 'It's from a – grateful patient,' she said.

'Oh,' said Lisa reflectively. 'Do you dislike her as much as that?'

'I was trying, till this came, not to dislike her as much as I know she dislikes me.'

Lisa considered briefly; then said, in her placid voice, 'Well, I dare say it means a lot to her to take her pride out of pawn at the expense of yours. And after all, unless she's an exceptional woman, you can probably afford it better.'

Hilary wrote her letter of thanks next day. It must contain, she decided when she re-read it, the highest concentration of bromides ever compressed into two sides of note-paper. She posted it with the sense of riddance people feel on dropping something unsavoury into the fire; and deposited the dressing-case in the box-room, hidden in a suit-case she seldom used. A few years hence she might rediscover it with feelings of grati-fied surprise. Such things happened, but were, she felt, sufficient unto the day.

Summer ran out; the early sunlight began to be tinged with smoky scents of chrysanthemums and bonfires and faint frost on rotten leaves; tea was by twilight eked out with the fire. Between all these old certainties, distorting them like an abscess under flesh, the gathering poison of war swelled and tautened. The palliative of Munich was applied; the patient testified eagerly to relief after the first dose. Chrysanthemums and frost and crumpets got back their own taste again.

At the Cottage Hospital Hilary was invited into the kitchen to give the Christmas puddings a stir. She interpreted this, rightly, as a sign of grace, and emptied in her small silver under the Matron's benevolent gaze. When the last shilling was worked under she said, 'We'll have to be thinking about get-ting some children in.'

'I wish we could keep Christine and Betty,' the Matron said regretfully. 'If we only had the beds, *they* wouldn't complain, poor little things. But I've promised they shall come up for the Christmas-tree. Between you and me, I think it's going to be rather special this year. Mrs Fleming's promised to give it, and anything *she* does will be done very nicely, you can be sure.'

'Oh, really?' After this lapse of time the name brought only a vague discomfort in the nerves. 'I'm glad she's been taking an interest.'

'She's been a real asset to us this summer, I must say. Nearly every week something or other's come down. Remind me to show you the little woollies she knitted for the babies.' Hilary listened with an amusement which was only very slightly acid; here, too, it seemed, time had brought healing, the Matron's comfortable satisfaction was wholly unforced. She was continuing, 'Yes, I really must say, they both ... '

'Oh, Matron, could I *speak* to you for a moment?'

'Very well, Sister, though really, if I can't be out of the way for five minutes ... You won't go away without your cup of coffee, will you, Doctor? Just make yourself comfortable in my room, I shan't be long.'

Hilary went out through the flagged kitchen passage and opened the green baize door into the hall, prepared to dawdle a little, since the Matron's office provided no stronger incentives to comfort than a hard-backed chair and last week's *Nursing Mirror*. Round the corner, from the stairs, came the chirruping laughter of Christine and Betty, who were well enough now to have the run of the place. She paused a moment to listen.

'No, not that one. No, that's a silly one. Do the monkey face.'

A pause, followed by squeals of ecstatic mirth.

'Again. Again. Do it again.'

Hilary walked round the corner.

Squatting on the last few steps of the staircase, in a doubled-up simian crouch, was a man whose face it was at first difficult to see, since it was partly obscured by his knees. He was scratching his armpit, reproducing vividly a monkey's sporadic but earnest concentration. When he moved she glimpsed a prognathous-looking jaw and a hideously grimacing mouth beneath a mournful stare. Christine, hopping on one leg with delight, was handing him an imaginary morsel. He snatched at it and went through motions of peeling a banana so lifelike that she could almost see the skin when he threw it away.

'Go on. Go on. Now crack a nut.'

'Half a minute,' said the man, unfolding himself. 'I think someone's looking for you two.'

He got up. His face, after a few minor adjustments such as the removal of the tongue from inside the lower lip, had resolved itself into one at which she stared with unbelieving recognition. It had been like a trick done with mirrors.

Her first feeling was regret. He had seen her, they would have to converse, one had better prepare for the worst immediately. She could only remember having met two men with a fraction of his looks, and both had been, in different ways, insufferable. It was a pity, for she had remembered him chiefly with the impersonal pleasure one might feel at having saved some work of art from destruction; but the anticlimax would have to be dealt with, like other annoyances of a working day. She smiled, and waited resignedly.

He scrambled to his feet, wriggling his disarranged clothes back into place and vaguely stuffing down his tie. As he did so, he grinned at her over the heads of the children, guiltily but hopefully. She thought, in a moment almost of shock, But I can't have remembered him at all; why, he's hardly more than a child himself.

'It was my fault,' he said, 'entirely. I fetched them down.' Reaching out for Christine and Betty, he collected them, amid squeaks of protest, by the scruffs of their frocks. He handled them, not amusingly or indulgently like a grown-up person, but with the heavy-handed kindness of a bigger boy.

'It's all right,' said Hilary. 'I expect it's given the nurses a rest. How are you getting on yourself?'

The children had been jerking at their collars like little

dogs; now they recovered their freedom so suddenly that they had to run to keep from falling. They paused, one on each side; with the instinct of their age for the vagaries of adult attention, they were making off before he had opened his mouth to speak.

'Forgive me,' he said slowly, 'if I'm making a mistake. But I think we know each other, don't we?'

He was staring at her in an intense, puzzled concentration; not as men stare, with an eye to the reaction of the object, but with that self-forgetfulness which rarely survives childhood: in fact self-consciousness shortly overtook him and made him look down, none too soon for Hilary, who had found it rather unnerving. He was a tall, strongly made young man – taller, probably, than he looked, his perfect proportions made it unnoticeable – and his physical carriage had a kind of inbred assurance which seemed separate from the uncertainty in his face. He looked up again.

'Do you,' he asked anxiously, 'remember me at all?'

'Yes, of course.' She pulled herself together in time to smile. 'But I'm rather surprised if you remember me. You weren't very wide awake while I was there.' She thought, It's the white coat. There is only one woman doctor here, as no doubt he knows.

He said, with the same slow concentration, 'I knew your voice. As soon as you spoke, I knew who it was. But I've been here so often, and never seen you. They told me one of the nurses had left since I was there, and I thought it must be you.'

'I only call in now and again. I'm not a nurse, I'm a doctor.'

'Good Lord, a doctor. Why ever didn't I think of that.' He stared at her all over again; it would have been almost a relief to her, by now, if he had started to say the conventional things. Instead he added, as if an apology were the first imperative, 'You see, till after the operation there's almost nothing I remember.'

'That's quite usual. It's nothing to worry about.'

'But, of course, I remembered you.'

He paused. He had the air of having said all it can be necessary to say, and of awaiting some expected result. He looked suddenly strained, as people do when a shock, half felt at first, catches up with them.

Hilary was interested. She must, she thought, have stirred up by association some memory of the accident, submerged till now. Such resurrections were apt to be painful. She said, reassuringly, 'Bits of things may come back to you; or perhaps nothing will. It's quite normal to forget, it means nothing either way.'

He did not answer. The look he gave her – a compound of disappointment, diffidence, and the hesitation of one who does not like to own that he has missed the point – seemed so little related to the situation that she asked herself for a moment whether he had made a complete recovery after all. But he seemed quite well co-ordinated and alert. Presently he said, 'Yes, I see,' in the tone which means that one wishes one did; and came, suddenly and evidently, to the end of his resources. She became rather desperate for conversation herself. Since he was not her patient, a fact which had been heavily underlined, she could not ask him details about his symptoms; yet one would have said he was waiting for her to make some move or other. It struck her – she had not had time to notice till now – how curiously devoid he seemed of the kind of self-satisfaction his appearance had led her to expect. She eased the moment over with a little small-talk about the children; he responded quite readily and with cheerful humour, but she detected all the time a slight air of unreality, as if he were waiting for something to begin. Perhaps, she thought, he was hanging about for one of the nurses, who would, of course, be lurking round some corner waiting for her to go.

'Well,' she said, 'Matron's expecting me to coffee; I should be getting along.'

'Oh, but must you?' He looked as if it were the very last move he could have foreseen. His face was positively dismayed. 'I've hardly seen you yet.'

'Come and have some too; I'm sure she'd be delighted.'

'She wouldn't; she's death on visitors in the morning. I'm only supposed to be leaving a parcel.' He seemed suddenly to have shaken himself together. 'She won't be here yet, she was frightfully involved with something just now. Isn't there somewhere we can talk for a minute without being chucked out? Me, I mean, of course, not you.' He smiled, anxiously watching her face for sign of offence. She had never seen, in man or woman, such an exterior treated with such utter lack of exploitation by the personality within. It was almost uncanny. He wore his beauty anyhow, like old clothes. Curiosity, as much as anything, made her say, 'If you like we'll take a turn round the garden. But I mustn't be long.'

'Oh, fine.' They went out through the pointed stone archway, and into the drive between the laurels. The sky was coolly blue and clear, and rooks were cawing in a clump of elms not far away. He seemed in no hurry to say anything, but the pause failed for some reason to be strained; it seemed quite natural they should be walking in silence and that he should be immersed in thoughts of his own. At last he said, 'I'm afraid it must have seemed very odd of me not to have said good-bye.'

'Not very, in the circumstances,' she said, amused.

'It seemed very odd to me.'

A little moss-grown path branched off from the side of the drive. He took her elbow, casually and naturally, and steered her into it.

'Wherever does this go?' she asked.

'I don't know, I want to see.'

The laurels walled them darkly, then thinned. They came out into a little derelict box-garden, once squared and formal, now run wild. Marigolds had sown themselves in the undipped walks; there was a gardener's shed in one corner, against a hedge of arbutus; an old roller stood outside.

'What a gorgeously forlorn place,' he said. His voice was as attractive as the rest of his physical attributes, but when he pronounced the word 'forlorn' she noticed something else about it, a lack of the carelessness with which he treated the rest. It had a quality which suggested training, only a faint suggestion of the kind that remains when a skill has been absorbed and mostly forgotten. He had put the word into delicate quotation marks, and a train of images from Keats and de la Mare came into her head as clearly as if he had recited them.

'Let's sit down here.' He pulled off his coat and tossed it over the top of the roller. 'That's to save your nice white coat-tails. I'll sit on this.' A piece of dirty-looking board lay on the ground close by. He curled himself up on it, loosely, like a boy, displaying an indifference to his trousers which was, in its own way, as remarkable as his indifference to his face.

'Really I don't think I've got time to sit. Matron doesn't like being kept waiting.'

'You can tell her I was consulting you.'

'I certainly can't.' It slipped out before she thought. She was embarrassed, till she saw that it had meant nothing to him.

'Oh, but I am. I can't get over not having thought you might be a doctor.'

It was not till this moment that her suspicions crystallised into certainty. When he had failed so oddly to say the conventional things, she had wondered for a moment and at once been ashamed of herself. Now she knew, as if she had seen it written and signed; about her part in his recovery, as far as it had been decisive, he had been told nothing at all. She thought of the dressing-case, the covering note. The shock of disgust she felt was so strong that it was impersonal; her whole conception of humanity slipped downward with a jar. She was recalled to herself by hearing his low pleasant voice saying, 'Don't hover so distrustfully. There's nothing to stop you from getting up again.'

'This thing's covered in rust. Your coat will be ruined.'

'It's dry, it'll brush off. How women do fuss.' The word 'women', as he spoke it, was totally devoid of masculine provocation; it suggested, irresistibly, aunts, school matrons, and nagging devoted maids. She sat down, mechanically, her mind still concerned with its discovery. It was not for a moment that she thought, Then what does he want with me, after all?

A sharp consciousness of being stared at made her look down. He was gazing up at her with the same curious, strained expectancy that she had noticed before in the hall.

What *is* he waiting for? she thought irritably. What does he expect me to do now? Sing? Or pull coloured streamers out of my ears? As before, natural conversation deserted her. He sat and regarded her in silence, as if to do this were an entirely obvious reaction.

Choosing the first triviality that came into her head, she said, 'I've been away part of the summer; that will be why we haven't met. I went to Sweden.'

'Oh, really?' He looked at her, attentively, again; rather, she thought, as though he expected something Swedish to have stamped itself on her countenance. 'Do you like it there?'

Why not 'Did you like it there?' she thought; as if one flit-ted to and from Scandinavia at will. She said she had liked it, and explained why. When she ran out of ideas (which was soon, because he gave her no help at all) he asked her, 'Are there any good caves there? As it's so rocky, I thought perhaps there might be.'

'I've no idea,' she said blankly. 'I dare say in Norway; I was only there two days.'

'You don't go in for them at all?' There was a kind of defeated hope in his voice. She said, 'I'm afraid not,' thinking, I wonder whether he would strike one so oddly if he looked more average.

'Don't mind' – he looked, for the first time, a little embar-rassed – 'if I seem to ask you some rather stupid things. The fact is, when you were with me, I couldn't see properly, but I seemed to be seeing, and it's given me some rather confused ideas. I really should think before I start talking rubbish.'

She regretted her unhelpfulness instantly. It was rare for patients to retain such memories after so long, or, indeed, at all. Moreover, Sanderson was preparing a paper on traumatic hallucinations, and this was one of his own cases. If she could learn anything to the purpose, she ought certainly to send it in.

'It isn't stupid,' she said. 'It interests me very much. I'd like you to tell me about it.'

'Would you?' he said; and looked straight up into her face. Perhaps it was only his seriousness and his thick black lashes which gave him an air of unhappiness and doubt. His eyes, reflecting the clear sky, looked startlingly blue when she had supposed them to be grey. It was all a little disconcerting. Abruptly he lowered them and shifted his hands, which he had locked round one ankle. 'I don't think so, really. These things sound rather idiotic, don't they, in cold blood?'

'Not to me,' she said reassuringly.

He looked up at her again, and then discovered something unsatisfactory about his shoelace. Pulling it undone and retying it painstakingly, he said, 'Well, don't mind if it sounds silly, because it will. It's only that there's a cave I know fairly well because I've been there a number of times, and I suppose it's a natural thing if one's wandering a bit to wander to places one knows. Only I thought, part of the time, that we were there.' He tugged at the loops of the lace, knotted them together, and added, so indistinctly that she had difficulty in hearing, 'That was afterwards.'

'After what?'

She had no time to read the face which he turned to hers, and as swiftly averted. It might have expressed many things – incredulity, shame, even a mortal reproach. It gave her an unhappiness which pointed out to her her unfitness for this kind of research. She must have disturbed something which only a trained psychologist would be competent to deal with; this was what came of dabbling in other people's specialities. Above all, it was shocking to let oneself feel so personally about it. All she could think of to say was, 'Well, never mind.'

In a voice which was quenched to an almost colourless flatness he said, 'I don't think I can remember anything else.'

'You don't have to.' She spoke gently, and saw that there had returned to his face a kind of hesitant trust. 'You told me all I wanted to know.'

'Yes,' he said. 'I thought so, really.'

'I must go. Matron loathes cold coffee.'

He seemed suddenly to accept this without question.

'Just tell me one thing. Did I – behave badly, or anything? You know, the sort of thing I believe people do, shouting and swearing and being embarrassing about their pasts?'

'Not at all.' Here was comfortably familiar ground. Nearly everyone (except, curiously enough, the people with most cause for concern) asked this sooner or later. Suppressing the amusement which the word 'past' had given her, she added, 'Your brain just slowed down and you went to sleep.' She remembered, vaguely, some disturbance or other when she had first examined him, but could not by now recall the details, and would have reassured him in any case.

'Thank you,' he said. 'I had it rather on my mind.'

'The people who needn't always have.'

She got up. He made a movement as if to follow; then sinking back again, and smiling up at her, said, 'I've got cramp. Give me a pull.'

Good-humouredly she took his outstretched hand in both of hers; there was a good deal of him, and she did not want to be ignominiously pulled over. He got to his feet with a smoothness which did not suggest much muscular contraction, and stood for a moment looking down at her. He could not be much under six foot; one scarcely noticed it except at such close quarters. 'Thanks,' he said. He had spoken with a seriousness quite out of key with the rather ridiculous incident and, as if suddenly aware of it, picked up his coat, shook it perfunctorily, and put it on.

'The back's covered in bits. Let me brush it, you're not presentable.'

He stood there obediently, almost absent-mindedly, while she did so, and forgot to thank her, as if he were used to it. When she had finished he searched his pockets and produced, after some moments, the cigarette-case which she had last seen lying on the Matron's blotter. When opened, it proved to contain one cigarette, old and sad-looking. He made an apologetic face, and offered it to her.

'I'm so sorry,' he said. 'I only smoke at odd times.'

'If this is one of the times, for goodness' sake have a fresh one.' She became aware of the fact that she could very well do with one herself. He accepted gratefully, turning out to be unprovided with matches as well.

When they had got back to the drive he stopped and said, 'I'll see you again.'

'I expect so.'

'Let's not leave it so indefinite, though.' He reflected. 'How about – could you come over to lunch?'

'I don't think,' she said hastily, 'I dare not make any fixtures at the moment. I'm so busy, I shouldn't be reliable.'

'That doesn't matter. Give us a ring and come at a moment's notice.' But his air of confidence, this time, was a little forced. She could understand it. The voice of the Matron came back to her: 'Anything *she* does will be done very nicely, you can be sure.' She murmured vague platitudes about the work letting up, perhaps, in a month or two, and saw his face register relaxation as well as regret.

'Never mind. We'll manage something.' She saw that he meant what he said, and found that it gave her pleasure. I can't imagine why, she reflected; he's so erratic and unpredictable, he'd soon become quite exhausting; I suppose it's just the aesthetic factor.

'I do hope,' he was saying, 'I've not really put you in wrong with the Matron, keeping you here. In the surprise of actually meeting you I'm afraid I only had room for one idea at a time. Had we better think up a story before you go?' He seemed quite serious about it.

'Oh, she'll have started without me. There's no nonsense about her.'

'I know, poor old thing, isn't it a shame? I think I shall give her a bottle of curious scent for Christmas, called "Black Limelight" or "Ecstase" or something ... In a way, it was rather a shock. Suddenly meeting you, I mean. You see, actually, I'd become practically reconciled to the idea that I'd imagined the whole thing. I couldn't ask about you, because – well, not remembering what you looked like, there seemed nothing to ask. I imagined you quite different, I'm afraid.'

'I'm sorry.' She laughed because this was the sensible reaction.

'It's all right. I've got used to it now. In fact, I feel as if I'd remembered all along. It does seem odd, though, that I haven't heard the nurses mention you, or anything. I've talked to them quite a lot' (no wonder, thought Hilary, the Matron's been looking so unrelaxed lately) 'and I thought I'd got the low-down on pretty well everyone, not that one gets time to take in quite all of it, of course ... Good Lord, I must be crazy. I haven't asked you *now* what your name really is.'

'It's Mansell.'

'*Is it?*' He looked, for an unguarded moment, positively stupefied. Recovering himself with headlong haste, he said, 'You know, I do think I may have heard it, just vaguely, and forgotten again.'

Hilary was hideously conscious of blushing down to the neck. She knew, too well, that the change from an efficient and highly specialised department to the local product had not been easy to assimilate: she had not always suffered it gladly, nor in complete silence. She wondered which incidents, exactly, he had been treated to, and with how much embroidery. Not that it mattered, of course, in the least. She said, 'I dare say you have.'

'You know,' he pursued reflectively, 'I think nurses are an interesting study, very. I mean, seeing life so much in the raw, as it were, you'd think they'd become frightfully understanding about human nature, wouldn't you? I often think it's curious how they're not.'

The feeling of relief and well-being which swept over her quite startled her by its force.

'Well, they understand some aspects of human nature pretty soundly. And, of course, the brighter ones do gravitate more to the big places.'

'I suppose they must.'

They had come to the last bend in the drive. 'The last part,' she said, 'is just under Matron's window. I think I'd better go up it looking busy and by myself.'

'You could say you were talking to an old patient. That's what the nurses say.' He offered this information helpfully, without the least shade of irony.

'Well, good-bye,' she said, and then suddenly at a loss, 'I'm glad you're getting on so well.'

'I'll get on all right now.'

She was round the bend of the drive before this valediction reached her; and, when it did, the likeliest thing seemed to be that she had not correctly heard.

7

It looked like being a green Christmas. Hilary, who had no accompanying superstition about fat churchyards, but on the contrary had seen many chronic invalids and old people killed by cold, welcomed the mild, moist weather and the golden rags of autumn which quiet air left hanging on the trees. The place had become friendly to her, the blunt hills, with their grey out-crop of stone-roofed houses, their meandering lines of dry-walling, and the dips of soft, misty space between their shoulders.

She and Lisa got on increasingly well. It was a relationship owing much to unembarrassed silences, and to the mutual knowledge that either could seek privacy at any time without affront to the feelings of the other. The house was a newish one built round an old core; Hilary's two rooms, in the irregu-lar thick-walled part at one end, were almost self-contained, her sitting-room having its own glass door on to the garden, and, in one corner, a steep crooked staircase leading into the bedroom upstairs. They need never have met except at meals, but with increasing frequency spent their evening together by the log fire in the hall.

Rupert Clare had gone from Czechoslovakia to Berlin. When Hilary asked for news of him, Lisa said, 'He's been to a number of theatres. His private letters are all opened and read, of course, so they consist almost entirely of items like that, at present. So do mine.' While Hilary was still thinking of something to say, she added, 'We're used to it ... It doesn't make any difference.'

Lisa was not the kind of woman who makes such remarks as an invitation to comment, and Hilary offered none.

It was in the course of another such desultory conversation that Lisa said, 'Oh, by the way, what happened to that man who nearly died at the hospital – the one you had to rush off for a brain operation ... Excuse my journalese.'

'Well,' said Hilary briskly, 'for once it's accurate, we rushed him all right. Yes, he did quite well, in fact he's living a more or less normal life already. You may know the people. Fleming. The mother's a widow, I fancy. They live out Lynchwyck way.'

'Fleming? Oh, yes, I meet them sometimes at the Abbots'. The mother a very poised, buttoned-up sort of woman, and the boy – Julian, isn't it? – far too good-looking, and very ... what they call unspoiled. I suppose after this she'll manage to keep him in apron-strings for another year. Not that he'll mind, I dare say.'

Hilary said casually, 'I've run into him once or twice at the hospital, since. I was wondering what he meant to do with himself.'

'Oh, there's always vague talk of his doing something. It never seems to come to anything. Unfortunately the father – he was killed in the last war, I think – left him enough to be idle on. I'm afraid Rupert's made me rather allergic to drifters.'

77

'Yes, I expect so,' said Hilary; and observed shortly after that it was time for bed.

They neither of them had any plans for Christmas. Hilary, whom a vast family gathering in Shropshire was eager to receive, could not leave her practice. The family was used to doing without her, for since she took up medicine she had always been tied; but she herself, accustomed by now to the happy saturnalia of hospitals, looked forward to the festival with a sense of strangeness, which was only redeemed from gloom by the prospect of Lisa's company. Rupert, who was a Scot, was saving for the New Year the few days which were all he could hope for. The two women found in one another the excuse for decorating, saving their mail against Christmas morning, and such small follies which neither would have had the heart to pursue alone; and were mutually grateful.

On Christmas Eve, Hilary, coming in from an evening call, found in her sitting-room a huge pot of cyclamen growing in moss. The card attached to it turned out to be Julian Fleming's. On the back, in a neat, sloping fifth-form hand, was 'Are you coming to the hospital to-morrow?' She turned it over, wondering what it was that seemed odd; and realised that it was the mere fact of his possessing visiting cards at all. Such adult accessories seemed, somehow, out of keeping. When she had defined the thought, she found that it annoyed her and pushed it out of the way.

She had had two weeks of duty at the hospital since their first meeting, and during each of them had encountered him there a little too often, it seemed, for mere coincidence. He always contrived to leave with her, and to drag out their progress through the garden as long as possible. On these occasions, if he talked at all, it was about nothing in particular, and as unself-consciously as if they had been meeting for years; he had a fund of local gossip, and a nice undergraduate sense of fun. When he dried up completely, which he frequently did without any warning, it appeared not to embarrass him in the least. She scarcely knew why she found these moments so irritating; it was in fact the contrast between his face in repose and animation. Its structure was emphatic, vivid, and clear, with a subtle flare in the contours that seemed made to express a brilliant intensity. As soon as he spoke again it would all resolve into a pleasant, diffident adolescence. Waiting for this to happen was rather like listening to a pianist who always strikes the same discord in the same bar of the same piece.

Now and again he would stare. He did it, not quite stealthily, but with calculated suddenness; as if, she thought, he suspected her of being different when he wasn't looking. The times when she showed that she noticed it were the only ones when he became shy; so she ignored it. She found it less trouble to write it off as a nervous tic hanging over from the accident; which, incidentally, he had never mentioned again. Meanwhile the cyclamen had a place of honour in her sitting-room; the pot was too large, in any case, to be put anywhere else.

That night it grew so cold that Lisa had to bring extra blankets out of store, and Hilary woke early next morning, her eyelids pierced by a pale dazzle in the air. The window was covered with a lace of crystals; when she had thawed a space clear she found it was not snow that had fallen, but a deep, branching hoar-frost. It clung to the grass like thick white fur; the frailest things, the edges of small leaves, an old cobweb, a bird's breast-down caught in a strand of horsehair, were flowered with it; the most uninteresting conifers in the garden had a spun-glass web beside which the tinsel indoors looked tawdry and dull. Lisa and Hilary stood in the porch, tasting the tingling air and looking at the white woods feathering the hills, and found it hard to go in to breakfast and the parcels beside their plates.

The frost held over, pure and crisp, into the afternoon. Walking on grass was like stepping on the friable icing of a Fuller's cake. The round of visits whose necessity had kept her here and to which she had looked forward as a nuisance spoiling the day, provided enchantment at every turn of the road. And it was all here yesterday, she reminded herself, in the form of a clammy and depressing mist. A few degrees' drop of the thermometer, and the same trees and wet become imitations of immortality. Who was that idiot who used to say that the so-called sense of beauty depended solely on the recognition of biologically favourable conditions? It had been David; but it took her some moments to remember the fact.

She made so many detours through woods and over hills that, in order not to be late at the hospital, she had to drive like Jehu for the last quarter of an hour. She had nearly forgotten it completely, a lapse which would have cost her all the ground she had gained with the Matron. Everyone who had the slenderest connection with the place got invitations to the Christmas-tree ritual at three in the afternoon, and for the doctors it was a *sine qua non*. Lisa had dressed two dolls exquisitely, in brilliant peasant costumes. Hilary, whose mind did not run much on such matters in private life, wondered for the first time, when she saw them, why Lisa had no child.

Turning into the drive she saw that the Ruskin-Gothic mass had resisted, with stout Victorian common sense, the frail enchantments of the air. Nothing less obvious than a foot of snow would have made any impression on it. Only the red of its bricks looked dusky against the whiteness around, and its bulk more stolid; under its walls the garden hung in crystalline foam, like frozen spray about a rock.

She parked her car and went round to the steps. Before she could mount them, Julian detached himself from the porch and came to meet her. He had left his overcoat inside, but still had a thick woollen scarf thrown round his neck. It made him look very much the undergraduate.

Because she found herself unexpectedly pleased to see him there, she said conventionally, 'Thank you so much for the flowers. They were charming.'

With the smile whose lack of self-confidence never ceased to amaze her, he said, 'I'm glad if they were yesterday. You're not telling me that to-day flowers could look anything but rather grubby and crude.'

'They'll still be there to-morrow.'

'I wish I thought this would. The sun will be going down, by the time we get out of that racket.'

'I was thinking that, too.' She turned in the porch beside him, looking out. A buzz of conversation and laughter, and the shrill excitement of children already overwrought, came from inside. They stood for a minute or so in silence. Absently, it seemed, he broke off a sprig from a yew-bush that grew beside the porch, its fine leaves exquisitely and intricately frosted, and turned it over in his hand; then suddenly dragged it through his fingers, shredding off the bloom with a kind of painstaking and deliberate brutality. When he had finished he snapped it across the middle, crushed it, and threw it away. Hilary found the gesture irrationally disturbing. She did not believe in irrational feelings, on principle.

'I daren't be late,' she said. 'But don't let me drag you in.' She hoped that he would take the hint; she had no desire that they should make so public an entrance together.

81

He looked at his watch. 'It's only five to. Don't let's go for a minute.'

He spoke without insistence, but she paused for another moment, watching the garden glitter and the blue shadows lengthen, almost visibly, in the deepening sun. Julian broke another sprig from the yew, turned it round to catch the light, and stripped it, ruthlessly and systematically, like the first. Looking up from this, he said brightly, 'Did I tell you I found Matron that scent? Just the stuff. It's in a little black bottle with an enormous stopper, and it's called "Nuit de Lesbos". It's on the tree.'

'Oh, Julian, how could you?' The name slid out without attracting the notice of either. 'I'm sure it isn't appropriate. What does it smell like?'

'Just like the specification. I think I must be there to see her have it ... Let's not go in at all. Next time this happens one might be in town. Or dead.'

He had spoken quite lightly and without significance; but it was the winter of 1938. Hilary felt as if, without warning, a tight hand had constricted her throat. With extreme flippancy she said, 'Try to work up a bit of Christmas spirit. You're being anti-social.'

'Yes, I know. That must be the word I was trying to get hold of. Well, let's go ahead and have a simply *won*derful time. We ...'

He stopped, and turned round quickly. There had been a step in the hall; but in hospital halls footsteps are the rule rather than the exception, and she had not attended. Now, though the massive pitchpine door, half-open, was in the way, she knew at once who was coming, and was amazed by her own folly in not having expected it.

'Hallo, dear,' said Julian, going to the inner door. 'I've virtually arrived. A matter of instants.'

'Julian, you absurd boy. What *are* you doing, day-dreaming out here? They're just beginning. The Matron's been asking where you are, and the poor little nurses look *most* hurt at being deserted.' Hilary thought how different the voice sounded, relaxed and expansive, from the one she remembered; and yet, after all, how like.

'By way of being thoroughly anti-social,' said Julian, 'I've been detaining the guest of honour, as well.' One could not have said exactly that his manner had changed; it had only become very slightly overdone. He set back the door with an unnecessary little flourish. The two women were left confronting one another, an encounter for which only Hilary had been at all prepared. With the instant perception which at such times outpaces thought, she knew that Mrs Fleming had supposed the remark about the guest of honour to refer to herself, and that Julian had just realised it too late. Everyone snatched up the situation with great social address; in actual terms of time, the jolting pause of which they were all conscious had no existence at all.

'Why, Dr Mansell. I was thinking that surely we should be seeing you to-day. How very naughty of Julian to keep you hanging about here in the cold. I often tell him he makes himself far too much at home here, considering that he was only a patient for about twenty-four hours. You mustn't let him be a nuisance to you.'

She looked at him, as she spoke, with affectionate, whimsical apology. The fact that neither the words, nor the look, would have needed any essential alteration if they had been directed at a child of ten, was scarcely apparent, so gracefully was it done. Julian received it with his pleasant diffident smile.

Hilary said, 'Not at all; I was just lingering to admire the garden.'

'Quite lovely, isn't it?' Mrs Fleming came out a little way into the porch, a gracious figure, dressed with dignity and taste in soft blacks and greys; she inclined her head slightly, as if a florist had submitted for her approval a well-chosen vase. 'I expect it's rarely that you have time for such things, in such realistic work as yours.'

'I like to remind myself, sometimes, that this is just as real as anything I see when I'm working.' Hilary smiled socially. In the moment of using it as a conversational pawn, the beauty outside had seemed to withdraw itself from her, its secret gone.

'I can see you're a thoroughly balanced person. And that's a very enviable trait, as I was saying to Julian only this morning. He's a quite hopeless romantic, I'm afraid. As soon as I missed him I knew just where I should have to look for him. Take your scarf off, dear, before we go in; it's quite oppressively hot inside. Of course' – she turned courteously to Hilary – 'one quite realises that sick people need it. I think if we go now we shall be just in time.'

Hilary paid her respects to the Matron, and was drawn into conversation by Dr Lomax, who had a bald head continuous with his neck, and a face like an overripe cherub's. Hilary liked him, in spite or because of the fact that he had a way of looking at her as if he knew a joke about her which was vulgar, but not unkind. Dr Dundas, the senior honorary, was invisible; *ex officio*, he would be Santa Claus. She wondered how much of his black jowl would overflow from under the cotton-wool whiskers.

She was just considering whether there would be time to greet any of her own patients before the show when a voice said 'Hallo,' on a level with her elbow. She looked round, but she was not being addressed. It was Christine, in a very short, very grubby red satin dress, trimmed with moulting marabou, and with a salmon-pink velvet bow in her straight thin hair. She had caught hold of Julian by one sleeve and a handful of the back of his coat, and was making an earnest attempt to swarm up him from behind.

Julian glanced over his shoulder, winked, and said, 'Happy Christmas, pig-face,' under his breath. He reached back an arm and shoved her, gently but firmly, down again. The slight movement had attracted Mrs Fleming's attention: she looked down with a gentle inquiring smile. Christine slipped shyly round to Julian's far side, where she gripped his elbow with both hands and gave herself a swing.

'Well, Christine, dear?' Mrs Fleming leaned forward; Hilary caught a discreet waft of violet from her furs. 'What a shy little girl she is to-day, hiding there. Aren't you going to let me admire your pretty frock?'

Christine stopped swinging, and sidled a few inches forward, dragging one leg and pulling at the top of her stocking so that her grey cotton knickers showed. Now that the front of her dress was visible, it looked worse than the back. Her family, Hilary remembered, was the worst in the village. Under her streaky fringe she shot a slant look across the ward; Hilary, following it, saw Betty, her hospital bedmate, carefully shepherded by a trim mother, and dressed in clean pale blue rayon. The parents, of course, were not on speaking terms.

'We *are* a smart little girl to-day,' said Mrs Fleming, with gently heartening kindness. 'And what did Santa Claus bring you this morning?'

Christine hooked one finger into the hem of her knickers, extended a loop of threadbare elastic, and let it go. She had become so small and skinny that the dress seemed almost to fit her. She looked at the elastic as if she had made a scientific discovery, and said nothing at all. Retreating, she effaced herself between Julian and Hilary, and traced a pattern on the floor with a dirty sand-shoe split at the side.

Julian had been looking thoughtfully at the tree, and had appeared not to notice. Presently, however, with a caution that verged on the furtive, he dug her in the ribs, and, when he had caught her eye, made an appalling face, like a chimpanzee with a gumboil. He did it very swiftly, and at once put on an expression fit for morning prayers in the college chapel; but Christine straightened her spine and grinned.

'Really, Julian, what a shame to terrify the poor little thing. Do try to be civilised, dear; you're not at Oxford now.'

The voice was so soft that Hilary only just caught it. Under its semi-humorous surface it had a quality that she remembered from earlier in the year.

Julian looked straight in front of him for a moment, then turned to his mother and smiled. It was a smile into which one could imagine almost anything; defence, embarrassment, apology, and, through them, a gentleness in which there was something incongruously mature. Probably it was only the incalculable x of his beauty that prevented him from looking simply sheepish. Hilary, who would rather have been elsewhere, compromised by looking away.

A burst of clapping came like outside air through a suddenly opened door. A door had in fact opened to admit Dr Dundas, hugely hooded, booted, and bearded, with his sack. He was very tall and gaunt with a double bass voice, and the fact that normally he never employed three words if a monosyllable would do instead, gave added piquancy to the patter which he growled at each recipient. Everyone was delighted, except a small boy of three in a cot, who panicked at his approach, and, tense with hysterical screaming, ignored the parcel he dropped at the foot of the cot before moving hastily on. Suddenly the screaming stopped. Hilary saw that Mrs Fleming had let down the side of the cot, and sitting on its edge, had taken the child in her arms. Something brittle seemed to have become flexible in her, some contraction sprung free. Her shape, and the baby's, seemed to fit one another like complementary things. He gave a few fading whimpers, waved a fist uncertainly, and plunged it with profound physical pleasure into the furs at her neck.

Hilary, who had already been reproaching herself for the unpleasantness of her recent feelings – it was not like her to make much out of little – was made remorseful by the sight, and at once felt more comfortable. Looking round with a general feeling of relief, her eye happened to encounter Julian. He was not watching the pretty little scene at the crib; it was evident that he had just turned away. His mouth had a line which was as near to sulkiness as so sweet-tempered a face could easily harbour; a little neglected, a little put about.

Hilary went quickly down the ward to an old woman who was a patient of hers. With eager enthusiasm she admired Santa Claus's gift of a blue bed-jacket, and helped to put it on. When it came to tying the bow she succeeded somehow in pulling off one of the ribbons. The old lady took it in a Christmas spirit, remarking that the last person to do a thing like that had been her husband, but that was a good while ago.

The present-giving was over. Christine was parading with the finest doll, one of Lisa's; the Matron was a kind woman at heart and no fool. The nurses were comparing their soaps and bath-salts in a corner. Mrs Fleming was still on the cot with the baby; she had unwrapped his rabbit for him and was showing him its paces. Suddenly Dr Dundas's boom rose above the general gabble, like the voice of Elijah interrupting one of Ahab's dinner-parties.

'*Now*, Matron. What about a Christmas-box for Santa Claus? Don't be shy, don't be shy.'

The staff, who knew what was coming, began an anticipatory giggle. Dr Dundas, still in full canonicals, but handling the Matron's eleven stone like eight, swept her under the misletoe (not far from which she had by some coincidence been standing) and kissed her resoundingly, courteously snapping his beard under his chin for the purpose, and receiving a furore of cheers.

Hilary's old lady cackled delightedly; Christine and Betty were in ecstasy. They had taken advantage of the mêlée to gravitate together, and, social barriers forgotten, were jumping on a leg apiece.

'Now somebody else kiss somebody else,' squealed Betty, when Santa Claus, with an air of definite finality, had replaced his beard. She was at the hectic stage of elation which precedes crossness and tears. 'Go on, Monkey. *You* kiss a lady.' She hurled herself at as much as she could reach of Julian's back, catching him off balance and making him stumble a pace forward. 'Kiss a lady. Go on.'

From somewhere in the background came a hissing sound of 'Give-over-Betty-this-minute-and-let-that-gentleman-alone-the-very-idea.' Betty wavered; but the patients, well warmed up, had begun a round of applause.

Julian had been standing laughing with everyone else, semi-submerged in the crowd. To find himself isolated on the floor and a centre of interest, seemed for a moment to take him as much by surprise as Betty's impact in his rear. Almost at once he gave his friendly casual grin, said, 'All right,' and shot out an arm to grab Christine; but Christine's shyness had suddenly returned. She ducked, squeezed between two visitors, and ran away up the back of the line.

'Not *Christine*, silly.' Betty had subdued her voice to a piercing whisper, which made it, if possible, more penetrating than before. 'Christine doesn't count. A *lady*. Go on, you're scared.'

By this time everyone was looking. Dr Dundas gave a deep eupeptic chuckle, and the Matron a dubious but indulgent click. From the group of nurses a few yards away, Nurse Jones, looking very pink and round and pretty and absently clasping a jar of eau-de-nil bath-salts to her bosom, had drifted in a preoccupied maiden meditation towards the empty space on the floor.

Julian continued to smile; a nice-mannered, party smile. Whether he was aware of Nurse Jones's presence it was impossible to say. Hilary watched him, feeling first amusement, then a sudden painful unease. Though he could scarcely yet have been said to hesitate, and looked quite cheerful and at home, she found herself shoving him along with her will as hard as Betty had with both fists. As if he had felt it too, he turned and caught her eye. She responded, instinctively, with a tolerant, vague smile.

Julian moved. With a long, swift, graceful stride, he crossed the floor to her, made an eighteenth-century bow, said, 'Madam your servant,' and handed her out under the chandelier. He kissed her, briskly, cheerfully, and inaccurately, bowed again, and let her go. It went very well; almost as well as Dr Dundas. He stepped back into his place, relaxing comfortably, and smiled at her from the midst of the crowd. He looked both grateful and relieved.

Hilary smiled too, in the correct Christmas-party manner. It had all happened so quickly that by a kind of delayed action she only felt the kiss after she had got back to her place. In the same moment she saw Mrs Fleming, looking gracious and benevolent. To Hilary she looked like the lady of the manor unbending to exactly the right angle at a servants' ball. It was an expression so characteristic that on her it must be considered innocuous. Hilary thought so; but found, suddenly, that the processes of thought were curiously beside the point. Still reasoning, she found herself shaking the Matron by the hand, murmuring something about an urgent visit and a delightful time, and making her way down through the garden to her car.

The sun was still far above the horizon; in its slanting light the effects of the frost looked more beautiful than in any part of the day before. Hilary drove home by a long detour, arriving back at the fall of dusk. She explored one or two wild lanes where she had never been before; it was this, she thought, which made the house when she got to it look strange and different, as if she had been away not for a few hours but for weeks. Or it was the frost, perhaps. She went through into her room and this again looked different, though Lisa had built up the fire into a lovely seasonal picture with fir-cones and apple-wood logs. The cyclamen in the pot were expanding in its warmth. Their little card was still hanging round them by a silver thread; now that she had acknowledged them, it could be thrown away. She broke it off and turned it over, and looked at the writing at the back, even and clear, slanting a little with a regular thickening of the down strokes; a young, well-brought-up hand of one to whom the written word is not the natural means of expression. The kind of person, she thought, whose letters tell you nothing whatever about them. She swung the card by its silver cord and watched it curl in the red of the fire.

That evening, as they sat over coffee and the frost melted in a south-west wind, it occurred to Hilary that it would be, for some unexplained reason, a good time to hear Lisa talk.

Lightly, and scarcely hoping that it would draw anything,

she said, 'You've been very nice to me all day. Particularly considering that I'm here instead of the person who ought to be.'

Lisa answered with something friendly and unimportant; paused; appeared to have finished; then said, slowly, 'In any case, I can't afford ideas like that. You see, we've each tried living with the other – the other's kind of life, I mean – and it nearly killed us each in turn. Only the difficulty was that at the end of it we were still in love. So the present compromise is by way of being the last resort. It wouldn't do to get discontented about it.'

As she talked on, in her easy quiet voice, Hilary had a clear picture of a relationship predestined, one would have said, for inevitable disaster. Rupert was a wanderer by instinct and vocation, extrovert, gregarious. 'He plunges into new people,' Lisa said, 'like a boy working the handles at a fun fair.' Lisa had, as she herself described it, the temperament of a cat. Hilary agreed with this comparison; she had always thought its colloquial use was based on wildly inaccurate observation. Lisa did in fact possess every feline quality except the cat's self-sufficiency; and of this her reserve offered a colourable imitation. For the rest, she had the love of solitude, the passionate attachment to places which she had made her own; the instinct for quiet which looks like secrecy and partly is so; the power of absolute relaxation. She and Rupert had come together by a violent attraction of opposites, overlooking, in the temporary insanity of their state, the fact that opposed ways of life do not fuse like personalities. It was she, of course, who had made the first attempt at adaptation. She had trailed with him to one European capital after another, scarcely alone with him except in their littered overpacked hotel bedroom at night, her days unoccupied after the first week's sightseeing, cut off from the domestic rhythm to which she was adapted and from the little creative jobs of a growing home; refusing herself a child because of the separation it must involve. Needing a handful of friendships slowly and completely evolved, she was beset with swarms of acquaintances, who gave her the sensations of a railway journey in which people are continually pushing past one's knees. Disliking alcohol, not on principle, but because it happened to make her depressed and irritable, she was for ever having to drink with chance-met persons, who, for Rupert's sake, must be entertained. It had been after a cocktail-party in Rome that they had had one of those quarrels so destructive that, however absolute the for-giveness after, the memory remains like a visible scar. Appalled by it, they had comforted one another, as Lisa put it, 'like mur-derers, with the body under the stairs.' A few weeks later she had realised that she was pregnant.

Thus confronted with an inevitable fact, they had both found its decisiveness a relief. It had been early summer, and Lisa had stayed on for another two months; Rupert was due for a holiday and hoped to travel back with her. Everything had been ready for the journey, when Rupert's editor had telephoned to say that the correspondent in Moscow was invalided home, and Rupert was to take his place.

A refusal would have checked his career and probably fin-ished it. Lisa had set out alone, her reason acquiescent, her emotions in violent revolt. She was a poor traveller at any time; the Channel crossing had been a particularly bad one. On the train journey to London she had known that some-thing was wrong, and gone straight to a hospital, where she had a miscarriage a few hours later.

No one had thought to warn her of the emotional trauma with which frustrated nature responds to this event. (She was quietly amused at Hilary's violent indignation about it.)

Confined in a solitude which for the first time she would gladly have avoided, because her means excluded her from the general ward, she had taken everything she felt at face value. On the first day when she had been allowed to sit up, she had written to Rupert asking for a divorce. They had had the intimacy in which people entrust to one another an unlimited power to hurt, and Lisa had wasted none of it. The necessary evidence had arrived a fortnight later, without an accompanying line.

Lisa had gone back to the house in Gloucestershire, which, Hilary now learned, was her own, the legacy of an aunt who had brought her up after her parents died. It had been her home for most of her childhood; and in returning to it, and to her own instinctive kind of life, she had found a relief which she had almost been able to pretend was contentment. But within a few weeks of the divorce decree being made absolute a friend of many years' standing asked her to marry him. It had been her reaction to this which had awakened her to herself. She realised that during all the intervening time she had been stunned, that the loss of Rupert had never, till now, had reality in her imagination at all.

At this phase of the story, Hilary thought again how apt the comparison with the cat had been. Just as a cat rouses instantly from a motionless torpor into decisive action, Lisa had packed and gone to town. It was no more than possible that she might find Rupert there; his series from Moscow had stopped recently, and this was all she knew. Arriving, she had gone for lunch to the chop-house he generally frequented, and he had been there. At this point her account grew rather vague. 'The hotel was just like all the other hotels, except that you could drink the tea. We sent the bill to the King's Proctor with a nice little note to say we were sorry he'd been troubled.'

When they had been able to rouse themselves to a partial sense of realities – it appeared, indefinitely, that this had been a matter of some days – Rupert had managed somehow to get himself transferred to a political assignment at home. They had taken a flat in London; and, for nearly as long as Lisa had done before, he had managed to blind himself to the fact that the work was wholly uncongenial. It was the time when the Abdication crisis was blowing up; the general tension, and personal parallels which were lost on neither of them, had had its own emotional effect; they had exhausted themselves and one another with stresses not like those of marriage, but of a violent love-affair which tragedy must inevitably close. The reaction had come after. Rupert's successor abroad had turned out to be, comparatively, a failure. His articles were to Rupert a daily exasperation. Neither he nor Lisa dared to discuss them. She guessed that the paper wanted him back on his old job; she was afraid to ask him, and he never told her. Their tenderness to one another became watchful, patterned with silences and edged with fear.

And then, as once before, decision had been forced on them by circumstance. Rupert had split with the paper, on a point of policy in which he felt his integrity to be involved. The issue was clear, and Lisa wholly with him. But when he came to look for work elsewhere, there was nothing to be had except the work in which his reputation had been made.

'And so,' said Lisa, 'we were back where we'd started, asking ourselves which of us should destroy the other. Only we weren't capable any more of being destroyed independently. And we wanted one another alive to come back to, even if it were only for a few weeks of every year. And ever since then, that's how it's been.'

Hilary said the little which, to Lisa, it was wise or indeed possible to say. There were a number of things she would have liked to know; whether, for instance, Rupert was faithful to her, and, if not, how she felt about it. As if she had reflected aloud, Lisa said in her quiet commonplace way, 'He tells me most things. It makes him feel better; and me too, oddly enough. Personally, whatever he says, I don't feel I've got the right to consider myself more than a mistress with special privileges. But it's so much better being that to Rupert than everything to anyone else I've known.'

Hilary smoked in silence for a minute or so. At last she said, 'Wouldn't it be a good idea to have another baby?'

Flatly and without emotion Lisa said, 'Oh, I did. A few months before you came. It was born dead, and they wouldn't let me look at it.' She bent and threw a fresh log on the fire. 'I suppose if Rupert were there, I could bring myself to go through it again. But not without him. I think for some reason it must be meant.'

'Things like that aren't meant,' Hilary said. Having been much moved, she spoke rather shortly. Lisa smiled at her; by now they understood one another pretty well.

'I mean,' she said, 'that perhaps after all it's something in me. If you have a child it ought to come first; that's how the race goes on. Once I could have done it. But some things go deeper with time.'

'Judging by what I've seen,' said Hilary, 'though I may be wrong, I think you'd probably make the ideal mother. Children stake out their own claim. A compensating balance might save your soul, and the child's as well.'

Lisa looked at her curiously. 'You may be right,' she said. 'It's a point of view I hadn't thought of. I wonder what makes you sound so sure.'

8

The week between Christmas and New Year carried its usual freight of hangover and reaction. Everyone who had been saving up ailments, to avoid fuss over the holiday, brought them along to the doctor. A heavy kind of cold, which had begun to be epidemic, developed as it gathered impetus into full-fledged influenza, the type with sinus and antrum complications. For the first time since she had taken the practice over, Hilary had too much to do. She thrived on the work and blessed it, not wholly unaware.

On the twenty-seventh of December Lisa heard from Rupert that he would be able to get to London, but would not get a chance to leave it; she went about singing to herself, and doing mysterious things to clothes which Hilary had never seen her wear.

On the twenty-eighth a note arrived for Hilary. It was from Mrs Fleming, asking her to an informal dance to see the New Year in. It ended, 'Please forgive this late invitation; we had meant to ask you on Christmas Day, but you were called away so suddenly that we missed our opportunity.'

Hilary read the note again. As if it had been an impersonal

accident, like an urgent case at the wrong moment, she asked herself why, in the name of misfortune, this nuisance should happen now. It upset everything. Of course, she ought to accept it; as a gesture to herself (for, if it had been anywhere else in the neighbourhood, she would certainly have gone), and a reparation between her own conscience and Mrs Fleming, a pleasant and harmless woman, not perhaps quite of her own type, but none the worse for that, against whom she had allowed herself to harbour a pathological prejudice. Yes, she said to herself, she would write in the evening.

That day's work turned out to be the heaviest yet. It left her tired, and with the beginning of a headache. It was not till she got up to her room, thankful to rest, that an uneasy feeling of some impending reluctance defined itself in the note which stared at her from the mantelpiece. When she walked over to get it, she saw her own face in the mirror behind it, weary, unadorned, and stamped with the haste and anxieties of the day. The thought of any social activity at all would have been a burden; the thought of this one, she found, was like the thought of entering for a marathon. She did not try to explain to herself what, exactly, she expected to be the cause of the additional effort, She only knew that she could not and would not go; it was too much to ask of anyone.

She phrased her refusal in the nicest terms, explaining that she suspected herself of coming down with influenza, and was finding the work as much as she could manage. It might quite well be true; headache was an early symptom of the prevailing type. It left conscience palliated. She posted it, and went with aspirin and immeasurable relief to bed.

In the morning the headache had gone; which, said Hilary to herself, went to show the value of dealing with one's correspondence promptly. Lisa had left for town; she had the

97

place to herself. Equipped with a detective story which blended wit, style, and complex homicide in suitable proportions, she stretched herself in a long chair, rang for tea, and prepared herself for two hours of triviality and peace.

She was hardly through her first cup when there was a tap at the door. Her reluctant answer brought in Annie, who peered at her, before uttering, in a way for which Hilary could find no ready explanation.

'Is it urgent?' she asked mechanically.

'I couldn't say, Doctor. It's that Mr Fleming. He says he hopes you're better, and to give you these.' She advanced with a huge sheaf of forced chrysanthemums, taking advantage of a closer view to inspect Hilary again.

Hilary took them helplessly. Annie was a treasure, but, as the household had cause to know, totally lacking in urban finesse. Little imagination was needed to picture the all-revealing gawp of astonishment which had, in fact, scarcely yet left her face.

'But, really, I—' Hilary wandered vaguely round the room, ostensibly seeking a suitable pot. 'Has he gone?'

'No, Doctor. He said if you weren't in bed could he come in and see you for a few minutes?'

'Oh.' She had just time to reflect that these delicate attentions might have caught her unprepared in the hall, with Lisa there. 'Yes, ask him in. And bring another cup, please, and something with water in it.'

Annie went, with another searching look over her shoulder. Presently, a voice out in the hall said, 'Oh, *good*. Thank you.' The sound made him present before he walked in at the door.

'Hallo.' He lengthened the word and stressed the last syllable; a long and eloquent sentence expressing gratitude at being admitted, delight at seeing her, concern, sympathy, and relief, could not have conveyed any of them half so well. 'I hope you don't mind.'

Suddenly she could not remember what all her hesitation had been about. 'I should think it would be more to the point if I asked you whether you minded coming all this way for such a fraud. And flowers, too. I ought not to be able to look you in the face.'

He came up to her, surveying her with great gravity out of long blue-grey eyes. His intentness and his unconsciousness of himself underlined his beauty till it seemed too improbable to be true.

'Quite right,' he said. 'You're behaving very badly. You ought to be in bed. Now sit down and rest, or I shan't stay even the minute I'm going to.' He took her by the elbows from behind, and steered her into a chair.

She subsided, and heard the cushion being patted into place behind her. Having arranged her to his satisfaction, he took the chair on the opposite side of the fire, and, leaning forward with elbows on knees, looked at her again. Becoming quite concerned on her own account, she tried to remember, unsuccessfully, whether she had done anything about her face when she came in.

'Don't make me more ashamed of myself than I am. I'm pretty sure now it isn't going to be 'flu after all. You're going to have some tea with me, aren't you? I've only just begun.'

'Well, if it really won't stop you from properly resting ...'

When the flower-pot arrived along with the cup, he said, 'Now just you stay put, I'll do it,' and did so, tidying up carefully after him and putting the loose bits on the fire.

'They're magnificent. Do you grow them?'

'They're not bad this year. As a matter of fact, these were supposed to be for the church next Sunday. Don't tell a soul.

There's much more point in giving them to you. Haring about dying on your feet and looking after everyone except yourself.' He stood back to admire the effect, which was quite creditable.

'For heaven's sake. I've had just enough work to be good for me, for once.'

He said, thoughtfully, 'You know, you quite make me wish I'd gone ahead with it myself. I did think of it, at one time.'

'Why didn't you?'

'Well, I read English. It would have meant starting more or less from scratch.'

'It's been done. I met a man once who did it on his retiring gratuity from the Navy; he was forty when he began.'

'Really? Pretty good. The only thing is, I was never very hot on the science side.'

'So what did you decide on in the end?'

'To tell you the truth, I've more or less let the question lapse for the moment. You see, as they keep telling me I can't take on anything needing sustained mental effort for at least a year, there doesn't seem much point in getting too many ideas.'

Hilary looked up sharply. She was shocked out of all discretion.

'Did Sanderson tell you that?'

'Not him actually. But it seems to be the general idea.'

She said, slowly, 'He doesn't generally insist on that. Of course you'd need to take care physically for a bit. But you don't want to be a middle-weight champion, or anything, do you?'

He laughed. 'Well, no, I don't think so. I'd be cruiser-weight, anyway. People don't think so, but I've got big bones, that's where it goes. Oh, yes, and talking of bones reminds me. I was going to ask you a bit of a favour; only I didn't mean to to-day, in case you were feeling rotten.'

'What was it?' She could not make up her mind whether he had sidestepped the subject deliberately, or simply been dense. 'How do bones come in?'

'In a big way. I was wondering if, just for one night, you could possibly see your way to lend me a skeleton.'

'A *skeleton*!' She gazed at him, with bewilderment followed by inward exasperation. There he sat, charming, diffidently eager; filled, one would have said, with purpose, planning heaven knew what adolescent crudity; she could not bring herself to ask him. 'But I haven't got one. I'm not a lecturer in anatomy.'

'Oh, I see.' He looked quite dashed. 'I thought most doctors had one tucked away somewhere.'

'My dear boy! Seeing that an articulated skeleton can cost anything up to seventy pounds, and the simplest way of moving one about is to borrow an ambulance and lay it out on the stretcher, it isn't a thing one acquires casually. *Must* you have one?'

'Well, not really. It would have been ideal, but I expect I can fake up something or other.'

'You know,' she felt moved to say, 'it isn't my business, of course; but sometimes these rags don't turn out as funny as people think beforehand. I remember one where the victim pretty nearly died of shock, and no one would have taken him for a nervous subject.'

'But I don't want it to terrify anyone with. Good heavens, what a frightful idea.' He looked quite reproachful before relenting enough to add, 'Of course, I ought to have explained. It's for a stage prop. But we can manage without.'

'Oh, I see.' It seemed at once that for some reason she ought to have known. 'Well, I apologise; but if you knew what some medical students are capable of . . . What exactly do you want it for?'

'Actually, for the Lynchwyck Dramatic Society. I'm producing for them this year. Some of them aren't at all too bad, in the right sort of stuff. Of course, they've the usual yearnings towards Sheridan and Coward – attraction of opposites, or something, I suppose. I don't doubt they'd be ready to tackle *The Way of the World* if it wasn't for the rudery. But once you've jollied them out of all that, it's amazing what you can get out of them. I've got two chaps from the aircraft works that are perfect naturals, and one who can really act. They'd rather set their hearts on a real skeleton. Of course we could have the thing screened from the audience and use a bit of suggestion; in fact I'd prefer it myself. But you know how it is, a few slap-up props are good for morale. It's more for the effect on the cast I want it, than anything.'

'I wish I had one for you.' She spoke mechanically; she had been, for a few moments, quite startled by his change of tone. It had been almost a change of personality. She recognised in him for the first time what she had unconsciously missed most, because in her own world she had been used to taking it for granted; the voice of a man talking with casual confidence about a job. Her recent patronising amusement felt suddenly like impertinence, and would have embarrassed her in the company of anyone less easy. She said, 'Have you done much of that kind of thing?'

'Oh, well, on and off, you know. I produced at school, and acted a bit. And then I was in Ouds.'

'Really? I might even have seen you, then. No, I suppose not; the only one I've seen in the last four years was *The Tempest*, one of the summer ones. You weren't in that.'

He grinned. 'Don't you remember me? Well, I *am* hurt.'

This was more than awkward. She cast her mind back: the Ferdinand, fair and much too small; the Prospero, broad, and the voice too deep; the Trinculo, definitely not. Perhaps she might have missed him in a minor part. She said, apologetically, 'I came in too late for a programme; and there were so many beards.'

'Not on me.' Far from being hurt, he was plainly enjoying himself immensely.

'Well, I give up.'

He leaned forward, and suddenly dropped his arms so that they hung beside his knees. His face, thrust out, took on a mournful and malevolent stare. It recalled to her the face he had made for Betty and Christine; but this time it expressed, with startling vividness, the tragic lostness which one glimpses sometimes in the eyes of a monkey sitting quiet in the corner of its cage.

> *'I prithee, let me bring thee where crabs grow,*
> *And I with my long nails will dig thee pig-nuts . . .'*

Even after she had heard, and remembered, the gross and forlorn voice whose sullenness had been so curiously moving, she exclaimed, 'You're pulling my leg. Don't try to tell me the Caliban was you.'

'And you never knew me again. You can't imagine what that does to me. And I had such cute green gills. I made them myself, out of pig-bladder.'

'Well, now that I've got my breath, let me congratulate you. You were far better than the Stratford man the same year.'

'Who, Streatley? I think he was all right, if you see it funny. Shakespeare may have done, at that. The Elizabethan sense of humour was so much tougher than ours, one's apt to over-interpret what one can't swallow, don't you find? Still, I must say I feel a sort of sadness for the poor beast, myself.'

'But the face. Was it a mask?'

'Just greasepaint. I pooled ideas with the chap they sent down from town, and did it myself, after the dress rehearsal.' He added, with modest satisfaction, 'The gills were mine. He was rather agin them, but he admitted in the end they were a help. I always think there ought to be something a bit fishy about Caliban, don't you? After all, he *smelt* like a fish.'

'What else have you done?' Surely, she thought, they could hardly let him get away with grotesques very often; the puzzle was that he should ever have wanted to.

'I was the First Madman, in *Malfi*. That was *great* fun. I had a sort of cheese-coloured face, paralysed down one side. Like this.' He illustrated with unpleasant realism. 'Oh, and Oberon the year after.'

'But I remember reading about that. Was *that* you?'

'I was after Bottom, really, but they weren't having any. Still, Toller was very good, and I'd had a lot of fun, so I couldn't grouse. There's something in Oberon, too, if he isn't prettified; great mistake, that. I believe I've got a couple of snaps some-where, if all this doesn't bore you stiff. But are you feeling tired?'

'Not at all. Let me look.'

He fished a thick, rubbed leather wallet out of his pocket. 'I expect there're here. It hasn't been turned out in years. Yes, here we are.' He handed them over; the work, she saw, of a competent amateur, no doubt one of the cast. 'It looks a strong make-up,' he said, 'for the open air. But the audience wasn't very close; and of course the lighting came on half-way through.'

'It's very striking,' she said, covering an inward disappoint-ment. 'But I still wouldn't have known you. I should have thought your own face would have done, with a few quirks here and there.'

'I tried it. But I didn't fancy it.' He spoke with an off-handedness which was, somehow, more definite than emphasis would have been.

'Did you keep any of the clippings about it? The one from the *Observer*, for instance? I'd like to see it again.'

'Very likely.' He produced a strip of newsprint, and handed it over. When she had taken it, he looked for the first time embarrassed and fidgeted aimlessly with the papers that were left. She ran her eye down the cutting, confirming the impressions she had retained.

... No such allowances, however, had to be made for Julian Fleming's Oberon. Here was a fresh, strong, and consistent interpretation. If it owed something not only to Shakespeare but to the dark Dionysus of the *Bacchae*, the theft justified itself. A few technical faults, which experience will remedy, were offset by imaginative coherence, a fine presence and a delivery which wasted nothing of the great incantations. One hardly expects, by now, to find anything new brought to the Promontory speech; this young actor conveyed into it something Orphic which, contemporaneously, might well have scared the Imperial Votaress from her compliment, and more than half scared one member of the audience at least. It seemed a pity to handicap a flexible and subtle performance with a make-up so heavily stylised that it approximated to a mask; enough came through, however, to set up a standard inimical to indulgence elsewhere, and ...

She looked up. 'I know less than nothing about the theatre from inside. But I should have thought that after a notice like this in a London paper, you wouldn't have much difficulty in breaking into the professional stage.'

He said, with what seemed complete indifference, 'Oh, not by now, I should think. They have short memories, you know.'

She said quickly, 'You had an offer, then?'

'Vaguely. But there were – various difficulties. I hadn't had my viva, or the result of my finals, or anything. And so on. Oh, well, there were any amount of things.' He took the cutting from her and put it back. He would have taken the photographs too – he had a look as if he suddenly wanted to close the subject – but she withdrew them, and sliding away the top ones, took out the one below.

'This isn't Oberon,' she said. 'What is it?'

A second glance made obvious what it was; a flash, taken during performance, of one of the Boar's Head Tavern scenes from *Henry IV*. Beside an unconvincing lath fireplace, Falstaff, crudely whiskered and padded, with bloat lines pencilled on a youthful face, was standing with a tankard. Near him on a long settle Prince Hal was lounging, long-legged in silk hose, one hanging scalloped sleeve brushing the floor, smiling up with lazy impudence into his face. He looked slight and graceful and immensely young; it must have been taken before he was fully grown.

'Well,' she said, 'here at last is something I *can* recognise you in. Was this one of the plays at school?'

'Which? Let's look.' Not only his face, but his voice had altered; both had a guarded lack of expression she had never known in him before. He leaned forward, took the picture before she had made any movement to return it, and gave it a cursory glance. 'I thought it was another from *The Dream*. Really, the rubbish one does accumulate if one doesn't have a purge from time to time. No wonder this wallet won't shut.'

He made as if to put the photograph back, but, instead, leaned out of his chair and tossed it into the fire. It struck the unburned end of a log, glanced away, and fell into the fender. Hilary picked it up.

'What did you do that for?'

'Sorry. I didn't mean to make a mess of your fireplace.'

'Don't throw it away. You'll be glad to have it, later on.'

'I really can't think of any reason why.'

He spoke with the appearance of lightness; she sensed, below it, a tension which she tried to ease by continuing to talk.

'Oh, nothing seems so dead-and-done-with as the fairly recent past. But you don't want to throw out the baby along with the bath water. In a few years you'll be sorry not to have a complete record. What about your memoirs?' She smiled. 'You'll want this for the chapter on Early Successes.'

'Very funny.'

She looked up, quite at a loss. He had spoken with a bitterness which was made doubly disconcerting by his evident impression of having adequately concealed it. That he should suspect her of amusing herself at his expense not only hurt, but bewildered her; it seemed both unreasonable and unintelligent.

'It wasn't meant to be so funny. Quite a lot of people have started in Ouds and got to the West End. Why not you?'

'Why not indeed?' He had recovered an almost convincing flippancy. 'When I open at His Majesty's, I'll send you stalls.'

'I'll hold you to that. I shall keep this, and give it you then. Don't laugh, I mean it.'

'I've got to laugh. But it isn't rudely meant.' He added, under his breath, 'Early successes. Great God.'

She had been watching his face, and, before she could prevent herself, said without the defensive impersonality which had become a habit with her, 'Things stop mattering. I promise you they do.'

'I don't quite see what you mean.'

His face had frozen. She regretted her folly; but the conversation had to be rescued. 'Oh, I mean any of the contretemps that loom at the time. For instance ...' She related a story against herself, about an indispensable object she had dropped on the theatre floor on the first occasion when she had assisted Sanderson. It was a fact that she had minded a good deal. The operation had had to be held up for five minutes while it was re-sterilised; and she had been the first woman ever to be taken on Sanderson's firm. 'I couldn't get myself inside the theatre for a week afterwards, even to look on. I imagined everyone talking about it. Then months later, when I knew him better, I mentioned it to him by way of a joke, and he didn't even remember. People don't; they've enough troubles of their own.'

He said, slowly, 'It was nice of you to tell me that. It isn't much to the point, I'm afraid, but it was still nice of you. You don't really want this thing, do you? You're welcome. Only stick it away somewhere, if you don't mind.'

She went over to her desk, and put it in a drawer. 'About this skeleton; if you can't get one, would a skull be any help? Now I think of it, I have got one of those.'

'No, do you mean it? But that's terrific. I can suggest the body perfectly well, under some sort of rags. And the hands, threaded cane would make those ...' He was well away at once, as if nothing had happened. Relieved, she would have looked out the skull for him then and there, but of this he would not hear. 'Grubbing about in cold box-rooms, when you're not feeling good. The show isn't for a fortnight. Mayn't I come and collect it, some time next week? That is, if you don't find me an intolerable nuisance, dodging in and out?' His doubt about this was evidently genuine. She reassured him, and to her own rather disgusted surprise (for she detested third-rate amateur acting) found herself telling him that she was looking forward to seeing the show. She expected a naive gratification, but he looked doubtful.

'Well, I suppose I shouldn't daunt you, charity and all that. But your time's rather precious, it really doesn't seem fair. It's just a romp, you know. The most I hope to do is to get the lines heard and keep it moving. It's a draughty hole, too.'

'I'd still like to come. What's it called?'

'*High Barbary*. It's piratical – hell's bells and buckets of blood. Plenty of good type-casting parts, though. And the fellow who does Morgan has really got something. He's the test pilot at the aircraft place. Wouldn't think it would leave him the energy, would you? He's half promised to take me up one day. Don't mention that at home, though, will you? You know how it is.'

'Don't be crazy,' she said, with a warmth that surprised herself. 'You're not ready for that sort of thing. The internal strains are terrific. You couldn't choose anything worse.'

'I thought you were all for me leading a normal life.'

So he did get it, she thought. 'Do you call stunt flying normal?'

'I don't know. The ordinary kind feels good. All right, if you think so. But it would have been something to look forward to.'

After he had gone she found that it was this sentence, with its lack of emphasis and its disturbing note of weary reconciliation, that stuck most in her mind. Thinking about it, she went to her desk and took out the snapshot again. The pose, the charming effrontery of the smile, looked wholly confident and effortless. What a part for him, she thought. He'd give it all the glamour that Shakespeare meant it to have; and take the prig speeches somehow in his stride, instead of letting them get him down all through the fun, as so many Prince Hals do. He has a nice sense of values – about dead dramatists ... But he prefers Caliban with gills made of pig-bladder. I suppose it must be some kind of inverted vanity. Young men are full of maggots in the head.

The picture was still in her hand. She found she had now been looking at it for several minutes; and, shutting the drawer on it smartly, closed the top of the desk, for emphasis, as well.

Lisa stayed in London four days instead of two. She came back with an air, which Hilary had come to recognise, of trying to be present but not wholly succeeding. But by next evening she was herself again – or, at all events, the self with which Hilary was familiar – and, coming to announce that dinner was almost ready, started, stared, and exclaimed, 'My dear, what *have* you got there? Are you meditating on your latter end? I warn you, if Annie sees it you'll have to be on the spot to render first-aid.'

'I'm sorry.' Hilary followed her eyes and laughed. 'I really ought to have put it away. Familiarity breeds contempt. I hope it didn't give you a jolt.'

'Considering what the news has been like lately, I shouldn't have thought you needed a *memento mori*.'

Rupert has been talking to her, Hilary thought; and put the thought away, as most people then were putting away thought that could serve no further good.

'I want it for a quite escapist purpose, really. It's going to be a stage property in a play about pirates. I promised it to that Fleming lad.'

'Oh, he acts, does he? Well, I'm not surprised.'

'He does, I believe. But he's only producing this time.'

'If he has the smallest spark of talent I wonder what he's

doing here. He couldn't need much, with that maiden's prayer of a face. But I suppose even for that one needs a certain amount of drive.'

It was not usual to find oneself making excuses for Lisa, in order not to be annoyed. It was, indeed, so unreasonable that Hilary made herself particularly agreeable all through the ensuing meal. After it she explained that she was behind with her records, and spread them out ostentatiously in her sitting-room lest anyone, including herself, should doubt it.

He'll probably forget to come, she thought when the clock struck eight-thirty; but a few minutes later she heard him being shown through.

'Are you busy?' he asked, looking respectfully at the day-book.

'No, I've finished now. It's more comfortable doing it here than at the surgery.'

'Yes, I should think so. Have you been looking after yourself?'

Good heavens, she thought, has he got it into his head that I enjoy bad health? It serves me right. 'I'm fit enough to push a house down. Look, there's your skull.'

'My word, what a beauty.' He turned it over, lovingly. 'Isn't it *clean?*'

'We prefer them that way. I hope it's realistic enough.'

'I should say so. I only mean it seems too good. All polished up, and the lid fitting so beautifully. "To what base uses do we come, Horatio."'

'You can keep it, ready for that.'

'Hark at her, sweetie-pie.' He addressed the skull, which returned a gap-toothed grin. 'She thinks the milk isn't wiped off our mouths yet.'

'Wouldn't you like to do it?'

'I'll tell you in ten years. You know' – he twirled the skull intimately between two fingers – 'one knows simply everything about Hamlet at, say, nineteen. But everything – from the outside. It looks fine. Then one reads it again, after something's happened, or something. And the outside has a little crack, if you see what I mean, through which you get a minute glimpse into the interior. Then you feel a bit of a fool, if you've any sense at all, and you put it in cold storage to take a look at when you're thirty.'

He gave the last word so airy a remoteness that it might have been 'fifty' with equal effect. The clean white chops of the skull grinned quietly at Hilary from between his hands.

'I expect you're right,' she said.

He wandered over with his burden, and, ignoring the second chair, curled himself on the hearthrug at her feet.

'I wonder just what sort of hell it was,' he said, 'that Shakespeare went through. The private part, I mean. I think it will be a pity, really, if anyone ever digs up the facts. Not that they'd tell you anything, I dare say. But meanwhile, everyone who reads *Hamlet* will always be able to think maybe it was something like their own. And that's rather steadying ... I expect.'

'Yes,' she said.

She looked down at him, for he was looking at the fire; the skull lying slackly on his knees. She waited, quietly, hoping he would say more; but presently, without self-consciousness or jar, he collected himself into the moment. Lifting the hinged vault of the skull, and peering with interest into the cavity, he asked, 'Is that what they did to my head?'

'My *dear*!' Carried along by laughter, it slipped out unawares. 'Not that size. Give it to me.'

He uncurled and shifted himself to lay it in her lap, resting his arm there along with it. She showed him on the temporal bone the area of Sanderson's flap, as nearly as she could remember.

'Quite a good slice, though,' he observed with unashamed importance. 'Could you still find it on me?'

'With that thick hair? Not by looking; one could still feel it, I expect.'

He laid his head confidingly on her knee, so close to the skull that they almost touched brows. She put it down quickly on the floor, and drew her fingers through the heavy dark sweep of hair across his forehead. Faintly she traced the elliptical edge of the incision; the union had been the least degree uneven, so that it was palpable still, but it felt sound enough. As she explored it with the delicate stroking movements that were necessary to find so slight an outline at all (for the external weal had vanished long ago) she felt a difference in his weight and pressure, and saw that he had relaxed sleepily, and closed his eyes. Abruptly she took her hand away.

'Don't stop,' he murmured placidly. 'It feels nice.'

'Don't be such a baby.' She laughed, and pushed his head away; but she had stood his hair on end, and had to smooth it back again. He submitted with undisturbed docility.

'Did you find it?'

'Just. It's going on nicely. Don't knock it about.'

'Oh, I'm really very tender with it. I'm developing a permanent crouch from avoiding the low beam in the hall.' Recovering the skull, from which he seemed loath to be separated, he remarked, 'Queer to think one has this all the time, inside, isn't it? I wonder what mine looks like.'

'I have the advantage of you; I've seen an X-ray.'

'Nothing's hid from you, is it? Quite alarming. Did I look just the same?'

'Not really. This is a narrow one; a woman's, probably. The malar bones and the jaw would both be broader. And I don't think I shall give it you, it's making you morbid.'

'Oh, no, but why? It's interesting. I mean, to know that everyone has a second face hidden away that nobody's ever seen. Except, of course, for an occasional witch-doctor here and there.' He smiled up at her, a strand of hair which had resisted her ministrations falling down over one eye.

'Well,' she observed, 'it may be interesting to know; but to get much enjoyment out of it one would need to be pretty seriously dissatisfied with the face on top.'

He said nothing, but fiddled with the jawbone of the skull. Presently he exclaimed, 'Good Lord, this hinges too, you never told me,' and made an elaborate business of closing it again. She saw that he had flushed to the roots of his hair, and was stooping to hide it. How is one to cope with him? she thought. To ease things over she embarked on an anecdote about a skeleton, not remarkable for subtlety, retrieved from her early student days. It was received with a most flattering hilarity.

'I'll have to go,' he said presently, 'after wasting another of your evenings. Sling me out, you know, any time. Shall I put "Skull of mutineer kindly lent by Dr Hilary Mansell" on the programme?'

'Not unless you want to get me struck off for advertising. Shall I want a ticket, by the way, or do they collect inside?'

'They do, but I've reserved you a seat, of course. Oh, Lord, that reminds me, I'm forgetting all my messages. Mother says she hopes you can come round to our place to tea first, then you and she can go together. Is that OK?'

'Why, yes, I think so. Yes, please thank her from me and say that unless something urgent turns up I'd be delighted.' There was no possible way of evading it this time; and, in any case, the desire to do so seemed increasingly silly and ungracious. 'About five?'

'Well, if you *could* make it earlier. Just so that I'll see you before I have to leave.' He had become a little constrained; and would have borne off the skull naked under his arm if she had not pointed out to him in time the paper and string she had prepared. When he had gone she got out her engagement book, and drew on the half-page for the evening of Saturday week a thick square frame, enclosing a blank.

9

The house was a smallish, but very pleasant combination of the Georgian style with the Cotswold tradition. It had a shell portico, broad windows, and the stone-tiled Cotswold roof which, being pegged together, moulds itself ever so slightly with age, like an integument, over the supporting beams, letting their bony structure appear. Patches of gold lichen, their colour warm in the last light, patterned it here and there, and on the ledge above the porch stonecrop had taken root. She rang, and was taken by a well-trained maid into a room whose proportions were as perfect as the period of the house had made her expect. The contents had taste, good spacing, and the air of having accumulated effortlessly over some generations, by contrast with which the best efforts of interior decorators appear over-slick. From the pool of light under a parchment-shaded standard lamp Mrs Fleming came forward to meet her; behind, in the shadows, looking very neat and well-behaved, Julian was already on his feet.

'How splendid that you were able to get here in good time.' The outstretched hand felt fragile and its faint pressure made Hilary's naturally firm grip seem a little over-hearty. 'I hear you've been having a busy time. We were so sorry about New Year's Eve, but of course we *quite* understood.' Hilary made suitable responses. In the early days of her training, elderly relatives, and some of her mother's friends, had had the same air of making well-bred allowances for an odd way of life, and she had learned to take it in her stride.

'Things are easing off a little,' she said, 'they often do, just before the spring rush begins. I've been looking forward to my evening off.' As soon as this homely expression was out of her mouth it seemed to her that she had chosen it with conscious challenge; and that the slightest contact of their two personalities would throw up, inevitably and always, effects like this.

Mrs Fleming said, 'It's very good of you to give it up to us. I'm afraid it isn't going to be a very exciting evening for you; in fact, I was just saying to Julian that I felt sure you would prefer a quiet dinner and a little music, to rest you, instead of being dragged off to see amateur theatricals in a draughty hall. He expects everyone to share his enthusiasms.' She smiled at him with affectionate indulgence, as if he had insisted on littering the floor with clockwork trains.

'I couldn't possibly let her off.' Julian was still standing a little in the background, with the shy deprecating smile which, lately, she had less often seen. He was wearing a dark suit and, because she had generally met him fresh from the road, looked by contrast very well brushed and combed down. 'After all, a vital member of the cast is appearing by her permission.'

'What do you mean, dear? Is one of them a patient of yours, Dr Mansell?'

'He means the skull,' said Hilary, 'I expect.'

Mrs Fleming gave a delicate shudder. 'That horrible thing. I made him take it straight down to the hall. It made me feel quite uncanny to see it about his room. Of course, it was *very* kind of you to lend it. It's a very fine specimen, Julian tells me, though I'm afraid one looks just as gruesome as another to me. But I expect to you such things are all part of the day's work, aren't they? I do hope it won't get damaged in any way.'

'It won't matter a bit if it does; I never use it.'

'You mustn't be so good-natured, or Julian will be taking advantage of you right and left. He has no conscience at all about these productions of his. Still, I think these little entertainments do give pleasure to the local people. They have so few outlets, and when the performers are all relatives and friends of the audience the standard is fortunately not very critical. Do make yourself comfortable here by the fire; I'll ring for tea at once, now you're here. Julian, dear, take Dr Mansell's coat.'

Julian did so. He had been hovering for some minutes, as Hilary had been aware, in readiness to perform this office, but hesitating to interrupt.

Tea arrived, and was dispensed by Mrs Fleming behind faultlessly polished silver; Julian kept the little scones and wafer sandwiches in motion with unobtrusive assiduity. It was, Hilary reflected, like a scene typifying the English Home; Hollywood, with the help of technical advisers, could hardly have made it prettier. There was small-talk about the London plays of the moment, which developed into rather tricky going, because Hilary and Mrs Fleming had, it turned out, each visited those which the other had carefully avoided. Mrs Fleming was charmingly tactful about Hilary's selections, saying that she had heard they were most interesting and unusual, and that it was very enterprising of her to go; making her feel as if they had been censorable eccentricities at Sunday theatres, instead of such ordinary current successes as offered mild controversy and mental stimulus. Anxious to make the *amende honorable*, she assured her hostess that friends had spoken of *her* plays in the highest terms, and found herself assenting to the opinion that with so many terrible happenings in the world, it was such a pity to put on plays that produced a sense of strain. As she was meditating, fascinated, on the ease with which they had thus dismissed all surviving Greek tragedy, the major efforts of the Elizabethans, Ibsen and an odd Russian or two, something made her look up, and she surprised Julian watching her face. She busied herself quickly with her teacup; he had looked so painfully young and unprovided with the world's armour. She thought of the kindly, aloof humour with which this situation would have been met by other young men she knew – if, indeed, they had put themselves to the trouble of noticing it at all. There seemed nothing to do about it but drink her China tea and remark, brightly, that they always went on that principle very strongly in the hospital Christmas shows.

'Yes, indeed. I was taken to one by a friend whose son was a medical student at the time. I remember it was most high spirited, but the jokes were rather difficult for a lay person to understand.' Her voice conveyed a suspicion that it was probably better so. 'And did you take part in them yourself?'

'No, none of the women did. It was considered more fun to have the female parts taken by men. The beefier the better, of course.'

'Oh, yes,' said Mrs Fleming. 'Of course. How amusing.'

There was a slight pause, into which Julian rushed headlong, apologising for the fact that he would have to be getting along, that he had some props to check up on, that one had to allow a bit of a margin, and that he had promised to make one or two people up. While he was speaking a silvery insistent bell somewhere in the house began to ring.

'Yes, dear, run along,' said his mother. 'I'm sure Dr Mansell will excuse you. But just answer the telephone before you go.

Clara does so muddle the messages sometimes.' The conversation turned to maids, a topic on which Mrs Fleming's views were highly representative. They were still on the subject when the door opened and closed quietly, and Julian came back into the room. He looked so reluctant to say anything that Hilary was sure an urgent call had come for her. But it was not at Hilary that he was looking.

'Yes, dear?' said Mrs Fleming. 'What was it? I hope it's nothing unpleasant; you look quite upset.'

'Well,' said Julian slowly, 'something rather upsetting's happened.' He put up his hand and straightened his tie. 'It seems Tom Phelps had engine trouble with a plane he took up this afternoon. He managed to make a landing, but he was the other side of Bristol when it happened, and had to come down at Filton. He's just rung up the works to say he's not been able to get the plane fixed, and he can't be back here before tomorrow.'

Hilary looked at him curiously. It was, no doubt, a moment for exasperation, for dismay, even, possibly, for despair; but he was betraying none of these comprehensible emotions. He looked, in fact, anxious, wary and nervously apologetic.

'Oh, *dear*,' his mother was saying, 'how very vexing for you all. I suppose, with that possibility, he wasn't really a very good person to have. But you said he was so much the best, didn't you? It's so late now to put it off, isn't it? What *pity*.'

'Yes,' said Julian, looking at the middle distance. 'It is a bit of a nuisance. We can't call off the show now, of course. I'm afraid the only person who knows the lines is me.'

There was a little silence. Hilary was about to fill it with some encouraging commonplace, when something stayed her. She scarcely knew what it was; Mrs Fleming was perfectly composed, almost too composed for the moment, and oddly long in replying; but no doubt it was a principle with her to meet the minor crises of life with calm. And if Julian was looking as if he had been sent for to the headmaster's study, worry about the play could account for that. Mrs Fleming looked up from her lap. 'But, surely, dear, that will be a very difficult arrangement. You've made yourself responsible for so much of the organisation, I should think it will cause a great deal of confusion if you take an important part on the stage as well.' Her voice had the unmistakable note of a good hostess avoiding unpleasantness in the presence of a guest.

'Well, I hope not. Most of the organisation's more or less coped with by now. We'll have to risk a few trifles coming unstuck. I mean, it's just one of those things. The show must go on, and all that, you know.' He gave a shadow of his deprecating laugh.

'Of course, you know best, dear, if you feel you can manage it. It would be a pity to disappoint the village. But I really can't imagine why you didn't arrange for a proper understudy, knowing what an uncertain quantity this man Phelps was. I thought it was *always* done.'

'In a sense,' said Julian, rattling something in his pocket, 'I am his understudy. In a way. I mean, the possibilities were rather limited ... It's Tom I mind most about, really. He was so keen, and he'll be so sick about it.'

Mrs Fleming was looking again at her ringed hands folded in her lap. Hilary sensed the approach of another silence, and said quickly, 'Never mind, he'll feel better than if someone incompetent was going to make a mess of his part.' Julian flicked at her, sideways, a look which was a curious mixture of appeal and apprehension. She had been about to say more on the same lines, but changed her mind, and said nothing.

'One has to allow, don't you think, for the rather different mentality of these village people? They're so touchy, you know, Dr Mansell, and so suspicious of anything that's done for them. They're quite willing to accept a certain amount of help with organisation; but if people like ourselves seem to be trying to take advantage of it to come into the limelight, they resent it at once. They think of it as ostentation. Julian's become so used to the free and easy life at Oxford, where a little egoism is considered rather amusing, that I'm afraid he sometimes forgets to allow for their point of view.'

'Oh, but surely not.' Hilary was so angry that the falsity in her own careful voice made her feel quite sick. 'It will be announced, won't it? I should have thought it would rather add to the excitement of the thing for them. Particularly when they get a much better ...' Julian had not even looked at her this time, but she did not complete the sentence. 'If they get value for their money they won't worry about who it is, do you think?' She felt, rather than saw, his tension relax.

'Yes,' he said quickly. 'It's just a question of getting on with the job.'

Mrs Fleming had risen in her chair. 'Well, dear, Dr Mansell is quite right; we shall just have to look at it in that way and make the best of it. Don't be late back, will you? I shan't wait in the hall, now that you'll have your costume to change. I'll have something cold left out for you; I shall probably go straight to bed.'

'All right,' said Julian. He looked like a boy who has been beaten for a recognised offence, and is taking it with conventional good manners. 'I'll get out the car for you.'

'And please remember, dear, that you have to be careful of yourself, and don't get carried away with any rough horseplay on the stage. It will make me very anxious if you do.'

'We don't really. It's just effect, you know.'

'Will you excuse me for a few minutes, Dr Mansell? There are one or two things I must see about before I go ... You had better be hurrying, hadn't you, Julian, now you have all these extra preparations to make. I hope it will be a success, in spite of everything.'

She went out of the room, quietly and erectly. Hilary was left to make such suitable conversation as might occur to her. Lacking time for meditation, she only said, 'I'll keep my fingers crossed for you. The best of luck.'

'Thanks,' said Julian. He went over to one of the windows, closed the curtain, and proceeded methodically to the next. 'I suppose I'd better be getting along.'

'What sort of a part is it?' She felt both of them unequal to the kind of talk with which silence would inevitably be filled. 'The dashing hero, or what?'

'Good Lord, no.' He spoke with an instant, spontaneous revulsion, which gathered force from being largely suppressed. 'Captain Morgan. An extremely dirty villain. Tom did it very well.'

'I dare say we shall find he isn't indispensable.' He would not turn to meet her smile.

'We'll rub through, I expect. I hope to God I can get into those boots of his. If I split the coat it can't be helped ... Oh, *Christ*.'

'Whatever is it?'

'The beard. That fixes everything.' He turned round to face her, like someone confronted with irretrievable catastrophe, his studied restraint forgotten. He looked almost desperate. 'I might have known. Something like this was bound to happen. I *told* the damned idiot not to take it home.'

'Is that so awful?' His sense of disaster had infected her in spite of herself. 'Is there a lot of talk about it in the play?'

'Oh, probably. No, perhaps there isn't. But it's – oh, well, it's just an essentially bearded sort of part. He was called Blackbeard, even.'

'Well, that will be quite simple to cut.'

He said half to himself, as if he had not heard, 'What on earth can I have instead?'

'Instead of a beard?'

'I must have something . . . Blast him, he would do it. Just to play a damn fool joke on some girl.' It occurred to her that, except when he was semi-conscious on the theatre table, she had never till now heard him swear.

'But does it really matter so much? I don't suppose anyone in the audience will know he was bearded – I didn't. And if they do they won't care.'

'Well, I do. It's – it's completely offputting. Don't you see, it will mean making-up practically straight?'

'But why not? You'd have a few lines, or something, I suppose.'

'*That's* not enough!' He almost snapped it at her. There was a pause. He said, awkwardly, 'Actually, I never feel myself on the stage unless I look different. I really don't know why.'

If he did, she thought, it was no time to be asking. She said, matter-of-factly, 'You know a good deal about make-up. You'll think of something.'

'I shall have to,' he said. He walked away from her, to a glass that hung on the wall. She saw him put up his hand to his face, but his back was to her and she could not tell what he was doing. Presently, with a look of one who has solved something, he turned round. 'I wonder – have you got your bag here with you, by any chance? Your doctor's bag, I mean?'

'No. But I've got my car. What is it you want?'

'Oh, no, but what a frightful sweat for you.' His face had

lightened, however, with relief. 'No, I couldn't possibly. Dragging you about at this time of night.'

'I had to pick something up from the surgery, in any case, on my way back.' She had rightly judged that this would do for one so ready to be convinced. 'What shall I bring?'

'I oughtn't to let you. But if you really mean that . . . It's just a roll of strapping, the narrow sort. I had some, but it went bad with keeping.'

'That's simple. I'll give you a lift to the hall – it will be on my way – and bring it straight back to you there.'

'It would make all the difference. You always seem to be on the spot when one's in a jam.' He had almost recovered his normal smile.

'I'd better make my apologies to Mrs Fleming, hadn't I, before I go?' She tried to make this necessary remark sound trite and meaningless, and hoped she had succeeded.

'Oh, yes, of course. I don't know exactly where she is at the moment . . . Don't worry, I'll just run up and tell her.'

He was gone scarcely more than two minutes; long enough, however, to give Hilary time for reflection. If she had not put her patched-up relations with Mrs Fleming finally beyond repair, there seemed very little she had left undone towards it. She shrugged her shoulders; the milk had been spilled in a decent cause. After thought, she felt no more inclined to sacrifice Julian on the altar of social finesse than she had felt at the time, and would have done the same again. Besides, what had it all been about? Sectarian scruples about the stage would not be likely to draw any fine line between acting and production, and Mrs Fleming had not the sectarian air. It could only be supposed that her stated reasons were the real ones. Chewing over her indignation, Hilary found herself thinking, If he were my son . . .

He was back again, with a face of determined unconcern, and a large japanned make-up box under one arm.

'She says,' he remarked with very plausible ease, 'that you shouldn't let me make such a nuisance of myself, but that it's extremely good of you and she'll see you in the hall.'

She turned her own car while he got out Mrs Fleming's and drove it to the door; after which, directions for negotiating the drive and the gates filled in, for a few minutes, the encroaching pause. When they reached the road, and the pause engulfed them, she tried to look like the careful kind of driver who would expect silence in any case. Obliquely, in the windscreen, she saw Julian trying to look like a careful driver's considerate passenger. It was no use. The silence was becoming corrosive. It was evident that he was not going to break it with anything to the purpose. She should not, she said to herself, have expected it. 'Have you got many people to make up?' She could almost hear him sigh with relief.

'Well, the principals completely, I expect, and some general touching up. I've dared anyone to lay hands on a liner till I get there. You've no idea what they get up to. The women are self-supporting, thank goodness. *They* soon pick it up.'

'Are there many?' she asked, lest the protecting trickle of talk should stop.

'Only two. A dusky maiden and a distracted heroine. The Creole is one of the secretaries at the factory. She's made an intensive study of Dorothy Lamour and does it ever so sweetly, particularly in the places where she's supposed to behave like a hell-cat. And the younger of the local schoolmistresses is the heroine.' He smiled to himself.

'Is she good?' She found herself less eager than was reasonable for one of his sudden spurts of enthusiasm.

'Good as gold. The only thing is, one feels she'd make a

better job of repelling Morgan's dishonourable advances if she could bring herself to admit knowing what they mean. I've been on the point, once or twice, of suggesting she should go home and ask her mother to tell her. There *are* limits to a producer's function, after all.'

They laughed. A laugh is well enough in itself, but has a way of snapping the conversational thread. Presently Julian opened the make-up box, and proceeded to check the contents. She knew him well enough by now not to doubt that he had done this already, with a good deal more efficiency, before starting out. There was still six minutes or so to go. It felt like the prospect of an hour.

A car passed them. Julian said, 'Not dipping headlamps like that ought to be worth five pounds.' They agreed that driving tests should be carried out at night. Four minutes. The fringes of the village began to appear.

With the tail of her eye she saw him glance at her quickly, and then look straight ahead.

'I suppose you gathered, all this Morgan business was rather unpremeditated. I'm sorry about it. I'm afraid I rather let you in.'

Hilary lifted her foot on the accelerator. I ought to have known, she thought, he'd leave it till the last moment like this. She said, with cheerful vagueness, 'Oh, I'm used to families. I belong to a large one.'

'I ought to have said something before you came. I never thought of anything cropping up ... It's hard to explain, really. Why she has this thing about my acting, I mean. It's not that she's narrow-minded about the stage, or anything. It's just me. I think it must be just natural apprehension at the prospect of my making a fool of myself in front of a number of people. She's frightfully un-exhibitionistic herself, and I suppose she extends it to me. That often happens, I believe.'

'Oh, but naturally. Stage-fright on someone else's behalf must be much worse than on one's own ... I suppose one would still feel that about someone belonging to one, even after they'd done pretty well for quite a time.'

'You mean Ouds? Well, you were up yourself, weren't you? It doesn't amount to so much to anyone out of touch with the place. That's another thing I ought to have told you; I – really haven't often mentioned it. A few lines in a paper easily get overlooked. It was a bit awkward about Oberon, because unfortunately it made a headline, which I hadn't thought of. However, I was down by that time, and I've more or less stuck to producing since. It's a pity to upset people, I think.'

'I believe,' said Hilary, 'I ought to have turned left just now. However, we'll be there in a few minutes ... Even allowing for families, you don't strike one, somehow, as likely to be a source of anxiety in a village hall.'

'Well, I rather seem to let myself go to you. Perhaps it's because you're the only person who's seen me, literally, with the lid off. Or something. But after I had, I ought to have warned you. Not that anyone could have coped better if they'd known.'

'Oh, I've had to do a certain amount of coping on my own account. You see, my mother made a great success of her domestic and family life, and she'd rather set her heart on my doing the same. She's forgiven me now, but I don't think she's ever quite got over having a daughter who she feels has entirely wasted her vocation as a woman.'

'I should hate to seem rude to your people in any way. But if anyone else had felt that about you I should have said they weren't right in the head.'

The brakes squeaked.

'Oh, hallo,' said Julian. 'Are we there? I wasn't noticing.'

Hilary herself had only noticed in time to overshoot the hall by ten yards. She backed. Through the open door beyond the railings came the sounds of purposeful confusion. A voice said, 'Ah, here's Mr Fleming now. Ask *him* if you don't believe me.' Julian, opening the car, remarked, 'Looks about time I came.'

'I won't be long. If you're not about I'll leave it with someone at the door.'

'No, don't do that, they can fetch me. Oh, just one thing. If you did happen to have a black eye-shade – for one eye, you know . . . ? Sounds crude, but I think I could work it in.'

'Yes, I believe so.' At all events, she knew of a chemist who would sell it her after hours.

'Sometimes I wonder what I'd do without you.' He swung in through the doorway, the voices surging, in an eager wave, to meet him.

It was five miles to the market town, along a good main road. Hilary extended her car; it gave a focus to attention, and kept the mind from unprofitable exploration of itself.

There was no need after all to ask for him when she returned. He must have seen her through the open door as she stood looking, rather nervously, for some messenger not frantically preoccupied; for she saw him almost at once, jumping down from the stage level in the wings. He had changed into his costume, a traditional affair with a waisted coat, ruffles, and a cutlass belt; and must have miscalculated the size of Tom's feet, for he was wearing tall thigh-boots which seemed not to incommode him. Though a strong smell of greasepaint preceded him, he had not made himself up yet, and had left his frilled shirt open, in readiness, at the neck. The things had not come from the kind of establishment which cleans its costumes after every hiring; but, on him, this had merely the effect of making them look as if they had belonged to him for years. Already his stance and instinctive movements seemed to be of the period, so perfectly that she did not think of it till afterwards. A few yards away a young lady in ringlets and yellow velvet, whose refinement marked her out at once as the distracted heroine, had looked up from the typescript she was conning to eye him wistfully.

'You *have* been quick,' he said appreciatively. '(Check the cutlasses on the stage, Dick, if you've a minute, will you? We don't want to be one short again.) Now I shall have time to get down to it. You know, you've definitely saved my life.'

'I'm glad,' said Hilary, smiling at her own thoughts, and turned to go.

'Aren't you going to wish me luck?'

It had occurred to her, but she had been so impressed by his competence that she had felt it to be rather insulting. Now she perceived, under the convention of flippancy, an actual appeal. She longed, helplessly, to meet it.

'You know I do.'

'Yes. Thanks.' He stood looking down at her, his hand on the sword buckle at his belt.

'Oh, Mr *Fleming*.' A voice of lingering sweetness, and a waft of scented leg-tan, heralded the Dusky Maiden, tightly and briefly wound into magenta cretonne, with a hibiscus flower over each ear. 'I *can't* seem to get the hang of my sarong. It feels all anyhow. *Would* you tell me if it drapes properly at the back?'

She rotated, sinuously. As Hilary disappeared she heard him say in an abstracted voice already receding, 'I shouldn't worry, it looks pretty firm. So long as you've left yourself enough room to bend.'

Hilary filled in the next half-hour with a visit that would do as well to-day as to-morrow, and arrived at three minutes to curtain-time. The yeomanry had settled in, two benchfuls of small boys were scuffing joyfully at the back; the gentry were appearing, adding their smells of fur and Elizabeth Arden to the basic ones of varnished pine, chalk, prayer-books, and stale tobacco; and a thin lady in pale blue with a fox-stole was playing 'What Shall We Do With The Drunken Sailor?' very archly on a piano just under the stage. Hilary recognised from afar the back of Mrs Fleming's hat, with an empty seat beside it. She had been so preoccupied that she had actually not considered, till now, what she was going to say when they met.

Fate was kind to her. They had no more than exchanged guarded smiles when the curtain was agitated from within, and yielded up a pink young man in a bow-tie. Amid breathless silence, to which Hilary was happy to contribute, he embarked on a speech beginning, 'Ladies and gentlemen, owing to unforeseen circumstances ... ' Its conclusion was greeted with social clapping from the front, interested clapping from the centre, and a furore from the small boys' benches at the back.

The play was a rip-roaring romance, vintage 1910, and struck Hilary at once as a sensible choice. It called for no subtleties of emotion or technique, offered plenty of parts in which the local accent could flourish unreproved, and allowed the whole cast to be excitingly involved. Before any of the principals were on, she had become aware that it differed from the amateur plays she had seen before in some particular which, since many of the players were raw enough, she could not at first define. Presently she realised that it was moving at almost a professional pace.

While she was making this mental note the hero came on. She had quite forgotten that there would have to be one. He was a healthy and self-conscious young blond, very presentable except for a slight tendency to knock-knees, which he underlined by refusing ever to balance his weight on both feet at once. His modest declaration to the captain's daughter was interrupted by the sighting of the Jolly Roger just as the tender moment approached; an agonised fear that it might be sighted ten seconds late, letting him in for an unrehearsed embrace, had been written all over him so clearly that Hilary found herself sighing with relief. Action stations were called; the heroine cowered virginally in lurid light from a porthole; the stricken captain was borne in to entrust, with his last breath, the secret of the hidden bullion to her charge; the dreaded name of Morgan was heard without, and the heroine, blenching, clasped a horse-pistol to her bosom.

It was an entrance which the dramatist had been at pains to work up for several minutes beforehand; and during one of these minutes Hilary slid a quick glance at Mrs Fleming. She was looking, with composed attention, at the stage, and folding her programme into small pleats with great accuracy, as if some important use depended on her precision. Offstage, an evil and wholly unfamiliar voice snarled, 'Stir, stir, you yellow scum. Break in this door.'

The door swung open. His hand on his cutlass hilt, Julian strode in. Hilary knew him by his clothes, which she had already seen.

She had been prepared, by more than the needs of the play, for some degree of transformation; but had confidently, perhaps a little amusedly, looked forward to recognising him through it. Instead she simply found herself receiving, along with the rest of the audience, a shock of fascinated repugnance. The face, on what might be called for convenience its good side, looked a vicious and hard-bitten forty-five. The other side was traversed, upward, by a great drawn scar which, disappearing under the eye-shade, hinted vividly at some hideous mutilation of the concealed eye. Below it, as if by a contraction of the scar-tissue, the corner of the mouth was pulled into a permanent dog-like grin.

From where she sat, a few yards away, the mechanics of all this should have been, and to some extent were, apparent; but it needed concentration to work them out. He must have counted on a near view, and been at considerable pains to meet it. She wondered where, in his brief and sporadic experience, he had managed to pick up the technical knowledge. He could hardly have worked more finely for a close-up on the films.

She was so set aback, and so absurdly shocked (remembering that glimpse in the wings) that it took her some time to settle into following the scene. She tried to find her way back as quickly as possible, feeling her too personal thoughts a kind of failure in co-operation; for she sensed, at once, that he was in need of all he could get. Perhaps, she thought, nobody else could tell, as she could instantly, that he was painfully tense. Superficially, against the fidgeting of the others, he conveyed an air of complete assurance merely by remaining almost motionless in an effective pose, and using gesture sparely and to the point. It isn't fair, she thought – scarcely knowing the strength of her own emotion because the purely dramatic response around her confused it – we ought to be shot, both of us, for coming at all.

She had mislaid hopelessly the thread of the plot, which was beginning to ramify. At the point where she picked it up, he was having a showdown with the hero, and offering him the choice between freedom with dishonour, and several horrid deaths. Her attention focusing, she became aware that the hero was doing unexpectedly well; and then that she had ceased to receive from Julian that telephathic sense of strain. She did not at first connect these phenomena. She had been on the whole a passive playgoer, for whom one actor was good and another not; it had not occurred to her to ask herself how far one member of a cast was supporting another. Now her quickened perceptions recognised this process for the first time. The hero must have been Morgan's senior by quite ten years; but it was like watching a fire of damp coal being stirred by artful application of the bellows. His mild defiances, feeding on their effect, became almost dashing; he even straightened his knees and managed, for minutes at a time, to get himself poised successfully between them. His exit, on a resounding line, got a tremendous hand.

From this moment, the audience was won. The plot thickened; the funny man was chased by a whiskered pirate amid side-splitting appreciation; Morgan had a passage with the Dusky Maiden, displaying brutal indifference to her discarded charms and wresting a knife from her grasp with a difficulty which depended for its illusion largely on his own efforts. The lady was not at ease on the emotional peaks; and Morgan, exhausted perhaps by his efforts with the hero, gave her little assistance in climbing them. But the scene, after all, required him to be impassive.

The interval came soon after. Hilary, finding that refreshments were being sold in aid of whatever charity they were supporting, hastened, perhaps too eagerly, to leave her seat and find Mrs Fleming coffee. She came back, having killed five minutes of interval-time; and now some sort of comment could no longer be delayed.

'They're all doing very well, aren't they? And enjoying themselves, too; country amateurs are generally so cowed and conscientious. Do you think it's because there's such a high proportion of men in the cast?'

'I believe this society is unusual in actually having more available.' Mrs Fleming's manner was, irreproachably, that of a perfect hostess; nothing might have happened at all. 'So many come from the new aircraft works. No doubt, as it gets larger, it will become socially quite self-contained.' She seemed to approve this prospect. 'I don't know how far Julian influenced the choice of play. He has very little experience in producing women, of course.'

Lowering her voice discreetly, Hilary remarked, 'I should say, considering his material, he was probably quite wise.'

'I don't believe the level of talent was very high. But there must have been some disappointments, I'm afraid. When he gets carried away by an idea, he doesn't always make as certain as he should that no one's feelings are upset.'

'One can't always, can one, if one means to get results.'

She had spoken unthinkingly, out of her experience and instinctive way of thought; but as soon as the words were out of her mouth, she saw in Mrs Fleming's face that she had confirmed a conclusion, ratified a judgement on herself. Something like this had been expected of her, and she had supplied it. Perhaps, she thought, one generally did give other people what they expected: perhaps she, too, was conditioning Mrs Fleming's responses, perhaps her own summary was as incomplete and as unfair. What was the use of recognising these things when one could do so little about them?

Having received no answer to the spoken question or the unspoken one, she went on, 'He certainly seems to have pulled the cast well together.'

'He gets on well with most people.' Mrs Fleming attended to her coffee-cup. Her voice had been neutral and, apparently, quite indifferent.

'And he's giving a very capable and unselfish performance himself, don't you think?' Something had sooner or later to be done with an omission which was becoming so oppressive; she got it over.

'Acting used to be quite a little hobby of his, some years ago.'

Finality of tone could hardly have gone further. The rest of the conversation consisted of trivialities about the costumes and the inconveniences of the hall.

The curtain went up again and the play pursued its hearty and predictable course. It was not till the last threads were being tied that Hilary had time for her own conclusions. She remembered his lack of all but vicarious rehearsal; the quality of his support, of the play itself, the continual temptations to burlesque which both must have held out to anyone with a sophisticated technique. She remembered Caliban, an association which was still unreal because already, before she met him, she had ceased to think of it as a rendering at all; it had become part of her permanent conception of the play. With hesitancy akin to fear she thought – But he must really be good; not by these standards, by others that I don't sufficiently understand. What shall I do? For she had ceased, by now, to question her own sense of responsibility present and to come.

The curtain was coming down. She clapped, like everyone else, with palm-scorching energy, feeling a little fidgeted as she did so by she scarcely knew what. As the curtain rose again on the assembled cast, she identified the source of her irritation with Mrs Fleming, who in the midst of all this had been making, most uncharacteristically, furtive efforts to touch up her face. At this moment Hilary realised that she had been, if not weeping, at least so near to it that she distrusted the light. It was a discovery so unsettling, so destructive of all the adjustments she herself had been trying to make, that she scarcely noticed Julian being stamped and yelled for, and saw him appear in front of the curtain with vague surprise.

Luckily there were many more curtain-calls after, and a full-length rendering of the King, to which Hilary accorded a rigid eyes-front. At the door of Mrs Fleming's car they said all the right things to one another; their courtesies, thought Hilary, were hygienic to the point of sterilisation. Mrs Fleming started the car immediately; she had already remarked, on the way down the hall, that Julian would have no difficulty, when he was ready, in getting a lift.

Hilary's own car was parked in an alley beyond the stage door. She walked round to it at leisure, lighting a cigarette on the way to settle herself. She had almost reached it when she saw something white moving weirdly inside. Recovering from the unpleasant start it gave her – her nerves were not quite what they ought to be to-night – she threw open the door. The white object, which revealed itself as an indescribably streaked and filthy towel, was lowered, and from it emerged Julian's face, recognisable and tentatively smiling. The car reeked of greasepaint. Out of one of his hip-pockets (he was, of course, still in costume) trailed the fall of lace from his neck, which he had taken off to assist operations. He said, shyly, 'Hallo,' and stuffed the towel into the pocket on the other side.

'Well!' said Hilary, trying to pull herself together; she had counted on a longer breathing-space than this. 'You made me jump, for a minute.'

'Sorry.' He eased out his long booted legs to stand aside for

137

her, and hovered uncertainly with one foot on the running-board. 'I just looked in to say good night. I never thanked you properly; there wasn't time before.'

Even by the dashboard lighting she could see that his face was still very far from clean. A rim of brown clung along his hair-line, his cheekbones were high-lighted with removing-grease, and his eyelids, heavily blue, were further smudged with black from the liner. Aware perhaps of this, he fished out the towel and gave himself another scrub with it, shifting the grease but little else. The general outcome was a rather touch-ing effect of innocent dissipation.

'Come in and sit down for a minute,' she said. 'It's cold.' He climbed back again with willing promptness, and shut the door. It was a moment which found her quite incapable of the constructive thought she had meant to give it. She could only remember that he must be the only member of the company for whom no one was waiting, somewhere or other, with a good word.

'My dear,' she said, 'if you're not pleased with yourself to-night, you ought to be.'

'Was it all right?' Under the sketchiest pretence of casual-ness, he expanded so simply that she could no more have kept herself from giving him what he had come for than from con-tinuing to breathe.

'Of course it was. I don't only mean you, I expected that. The whole thing. It moved so well.'

'That's a relief. We were nine minutes over time, but it was twenty at the dress rehearsal. They were quite snappy on their cues to-night. You've no idea how difficult it is to get it out of their heads that the audience needs a good five seconds to digest the last fellow's lines. Which was why they wanted to do *Hay Fever*, I suppose.'

'Well, they had fun with it in the end. I certainly did. Didn't you?'

'M-mm.' He stretched, and linked his hands behind his head. 'You can call it that. It's a funny thing, it never feels at all that way while it's going on. Even if nothing goes wrong, and you feel more or less on top of things, I wouldn't say ... no, you can't call it enjoyment, not at the time. More like walking a tight-rope, really. I suppose that sounds a fatuous thing to say after a romp like to-night; but you can't help feeling it. And yet, when it's all over ... I wonder ... I suppose you wouldn't have a spare cigarette about you? I didn't think to bring any and now I suddenly feel like one.'

She gave it him, wondering for how long he was proposing to settle down. He must surely have things to see to; besides, it was scarcely warmer in the car than outside. The cigarette, which he was enjoying in the conscious way of the sporadic smoker, looked queer with the rest of his externals, and added to his rakishness something insidiously forlorn.

'Of course,' he was saying, 'the most hair-raising contre-temps were going on practically all the time. Peters had to do some pretty quick thinking when that ladder came down. It was rather good, the way he turned it into a laugh. When I saw him ...' And so on, for several minutes. He was, obviously, bursting with gossip of the kind which there would be nobody else to hear. It seemed the cruellest heartlessness to turn him away; and she dared not think how little she wanted to. But what was one to do with him?

'Would you like a lift home?' she asked, after she had assured him for the third time that nobody in the audience had noticed whatever it had been. 'I can easily take it in on my way.'

'Thanks very much, but I don't think just yet ... I mean, there are one or two things ... I'm keeping you, aren't I?'

'I've nothing to hurry for.' Yes, she should have realised that he could not go home yet. In fact, for the next half-hour or more he had, probably, nowhere in particular to go. It seemed a little hard. But if he was hoping that she would take him home with her (and she suspected increasingly that he was) he would really have to think again. This was deep Gloucestershire, not Oxford at the end of term. People would be talking.

'It feels so odd,' he said wistfully, 'just solemnly packing up straightaway and going home. But they're like that, here.'

'No party?' she asked, instead of changing the subject as dictated by common sense.

'No party. The aircraft crowd will be fetching up at the Crown, of course; but they'll be happier on their own. If there were anywhere else, I'd say come and have one with me. I owe you a drink, to put it mildly. But I expect you're dying to get back to bed.'

'It isn't as late yet as all that. The heroine looked nicely terrified, I thought. Perhaps her mother told her in time.'

He grinned. 'She hadn't been as near up to my face before. I think it caught her sort of unprepared, from a foot away.'

'It caught me unprepared, if it comes to that. It really was appalling.'

He looked delighted.

'That was entirely thanks to you. I'd have been nowhere without that strapping. You have to catch it with a dab of spirit-gum at the ends, or it starts to slip when you get warm. Then you work on the scar over the top of it; the difference in texture is just right. I've had the idea in mind for some time.'

'Whatever gave it you, in the first place?'

'I saw it once in the street. An ex-soldier, I should say.' He drew calmly on his cigarette. 'Looked like a gunshot job. The original took in the whole corner of the mouth as well, but that would have made speaking too difficult. Interesting thing, though, a certain amount of one-sided tension is quite a help if you want to alter your voice. I didn't know till I tried.'

'Julian, a head keeps peering out from that door and then vanishing. Do you think they're looking for you?'

'Oh.' He gathered himself together, reluctantly. 'Yes, I suppose I shall have to go in, anyhow, and say good-bye to people. And change. After that' – he looked at her ingenuously out of blue dark-rimmed eyes – 'I think I shall probably go for a quite long walk.'

'Don't be ridiculous.' She had to laugh; he had done it with such infuriating efficiency, and she could not even tell if he knew it or not. 'You're coming back for some supper with me. Then you can walk home, if you still want to. Or there's a bicycle you can borrow if it's worn off.'

'That would be *simply* marvellous. But I feel I'm rather planting myself on you. In fact, I know I am.'

'I want to talk to you.' (Odd how one could trip on the moment of decision before one knew one had reached it, like a threshold in the dark.) 'How long will you be?'

'Five minutes, inclusive. We're leaving all the clearing-up till to-morrow, and I can finish my face on the way.'

He was back in six, dressed after a fashion and fixing his tie as he came.

'I'd have been quicker,' he apologised, 'but I had to co-opt two men to get me out of my boots.' As she started the car he wedged a large tin of grease between his knees, and proceeded to use it with what, considering he had no mirror, seemed creditable efficiency. 'Am I respectable?' he asked presently. 'If it's not taking your eye off the road?'

'Presentable, anyway. You don't look very respectable, for some reason. I think it's because you've left some mascara on.'

'Mascara!' He threw back his head and crowed with laughter. Even when he was unhappy he remained childishly easy to amuse. 'Lord love you, hark at the woman. You want to be careful who you say a thing like that to. Mascara. Well, well.'

'Whatever it is, it's still there.'

'I only need have done one eye, but I forgot. A bit like blacking yourself all over to play Othello; I must be losing my grip. Anyone would think, to hear me talk, that I was going to be doing this sort of thing for the rest of my life, wouldn't they? Funny how I even feel, to-night, as if I were.'

'It isn't funny,' she said. 'You know that.'

She heard him draw the swift breath that precedes impetuous speech; but he was silent after all.

'Tell me; what *are* you going to do for the rest of your life?'

He said, with a little smile, 'The Lord will provide, I shouldn't wonder.'

This was too true to be good; but she was not sure if it had been what he meant, and in any case did not want to think about it.

'But is there anything else at all that you want to do, except this?'

He answered at once, simply and flatly, 'No.'

The road zigzagged through a village, and she had to give her mind to the car. She was glad of the interruption; it had kept her, perhaps, from saying too much. She waited.

'You're very good at putting up with people,' he said presently, 'aren't you? I suppose you get plenty of practice. You'll need it all to-night, if you don't look out. I get revoltingly garrulous after a show. I'll wake up perfectly normal in the morning; but while it lasts, it's absolute hell to keep it in.'

'You needn't; I like shop.'

'You said that as if you meant it. The worst of it is, there isn't any real shop to talk. Is it true what they say, that people who've had a leg off can still feel their toes?'

'Yes, sometimes; why?'

'That's rather the way I feel.'

'Except that the leg's still there.'

'That's worse, in a way.'

They had arrived. A light was showing in Lisa's window; she must have gone up to bed. The supper she would have left in Hilary's sitting-room would be – it always was – plenty for two. (Like all generous persons whose own appetites are small, Lisa grossly over-estimated those of other people.) She went out to get him a plate, and returned to find him stirring the damped-down fire into flame.

'Thank you,' she said. 'That's better.'

'I hope you don't mind. It occurred to me, too late, that I haven't known you seven years. It is seven years, isn't it?'

'That's what old maids who read tea-cups say. Come and have some food.'

'How did you guess,' he said presently, 'that I was as hungry as this? I didn't. But I am.'

'All that nervous energy. And think of the duel.'

'Let's not think of the duel, for pity's sake, if you want me to digest anything.' He applied himself to his plate – he was certainly hungry – and in a little while looked up to say reflectively, 'You are funny sometimes.'

His personalities always had a disconcerting suddenness that caught her with one foot off the ground. She contented herself with raising an eyebrow at him.

'You love to pretend you get it all out of text-books, don't you? I wonder why?'

'I quite often do.'

'Nervous energy!' The rim of black, still drawn along his

lashes, gave something spuriously sinister to a charming smile. 'All right, have it your own way.'

She led the conversation back to the subject of make-up and established it there with relief.

When they had finished they went over to the fire. By now it was blazing, and there seemed no need to move the lamp-standard nearer. He took the chair opposite hers, and when she offered him a cigarette, at first refused it and then changed his mind.

'I shouldn't keep smoking yours. It was funny, my not bring-ing any. Shows how long it is since I did anything.' He got up to give her a light, and at once settled himself, with the natu-ralness of old habit, on the hearthrug at her feet.

'Well?' he said.

Now that it had come to the point she felt quite unready. Weakly temporising on the brink, she said conversationally, 'How long will it be, do you think, before you get another part?'

'Never, I expect.' He said it as if it amused him, blowing a little cone of smoke into the air.

'You don't believe that.'

'At the moment, no. That doesn't stop it from being true.'

She put a needless log on the fire, bracing herself.

'Will you be angry if I say something I shouldn't?'

'There's nothing you shouldn't.' He leaned back against the chair beside her, his hands clasped round his knees. 'Go on. I should like you to, even though it isn't any use.'

'But—'

'Never mind that now. Go on.'

'What do you think it is? That you can act? I've told you so, and in any case my opinion's worth nothing compared with others you've had before. It's much more difficult than that.'

'Even so,' he said, 'it probably isn't as simple as you think.'

'It's never simple. It wasn't simple for me.'

'For you?' He looked up at her in a kind of blank wonder. She had seen the look before, when she had made some (it had seemed to her) ordinary statement about her life or background; almost, she had thought, as if he expected her to have emerged from a vacuum. It always vaguely troubled her.

'Why not for me? It happens to scores of people. Yes, getting my people to let me train took me more than a year. I was the youngest, you see; a sort of afterthought. I grew up almost like an only child. My father could have been my grandfather when I was born, and my mother wasn't young. I spent years wanting to be the sort of person they needed me to have been, but it wasn't any use. And they weren't selfish; if I'd wanted to get married, or take up music, or teach, they'd have made no trouble, I knew. But medicine was more than they could swallow; they belonged to the generation that talked about the New Woman, if you know what that means.'

'I know my Shaw. Go on.'

'My father thought that besides being unwomanly it was perfectly pointless, being a job in which no woman ever gets to the top. And my mother thought it so immodest that she couldn't believe I knew what it meant. Being fond of them, I could see it as they did, too. That doesn't help ... but this is the point: that even the best people don't always know what it is they're asking for. If they did, they wouldn't ask it. They thought I only needed weaning from this silly idea, to give them a nice home-loving girl about the place. I knew that all they'd get would be a slowly decaying corpse. They wouldn't really have liked it, when it came to the point. So in the end, I went.'

'Were you unhappy about it?'

'Yes, very, for quite a while.'

'What a shame.' He turned and stroked her knee. It was a caress entirely without sexual suggestion; a woman or a child could have made it. 'You were right, of course. One can see the results.'

'The result is that I'm a second-rate surgeon, just as my father thought. I'm only alive instead of dead. And you may be a second-rate actor, for all I can be sure of. But you see why I asked you not to be angry, don't you?'

'I'm not angry.'

'Well?'

'Well, there are several things. For one, both your parents were alive; it didn't mean leaving anyone quite alone.'

'That's true. But if it had, I still don't know. Yes, I do know. They'd have been even more alone, if they'd been alone with me.'

'And with a woman, there's something, isn't there, just in leaving home. With a man it's more or less understood that that will happen eventually.'

'Doesn't that help?'

'Not in this case. I don't know what it is, one could cope better if one did. I tell you, she has a thing about it. She – thinks I'd go to the bad in some way; she doesn't say so, but I know. It's impossible even to begin to talk to her about it. I have an idea why, but – well, I can't start about that now. Anyhow, I honestly think it would kill her, or crack her up in some way, if I went on the stage. You'll say that isn't reasonable; perhaps it isn't. You can't say, can you, why some people get better from a disease and some people die. But it's no good arguing, if that's the way it is.'

'My dear,' she said as gently as she could, 'believe me, people don't die so easily.'

He looked into the fire. 'Perhaps not; if one could afford to try it out. You see, I'm very fond of her.'

'Of course,' she said quickly. 'Of course, I know.' She had spoken as people make, sometimes, a swift movement to escape from a stab of pain. What she felt humiliated, it even frightened her; she threw her will against it, and reduced it to a dullness which could be half ignored. 'But it's amazing, you know, how family pride will react to a little success. When I'd no more than passed my first MB, my father was running round informing everyone to boring-point, poor dear. I think you'd find that the first time you played lead, and got a good notice or two, it would be the same.'

'No. There you couldn't be more wrong.' His voice had a certainty that asked not to be questioned; she did not question it. There was a silence. Presently he said, 'Besides, as I told you, it isn't so simple. I very much doubt whether, professionally, I'd stand a chance.'

This made her angry, and she saw no point in hiding it. 'That's an excuse you make to yourself. You must know that as well as I do. You should face the real issue, at least.'

'You mean that nicely, I know.' He spoke with a kindness that had unconscious dignity, and made her feel more rebuked than protest would have done. 'I think you'll believe me if I explain. If you're going to take the stage seriously, the only way to start is in rep. You can't pick and choose your parts there; that's just why it's good training. You don't get typed; anyhow, not much before you're forty. They're not going to take anyone my age to do character stuff all the time.'

'I suppose not; why should they? What you want is an all-round training.'

'They don't take people to train from the bottom, you know. They take them to act.'

'But I don't . . . You're not trying to tell me, are you, that you *can* only act character parts?'

'Yes, I am.'

'But, Julian, *why?*'

'I've never done anything else.' His face was growing closed and withdrawn. She tried to stir up her anger again, but could only feel bewildered impotence.

'But . . . it's absurd. Surely you don't need me to tell you that. You – you don't look peculiar, or deformed. You've a good voice, you've no eccentric mannerisms. Why on earth shouldn't you play straight parts? They must be much easier than what you've done. What's to stop you?'

'I don't know.' His mouth was as obstinate, now, as a lying child's. 'I just have a thing about it.'

'But you took Oberon and did very well.'

'That's not a straight part. I had . . . Oberon's non-human.'

'And there was . . . ' But she remembered his oddness over the photograph, and something warned her to hold her peace. Besides, it had been a long time ago, and, she deduced, in some way not a success. She thought again. 'Well, perhaps you have got a thing, or whatever you call it. But then it matters all the more to do something about it. For its own sake, I mean. People can't let their lives be governed by irrational phobias.'

'Oh, yes,' he said. 'It's easy to talk.'

A display of resentment would have shaken her far less than the unsuspected reserve of bitterness from which he spoke. Somehow she had succeeded in really hurting him. She could see that it would be wasting her time to ask him why.

'Never mind,' she said, smiling. 'You'll wake up one morning, sometime, and wonder what it was all about.'

'That will be very nice.'

He was perfectly polite. With a humility she had rarely

148

showed to anyone in her life, she said, 'I'm sorry. I'm just being tiresome and interfering. I only said all this because I thought you were good to-night; better than I've said. Now I've spoilt it, haven't I, preaching and nagging, and carrying on.

'Of course you haven't.' He seemed to come out of himself, and turned to her a face grown, in a moment, anxious and eager. 'Please don't think anything like that.' With impulsive swiftness he leaned up to her, and threw his arm across her knees. Now as before, there was no more in it than the coaxing gesture of a young boy. It made her feel restless, irritable, and unsettled; she could almost have drawn away, but found that her hand was on his shoulder instead. He tucked himself more comfortably round her, giving her a little squeeze. 'I'm not taking offence, I told you I wouldn't. As far as that goes, I had a pretty good idea beforehand what you'd be likely to say.'

'Then you'd much better not have let me.'

'Actually, I had a curious feeling that I should like you to. But, Julian, *why?*'

He had caught her own inflection so well that, in spite of everything, it succeeded in making her laugh.

'I wasn't going to ask why. I expect it was the same sort of feeling that makes people bite on a doubtful tooth.'

'Partly that. But I think it was more – oh, I don't know. If you keep things in entirely, it makes you – sort of unreal to yourself. You start to wonder if you're really there.'

'Yes, I used to feel that. You must feel it much more, being an actor.'

'Say that again.'

'I only meant that it's an actor's job to externalise himself. What's the matter with that?'

'Nothing. Nobody ever called me an actor before, that's all. It felt rather strange.'

'It feels quite natural to me.'

'Does it?' He spoke with an irony so gentle that it was subtly caressing. Not without a certain irony of her own, she thought: And he has a thing about playing straight parts.

Outside in the hall, the grandfather clock struck eleven, sounding clearly in the pause. He sighed and said, 'I'm afraid that means I ought to go.'

'Will anyone be sitting up for you? I don't think I ought to have asked you to come.'

'I didn't give you much choice, did I? No, it'll be all right, if I can really borrow that bike. I'll bring it back to-morrow.' He made no move to bestir himself. She knew that she ought to dislodge him; and thought, with the weakness of one becoming tired, that her knees would feel cold when he had gone; she had got used to him there. Another minute or so would do.

'Are you as good to everyone,' he said sleepily, 'as you are to me?'

'Don't be silly.'

'You would say that. I expect it comes so natural you don't notice it. Don't laugh, but I always remember ... oh, you know. I always shall.'

She had never felt less like laughing in her life. Their first conversation in the hospital garden had sprung, with an instinctive association, to her mind; she had never wholly for-gotten it, nor his look of shocked bewilderment when she had questioned him. In the moment when, now, he ceased to speak, her clearest thought was that then she had wanted something that Sanderson could send to the *Lancet*. It came back to her like an outrage.

'That was nothing,' she said; and the external facts, in which she had had such satisfaction, seemed suddenly so sterile that she felt it to be true.

'Nothing?' He was looking away from her, talking to the fire. 'All that time. And – everything. You must have been frightfully busy, too. One forgets one isn't the only person in the world.'

'It wasn't really so very long.' She cast back her mind. His whole spell of consciousness had been a matter of minutes; through much of it she had been plying him with the routine questions, and making notes. He had been dreaming, she remembered, when she came into the room. It was likely enough that out of the limbo of a jarred brain nothing remained with him but fragments of dream. She must have stirred the dream for a moment and deflected it, and it had coloured his imagination of her ever since.

He said, 'It made all the difference. I wanted to tell you. I was thinking the other day, perhaps people sometimes don't thank you, when they're well, simply because they don't want to remember making fools of themselves. So I thought I would.'

'You didn't make a fool of yourself, I told you that.' She felt her own memory entangled in his illusions. Had she really made some response that she had forgotten? She found that the thought brought her emotions to so slippery a place that she had to snatch them back in a panic. 'I don't suppose you remember as much about it as you think.'

'I remember enough,' he said under his breath, and laid his head against her knee. In his voice and touch she felt a nostalgia, a kind of undemanding weariness. She put her hand for a moment lightly on his hair.

'You're tired out,' she said gently. 'Go home to bed.'

'All right.' He had spoken like that in the hospital room, docile and uncomplaining. He got to his feet, and stretched himself. Just as she had foreseen, it felt chilly when he had

151

gone. She put on her coat and went out to the garage with him to find the bicycle. The night had cleared a little; it was moonless, but the stars threw the black edges of things against the sky. They tested the lamp and the tyres and wheeled it round; he propped it against the winter-dry myrtle hedge at the gate.

'Thank you,' he said, 'for putting up with me. I can't think of anyone else I'd have asked to do it to-night.' Without hesitation or embarrassment, as if he had done it often before, he put his arm round her shoulders; it might have been the preliminary to a confidence. 'God bless you. You're a darling. Good night.' He kissed her; quietly, affectionately, even comfortably, and let her go. She saw his head and shoulders against the dim sky, fixed as if self-consciousness had suddenly overtaken him; then they were gone and she heard the brittle sound of brushed leaves and the tick of the cycle-chain fading towards the road.

Hilary went in and smoked a cigarette by the fire. She began a second, put it out again, and, shaking herself out of her chair, went up to bed. But she was awake till a late moon, rising an hour or so before the dawn, confused the sleeping cocks and set them to a ragged, uncertain crowing.

IO

Oh, God, said Julian to himself, I hope it keeps fine.

He walked out on to the terrace, feeling with relief and dis-trust the sunshine which, here in the shelter of the house, was almost as warm as spring. After yesterday's rain, it seemed a turn of luck too good to be true; it probably was. He had known, at the time, that one ought to make some alternative plan in case of bad weather. None had suggested itself, and he had hoped for the best; which, of course, was simply asking for it.

The air was bright and clear; too bright to count on. It was still only eleven. Obviously, one would have to be armed with some possible scheme in case. If it wasn't too bad when he got there, there would be a certain amount of waiting about for it to clear, which would bring it near tea-time, and she would sug-gest having it there; but there had been so much of that, it wouldn't be decent. And supposing it were hopeless from the first. It would be ridiculous to take her an hour's run in the rain to Cheltenham, simply to eat in some dim café, and none of the cinemas were showing films worth crossing the street to see. The only reasonable or intelligible thing would be to put her in the car and bring her back here. It would stick out a mile.

No, there was no way round it. If it looked doubtful by lunch-time, he would have to say where he was going. That part was going to be difficult, in any case.

Well, after all, she would have to come here, obviously, from time to time. If only she hadn't been forced to come out in the open about the play. He had seen the whole thing ahead then, as he stood outside with his hand on the door, before he had walked into the room to tell them that Tom was out. Well, she must know that. She always handled these things well. If it came to the worst, it would probably pass off all right.

God, if it would only keep fine.

The weather had been uncertain since early morning; but, opening his eyes to sunshine and expectation, he hadn't worried much. That, though, was before he had known that this was going to be one of the days when something was wrong, and his mother hated him.

When he began to know, he had tried, as he always tried at first, to dismiss it as imagination. Then, as always, even after these years, he had searched himself for a cause. Could she have found out, for instance, that though she had made him sell Biscuit after the accident (old Lowe, of course, had backed her by forbidding him to ride) he slipped over to Pascoe's twice a week? She had taken it into her head to blame Biscuit for the crash; and remembering nothing himself, he could not disprove it. She had said that as long as he kept him, she wouldn't know an instant's peace of mind, and as this was evidently a fact, Biscuit had had to go. He had sold the horse to Pascoe for half what he was worth, because Pascoe couldn't afford him, would treat him properly, and, as one had known all along, let one exercise him now and again. But he had been terribly careful always, taking his breeches and boots in the car to change into on the way, and having a bath as soon as he got back lest the smell of horse should cling. Still, some fool might have seen him and said something; and, when he knew to-day that something was wrong, he had led the conversation round indirectly to riding, hoping it might come out. He would have been glad for it to be that; to be anything to which one could put a name. But it had been evident that she had not known.

If she had guessed, he would have admitted everything at once. He never lied to her when there was the slightest chance of being found out. The displeasure of his own conscience was trivial beside her displeasure, which could not, like moral guilt, be thought straightly about, nor righted by any logical process of amendment. It simply existed, till she chose to take it away. Yes, he would have owned up about Biscuit, and been suitably sorry, and then perhaps made her laugh a bit and got things right. But it had not been that, or anything that could be dealt with. It was the other thing.

It must be seven years now, seven years and a month or two, since all this had begun. The time before it seemed in memory like a lost world, certain, unclouded, serene and secure. But even then he had been aware of something. It had passed quickly then, and, accepting as children do his original sin and wickedness in the eye of that perfection, he had been content to be forgiven and had never thought it strange.

He could only remember one incident which had had a definable shape. He had been six or seven, perhaps, and a lady called Aunt-Louise-from-America had come to tea. He had never seen her before; she had been one of those courtesy aunts, an old school-friend of his mother's probably. He had been fascinated by her beautiful make-up, longing to ask her how she did it, and by her delicious smell and the way her soft voice slipped upward in places where other people's voices went down. He would have liked to sit and look at her, but she had insisted on taking notice of him, which had made him so shy that he had escaped at the earliest moment after tea. Wanting, however, to study her again from a place of safety, he had gone into the hollow centre of the big deodar when she and his mother were sitting on the lawn. It had embarrassed him very much to find that she was still talking about him.

He had been about to slip away again, feeling silly, when he had heard his mother's voice, quick and defensive; as if she were standing up for him though she knew he was in the wrong. 'Oh, but he'll lose that as he gets older. I should hate him to grow into one of those too-good-looking young men. They're always superficial and untrustworthy. Julian's really quite a manly little boy.'

He hadn't known what 'superficial' meant; the grown-up form of 'cissy', he had supposed. What had he done to make her afraid he might grow up like that? For she was, though she had said not; he could tell by her voice. It had worried him so much that he had gone down to the village and picked a fight with Fred Saunders, but she hadn't liked that either because he had on his best clothes. For months he had dreaded Aunt Louise appearing again. Then he had forgotten about it, until the thing had happened which he was never likely to forget.

Since then, when something went wrong, he had always known that that was a part of it. Even when all was well, she kept him reminded – not directly, but by inference and remote illustration – that he had grown up with a handicap which would need a great deal of living down. He would need to be very careful, she had implied, to keep men from disliking him and the wrong sort of girls from making him look a fool – the right sort would probably distrust him at sight. (This was his own private and crude analysis.) He was, in fact, in a rather humiliating way not very good form. By the time he went up to the University, he had accepted this as unquestioningly as he might have done a speech impediment, lack of money, or reach-me-down clothes. It had been an agreeable surprise (though she had been right about the girls) to find people so decent to him on the whole. But then he had found out quite soon, with vast relief, how easy it was to be the kind of person no one takes very seriously.

Not being taken seriously was obviously the way to live; and it had been obvious, too, what to do with the rest of oneself which this simple recipe did not employ. Provided one did it well enough – if one's technique had the polished surface which gave invulnerability – one could get away with anything on the stage. If the disguise were really impenetrable, one could get an emotional response from other people honestly, without loss of self-respect; one could escape from anything, plunge into anything; one could become real.

He had given it up when it had seemed that, if he did not, she would altogether cast him out. It had always had the guilty sweetness of a forbidden indulgence. But he had thought then that there would be security, that the moments when something was wrong would cease. They had not ceased; the thing had gone on, descending out of clear weather, falling like rain on the just and the unjust of his days; a sending, a curse. He never knew what had brought it, nor, when it was lifted, the cause of his absolution. There was only the central core of it at which he guessed.

He had been over it a thousand times, eliminating every possibility except one. How often, in these moments of exile, he had walked up to the stiff, straight-faced photograph on the wall, searching it with the acuity of hatred for a resemblance, a characteristic expression, a typical gesture to avoid. But what? There seemed no common factor. A clean, squared, military face with a clipped army moustache, disciplined, conventional; a stiff upper lip over a well-bred sentimentality. 'All this emotion,' the face seemed to say to him. 'Not quite the thing. Not what I expect in a son of mine. A brisk walk and a cold bath, my boy. That's the secret.' But the picture must be thirty years old. They used to expose the plate for three minutes or so, with the sitter gripped in an iron frame and a light glaring into his eyes. What could one hope to learn?

Now and again, in the night, he had thought he knew what was meant by 'after death, the judgement'. Expelled from the body, one found oneself absolutely alone in absolute space; and then, if one could remain alive, one lived. If not, that was the real death, and the moment of it damnation. But if one could cohere for the appointed time, one was admitted to heaven. People had odd conceptions of heaven; draughty and vast, with hordes of saints like a Bank Holiday. Heaven was warm and enclosed, secure from intrusion; the branches and leaves of the tree of life encircled it, the sun through the leaves making it warm and sleepy; the river flowed through it, sun-warmed, and one could live and breathe in the river like a fish in a summer stream. As long as he could remember, he had thought of heaven like this.

As for hell, he knew now about that too. After Biscuit had thrown him, he had not known at first that he was dead. His soul had loafed about, aimlessly, like an out-of-work at a street corner, among the jumbled residue and junk of life. Once he had been aware of cold, and had known then that something was amiss; but he had escaped from the cold and dreamed again. But presently the dreams had ceased, and he had known that he was dead and that the judgement was beginning. It was just as he had imagined. He was alone, a minute pin-point of self in the infinite black shadow of God. God's face was turned away, because his soul was not yet proven. He must walk, like St Peter on the sea, a certain way through the emptiness by his own power, before God would stretch out a hand. With a thrill of horror he had known that he was not ready. He should have died hereafter, there would have been a time for such a word. The fear of the ultimate loneliness was tearing him apart; God was receding, not approaching; and he began to sink.

But all was not lost, for he could see beyond the great ring of eternity the mediatrix who could cause the cup to pass away. He had called to her, silently in the silence, knowing that with the call power went out of him and the last hope of salvation from himself. She had turned a little, and then she had turned away; and he had understood immediately that this was one of the times when something was wrong, and that it had been inevitable, always, that this should be the ultimate end.

The gate of hell had opened, then, below him. Already the pull of its descending spiral was making his soul tenuous and mis-shapen; in another instant its disintegration would begin. At the very last, some reserve in him held him together for a despairing thrust upward, such as the drowning make: and in this penultimate moment, the Other had come, to whom in his extremity he had forgotten to pray. Unremembered, unimplored, moved only by the mercy which was her being, she had come to him from her own place, hidden in its shadow like a veil, and lifted him out of hell by the hand.

Because she was there, pain and a heart-wrenching sickness had been like friends assuring him of safe return. For a little while he had been afraid to let her go, lest he might drift away again into the dark; and she must have known this, for although he could not speak, and did not know even the place in which they were, she had been close and consoling and had refused no comfort for which he had asked her; of this he was sure, though it was growing hard, now, to keep the fragments of true memory apart from the rest which was also, but differently, true. He could bring it all back, even now, if he shut his eyes.

When, after so long, he had found her again, it had startled him at first to find her so different in daily life, her charity so armoured and disguised. It scarcely seemed, sometimes, that she remembered. But the armour had never deceived him. It made one, superficially, a little shy and uncertain how to approach her, and he wondered sometimes if, supposing one had met her first in the ordinary way, one would have understood her at all, or would not even have been a little scared of her. Such speculations were pointless, for they had met as they must.

'Thou art so truth, that thoughts of thee suffice to make dreams truths, and fables histories ...' He remembered the rest, and caught himself up quickly. If he began to let himself think like that, when he was with her he would remember it and wouldn't be able to look at her, wondering if she knew.

Nothing was so strange about it all as the need of external behaviour, having to keep in mind what stage of an outward acquaintance they had got to, and observing the social rules. It was practically impossible to think of her as an entity of the polite world who had a right to expect that one should return her hospitality suitably, and even, of all impossible incongruities, invite her home. (But please God, not to-day.) It was a violation of her mystery; one should go to her, always. But even if she knew that, she couldn't say; and neither could he.

The sky seemed as clear as ever. It would probably be all right. At least there was no need to worry about it yet.

'Julian.'

'Hallo, dear.'

He saw at once, as his mother stepped out on to the terrace, that he was forgiven again. She was dressed for the garden in the old cardigan and tweed skirt he knew as well as he did the parting in her hair. Suddenly everything settled, the sunlight even seemed more stable and lost its threatening sharpness; his thoughts rested, thankfully, on the surface of things.

'I was wondering where you'd got to. The Laytons want us to go there to dinner on Tuesday. I told her I was sure you were free.'

'Yes, of course.' The Laytons were a bore, but in his reassurance and relief he was glad to appear delighted. 'I'm not doing anything.'

'We really must go into Cheltenham, I think, one day this week, and get you some white shirts. I've just been going through them; that Oxford laundry must have been disgraceful.'

'I suppose it was rather fierce. What are you going to wear?' He always asked her this, knowing that she liked it.

'I think the grey; they have seen it once, at the Abbots'; but I haven't worn it there. Of course, if I wore the blue, it goes with the little jacket we chose in town. But I can't make up my mind if it's really me.'

'Of course it is. That's why I made you have it.'

'Well, dear, I'll wear that if you like. I chose it to please you; I had meant to get something much quieter. You give me extravagant ideas, I sometimes think.'

'Nonsense, you can carry it off. It looks rather regal.'

'But, you absurd boy, I can't look regal at the Laytons'. I'd better wear the grey.' He knew that she wanted him to persuade her, and did so.

'Where's your jacket, Julian?' she asked, when the point was settled. 'That pullover's far too thin to wear out-of-doors this weather. I don't want to have you ill again, after all I went through last year.'

'I was just going in. Unless you'd like anything done out here.'

'I'm just going round the garden. Run and fetch your jacket, and you can come with me. It's so beautiful now in the sun.'

Yes, it was beautiful now, in the sun. Immediately it had come out from the silver edge of its concealing clouds, how easily the cold mist could be forgotten. As they went down from the terrace into the wilderness-garden below, he almost found himself wishing that he weren't going this afternoon, in case any awkwardness should crop up about it. Soon, of course; he had been looking forward to it a good deal; to-morrow, perhaps. And yet, as he knew from experience, once on the way he would be glad to have made the effort; like acting, or slipping off to ride Biscuit, these truancies gave him a mingled sense of value and of guilt. Sometimes he had gone when it was very difficult; when, having made no arrangement beforehand, there was no need, and when the worry involved outweighed all anticipated pleasure. He didn't know why; only that if he failed the impulse, he would not feel, as one should, good and unselfish, but defeated and accused.

'Look,' he said, 'I thought we should find something here,' and showed her the first violets in a sheltered dip of the long grass. She said, 'How quick of you, dear, I should never have seen them,' and then, 'It's a shame to pick them, let them grow.' But when he had robbed the dark leaves of the fragile hope they had been hiding, and put it into her hand, he knew that he had pleased her after all.

By lunch-time a few small light clouds were drifting across the sun, making wings of shadow on the hills. But there was still no sign of anything serious; he would chance it, he thought. It would always be possible, if things took a turn for the worse, to ring up from somewhere.

'See what's come for you,' his mother said, as they sat down. 'The post gets later and later. It's that new postman; I'm sure he finishes this end so that he can drink at the Crown.'

Julian deplored the postman, excused himself, and slit the thick envelope along the top. He would rather have kept it, but she wouldn't have liked that. They always opened their letters at the table; it was a nice, sociable custom, she said, and gave one fresh things to talk about. He had recognised at a glance the rickety spacing of Chris's typewriter, and fished inside for the letter, leaving the wad of typescript where it was. So Chris had finished it at last, he thought (carefully concealing his quickened interest); if it shaped up to plan it ought to amount to something. If only he had managed, this time, to get the hang of speakable dialogue. Chris's stuff always read well, of course – too well.

'What a fat, intriguing envelope, dear. Is it a catalogue, or what?'

'No, it's from Chris Tranter. You've met him, I think. He came on the barge with us at Eights. Thick, fair man with a square face.'

'Oh, yes. He brought me an ice, but it had melted. I remember he was quite mute until the boats came by, and then gave a perfectly deafening bellow almost in my ear.'

'No, that would be Fox. Chris would talk till the race started, and then go to sleep.'

'How odd. Never mind, dear, read his letter and then you can tell me the news.'

Julian skimmed the page; he could read it again, properly, later.

... so I haven't altered the structure, essentially, except to write in a short scene for the brother and the prostitute in Act II, which I think gives the note better for what is coming. The rest is cut pretty near the bone, but I'm open to suggestion. As I said before, what I principally want from you is to vet the speech-rhythms. I'm a hopelessly visual type and shall never cure myself of primarily seeing words. You are almost completely auditory; so just mark the margin against anything you personally would find difficulty in putting over. Thank God I won't be there to see you trail off with that gluey expression as if you were being choked with bread sauce. By the way, when are you coming to town; surely the component parts of your skull are properly gummed up by now? There's a man I want you to meet, because, seriously, if this play gets taken I want to put you forward for Anthony; you're the only person I shall ever really see in the part. Don't write back and say you'd rather do Old Ike, because that one's wearing thin. I presume by this time you have managed to sell the acting idea to your people in some form or another; so unless you are absolutely set on rep. I don't see ...

'I always think it's so odd of people, don't you, to type their letters? It seems so un-intimate and casual, doesn't it?'

'Oh, I don't know.' He returned the sheet unobtrusively to its envelope. 'It would be rather a waste of time for Chris not to type his, because no one except Chris would be able to read them.'

'Has he any interesting news?'

'Nothing special . . . He doesn't get about very much.'

'He must be tied by his work, I suppose?'

'Sort of. He works quite hard.'

'You're not very communicative about him, dear. Don't you like him as much as you did?'

'Oh, yes. Of course. Chris is all right. He's in the Civil Service, actually. The Treasury, I think.'

'That certainly doesn't sound very exciting. Does he send you all his statistics? The envelope looks thick enough.'

He laughed accommodatingly. 'Well, not quite. It's only something he's written he wants me to look over.'

'Well, dear, that's *very* interesting. You made him sound quite dull. Is it novels he writes, or short stories? I should like to read it. Perhaps I should be more impartial than you would, being his friend.'

'I expect you would, really.' He knew that Chris had a violent hoodoo about displaying unaccepted work, and would never have sent it even to him without practical purpose. 'I don't know if you'd care much about it, though. He's rather leftish and strong-spoken, and there's a sub-plot that . . . '

'Oh, he's discussed the book with you already, then?'

'Just vaguely.'

'Well, my dear, I think for anyone of my generation you could call me quite broad-minded, don't you?'

'Oh, why, yes, of course. I was just thinking that perhaps—'

'I should find it so much more interesting, knowing it was by a friend of yours I had actually met. What is it called?'

'*Hungry Harvest.*'

'What a queer title. It sounds almost a contradiction, doesn't it?'

'I suppose that was the idea.'

'Yes, I see. That's rather clever, isn't it? You're not getting on very fast with your lunch, dear, don't let it get cold. If he wants his novel criticised, I expect he would be quite glad to get two different points of view.'

'Well, there is that.' He kept his mouth full, hoping she would start another subject, but it didn't work. 'The only thing is, it's not properly finished, so he might not want it seen.'

'He must think very highly of *your* opinion, then, mustn't he? Does he want you to suggest an ending?'

'Not quite that . . . He just wanted me to say if the dialogue sounded natural.'

She looked at her plate. When she spoke, she was still looking down.

'If it's a play he's sent you, Julian, why did you tell me all this time that it was a novel?'

'I don't think I said, particularly.'

'You didn't correct me, did you? . . . I should have thought it would have been much better to have sent it to someone connected with the stage.'

'He will, I expect, when he's finished it.'

'I'm afraid I should be of very little assistance in criticising a play. I should never have made such a foolish suggestion, if you had explained to me in the beginning. Now we must really get on with our lunch, or it will be ruined.'

Julian rediscovered the food on his plate, and, to avoid comment, pushed it down. The room itself looked different, and he realised that the sun had gone in again. He scarcely noticed it, except as the reflection cast by another kind of weather. Everything had been going so well. He wouldn't be there at tea-time. Things must be got right, somehow, before he went.

'Chris keeps trying,' he said casually. 'I don't suppose he'll do anything with it. But his job's dull, and it cheers him up to have someone take his stuff seriously. He might get some of these left-wing amateurs to do it on a Sunday. I'll look it over sometime, he'll be offended if I don't.'

He stared at the envelope, from which the uneven lines of an ill-used typewriter looked dumbly back at him; and remembered the evening when he and Chris had discussed the thing together. He found that the prospect of reading it repelled him, now, as much as the prospect of finishing his lunch. Still, if it got things right ...

'Poor boy.' Her voice was a little warmer already. 'Yes, it must be an interest for him. Don't hurt his feelings about it; one can always find *something* to praise, can't one? There's too much fault-finding in the world, I think.'

'Yes.'

'I've had *such* a nice letter from the Matron of the Cottage Hospital. When people are so appreciative, it's a pleasure to do anything one can to help. There seems so little to send this time of year; but I think some time this week I shall let them have those old bound *Punches* – they're rather out of date, but they would pass the time, I expect, for people in bed.'

Julian thought swiftly. The Cottage Hospital was only five minutes or so out of his way; it might simplify things considerably.

'I'll run them down for you this afternoon, if you like.'

'It's hardly worth a special journey. One of us is sure to be passing before long.'

'I might as well.'

'The weather looks rather uncertain, or I might come with you, just for the run. What do you think? We could wait a little, and see if it clears.'

He got up, and walked to the window; not because it had not been clearly visible from where he sat.

'It doesn't look up to much, at the moment.'

'It was beautiful, not long ago. I expect it will change again.'

'We'd probably get a better run to-morrow. I'll use to-day for some of the pottering things.'

'There's the Women's Institute to-morrow. They're earlier in winter; it would leave us very little time. To-day would really be better.'

'I think it's definitely blowing up for rain.' He recognised the insistence with which she would sometimes pursue a point for no reason but that his response had had some reserve, and he gathered his resources together. For one brief moment he thought that after all he could ring up and put it off on the grounds that it looked like rain; it would sound fairly natural, and it wasn't likely that *she* was attaching much importance to it. But if he did, he would feel about her as he was feeling now about Chris. It couldn't be lived with. No, the thing would just have to be handled with tact. He turned back to the table, smiling.

'Let's think up something properly organised for to-morrow. Or shall we do something reckless and unpremeditated, to fill you with *élan* for the WI? I tell you what, I'll wander round this afternoon seeking inspiration, and spring it on you out of the void? No?' He leaned over the table towards her, making it as persuasive as possible. If he could only start out having left everything right ...

'Please don't be silly, Julian.'

Something shrank in him. He knew the tone, and even the words. How had he looked, what had he said? In any case it was too late; it had happened now.

'You have such an exaggerated manner sometimes, dear. I don't like it; it makes you seem insincere. I'm sure you don't mean to be, but it's an affectation, and you know how I hate

168

that. We'll think about to-morrow when it comes, though I have a great deal to do and I don't suppose we shall be able to fit anything in. I think you're quite right about the weather to-day; it would probably have been disappointing. Really I have a thousand and one things to see to, and this would be a very good time to get them done.'

She rang for the sweet, and, when the maid had gone again, talked on as if she had still been in the room. That was the worst of all, that she never allowed any crisis, any definition. Punishment would have seemed like forgiveness, rather then this withdrawal, which was a reaction of the whole self. The loneliness it left was absolute; there was no appeal, because, till the unknown moment of her return, nothing was there to receive appeals.

He said, when they got up, 'I don't think I shall be in to tea,' and would gladly have gone through every anxiety again from the beginning, if she would only have questioned him, or objected, or shown any concern for his comings and goings, or for his being at all. It seemed sometimes that if he had said at one of these moments, 'I am going to Johannesburg,' she would have answered, 'Very well, dear,' and gone quietly out of the room as if he were already there. She had written him off, for an offence not of word or deed, but of his own person; he knew this with the piercing certainty of childhood, whose condition it is to receive effect without cause.

As he would have done after this in any case, he went out to the garage to get out his car. It was a thin red MG, which he had bought at Oxford second-hand, but kept in shape with careful servicing. It would still do eighty, on a good road. He chose a good road, though it was out of his way.

The release of speed, the sense of power submitting, without the disturbance of any unknown factor, to his control, gave him a simulacrum, for a while, of peace and freedom and invulnerability. It wouldn't have lasted; but he remembered that this afternoon it had no need. He wondered what he would have done with himself, if he hadn't been going to her. Gone unannounced, he supposed, as he had done once or twice before. Or, if she were out, as had happened sometimes, gone to Mott's Cave. But, of course, there would be that too.

It had been an unpremeditated recklessness to ask her. Later, at night, it had seemed inconceivable to have abandoned so much, so lightly, to an almost certainty of wreck. But thinking it over, he had known that it had sometime to be done; and, when it failed, perhaps that would be the best. One could cling to one's myths too long and offer them too much power. It would have to go, once it had been made for ever impossible by the certain test. He put the thought from him, because he had a car to drive, and because to think even of the impossibility stirred a longing so intolerable that, unless he could succeed in forgetting it, he would arrive with nothing to say.

'Look.' Hilary pointed through the check curtain of the tea-shop window. 'It's beginning to clear. Cheer up.'

'Is it? Oh, yes. That's fine. I say, you're not eating anything. Try one of these things with jam on.'

Hilary looked round. If she had not been troubled for him, she would have reached by now the point of exasperation. She remarked restrainedly, 'No, thank you. I'm still smoking the cigarette you gave me when we finished tea five minutes ago.'

'Oh, Good Lord. I'm terribly sorry. I don't know what I was thinking about.'

'It's all right,' she said, smiling. 'I wasn't going to ask you.'

'You're very forgiving.' He roused himself; she could see him struggling back to the fluency with which he had been talking nonsense a few minutes before. 'No gentleman ought to think in the presence of a lady. Like spitting. It isn't done.'

'Don't consider it. A little accident like thinking can happen to anyone.'

'I feel so badly about dragging you out here in all this rain. You must have got awfully wet getting out of the car. I ought to have taken you back to our place. I kept thinking till the last minute it would clear.'

'So it has.'

'Yes, it would now we've passed all the views.'

'But that was one of the best parts, being so high and watching the rain come across the valley.'

'You're terribly good about all this. I should think in actual fact you'll look back on this afternoon as the year's high spot in discomfort and boredom.'

'If you lay on the suggestion so powerfully, I probably shall. I thought I was enjoying myself till you began upsetting my ideas.'

'It's a sense of guilt, really, at having enjoyed it myself.'

'I don't know whether you're giving me credit for brilliant deception or yourself for a thick skin. Would you really have enjoyed it if I'd been so bored?'

'Quite honestly, no. But one can't say, "Thanks frightfully for not being bored." Or can one?'

'If one must mean it, I don't see why not.'

He looked at her with a faint smile, and said nothing.

'I don't mind your thinking,' she told him. 'But don't think *at* me. That really is annoying.'

'Sorry, of course it must be. But it's rather fascinating when someone makes a remark that more or less epitomises them. A sort of heraldic device. "I don't see why not." Argent, in a bend gules a scalpel of the first. Crest, a head sutured proper with mantling of the second.'

'Good heavens. Wherever did you pick up all that?'

'Oh, you have to get a smattering, if you do anything about costumes. Otherwise you perpetrate the most awful howlers. I remember once . . .'

With a little encouragement he was well away. She listened

in quite genuine interest, but in still more relief. She had realised long since that he belonged to a type which mistrusts or fears its own capacity for introspection. Violently extro-verted activity would be his solution for all minor forms of internal strain. This afternoon he had talked the hind leg off a donkey, as well as driving within the bare margin of safety until the road surface had begun to compel discretion. (Fortun-ately he had not attempted these remedies simultaneously, and she had restrained him in neither since he had shown suffi-cient competence in both.) If these had failed him, something must be seriously wrong. He had never been distrait in her company before. With an older man she would very likely have asked what was the matter; but she had no confidence that, if he wished to keep his own counsel, he would know how to do so without embarrassment to them both.

It struck her afresh how urgently his temperament, as well as his abilities, required the outlet of the stage. It would give him extroversion without suppression; how could anyone with a lifetime's knowledge of him fail to perceive it? No one could, she thought, without self-imposed and deliberate blindness.

'. . . so I had to go over them all,' he was saying, 'with a pot of gold paint, and of course when it came to the time, not a damned one was dry. Everyone was careful, and nothing hap-pened till we got to the part where . . .'

I take it all too seriously, she thought, masking her preoc-cupations with a show of lively attention. If he had a face like a peeled rabbit and no chin I suppose he could be enduring the agonies of Hamlet, and all I should feel would be guilt at not feeling more, plus a longing to get home. As it is, he only has to look a little absent-minded – when probably it's nothing at all but a certain embarrassment at having bungled the expedi-tion . . . Why is one such a fool?

'... and it wasn't till he'd got right downstage and was starting the big love scene that I noticed half his nose was gilded, the side facing the audience too ...'

Or if he'd only pose a little, she said to herself; or present his profile as if he knew what he was doing; if he would thank one only a little less sincerely for not being bored ... But the anecdote had come to an end, and it was time to be amused.

'The sun's definitely shining,' she said presently. 'If we're going to do this cave of yours, don't you think we ought to get on?'

He looked across at her quickly, eagerness struggling with doubt in his all too expressive face.

'We *could* do it, easily, before the light goes. But, honestly, do you want to? I mean, don't mind saying, whatever you do. Are you feeling damp, or cold, or anything? Don't let me just drag you around. If you like, we could go into Cheltenham and see a flick.'

It was almost on her tongue to ask him what was showing. A good film might take him out of himself, she thought. Though the rain had ceased, the weeping landscape made any thought of inner earth strike like a chill. She could not have said, afterwards, what impulse it was that came to turn her from so reasonable a choice.

'There are so many films. I'd rather see the cave. Just wait while I tidy up, and we'll catch this fine spell while it lasts.'

She went out to the ramshackle little cloakroom in the garden, where the cracked mirror informed her that she might well have called it into consultation before tea. He had not put up the hood till after the rain began, and the wind had reduced her face and hair to a state of nature. Her ill-founded confidence in them must, she supposed, have been reflected from her companion; she had remarked in him before an imperviousness to details like this which would have pointed to complete indifference in anyone else. Sometimes she had been tempted so to regard it, for the sake of finality and peace.

The door had a rough, ill-fitting lock; the key stuck, and she had a few minutes' trouble in releasing herself. Her efforts recalled some distant but unpleasant memory, which at first she could not place, till she remembered that the same thing had happened to her once as a young girl. Then, it had been in a windowless London basement, and she had hammered on the door (which the attendant had opened for her almost immediately) in a reasonless stifling fear. This place was light, and the casement would have let her through easily; so that it seemed an odd thing to recall after so many years.

When she got back he was waiting for her in the car. He had quietened down in the interval; and presently a steep gradient, full of sharp bends, demanded concentration enough to keep him silent altogether. Before long they reached plainer ground, but such thoughts as the pause had engendered seemed still to be containing him; though now and then, with an obvious effort, he would throw off a perfunctory comment on something they passed. She made no attempt of her own to develop conversation, because his erratic restlessness appeared to have left him; she noticed that his management of the car had toned down into a rational kind of enterprise, which was no doubt his normal style. Presently, however, they came to a clear stretch, and with an air of thoughtful deliberation he began to accelerate. The needle climbed smoothly. It occurred to her that all through the drive, even during periods of time when she had been rather too conscious of the car for perfect comfort, she had been very little conscious of his movements; and it was borne in on her suddenly that his confidence was based on a first-class technique. It came as a curiously new thought to her that for a number of things twenty-three is the prime of life. But, of course, it was the better part of a year since she had first met him: by now he must be twenty-four. This thought made her recollect that she had not passed the interval without undergoing a birthday herself.

The finger of the speedometer had slid, unnoticeably, up to seventy. He sat at the wheel with a quiet that looked like indolence, his head tilted back a little, his eyelids relaxed. Without any difference of expression he said, almost as if he were continuing a conversation, 'Do you know Leonardo's "Madonna of the Rocks"?'

'Yes,' she said, trying to recall how many years it was since she had seen it. Its image rose still vivid in her memory; a melancholy, mysterious and faintly sinister evocation. It had had a quality for her, which still remained, of answering the dropped thought with a little echoed whisper, a little heart-chilling delay, like that with which the mine-shaft or the unplumbed well receives a stone. 'I wondered, when I saw it, whether there used to be any legend to explain the setting.'

'Why not?' he said. 'Oh, yes, I expect there would always be a legend.' The needle, which had dropped to fifty while they spoke (he had the good driver's knack of compensating, almost unconsciously, for lapses of attention however slight), started to move upward again. Perhaps it was for this reason that such further comments as she had felt like offering seemed just as well unmade. Presently the road began to wind a little, and he slowed down to forty.

'One of the many things I dislike about Pater,' he said, 'is the extraordinary coarseness of perception with which he lifts the imagery that essentially belongs to her ... to this picture, I mean ... and uses it for effect about that other diabolical creature. You know the passage, of course.'

She enjoyed, for a moment, a Beerbohmesque vision of Pater being informed by Julian that his perceptions were extraordinarily coarse; but, deciding on a quick glance that he did not look a receptive subject for humour, she kept it to herself.

'You mean,' she said, '"She is older than the rocks on which she sits"? The part about the Gioconda? Does she affect you as strongly as that?'

'Personally,' he said, with rather excessive flippancy, 'she affects me like a near view of the Bottomless Pit.'

'I admit I find her rather malign myself.' There had been an overtone in his voice which she had found indefinably disturbing. 'Somewhere or other – I can't remember where – I came across a theory that the Madonna of the Rocks is a kind of reverse of the medal; the beneficent aspect, you know.'

'I don't think I care for that theory very much.' There was a car a little way ahead of them; he devoted himself to passing it, efficiently and very correctly, as if some weighty enterprise hung on the achievement. It took him a couple of minutes, after which he said, 'Beneficent, yes,' and relapsed into silence again.

Hilary felt no disposition to interrupt his thoughts, being suddenly absorbed in her own. For some undiscovered reason the memory of David had returned to her after an absence of months, bringing with it a sense of flatness and banality never felt, or at all events never acknowledged, before. Her thoughts wandered on, with the looseness of association which comes from want of desire to follow their processes too closely: How much men lose, as they collect experience; but it gives them a certain capacity for protection, when they care to use it, and to do them justice, they quite often do. But to be at the mercy of a fresh, inchoate imagination, to be its raw material, a tambourine to take the rap when the spirits answer ... What am I thinking, and why? We'd better talk.

'Why are we going down there?' she asked. 'This looks like a private road to a farm.'

'It is. It's Mott's Farm. The cave's on their land. It's only been discovered about fifty years.' His voice had become suddenly brisk and factual. 'The story is that one of the young Motts was out rabbiting with a dog, and the rabbit dashed into a hole in the side of the hill, with the dog after it. So the lad brought his father along to help dig out the dog, and after they'd been at it for a bit one side of the hole collapsed inwards, and there was the cave. We'll have to call at the farm for the key. In summer they do a line in conducted tours, but they don't bother conducting me, I've been too often. Here we are. Don't get out, I shan't be a moment.'

He had stopped the car at a five-barred gate. Beyond it was a farm-yard, containing hens and a midden, around which Julian picked his way with the neatness of one who knows the hard places. She saw him knock at a green door in a grey house, pause a minute or so in chat, and reappear.

'I've brought you one of the vicar's leaflets,' he remarked. 'Mrs Mott insisted. Don't read it now. It's frightfully informative and bright.'

'Thank you. I'll keep it till I get home.'

The lane had degenerated into a track, with a glutinous surface which sucked at the wheels. They bumped and slithered across a couple of fields, and fetched up under the sheer flank of a hill, whose base was stripped and broken as if by the erosion of water. Here and there a thin crust of turf clung to the rock, and it was in the middle of one such surface that the outer arch of the cave, evidently the recent handiwork of man, had been cut away. Within it, a lintel and posts of rough timber enclosed a still rougher door, fastened with a padlock and chain. Julian unlocked it and swung it back; the hinges, rusty with late disuse and rain, moved with a heavy groan. The sun was declining, and the long blue shadow of the hill-side, speaking already of dusk, seemed to make still deeper the blackness within. Peering, Hilary saw that after a few yards, the mud-caked rock of the floor disappeared, abruptly, into nothing. She experienced, suddenly, a powerful disinclination to go on.

'It looks a bit like the mouth of Tartarus, doesn't it?' said Julian contentedly, 'till you get a light. It isn't really very deep; at least, the first part isn't. Look.'

He reached up to the inner side of the lintel, and a switch clicked. The void ahead became defined in a yellow, melancholic glimmer, rising from the depths. She saw a rickety-looking ladder spanning a ten-foot drop. The cavity was steep, narrow, and evil-looking, like the mouth of an oubliette. At its foot, the walls were visible on every side save one, where a boulder partly concealed a fissure in the rock.

'I'll go first, shall I?' he said, 'to steady the ladder. It's inclined to wobble.' He eased his long limbs down it with his usual effortless grace, and stood waiting for her at the bottom.

Hilary, annoyed by the consciousness that people do not appear at their best in foreshortened views from the bases of ladders (and this one had uncomfortably wide-spaced rungs) found that she disliked the cave more strongly than ever, but felt also that to let this appear would be not only unkind, but faintly old-maidish. Craning down to look for footholds, she was relieved to see that her escort, though keeping the ladder firmly braced with a foot and arm, had modestly averted his eyes. When he turned to hand her down, he looked so full of quiet anticipation that not for anything would she have let him see how much the place oppressed her. They were out of sight of the sky, and only a little reflected light gave a cold blue-greyness to the small patch of roof overhead. There was a chill, wet smell; the smell of limestone, which is so much danker than the smell of earth. Somewhere out of sight water was dripping, not musically, but with a dull, smothered thud.

'Through there,' said Julian. He spoke like someone who produces, as a birthday surprise, a not unworthy gift.

She flattened herself and edged through the crack behind the boulder. In this still more confined space a stifling sense of imprisonment pressed on her like a physical weight. Because it was irrational, and she did not approve of irrational fears, she went on with a new determination. A dry little voice in her head, clinical and detached, remarked, Quite a number of people have sub-acute claustrophobia. It was odd, she said to herself, never to have diagnosed her own case before, but really quite interesting.

'Is it as narrow as this all the way?' she asked, turning her head to look for him. He was close behind her, backed to the rock. The question seemed to amuse him; he returned a proprietary smile.

'Go on round the next bend, and you'll see.'

She rounded a sharp buttress and realised that the light was coming, now, not from behind, but before. The crack widened. She came out into the cave.

It was, she had to admit, an impressive transformation scene. The place must have been twenty feet high, and not much less across. Here and there, along its irregular sides, the lime deposits of millenniums had dripped their characteristic fantasies; petrified cascades, pointed fringes like the beards of dragons, strong rods and thin-waisted stems of water-polished stone. Curiosity, and the relief of wider space, pushed into the background the discomfort of her nerves. She went forward, realising that what she could see was only an unknown fraction of the whole, for the string of electric bulbs stapled into the roof disappeared downward, and evidently continued round a bend.

'Do you like it?' said Julian close behind her. He spoke in the half-whisper that people use in an empty church.

'It's amazing.' She answered in the same voice; his, or the place, seemed to enforce it. 'I'd no idea there was anything here on this scale.'

'It's rather off the track. There are so many showier ones, nearer the big towns. I like this better, myself.'

He looked past her, down the broken perspective of shadow and dim light. His eyes seemed to have deepened and darkened, and in his face was a curious look of remoteness and of rest.

'The lower half's the best,' he said, moving forward. 'Mind how you go, it's uneven here and there.'

Just beyond the bend the floor sloped sharply, and the arch was divided by a thick pillar of rock. Passing this, she saw beyond her the dark sheen of water. More than half the wide oval of this inner chamber was a pool. Cold and unmoving as its containing stone, it stretched from a saucer shallowness, where the dull light easily found bottom, into impenetrable depth against the rocky wall. It set her mind seeking a phrase: 'the dark backward and abysm of time'. It would not have astonished her if from the farther depths a blunt saurian head had reared itself to blink at them with white eyes. She said something of the kind to Julian, who was standing, silent, beside her. He laughed softly.

'You never know. This is only the front hall. There's

another cave, with an opening under the water-line. A few years ago, in a big drought, some men saw the mouth showing, and managed to get through. They found something bigger than this, and their impression was that there was more, under more water, beyond. Nobody can say how far it goes.'

She felt a little shiver move over her body.

'That's rather frightening, isn't it?'

'Why?' He was smiling. 'It's rather fun, I think.' As if to justify this unsuccessful essay in expression, he added, 'When you were little, didn't you ever play at caves?'

'No. Do most people?'

'Oh, I should think nearly everyone. What else would one do about the tiger under the bed?'

'Mine was a tent. And camp-fires round it.'

'You must have been one of those frail creatures with a night-light.'

'I'm afraid I was.'

'I suppose it's race-memory, or something. Geologically speaking, it's only yesterday that the tiger was real. And so was the cave – this one, among others. People lived here. It's in the vicar's leaflet.'

'I don't think I should do well as a troglodyte.'

'Don't you?' he said, and looked into her eyes with the same strange withdrawn smile he had turned on the dark recession of the rock.

She felt indefinably disturbed by a change in him which, also, eluded definition; and tried, for the sake of reassurance, to dispel with bathetic brightness a mood which was beginning to tinge her own. 'One imagines a squat creature with matted hair and a prognathous jaw.'

'I don't think so.'

Her attempt had not brought conviction even to herself;

she had not been able to raise her voice from the sub-tone with which they had all along been honouring the genius of the place. On him it had clearly had no effect at all.

'You haven't sat in the chair yet. That's very important.'

There was a flat, square rock near the water's edge, with a fall of stalactites behind it; a sunken plane in its centre gave it the rough likeness of a throne. He motioned her towards it, with a quiet ceremoniousness. His gestures were, always, more expressive than he knew. An unknown apprehension and reluctance stirred her, mixed with another force, which was not reluctance nor apprehension, but less to be trusted than either. She had an impulse to laugh, to say something unforgivably trite and crude which would make him flinch, and slam against her the door of this secret world whose darkling welcome was more disquieting than the water with its drowned labyrinth below. But she moved forward instead, and, smiling to keep herself in countenance, sat down in the bed of the stone, leaning forward a little from the sharpness of the ribbed limestone, her hands on the rocky arms.

He took a step or two towards her, then stood still, looking at her from a yard or two away. The intentness of his face frightened her. Till now he had kept intact a surface, at least, of commonplace. She tried, for self-protection, to reflect how absurd a picture she must make in her modern clothes, her parchment-coloured woollen dress and the dark blue coat hanging unsleeved from her shoulders, against this setting for a mermaid or a titaness. But her sense of humour failed her; she could feel nothing but a certainty of power to which her soul had not assented, which wisdom – or fear – warned her to evade.

It was the place, she thought, the absolute exclusion of familiar light and living, the stillness: she understood, for the first time in her life, what the phrase 'a stony silence' meant. It must be her own strong reaction to the cave, a compound of formless dread and pride in quelling it, and over-gentleness for his mood, which was adding force to this illusion. She must break it now; they must escape to the safe clichés of daylight, the red sports car, the vicar's leaflet, which explained everything it was useful, or good, to know.

All this went so swiftly through her mind that the pause had scarcely had time to become significant. She saw in his eyes that convention, the fear of ridicule (perhaps only of his own) still partly held him; but so unsurely that a look from her, a gesture, accepting the dream, would loose him from them altogether. She saw that a bald denial would be destructive cruelty already; he had betrayed himself too far.

Without moving from where she sat she said gently, 'The light will soon be going, up above. Don't you think we should leave soon?'

'I suppose so.' It had happened as she had meant; without violence, reality was strengthening its hold on him again. But when she made to rise, he motioned her back into her seat.

'Just a minute. There's something you must see before you go. I nearly forgot.'

He moved to the column of rock that divided the inner from the outer cave, and touched something she could not see. The place was filled with what seemed, by contrast with the yellow beading of sparse light, a dazzling colour-filled effulgence. There must have been three or four flood-lamps concealed, with their reflectors, in jutties and coigns of the stone. The deposits on the walls leaped into vivid ivories and rusts and greens; the water of the pool was a profound, hyaline blue. She blinked, and exclaimed in admiration.

'A bit obvious, but not bad theatre, I admit.' He had raised his voice to an almost normal pitch; an echo, hitherto unheard, caught it and played inhumanly with it in the vault above.

'It looks like a decor for *Swan Lake*.' She felt safe and confident again; the memory of that short silence was already fading.

'I've never used it before. But I remembered, from my first conducted tour. I felt you ought to have the entire ...'

Darkness, deep, dazzling, absolute, and suddener far than the most sudden death, annihilated the scene. His voice, as if it too had been a visible thing, stopped in mid-syllable. There was a pause; the half-incredulous pause that happens in any human company when electricity fails. Then Julian said, in the protesting bewilderment which someone always displays at such a moment, 'Damn. I suppose I can't possibly have blown a fuse.'

He had spoken aloud again; sounding in the hollow of invisibility, the echo repeated him with an effect grown suddenly devilish and malign.

'You must have.' She lowered her own voice, out of its reach.

'There were two switches ... Oh, Lord. I suppose I should have turned off the other lighting first. God, what a fool. I might have known the wiring probably wouldn't carry both.'

'Try the switches again.'

'I have. They're both dead.'

Slowly, like a wild beast whose cage has been opened and which looks out at first with hesitation before it springs, there advanced on Hilary the image all this time thrust back, the huge imponderable mass of the hill piled, earth and rock and boulder, three hundred feet above her head. She imagined the unseen roof slowly bowing, the first thin fissure widening, the thunderous, obliterating descent of a million tons. Her fingers clenched themselves on the rock. One must have control, one must rationalise . . .

'I really am most frightfully sorry.'

If this nether darkness had fallen on his own room at home, he could scarcely have shown less sense of insecurity and awe. He was begging her pardon for another contretemps, nothing more. While he spoke, the infection of his confidence thrust back her advancing horror. It was chiefly to make him speak again that she said, 'Have you got a light?'

'Let's hope so.' His voice was nearer; she could hear a soft jingling as he searched his pockets. The sound was travelling past her, receding.

'I'm here.' She rose to her feet, to go and find him.

'I know. Stay where you are.' He was nearer again. 'I shouldn't walk about; you might get your feet wet.'

She had forgotten the pool. Its ancient and wicked secrecy, the undiscovered bourne behind it, added themselves to her nightmare. A water-drop splashed into it; she imagined the ripple of something rising from the submerged inner cave.

'Where are you?' The echo, lying in wait, pounced on the last word. 'Ou, ou,' it chuckled; a gloating sound.

'Here.'

The scrape of his shoe sounded beside her. So great was the comfort of having him within reach that she could hardly keep herself from gripping him. Lest he should pass, she said, 'I'm still where you left me.'

'Good.' She heard, closer, a soft brushing against the stone. 'Oh, yes, here you are.' His hand passed over her shoulder. His touch was light and impersonal; he was checking his orientation. She longed to keep him, but was ashamed. The picture of the cracking roof grew again in her mind.

'Did you find any matches?'

'I'm horribly afraid they're in my top-coat in the car. How about that lighter of yours?'

'Yes, of course. It's in my bag.' She felt for the place where she had put it down, and fumbled through it, cursing inwardly her habits of accumulation. At last she found the thing, and not till then remembered, with an inward sinking, that yesterday she had been thinking that it needed to be refilled. The flint sparked brilliantly, a dazzle revealing nothing; at the third attempt the wick brought forth a tiny bud of flame, sufficient scarcely to define her own encircling hand. It went out. Nothing would revive it.

'Why didn't I think?' Even the momentary gleam had a little heartened her; she talked to prolong its effect. 'I ought to have had something ready to catch from it, a letter or something. We could have got most of the way, with that.'

'You talk as though we couldn't get out without it.' She could hear a smile in his voice. 'I must seem pretty dim, I know, but I'm not as dim as that. I know this place like the back of my hand. It would have been quicker with a light, that's all. Come along. Just hang on to me.'

His hands felt for hers, and held them. Before she could rise he said, softly, 'What is it?'

'Nothing,' she said. 'I just feel a little strange.'

'I expect so.' He stood there, without moving.

'I suppose it's simply the dark that makes one feel shut-in.'

He said, with a quiet tranquillity, 'When we're tired of being shut in, the door's open. We've only got to get there.'

'I know. It's foolish of me.'

'No, not foolish. I felt strange, too, the first time I came here. Sit quiet a moment, and get used to it.' She felt that he had lowered himself to some projection of the stone beside her knees. 'It feels natural, presently. I know; I've been here in the dark before.'

He was still holding her hands. She was aware of something felt too briefly for certainty at earlier times; the physical sympathy which is not foreseen, which has power to subdue to itself the antagonisms of the mind, and, sometimes, almost of the spirit. But between them there were no antagonisms to be subdued. She wanted to say, 'We must start now,' and get to her feet; but the thought of the journey ahead, groping and stumbling, was hateful to her, and in their stillness her fear was comforted. She said, to say something, 'Did the lights fail then, too?'

'No,' he said. 'I could see better without them. I can now.'

He spoke without emphasis, very quietly. She could not answer him. It was he who went on, in a moment or two, a little too easily and a little too fast. 'It came so suddenly, after the flood-lighting. Is it better now?'

It was, in the end, only to lengthen this precarious moment of balance that she found herself saying, 'I sometimes feel afraid that the roof will fall.'

She heard him draw in his breath, softly and guardedly. He said, 'We should be here for ever.'

'Don't. You frighten me.' But she had felt no fear, or not the fear of which she had spoken. He said, gently, almost humorously, 'Do I?' She felt his hands tighten a little over hers.

'We must go,' she said.

'Yes.' But he did not move. She tried to brace her will to withdraw her hands. As if to forestall her, he began to talk again. 'It's nothing to mind about. Everyone has moments about the dark. All the best people; you're in good company. Even Shakespeare had.'

'Do you think so?'

'I know; don't you?' He laughed briefly, as people do for their peace of mind. He dropped her hands; she felt that he was leaning against the rock beside her.

> *'Why art thou yet so fair? shall I believe*
> *That unsubstantial death is amorous,*
> *And that the lean abhorred monster keeps*
> *Thee here in dark to be his paramour?'*

Her vague emotions focused into a sharp anxiety. He had given the lines an edge of delicate mockery; but she remembered too much not to be deeply disquieted for him. It infringed all his taboos. He was doing violence to himself, she thought, to comfort and divert her. It would recoil on him. She said, lightly, to release him, 'Must I die so soon?'

> *'For fear of that, I still will stay with thee,*
> *And never from this palace of dim night*
> *Depart again . . .'*

She listened, with suspended breath. His voice had altered; the verse had moved into the circle of its own dark stars. It was a faultless, disciplined delivery; there was something terrifying in the control which directed, inflexibly, the emotion which her instincts recognised, letting nothing escape from the perfect service of the form. The shock of it was beyond what she had power or will to withstand. She was aware of nothing clearly, except the necessity of seeing his face; and, scarcely knowing what she did, she put out her hands to serve her instead of eyes. They touched his hair and his forehead, and there was a silence, perhaps as long as two beats of the verse, which the soft drip of water measured as clearly as a drum. But he continued: his voice, though it had become a shadow without substance, still kept unbroken the shape and texture of the lines, as if these were a responsibility which could not be set aside.

> '*Here, here will I remain,*
> *With worms, that are thy chambermaids; O here*
> *Will I set up my everlasting rest,*
> *And shake the yoke of inauspicious stars*
> *From . . .*'

The words were extinguished, like a steady but exhausted flame.

In a complex recurrent rhythm two chains of water-droppings falling sometimes together and sometimes divided by an instant or so of time, made a thread of sound which traced itself like a visual pattern over Hilary's brain, as her eyes looked downward, through the refusing darkness, at the unseen head she had caught against her breast.

Nothing is inevitable, she thought, in the pause of realisation which no other sound nor any movement disturbed. It is a terrible thing I have done, out of weakness and self-love. It is the sin of witchcraft. I have betrayed him to the power of darkness, which I could have destroyed. Even though he would never have forgiven me, I should have destroyed it. She knew that she had betrayed herself to it also.

He was still, his face hidden. She slipped her arm about his rigid shoulders and felt, without hearing, the violently controlled breath which she had never recognised, till now, except as the index of scarcely endurable pain. 'Julian,' she whispered. 'My dear.' But he did not answer. She bent her mouth to his hair – it felt soft and warm, like a child's – but found no response except a sense of tension drawn so far beyond the natural breaking-point that she dared venture no more. In the presence of this voiceless need, to which she could have refused nothing if anything had been clearly asked, she could only measure comfort in cautious crumbs, as food is measured to famine. Moved by some such feeling as this, or by the half-felt chill of the place, or by his stillness, which was of the tautened kind that is like a tremor to the touch, she lifted a hanging fold of her loose coat and gathered it round him.

He caught in his breath (the small movement seemed to pass, like a shudder, all through him) and the arm with which he had gripped her waist fell loosely round her. Silently in her arms his hard immobility changed to a death-like relaxation. His head fell back against her shoulder. She experienced a moment of intense sweetness and exaltation, followed by guilt and remorse, like the guilt of murder. Blindly, between expiation and helpless love, she stooped and began to kiss his forehead and brows and his closed eyes.

What shall I do? she thought desperately, how shall we escape from this? For one thing was clear among so much unknowing, that none of it could be endured or lived with when they brought it back into the light of day. And even that, she thought, I might have remembered in time. But even while the thought passed through her, she was stroking the hair back from his forehead and rocking him softly in her arms.

At last, slowly, he raised himself a little, and, putting his hand behind her head, began to draw it down. As all this while she had not dared to do, he was lifting his mouth to hers. She held him closer in a piercing tenderness and a longing mixed with fear.

A searing glare, blinding and brutal as a sword-slash, outraged her wide-open eyes. The cave, the water, everything was defined in the shocking indifference of light. Its extinction had seemed friendly and benign, compared with this moment of its return. She flung up her hands to her face to shut it out. The tight pressure of her palms made coloured moons and flowers against her eyelids, swimming across the image of Julian's face as she had seen it in that first instant stolen as it were whole from the darkness, a blind face lifted from her arms in an abandonment so final that it was like despair.

There was a swift movement beside her, and she felt him gone. She could not bring herself to uncover her face. There is no bitterness like that of the tragedy that ends in farce.

The fierceness of the light was suddenly tempered. Lowering her hands, she saw that he had run over to the switches in the rock; he must have left them both on before, and had gone now to turn off the floodlights in time. Scarcely yet in command of herself, she was staggered that he should have reacted in seconds to this necessity. Had all men the power of escaping into action even from such a moment as this? She herself had not even thought which lights were burning; she was shocked, approving and profoundly envious. These swift reflections braced her. She got to her feet.

He was coming back towards her from the central arch. When she looked at him everything she had felt before swept over her like a returning wave. His eyes were narrowed, painfully, against the light, and he stumbled on an unevenness of the stone. His face was drained, as if he had been sleepless since yesterday. Without looking at her, he put up his hand and pushed his disordered hair back from his forehead.

'Someone must have fixed the fuse.' His voice was even, though he could not conceal the fact that he had been unable to finish even so short a sentence with a single breath. After a moment he added, 'Smart work.'

As soon as the last two words were out of his mouth she knew what he wanted. He wanted the impossible. Her emotions, her intelligence, her whole adult apparatus rejected it. But, behind these, something accepted; remembering, from a time which had had no use for tactful regression, the bald decencies of the schoolroom. He was intolerable, she thought. But he was probably right.

'I suppose,' she said, 'the fuse-box must be over at the farm. Or perhaps it was something at the power-station.'

'Might have been that. We'd better get moving before it happens again.'

'Yes; it must be getting late.'

'Look, you've dropped some gadgets out of your bag.' He bent to gather up a handkerchief and a compact from the floor; she must have spilled them when she was searching for the lighter. He turned the compact over, fiddling inexpertly with the catch.

'How's your claustrophobia?' he asked politely. 'Passing off?'

The effrontery of this almost took her breath away. But she recalled the convention again; one had always been brazen in proportion to the crisis. He had almost dropped the compact in the act of returning it to her.

'It was only a spasm,' she said. 'Not the real thing, that some people have. But I think it would have been worse, this time, if I hadn't had someone with me.'

They were passing through the arch into the upper cave. Partly shadowed by the pillar, he was looking straight in front of him; but she saw in his face, as they came out into the light again, a gratitude and relief which made her feel sufficiently rewarded. He concealed them almost immediately, remarking that the place struck chilly after a while.

It was an astonishment to find, when they reached the surface, the westering sunlight still lying low and golden across the countryside. After the dimness below, even its reflection, seen from within the hill's shadow, was almost blinding. In a few moments, however, it revealed to her vividly that Julian was in a state of picturesque dishevelment that would scarcely pass unnoticed when he went to return the key.

'The wind still keeps up,' she said when they got into the car. 'It seems hardly worth tidying oneself just to be blown about again. However ...' She got out her comb and put in some sketchy work with it. 'How about you?' She held it out carelessly.

'Oh, thanks,' said Julian. 'Might as well.'

There was no need for him to walk over to the farm; Mrs Mott, who must have heard them coming, was at the front gate.

'Well, there, Mr Fleming, you've got back. I was in two minds whether to send one of the men up along. When George made it right he come in and said, "The light's come on in the cowshed, reckon that's bound to be on now in the cave. It must have given the lady a proper turn, but she'll be over it by now," George said.' She looked at Julian with hesitant reproach. 'Mr Mott reckoned someone had interfered with that floodlighting.'

'I'm afraid he was right, too.' Hilary was relieved to see that he had recovered the power to smile.

'You never should have touched that, Mr Fleming. Only Mr Mott has to do with that. Not even our eldest boy don't have to do with it. We'd never have known nothing, only it was milking-time, and George was in the cowshed. So he come back in and said ...'

They managed, somehow, to get away.

To take in the hills they had to come by a long detour. The journey back was a matter of half an hour. They talked very little, dropping into the silences only the small pebbles of talk which sufficed to keep it from dangerous stagnation. There was a softness in the air, whose influence brought from the birds that thin flute-like singing which, more than budding hedges, declares the relenting touch of spring. The last sunlight lay flat and green-gold on the sides of trees and the westward curves of the hills. Before they were back it had crept upward to touch only the tops of high things with a wan fire, while in the valleys and deep lanes everything was umber and cobalt and smoky grey. The lamps were burning already in the windows when they reached her house.

'It was a lovely run,' she said at the gate. 'Weren't we sensible not to be put off by the rain?' I suppose, she was thinking, there must be some happy mean between the conversation of a lover and a well-meaning aunt; perhaps it needs longer in rehearsal. 'Come in and have a drink, won't you, before you go?'

'Thanks terribly, but I think I'd better not. I ought to be getting back, I'm afraid.' For the first time since they had left the cave he managed to meet her eyes. She had an absurd impulse to tell him that he need not, that he could leave it till another time. 'Thank you for coming. I'm afraid it's been rather a frost for you really, what with one thing and another. I'm – sorry I couldn't fix things better. I ...' His eyes fell, defeated; he pushed the gate which, forgetting his intention of opening it, he had been holding shut in her path. 'I hope when the days get a bit longer you'll come again.'

'Of course I will.'

In spite of herself she had allowed her voice to say more than the words. For a moment, in the unguarded twilight, he turned to her a face of longing and hopeless trust. 'Good-bye,' he said, swung to the gate and went back to the car without looking behind him.

The lights in the hall were on, but Hilary went silently round the house to the door that led straight to her own room.

12

The moon was in its last quarter. It came up stealthily, between two and three in the morning, taking Hilary by surprise and deluding her, for a little while, into the belief that the dawn was breaking, for she had lost count of time. She had forgotten even to be impatient with her own inability to sleep, though she had always maintained that insomnia could be controlled by a reasonable use of the will. She had not reproved her thoughts, or rationalised them, or tried to convince herself that they were otherwise. Simply, she had not been thinking about herself at all. The pale light slid into the room, catching a glass candlestick with a faint prismatic blue and green that disturbed her half-shut eyes. She opened them, and saw through the window, against the luminescence of small clouds, the dark crests of trees. A voice which she had not summoned sounded in her head with a thin, intolerable clearness, like that of the moonlit glass:

By yonder moon I swear,
That tips with silver all these fruit-tree tops . . .

She raised herself on her elbow to see if it were true, if any reflected light shone on the black branches, till she remembered that what had been meant must have been the whiteness of the flowers. But it was her memory that had shown her the fine bareness of the twigs, for her eyes were filled with tears.

The definiteness of this physical fact brought her mind back, at last, to a belated self-criticism. A habit of truthfulness, inherent in her and fortified by her work, made further evasions impossible. For some time already she had been pampering, under the disguise of common sense, an arrogance that had refused to let her see her own part in one of humanity's classically comic situations. Even now she made some attempt to hedge her pride with irony; but it was a thin hedge and concealed nothing.

In search of an antidote, she tried to see the thing as she might look back on it in a few years' time, when it would have become a memory, making for tolerance of other people's follies. At some point in this not very successful enterprise she found herself thinking again of David, not as a lover – she did not avoid this thought; it had simply faded, like an old photograph left in the sun – but as the background of her surface disposition, which he had helped to form. With David, she had done what had seemed at the time an admirable amount of mental tidying up. She remembered telling him, once, about an adolescent crisis whose confusion and fear still faintly lingered; the effect had been very satisfactory. Yes, he had said, of course, quite so; and had used, with a cool and cleansing indifference, the correctly classifying terms, following them with a story of something similar that had happened to someone he knew. From that moment the memory had been sterilised, dead, as safe to handle as something in a tank of spirit on a laboratory shelf.

She fell back defeated from an attempt to imagine David at twenty-three; she could not conceive of a time when it would have been in her power either to hurt or comfort him. Only his intolerances would have been cruder, lacking the airs of toleration which he employed, often with some skill, to give them a finer cutting edge. Nor could she envisage any situation in which he would not have known, and been able to state precisely, what he wanted, and when, and how, and why. She might as well, she thought with forlorn amusement, be a virgin, and a foolish virgin at that.

Reaching this conclusion, she decided that though folly was a luxury she could not afford, to-night was no time for pursuing wisdom; and, getting out of bed, went to her bag for five grains of medinal. As she settled back in the comfortable expectation of sleep, she reflected that she would have leisure for further thought; she knew, at least, enough of human nature in general to guess that it would be some time before Julian presented himself again. It would have been a relief to her, if she had not been sure that he would be unhappy in the interval. This was launching her mind on an endless circle; she made it a resolute blank, and fell asleep.

In fact she saw nothing of him for nearly three weeks. During the first, she thought what an excellent thing it was that he was being so sensible, and recalled the unfortunate way he had once had of reappearing just when one had looked confidently forward to an interval for meditation and rest. Half-way through the second week she began to miss him, intermittently, unpredictably, and with a force which was all the more unnerving, because it broke in on periods when she had managed, she thought, to dismiss the whole matter from her mind. At the beginning of the third week it occurred to her that he might very well have decided to stay away altogether, that she ought to support and applaud this choice, and that the first suspicion of it was already taking the light from the sky.

It was during the second week that, finding herself with a slack morning on the day when she was already free in the afternoon, she decided that it was time she went to town. She had some clothes to buy, and discovered a sudden discontent with the Cheltenham shops which had satisfied her for the past year. While she was in town (she did her best to make this into a casual afterthought) she would look up her nephew, Sam.

It had been with considerable pride that she had reached the status of an aunt at the age of nine. Sam, when he was of an age to appreciate the joke, had enjoyed it equally, and they had had a great deal of fun, when he went to school, arranging outings, which she had always preceded by a pompous and spinsterly note to his headmaster, executed in copperplate. It had been his father, whom her earliest recollections presented as a serious and responsible adult, who had always seemed to belong to a different generation. Sam was articled to a London solicitor now, and, since hers was a family in which established jokes died hard, when she rang up for him at the office she still went through a prim aunt-routine over the telephone. He shared rooms with a friend called James (if she had ever heard his second name she could never remember it), who had been up with him at Oxford. They were still excellent sources of university gossip, when one was in the mood.

Hilary found that, after a considerable lapse of time, the mood had overtaken her. She occupied her mind earnestly, however, with her intention of buying clothes. She had reached lately what she felt to be a reasonable degree of frankness with herself. It did not extend, yet, to admitting that she proposed a journey of a hundred miles or so, mainly in the hope of hearing Julian's name mentioned by a young man who had been at a different college and who in all likelihood barely knew him by sight.

Having in the end cleared almost the whole day, she shopped at first conscientiously, then with unforeseen enjoyment and uncharacteristic extravagance. After this she rang up Sam, the joke coming off even more successfully than usual, since, in Sam's presence, the senior partner answered the 'phone. Half-past five found them enjoying it again, retrospectively, while they toasted muffins over Sam's gas-fire. James, who was something in advertising or interior decoration (another point about which she was never quite clear), joined them soon afterwards. Thanks to his company, the talk drifted from family to Oxford with so little direction on her part that she could readily believe there had been none at all.

'I probably missed a chance of getting some uncensored information about you,' she said, 'a week or two ago. I ran into a man who must have been up with you, I should imagine, but I didn't think to ask him until too late.'

'M-m?' inquired Sam, partly extricating himself from a slice of the Fuller's cake she had brought with her (this was another part of the aunt routine which had never lost popularity). 'Name of who?'

'Fleming, unless I've remembered it wrong.'

'Fleming, Fleming.' Sam looked up, intelligently. 'Oh, Good Lord, yes, I know the chap you mean. Funny how one forgets, he was on my staircase. Earnest little runt with the most fearful stammer. If he told you what his name was, I hope you had your mackintosh on.'

Hilary put down the cup which, at the beginning of these remarks, she had found with disgust to be shaking slightly in her hand. 'No, I don't think that can have been the one.'

'Come to think of it,' said Sam helpfully, 'he might have got rid of the stutter by now. He was seeing a specialist about it, so that he could go into the Church.'

With successful vagueness Hilary remarked, 'I don't think it can have been. This one said he was producing a play.'

James, who in the opposite corner had been involved with a rather leathery piece of muffin, swallowed and sat up.

'My good Sam, I never knew anyone with such a parochial mind. Other colleges do exist, however regrettably, you know. As if she'd remember H. B. Fleming five minutes after she'd met him. What about J. R.?'

'J.R.?' Sam gave a complete reprise of the dawning process, with, for Hilary, a quite unnerving effect. 'Oh, yes, of course, the Ouds man. Quite likely, I didn't think. I was never as much in with that set as you were.' He turned to Hilary. 'Tall, strik-ing-looking chap? Black hair?'

'That sounds more like it.'

'You'd remember J.R.,' James decided. 'Wouldn't she, Sam? More than striking, really, in what you might call the Apollo class. No, come, Sam, you must admit that. Girl I knew said she always wanted to stick a pin in him to see if he was real.'

'And was he?' inquired Sam, unimpressed.

'Matter of fact, he was quite a harmless type when you knew him; you got not to notice it, somehow, after a bit.' After a vaguely reminiscent pause, he added, 'Lost his temper if anyone mentioned it. Funny, that.'

'Did he?' said Sam, interested. Hilary leaned back in her chair, and made herself unobtrusive, partly to listen, partly lest she should be asked for her impressions. Sam considered. 'Might depend on who mentioned it, I suppose.'

'No, nothing to it, really. I mean, just some typical light-hearted persiflage of old Prosser's; sort of thing anyone could have taken for granted, I'd have thought. Of course, he'd had one or two, we all had. Still I never knew it make him quarrelsome, any other time. If someone hadn't been quick, he'd have tipped Prosser off the window-sill into the quad. First-floor window, too.'

'You don't say? From what I heard ...' Sam looked discreetly across Hilary, with one eyebrow raised.

'No,' said James definitely. 'I happen to know. That got said because of the way he let Lavenham tag along. Whether it was laziness, or plain good nature, or what, God knows. No one knew. I remember Tranter saying he asked him once. Seeing there was nothing in it, I mean, and knowing him pretty well, he felt he could.'

'Did he get shot out of a window too?'

'Not in the least, I gathered. Fleming just uttered some bromide to the effect that Lavenham was human like anyone else if you treated him in a civilised manner. No, he was like that. Put up with anyone sooner than upset them. Don't you remember those dim girls one used to see him having coffee with? Always a crowd, though. Safety in numbers, I suppose.'

'Queer type,' said Sam profoundly. 'He could act, I will say. Never did anything else, of course. Scraped a third, I believe.'

'Is he acting now?' asked James of Hilary. 'I've wondered from time to time when his name would crop up in some notice or other. He was good, I mean. Even for Ouds.'

'I believe only with some local amateurs; and producing, mostly.'

'Funny,' Sam ruminated, 'how these Isis Idols peter out.'

'The only thing was,' said James, 'they did say he wasn't very versatile. You know how he always went in for these weird characters, Caliban and so on. I remember, now I think of it, Toller told me once that he went all to fluff in a straight part.

They had an idea of putting on *Romeo and Juliet*, I forget which year; banking on Fleming for Romeo, of course. Toller said he wasn't at all keen even to read it, and when they got him down to it they could see why. Total loss, I believe. Stiff as a board.'

'Odd,' said Sam. He pondered. 'Psychological, or something, I suppose.'

'Oh, I don't know. Just a nice, aimless sort of bloke, really, I think, with only one line. Wouldn't you say so?' He looked to Hilary for support.

'Very likely,' she said. 'He seemed quite cheerful and amusing. James, do stop wrestling with that burnt muffin and have some cake while there still is some. I've always deplored Sam's greed from his earliest years; I remember when he was at school ... ' She had never, she thought, really appreciated enough the uses of the aunt-routine. The conversation, thus derailed, was shunted without further trouble to a branch line.

On the journey home she focused her attention on her shopping with renewed care. With regard to the rest, she had succeeded only in unsettling emotions she would have done better to take in hand, while illuminating nothing at all.

When Wednesday of the following week came round and she had still neither seen nor heard from him, she drove into Cheltenham for no other reason than to affirm to herself that she had never contemplated waiting in. One of her private patients was in a nursing-home there, which made the arrangement tidy and sensible.

She was window-gazing in the Promenade, and shifting her own shadow this way and that to avoid the light reflected in the plate-glass, when something among its passing images arrested her. She stood still and counted ten, slowly, before she allowed herself to turn. She had not been mistaken. Disappearing into the crowds on the pavement were Mrs Fleming and

Julian. He was carrying her travelling-coat over his arm; it was a mild day. It was evident that neither of them had seen her; after all, her back had been turned. It would, at least, have been evident, but for an inescapable certainty that as they passed Julian had looked round and then quickly away.

She walked in the other direction, and then back to her car. She was driving it and had reached the outskirts of the town before her feelings really overtook her. When they did she reminded herself that he had behaved with ordinary tact, that it had saved her a good deal of embarrassment (which was undoubtedly true), that she would not have wished it otherwise. Reason supported all this. It left quite untouched her shocked sense of betrayal and loss, and the shame of her own helplessness. As she drove back through the village she reaffirmed, definitely this time, that she would write it off and forget it, as no doubt he had decided to do. Men were impossible, of any age and of every kind.

By the time she reached home she had only one clear wish, to spend the evening talking to Lisa. Not confiding in her; that would have embarrassed both of them, for Lisa was temperamentally incapable, as she knew without experiment, of feeling anything for her present state except compassionate wonder; but to talk to Lisa would be good. They would talk about nothing in particular; village scandals, the latest book, the news, something on the radio; but, without any decisions of the intellect, life would become simpler. As the evening went on they would grow drowsy and inconsequent, potter about with bedtime odds and ends, and sleep well. It had happened before.

In the hall, the welcoming flame was rising between the tall firedogs; but no Lisa rose from the settle to greet her. There was nothing in that, though it brought a moment's chill because she had anticipated so clearly; but she had the instant feeling of the place being different, which comes sometimes only from one's own recent experience or mood. At first she put it down to that; but no, something was in the air. Literally: for it was a smell, which in a few moments she identified as that of a rank French cigarette, Caporal or Gaulois Jaune. Half of it was still in the ash-tray on the table, where it had been left to smoulder out. On the floor, by the settle, a splash of mixed colour caught her eye. Lisa's work-basket was lying there, on its side, with the embroidery-silks spilled out on to the carpet; her round tambour with the Chinese flowers was half in the fireplace. Hilary retrieved it and brushed wood-ash from the silk. She knew what had happened, even before she saw the battered portable typewriter on the table by the door. Lisa would not be at leisure this evening.

She sat down, aimlessly, by the fire, and wondered how long Rupert was likely to stay. So acute was her loneliness that it seemed, for a few moments, perfectly natural to be calculating hopefully that he could never get away from his work for long. When she noticed her own selfishness, it horrified her; but not so much as the state of mind which could make such thoughts an expression of her self at all.

She went up to the bathroom to wash her hands. There was a good deal of water on the floor in which the draggled bath mat had been left lying. She found herself thinking that he might really have cleared up after himself a little better. On her way down again she passed Lisa's door, and was aware of the kind of silence which is not the silence of vacancy. Lisa was waiting – they were both waiting – fearing that, having noticed nothing downstairs, she might decide to knock; she could imagine the man making a face of irritation, the woman smiling and shaking her head and motioning him to be still. When she had gone, the nearness of her intrusion would be a little joke they would share together before they forgot her existence again. After a time Lisa would say, 'I *must* go down. I've done nothing about Hilary's meal,' and he, probably, 'Oh, damn the woman. Surely she can see after herself for once.'

Down in her sitting-room she found that tea had been laid for her and the kettle put ready on the hob. This consideration was typical of Lisa and she knew it; but against all good sense she could only feel in it forethought to keep her out of the way. Though it was very late now for tea she put the kettle on, and sat waiting for it to boil, finding tears of self-pity not far from her eyes. It was humiliating, contemptible, and, she found, quite beyond her control. She would have been glad to talk even to Annie; but, as the kettle reminded her, it was Annie's afternoon off.

The steam rose sluggishly; to fill in the time, and to recover some of her self-esteem, she went up to her bedroom, attended to her face and put on a dress she had bought in town the week before, a dark green one with gilt accessories which made the best of her fair skin and reddish-brown hair. There seemed no need to look like an unwanted extra, even if she felt like it. The kettle was ready when she came down and the tea diffused its usual comfort; the solace of middle age, she thought mournfully, conveniently forgetting that it had tasted just as good after school hockey and on every intervening afternoon. She picked up a novel and was turning it vaguely when the doorbell rang.

She got up quickly to answer it, walking loudly across the hall so that Lisa would know there was no need to disturb herself. It was probably a tradesman or someone selling the parish magazine. She opened the door.

'Hallo,' said Julian. 'I was afraid you wouldn't be in.'

He gave a shy, characteristic smile which almost at once became mechanical; he was looking at her as if he had expected someone different, almost as if he had rung the door-bell for a bet and forgotten to be prepared with an errand. Her own emotions, which had made her feel quite ill in the first moment of seeing him, steadied at once. She could feel that the accident of her opening the door herself, or perhaps of her dress which was more sophisticated than the things she gener-ally wore, had overset some expectation in his mind like a muffed cue. It made her forget everything except the simple desire to smooth him down, and see him relaxed and easy again.

'I'm having a late tea,' she said. 'You're just in time to finish it with me.'

'No, but you're all dressed up. Are you just going out? I won't stop if it's keeping you.'

He was looking at her with something like awe. It occurred to her that almost every time they had met he had burst in on her when she was in her working clothes, or she had been dressed for driving. His constraint was flattering, but did not promise to assist conversation.

'No, I'm not going out. As a matter of fact I've just come in.' She led him through to the sitting-room. 'One really doesn't want a fire on an evening like this; let's open the window.'

The twilight looked deep blue against the yellow lamplight outside; the air that came in smelt of moist earth still warm from the sun, and of growing things. 'Make yourself some toast; there's plenty of hot water.'

He settled down on the rug with the toasting-fork; she felt sure that he had curled himself up with the same instinctive grace, and the same innocence of pose, in front of his study fire at school. It had occurred to her before that for him beauty of movement was not a visualised thing but a sense of inner well-being; it evinced a kind of pleasure, but a purely personal one, like that of eating or sleeping. The professional stage would, sooner or later, inevitably give him the kind of self-consciousness from which now he seemed wholly free. The anticipation saddened her. He was unusually silent. She searched her mind for something to say, but, herself at a loss, gave her attention to the teapot.

'I saw you this afternoon,' he said. 'You didn't see me.' He held the toast away from the fire, looked at it and turned it over.

As simple as that. 'Oh, were you in Cheltenham too? Or did we pass on the road?'

'You were choosing yourself a frock in a window on the Promenade. Is that it you're wearing?'

'No, they were a hideous lot.' She laughed, waiting to hear what excuse he would make, but having suddenly ceased to care.

'I didn't run after you because Mother had a train to catch, and we'd run it rather fine. So I thought I'd come round now, on the chance. It seems such a long time since I saw you.' He added, without allowing pause for reply, 'This bit's done, shall I butter it?'

She handed him the things. 'Is Mrs Fleming away then?'

'Yes. We generally fix things to go away together – it's awkward about the house, and so on – but one of her sisters has lost a husband – I mean he's dead – and she's gone there for a week, and of course they don't want to be bothered with me, so I'm sort of knocking around on my own. I'm supp— I'm probably going to town part of the time to stay with a man I know there. Man called Tranter, he was up with me.' He brought this out with a disjointed kind of haste and over-earnest attention to the toast. He seemed to feel that his presence called both for explanation and apology. Hilary reflected that for a woman with Mrs Fleming's high regard for the conventions, it seemed an odd arrangement to have left him alone in the house with the maids. She said, 'I hope you're a good housekeeper.'

'Oh, yes. I'll be all right. I've brought a lot of food back with me. Will you have this, and I'll toast some more?'

'No, I've finished, it's for you. Here's your tea.'

'Oh, thanks ... I'm sort of camping at home really, rather fun. The staff's on holiday.'

'Really?' said Hilary curiously. Convention, then, was satisfied; but this seemed more unlike Mrs Fleming than ever. Probably someone was coming in from the village by the day to 'do' for him; but even so ...

'Yes. Safety first, and so on. Mother has it fixed firmly in her mind that if we're all left alone together one of them will seize the opportunity to start a love-child and blame it on me. Quaint, isn't it? Particularly if you've seen them.'

He took a large mouthful of toast, having delivered himself with a carelessness which thinly concealed bravado. She could almost overhear him thinking that, after all, other people got away with remarks of this kind. All the same he had gone a little pink. Hilary, for whom the conversation in the house-men's common-room was still a recent memory, was gently amused.

'But who's looking after you, then?'

'Oh, I'm not that helpless. Good Lord, under canvas I've peeled spuds and washed up for thirty. And it's not for long.'

'No,' she said, 'of course.' A suspicion had risen in her mind which she was doing her best to dismiss. There was certainly something different about him to-night. He looked both guilty and a little above himself; just now, when he had been toasting, she had tried to remember whether she had ever noticed before that he had an unsteady hand. He had bolted the toast with scarcely decent speed; not, it was evident, from hunger but from absence of mind, for he refused a second slice. After a few minutes' desultory talk he got up and went over to the window.

'I was thinking,' he remarked, 'as I was coming along, that this is the best evening we've had this year. Listen to that blackbird. It's so warm, it might be April almost.'

'I know. All winter one longs for a day like this and when it does come it's too quick, and it leaves one gasping. Then when the light's gone one wonders how one didn't enjoy it more.'

'It isn't really gone yet. Don't you think, though, the evening's the best time? I suppose you wouldn't care to come out for a bit? We could park the car somewhere, and then walk.'

. . . I can't, I'm expecting a case . . . It would be dark before we could get anywhere . . . I think I'm really too tired . . . The number of suitable replies was almost infinite, a plethora, an embarrassment. It would be a pity not to select the best. 'Well . . .'

There was no sound from upstairs. In a little while Lisa would be coming down presenting Rupert for dinner and for good manners' sake, and both of them wishing her in Jericho. Julian turned, expectantly, from the window. He was standing quite easily and looking at her with the friendliest casualness. He was doing it very well. No doubt it was perfectly genuine. He had on a grey suit and a blue pullover. The blackbird continued, pensively, to sing.

'We shouldn't have time to get far,' she said.

'We'd have time for a turn around to smell the air. It's ever so much lighter outside than it looks with the light on. Come along. It will do you good.' He offered this statement with great assurance; with positive heartiness, as if he were persuading her out for a round of golf.

It would certainly do Lisa and Rupert good, she thought. How pleased Lisa would be to find her note. Besides, it would be unkind to refuse. He might think, perhaps ...

'All right,' she said. 'Just for half an hour. It would be rather nice to get off the main roads. I'll just get my coat.'

She wasted a few minutes in her room straightening the litter she had left when she changed and went over to the glass to brush her hair. Am I getting thinner? she thought. I look different to-night. It must be the dress. The spring is always upsetting. We could walk to the top of the Beacon; it will be good exercise. We might be in time up there to see the last of the sunset. I expect he wants to tell me some idea he's got about a play.

When she got down Julian had lit a cigarette and found himself a book from one of the shelves. He put it aside so abruptly that his ash, which must have been lengthening unheeded, fell between the pages as he closed them. It was one of her Penguin Shakespeares; when he slipped it back into place she saw that it was the first part of *King Henry IV*.

'Oh, hallo,' he said. 'You're ready.'

'Have I been long?'

'No. Not at all. Just one of those obvious remarks. Would you like to go anywhere special? Or shall we just follow our noses and see what comes?'

'If you like. Somewhere high up.' This was a choice of phrase for which, next moment, she could have bitten her tongue; but he seemed to have noticed nothing.

Outside the sky was cloudless, a delicate fading blue which

deepened in the east, and in the west was still tinged with slant light from the mist-drowned sun. As always on such evenings of early spring the earth seemed bent, like a child, on sitting up past bedtime. Birds which should have been roosting were singing still; in the rookeries, parliament was in full debate and no one called, 'Who goes home?' In a field they passed, a great cart-horse was rolling, kicking its fringed hoofs like a puppy in the air. The tops of the hills, from which the sunlight had just passed, were faintly luminous, as if a radiant film still clung to them like moisture after rain.

They began to climb almost at once, taking at first the high Roman road which had been superseded now, for heavy traffic, by the new one that followed the valley. It was still well metalled, and unfenced most of the way, giving glimpses of blue distant hills. Julian had fallen silent again, as he often did when he was driving. Looking at the horizon she did not perceive for some time the speed at which nearer objects were rushing past. At last the tug of wind in her hair brought her attention nearer home. The speedometer was just passing seventy-five.

At this hour, which could not be far from lighting-up time, it seemed to her a quite unjustifiable speed. She looked at Julian. He was driving with grave concentration and an air of detachment that looked dangerously like abstraction. She felt she ought to reprove him, on principle; she was not, to her own vague surprise, in the least afraid, though she was a conservative driver herself. After all she said nothing, finding a pleasure which she made no effort to analyse, in the passive committal of her life to the unknown quantity of his judgement and skill. They met nothing, and when the road began to dip at the end of the crest he slowed down smoothly and switched the headlamps on.

'I feel better for that,' he remarked, as he changed down into second.

'I'm glad,' said Hilary; her intention of irony had evaporated somehow from the words.

'I did once touch eighty in this car. Not bad, seeing it's more than five years old. Mind you I bought it in very good shape, and I've looked after it.'

'You touched eighty once to-night,' she informed him.

'No, did I? Don't call it "to-night", it sounds rather accusing. Funny, you can treble that in the air and just seem to be cruising. You didn't mind, did you? My licence is one hundred per cent pure.'

'Have you been flying, after all I told you?'

'Not a word at home. You told me to wait till I'd seen Sanderson, and so I did. Good enough?'

'Of course, if you've seen him.' She was a little hurt that he had told her only as an afterthought. 'He was pleased with you, I take it?'

'He seemed to be. He gave me a lot of very interesting advice and – information. I was thinking how about getting out and walking here?'

He was backing the car off the road as he spoke into a sparse wood of larches. It had been much thinned, so that grass and a tangle of wild growth had space to flourish between the mats of needles under the trees. Their young shoots were out already, the half-light deepening their pale green to a brilliant viridian. A bridle-way led through them, meandering gently downhill, with an old board marked Private at its mouth.

She said, 'Yes, it looks a good place'; the drug of speed had made her blood sluggish and almost deprived her of the wish to walk. 'Aren't we trespassing?' she asked. 'It looks rather like it.'

He put the ignition-key in his pocket; something seemed to

have amused him. 'I shouldn't worry. I've known the man it belongs to all my life.'

They went through a five-barred gate, with hinges over-grown as if it were never shut; along the ride the grass was very green, with a warren here and there velvet-cushioned with moss. There would be bluebells later in the year. The sun had set but the dusk was iridescent and clear and it seemed to grow no darker. She saw that a half-moon was up already, hanging, a transparent whiteness, in the deepening sky, very still, with no drifting cloud to give it the illusion of movement. The colour, not the strength of the light would slowly change, but not yet.

A rabbit bolted across the path and disappeared into one of the warrens. Julian said, 'I used to have rather a good ferret in the days of my youth. A yellow one, all the best ferrets are yellow. By the look of it I ought to be getting another. They made an awful mess of the garden last year; and I'm a rotten shot.' He branched off into a long and somewhat laboured anecdote about his school OTC, after which he fell silent and twitched aimlessly at such twigs as extended themselves in his path. Once he turned round to her with an air of sudden reso-lution, paused, and announced that last year had been a good one for bluebells. Hilary admitted to having noticed it; for fox-gloves too, she contributed. Silence descended again. She was beginning to find it something of a strain. In another minute or so, she thought, she would suggest walking back to the car.

Voices sounded; a village couple came into view, arm in arm and with clasped hands. In the moment of finding themselves seen they stiffened self-consciously and looked straight ahead of them; then, clearly deciding to put a bold face on it, remained linked and went on talking with muffled decorum; or, rather, the man continued to talk and the girl to listen.

When they passed Julian loitered behind, breaking off a sprig from a hazel-bush and, when Hilary looked round for him, examining it with a show of botanic interest.

'Well, really, Julian,' she could not keep from remarking, 'I hope it was worth the trouble.'

He caught her up, looking a little sheepish, then threw the twig away and grinned. 'As a matter of fact, it wasn't. He was just telling her a good back-answer he'd worked off on someone earlier in the day.'

'Well, why shouldn't he?' said Hilary, who often thought Julian took too much of life for granted. 'He probably can't afford to marry her for years. You needn't be so high-hat about it.'

'I wasn't,' said Julian meekly. 'I was only thinking.'

'Trespassing seems to be pretty general about here.'

'It's a sort of a right of way. We close it once a year, the usual thing ... Haven't you found out yet where we are?'

He pointed down through a gap in the trees. She had never seen the house from behind and had glimpsed it several times, already, without recognition, admiring the golden lichen on the grey roof.

'How stupid, I've no sense of locality at all. I didn't know your land went up this way. And we came so fast.'

She had exaggerated her surprise a little to please him. He stood staring down at the house as if he did not see it.

'It's nearer than it looks, the slope's deceptive. Why didn't you tell me last year that you resurrected me when I was as good as dead?'

'I?' She spoke first, and felt the shock afterwards. 'My dear, I didn't operate on you. I wasn't even assisting.'

'Yes, I know all about that. "A couple of hours' delay in diagnosis, with the rapidly increasing intracranial pressure"' –

he had given, it seemed unconsciously, a colourable imitation of Sanderson's teaching voice – '"but in the case we have here, early recognition of the signs, drowsiness, falling pulse-rate – er – depression of the respiratory centre" . . . or something like that. He didn't bother to tell me any of it, of course, just threw it away upstage to a couple of students, or something, he'd brought in to admire me. I was only exhibit A, I didn't have to say anything. Why didn't you tell me before?'

'But there was nothing to tell. Considering the training I'd had, if I hadn't recognised the condition I shouldn't have been fit to be at large. Fancy your picking up all that stuff.'

'I'm a quick study . . . You must have realised, the first time I met you, that – that I didn't remember. I'd rather have known.'

'It wouldn't have been natural to tell you. One just doesn't go telling patients that sort of thing.'

'Patients?' he said, looking away.

'Now you're being silly. One has to stick to the rules, even with one's friends. Besides, in my job it's – well, it's good form to take things in one's stride. Being dramatic about them is just as much not done as it would be in your job to have a real operation on the stage.'

'I'm sorry if I've seemed to be theatrical.'

'Oh, Julian, don't be so infuriating.' She turned round to him, laughing, though she did not feel like laughter; but he had looked away again. 'I only mean that in the nature of things we're bound to see it in different proportions. Wouldn't you rather I thought of you as a friend of mine than as a successful diagnosis? I hardly remember it, now, except incidentally as the way we happened to meet.'

'I understood you the first time, you needn't keep saying it. I realise you must be pretty well used to saving people's lives and not getting thanked for it. But I'm not so used to being one of the people.'

'Well, but as far as that goes I ...' She stopped; she had been about to say 'I did get thanked for it.' It was making things no easier, she found, to know what was on his mind, for she could think out no possible means of meeting him half-way. 'You did thank me, several times. It's so long ago, you've forgotten. Shouldn't we be moving? It's uphill all the way back.'

'How could I have thanked you, when I never knew?' He paused; some strong internal strain had sharpened the outlines of his face. His mouth had straightened; he looked, for a moment, older than his years. 'Please don't think hardly about it. You must have, of course. But people ... You see Mother's done everything important for me, all my life. My father was no good. He walked out on her, quite soon after I was born. She's never told me that, but you know how one picks things up, out of the air. When he was killed he hadn't been home for two years, I do know that much – not since my christening – and he was in France or Flanders all that time, so he must have done something else with his leaves. I've never asked, of course. I don't know who the woman was. I think she was on the stage. She must have been. It's the only explanation that seems to fit everything.'

'I'm sorry,' said Hilary helplessly. She, too, was convinced; it was a theory that agreed with her own observation of Mrs Fleming very well.

'She wouldn't like to think I knew this. She's always been careful to say the right thing about him to me, but I think I've known ever since I remember. One just does ... What I think is that when this business happened – last year, I mean – well, thinking it over, I suppose the idea of my owing my life to someone else while she stood around doing nothing, I suppose it was more than she could take. So she side-stepped it in her own mind, the way people sometimes do. There's something about it in psychology, isn't there?'

The effort of speech, now that it was over, was making him breathe as fast as if he had been running. To Hilary it had been scarcely less painful. She said, 'But of course. You were ill, you had a long convalescence. It was very sensible of her not to keep rubbing it in that you'd been in danger. Very likely Mr Sanderson advised her not to; it often has a bad effect.'

She was pleased with this improvisation, till she saw his face, and knew that he must have his own reasons for scepticism, which he could not declare. She felt no further capacity for bitterness about it, and only wished that Sanderson had kept his panegyrics to himself. This must have struck at something deeper than his sense of fairness, of right and wrong; it was she, she thought, who would pay for it in the end. She felt no bitterness about that either; there was something a little odious about having been put too much in the right.

She said, 'Besides, you're looking at it in the wrong way, and giving it a quite false importance. When people are worried to death, their minds don't work along the ordinary tramlines. After it's over, they want to forget everything and everyone connected with it. And so they should. Your mother's been charming to me, in any case.'

'That's not the same thing. You know what I mean.'

'You don't know yourself. Tell me about that ferret you used to have.'

'My God, do you have to treat me like a child?'

'I'm sorry. But you're being a bit difficult, you know.'

'I suppose I could have gone about it better. I wanted to tell you – well, for several reasons. You see, in a way, I knew. In a different way. But now it's – it's everything, and I don't know what it is I remember.'

'Stop trying. You're meant to forget, it's part of the healing process. Let it rest. All that matters is that it's turned out all right.'

'Yes,' he said slowly, 'it's turned out all right.'

A long way off, in the village below, a church clock chimed seven. He stood listening, it seemed with a strained attention, to the sound, as if it had been a signal which, when it ceased, would have to be obeyed. The last of the bell strokes died slowly away. He turned round to her, with failure in his face. The stress he had been under had not yet passed, but already, perhaps before he himself knew it, it was dispersing into the shifts and obliquities of defeat. He looked at her for a moment; she read in his eyes a hopeless appeal to her to help him out, mixed with shame at having made it, and with a reproach for her refusal, of which he was also ashamed. She turned away, feeling a primitive contempt which her civilised conditioning partly hid from her, and which her love and knowledge translated into pity, so that the humiliation she felt seemed centred only on herself. Revenging her unhappiness with a stubborn withdrawal, she set herself to admire the view.

'I forget if I ever told you about this man Chris Tranter, the one I'm going to stay with in town. He's rather an interesting type, I think you'd like him. He . . . ' The voice ran on, quick and constrained, with a surface of pleasant naturalness, which was not quite that of life. Technique was helping it out, the kind of technique that gets a player over a flat stretch of explanatory dialogue. But without the supporting conventions, it was not quite coming off. She listened, acutely and horribly conscious of every false intonation, without taking in a word of the matter it conveyed. In another minute or two, when he could think of nothing more to say, he would stop and she would have to reply. Somehow they would have to keep it up all the way home.

'He has the most extraordinary system of working,' Julian was informing her. Presumably she had been told already what he worked at, and wondered passingly what it was. 'He goes to bed quite early, about nine, and sets his alarm for 2 a.m. Then he makes some strong tea and ...'

The rest was lost in an interruption. Hilary had been vaguely aware, for some minutes, of footsteps on the path above them, and of loud, cheerful voices which, at an earlier period when distance still muted them, had been raised in song. Without conscious attention, the back of her mind had registered that the public-houses could only have been open for an hour. Now the evening peace, surrounding their small island of tension, was split by a burst of laughter, of the kind that accompanies a rude joke between men who are primed to appreciate it well. The tail of her eye told her that Julian had faced abruptly towards the sound. Turning herself, she saw its authors coming into sight between the leaves; an average pair, whom she placed at once as coming from the aircraft factory, some of the city importations of whom there were many in the skilled engineering grades. Their walking-out clothes had a touch of East End nattiness, not pushed to a point which could be called flash, and there seemed no offence in either of them beyond the absurd self-satisfaction belonging to their state. They were not outrageously drunk, and were making their way down the uneven slope with a large-minded carelessness, rather than actual unsteadiness of gait. Their lapels were conspicuously decked with white satin rosettes, causing her to remember that the church they had passed on the way had had a good deal of confetti outside it. Evidently these wedding guests had prolonged the feast on their own account. It was plain that, so far, their amusement was purely of their own provision. With the normal instinct of a woman anxious to let well alone, she turned away.

The movement brought Julian within her view. He was staring past her, tense and rigid with anger. His face was drawn with it, and looked almost grey. She could recognise that he was not in the mood for intrusions of any kind, and felt sorry for him; but her own stretched nerves mixed the feeling with impatience. People should not lose their sense of proportion so openly, she thought, with a tart humour. He could congratulate himself that it isn't more inconvenient.

It was at this point that the good companions, taking an expansive survey as they came into the open, perceived that they were not alone. To them the discovery brought neither embarrassment nor displeasure. The taller of the two, who had the kind of face one associates, for vague reasons, with a passionate support of league football (it might only have been the rosette), nudged his friend, who was rather undersized, waggishly in the ribs. The friend looked disapproving. He was evidently one of those people who develop, at a certain stage, a solemn anxiety about the proprieties. The fact that, unprepared for the nudge, he had almost tripped over, seemed to appeal to the large man as a joke good enough to share. He looked round in the hope of friendly acclamation, and, considering Hilary first, emitted one of those luscious, appreciative noises, something between a whistle and a tomcat passing the time of night.

Hilary interested herself in the landscape; of all such salutes it was the most innocuous, a mere reflex expecting no reply. That would, no doubt, have been the end of it, if the large man had not in that moment caught sight of Julian's face. It suggested, to his simple train of thought, interrupted spooning, the perfect essence of comedy. He giggled, winked, made a kissing noise, nudged the small man again, and seemed about to wander on.

'Just a minute,' said Julian.

He had spoken in so suppressed a voice that even Hilary had not heard it clearly; she could only pray that it had not reached its object. She was furious and quite prepared to let it appear. It seemed unthinkable that he could contemplate adding anything to what had happened already. She directed, full at him, the freezing stare she had had ready for the wedding guests in case of need. He did not see it; and would, she perceived at once, have ignored it if he had.

The large man had heard and expanded visibly. He viewed himself as the proud exponent of a sense of humour, boundlessly superior to people who couldn't see a joke; and also (for he had reached the euphoric stage) as a man who could, if necessary, look after himself. He made the kissing noise again.

Julian took a step forward.

'Be quiet,' said Hilary viciously, under her breath. 'Don't be ridiculous. Don't you see they're drunk?'

'Yes,' replied Julian aloud. 'Naturally I can see it. If you'll walk on a little way I'll attend to this myself.'

He had spoken with the crisp air of good breeding than which, when consciously applied, nothing is more offensive, while looking past her with intention at the men. She scarcely knew whether to be more exasperated by his tone, which though assumed with conviction, she knew to be grossly histrionic, or by the request to walk on, which suggested something in a novelette. In almost incredulous embarrassment she remained rooted to the spot.

He had certainly achieved his effect. The large man was impressed and resentful. He became, in his own sight, a responsible guardian of democracy. Striking an attitude, he remarked in a refined drawl, 'Di-da-di-da.'

Julian walked up to him leisurely. The little man, who had probably drunk rather less, looked from one to the other with growing concern and pawed at his friend's sleeve. 'Come on, Ted,' he muttered. 'Don't want a row. Got to get back.'

Ignoring him, Julian addressed himself to Ted, who was, Hilary saw, about his own height but considerably thicker.

'Look here. This isn't a parking-place for drunks. Would you kindly go out the way you came?' After reflecting briefly, he added, 'And if you want to vomit, or anything, do it in the bushes somewhere, will you, not on the path.'

A dark red suffusion made visible progress across Ted's square face, beginning at the neck. He thrust his chin forward.

''Ere, 'ere, that'll do. Who are you calling a drunk? Chuckin' your weight about. We've as much right to the path as what you 'ave. 'Cor struth. Get along home, that's what you want to do, and get your ma to wipe your pretty nose. Chuckin' your . . .'

In narratives where this kind of thing happens the heroine is as a rule scarcely aware, when the first swift blow is struck, of seeing the hero move. Hilary was aware of it all too clearly. The rather inexpert upper-cut seemed to travel to its goal through an endless suspension of time. It arrived, however, a little too soon for Ted, whose reflexes were slightly under par. It was just as well, since Julian was giving him at least three stone.

Hilary had little mind for such calculations. Through the thudding of blows, the tread of shifting feet, and the grunting breaths of the combatants, she was aware chiefly of violent nausea. She had never seen men fighting before, and though, from time to time, she had had to tidy up the results, she found

223

that it was no sort of preparation. The spectacle was made no pleasanter by the fact that Ted was too drunk, and Julian too angry, for such long-term considerations as avoiding punishment. A cooler student of form might have inferred that Julian had at some time undergone a school routine of boxing instruction which had lain fallow for years, while Ted (who looked about thirty-five but was probably younger) had been a passive patron of the heavy-weight ring and, occasionally, of all-in wrestling. They slithered about in the uncertain light, on the rough and increasingly muddy surface of the path, while the small man manoeuvred round them, uttering pacific, unheard exhortations, and reproducing involuntarily the movements of a referee.

It was not till Julian jerked his head sideways just in time to avoid a swinging right that she remembered his injury of last year. The fear that mixed itself suddenly with what had been, till now, her unqualified disgust, added a final touch of wretchedness to everything. Speculations about the state of his temporal bone raced through her mind along with the feelings, much magnified, of those who see their own dog being mangled in a gratuitous dog-fight for which it deserves in any case to be thrashed.

At this point, more by luck than judgement, Julian managed to plant a straight left on Ted's nose. She watched, sickened, a dark trickle make its way down into his mouth. It produced on him the effect this blow normally does on persons not trained to receive it coolly; he lost what remained of his temper, along with his head. His face, what with its expression and the blood, acquired a menace which, though not reflected in performance, made her stomach feel packed with ice. She had thought, a moment before, of simply walking away. Now she observed that Julian's left eye was puffing up. Ted had noticed too, and was doing his best to hit it again. Presently he succeeded, and the eyebrow above it began to bleed.

'Don't you fret, miss,' a voice was muttering beside her. 'Ted can't keep that up, not long he can't.' She was dimly aware that the small man had given it up as a bad job, and come to rest beside her, in search apparently of consolation. Ted had landed a vicious body blow. She saw Julian's teeth shut spasmodically, wondered if a rib had gone, and wished she had never opened Gray's *Anatomy*.

'Fact is, miss, I told 'im time and again. "You come on 'ome, Ted!" I said. "We don't want no trouble." I never see 'im the worse before, quite a quiet chap 'e is ordinary. What I mean, he didn't mean no offence to you and your friend. Bit above 'imself, see what I mean?'

'Yes,' said Hilary abstractedly. She was watching Ted avoiding, by inches, backward collision with a tree and imagining Julian being tried for manslaughter with herself as witness. 'Yes, I'm sure.'

'How it was, not being 'imself he took your friend up wrong. I mean, out with a lady, stands to reason your friend wouldn't fancy Ted getting fresh. That's natural. But Ted took him up wrong, see, took it like he was making out he owned the place.'

'Well, he does,' said Hilary dimly. Julian had almost missed his footing with a sharp incline behind him. It was not till she recovered her breath that she noticed her companion's horror and perturbation. 'But it's entirely his own fault for not saying so, and being so rude ... This is awful, can't we do *anything*?'

'Dunno, I'm sure, miss. They won't listen to *me*.' He made a reluctant move towards the arena, but changed his mind, remarking hopefully, 'You'll see, they'll be fed up with it before long. Mean to say, Ted's not been accustomed to it, no more than what your friend has.'

If they had, Hilary thought, they might at least have taken their coats off before they began. Julian's, with the advantage of a looser cut and better workmanship, was standing up to the strain, but Ted's had split all round the back of one arm-hole, so that the lining gaped through. A detached fragment of her mind brooded, apart, on the social injustice of this, and weighed the possibilities of repair.

Some latent instinct of self-preservation had advised Julian to keep out of a clinch. He had managed it more by agility and reach than skill, the chief benefit of training that remained with him being a capacity to keep steady under face-blows, of which he had now had several. Hilary perceived very little of this. She saw that a cool fanaticism had settled on his bruised face, and received a general impression as of a borzoi involved with a bull-terrier. Without noticing the change she was becoming less conscious of her own outraged taste and feelings, more aware of the clean lines of his body, the grace which was built into his bones and remained a part of him even in uncaring violence. The blood on his face, and his indifference to it, like that of a young savage to whom the war-drum has lent an entranced tolerance of pain, made a kind of shudder go down the marrow of her spine. She was not accustomed to such feelings, and they frightened her; but she found it impossible to look away.

Just then Ted, whose wind was shortening painfully, made a final effort to close in. But, his mind coloured by recollections of the all-in booth, he wasted a little concentration on making the correct all-in face. It not only slowed him down, but betrayed his intention. Julian was just in time to side-step him, much as a matador does a bull, and get in a rapid jab at his solar-plexus. In view of the indications, he might profitably have tried this a good deal sooner. Ted doubled up, tripped, fell headlong, and was enormously, excruciatingly sick where he lay.

As if cold water had been thrown on her, Hilary's confused emotions subsided into a chill disgust. She stood, viewing the spectacle, while her fellow-spectator made a clicking noise with his tongue, expressing polite disapproval, relief, and commiseration. Julian stood panting with his exertions, looking astonished and slightly dazed.

Breaking what could not, unfortunately, be called a silence, the little man observed to Hilary, 'Best thing, that is.' Further to enlighten her innocence, he added, 'Be more 'imself after that, see.'

'I hope he's all right.' She was moved to this less by concern for Ted than by goodwill to his unwilling second, towards whom, at some unnoticed stage in the affair, she had curiously warmed.

'Cor!' he replied reassuringly. 'I'll see after 'im.' Tactfully lowering his voice, he murmured, out of the side of his mouth, 'When you get your friend home, you want to put a nice bit of beefsteak on that eye. Draws it, see?'

'Thank you very much.'

'You're welcome. *Nah* then, Ted ...'

Ted heaved himself up to his knees. He had lost his florid complexion, and looked so like one of Hilary's patients that instinctively she advanced towards him. Ignoring her, he looked at Julian with a reproach that lacked the strength to be indignation. Responding instantly to this, Julian said, 'Sorry, I didn't set out to do that. Didn't think.'

Ted meditated, a green thought in a green shade. Presently he muttered, sourly, 'Wasn't low ... Had one or two. Acting silly.'

'Call it even,' said Julian. His naturally engaging smile

appeared, with confused effect, on his damaged face; he evidently found it painful. Having assisted the little man in getting Ted standing, he inquired, 'Can you get home all right?'

'Ted'll be OK,' said the little man, not without a certain odd dignity. He and Julian looked at one another for a moment in a profound, regretful non-comprehension, till Ted began to heave, wearily and half-heartedly again. The little man turned to his ministrations, and Julian, after a moment or so, to Hilary.

'Well,' he remarked quite cheerfully, 'may as well be getting along.'

She turned down the path beside him; it was hardly feasible to remain with the others, nor, in their presence, to walk off in the opposite direction. The path wound between the larches, and quite soon they were alone. She looked in front of her, sorting and arranging what she had to say. It would keep till he had summoned up the courage to apologise, which might supply her with further ideas. He said nothing at all, and presently began to whistle something from *Carmen* between his teeth. Hilary waited, with deadly restraint. He began fumbling in his coat pocket; anything, she supposed, for time.

'Damn,' he remarked with firm unforced annoyance. 'I could have sworn I had a handkerchief somewhere.'

He turned towards her, searching for the pocket on the other side. She had been walking on his right, too much absorbed in her anger to look at him. Now, in the light of a small clearing, she got a sudden close view. Fresh blood was still trickling from the smeared drying mass on his cut brow; the puffed and darkening eyelid was sticky with it; for a sickening moment she thought it was coming from the eye itself.

The cheekbone under it was dull red-purple along the high straight line of its ridge; so was the angle of the jaw. By some peculiarity of Ted's tactic or his own defence, most of the havoc was concentrated on one side; from the other he had looked almost normal. She could only begin to imagine what it would look like when it had had time to mature; and this was merely what happened to be visible. What had kept the boy on his feet through such a battering? As she knew from last year, he was neither physically insensitive nor naturally tough. She was, however, still too angry for her divided feelings not to make her more so.

Julian had found his handkerchief. He produced it, with a grunt of satisfaction, and lifted it towards his eye. She saw that it was no more than reasonably clean. Her carefully selected speech made way for a quick, cross, '*Don't* put that filthy thing on an open cut. Do you want it to go septic?'

'I've only used it once,' said Julian mildly. 'And I can't see out of my eye.'

'Well, use this one then.' She took a clean one out of her bag and held it out coldly. He took it, turned it over and sniffed at it.

'Oh, no, what a waste. It's got scent on it.'

'Keep it folded and hold it there hard.' It was not till he was obediently following these instructions that she had time to reflect how outrageous (and how unexpected) his self-possession was. No doubt he was putting it on; but if he could, it showed a very inadequate grasp of the situation. She paused no longer.

'You appear pleased with yourself.' Because an undermining concern still lingered she spoke even more acidly than she had meant to.

'Oh, no, far from it,' he assured her, briefly inspecting the handkerchief and putting it back again. 'On the contrary, I was just about to apologise.'

He said it very nicely. It dawned on her, with amazement, that his equanimity was not shaken in the least.

'Were you really? You astonish me. I thought you must have imagined that I was enjoying myself.' She edged her voice savagely, thinking, almost while she spoke, He ought to get that eye looked at immediately; it's impossible to tell, with all that mess . . .

'No, of course not. I ought to have taken him off somewhere else. Sort of thing one thinks of when it's too late. I'm afraid you're annoyed about it; well, of course you are.'

'Has it only just occurred to you' – she governed her voice with a considerable effort – 'that I might be annoyed?'

'Well, it should have, of course, but there wasn't much time.'

'At first I thought you couldn't be sober. But I doubt now whether you had even that excuse.'

'I never take anything,' he assured her with more concern than he had so far shown, 'when I'm going to drive. I take driving fairly seriously, as a matter of fact.'

Hilary boiled over. 'Then I should be glad if you'd also take seriously the fact that when I go out with anyone I expect some elementary standards of civilised behaviour.' They were walking sharply downhill, so that her remarks were violently emphasised by jolts caused by the unevenness of the path. 'It was completely inexcusable and disgusting.'

'I know,' he assured her. 'I really am most hideously sorry.' He spoke with feeling; with too much feeling; with an over-earnestness which it was impossible to mistake. In fact, he spoke like someone making a sincere effort to feel what he knows to be required of him. In the gathering gloom she saw him turn and regard her hopefully out of his serviceable eye. During this moment of preoccupation he collided sharply with a tree on his offside, and stood holding its trunk, dazed and unsteady. Forgetting the whole purport of the conversation, she found herself gripping him by the arm.

'Julian, what is it? Are you all right?'

'Yes, thanks,' he said, regaining his equilibrium. 'I didn't see the darn thing coming, that's all.'

'Well, look where you're going.' She withdrew to the other side of the path, but could not keep herself from watching him, from wondering whether only his one-sided vision had been to blame, and, eventually, from saying, 'You don't feel giddy, do you?'

He stood still, dutifully giving the matter his attention. 'No, I don't think so. I mean, when one walks into something one usually does, for the moment.'

'You don't remember, I suppose, whether you got a blow on the right temple?' She tried to use her consulting-room voice.

He put up his hand. 'It seems to be all in one piece. One doesn't feel it much at the time, of course.'

'I'll take a look at you, when you've cleaned off some of that revolting mess.'

'Is it as bad as all that?' There could be no mistake this time; if he had sounded unwarrantably cheerful before, his voice now was positively light-hearted. A train of recollections came unbidden into her mind; and perhaps it was this that prompted her reply.

'Seeing that you're barely recognisable now, I feel quite curious to know what you'll look like by to-morrow morning.'

This was an exaggeration, and she wondered afterwards what made her say it. But the effect was instantaneous. Ted's ministrations had included nearly everything except a split lip, so that the mouth still had that expressiveness which one generally missed, because the eyes had more. She saw it relax, as soon as she had spoken, simply and involuntarily, into a firm and peaceful line. A new confidence stamped it, a look of grave but carefree release. He remarked, conversationally, 'Bad show. It's a good job we're here and you haven't got to be seen about with me, isn't it?'

They had come to a wrought-iron gate in a stone wall. He opened it for her and they went on into a kitchen-garden, along an old mossy path between currant and gooseberry bushes. She scarcely noticed where they were, being too much filled with her own preoccupations. In spite of all that she had known before, she hardly found it credible that the hatred of his own beauty could have entered him as deeply as this, and would much rather have disbelieved the evidence of her own wits. It shocked her, and, joining with the rest of her concern for him, made her weapons useless in her hands. She said, trying to escape from it on to her own ground, 'I hope you've got some kind of antiseptic in the house.'

'Oh, yes; we've got a bottle of iodine somewhere, I know.'

'Iodine!' she said disgustedly.

'Why, is it out of fashion, or something?'

'It's better than nothing, I suppose.'

'Well, here we are. You don't mind coming in by the back door, do you? Are you going to clean me first and spank me afterwards, or the other way round?'

This passed all bounds, as she reminded herself in a last attempt at indignation. He was not even looking to see how she took it, merely accompanying it with a brief, affectionate, one-eyed smile. She maintained a frigid silence. He lifted a hand to the stone sill over the porch, searching, among the

232

moss and stonecrop, for the hidden key. His streaked face, upturned to the faint light, looked suddenly remote and self-contained. She found herself saying, 'You won't need any spanking when you've had iodine on that cut, I should think. I ought to have taken you to the surgery.'

He slid the big iron key into the lock; the green-painted door swung back, revealing darkness and a cool, stony smell.

'It only wants a bit of strapping. I've still got some that you gave me for the play.' He clicked on the switch, and stood back to let her enter. She felt the well-ordered emptiness of the house watching her, as it were, with raised eyebrows, a disapproving presence making her sensible of intrusion.

'Would you mind awfully,' he said, 'if I got the surface muck off in the scullery? Because if I use the bathroom I'm liable to make a bad job of the clearing up, whereas here they'll only think it's off a bit of meat.'

He opened another door and they went into a big, labour-wasteful, placid room in which everything had been cleaned and covered and scrubbed and stowed away. A huge stone sink stood under the window, smelling dank and clean, like a well. He ran the cold tap.

'Take off your coat first; it's bad enough already.'

He did so, following it up, stiffly, with his pullover and tie. She thought passingly how many men, emerging into shirt-sleeves, shrink into a self-conscious angularity. His body seemed always to have a life of its own aloof from the divisions of his mind, an arrogant self-sufficiency, careless and serene. 'Do you mind if I go on using your handkerchief? I'm afraid it's done for, anyway; I'll get you another.'

'Give it to me, you can't see what you're doing. I don't want water swamped all over the cut; it neutralises the iodine.'

'Thanks,' he said. 'Filthy job for you, I'm afraid.' But he

submitted comfortably and easily in her hands, with the pliancy of children accustomed to such offices.

'Am I hurting you?' she asked, as she removed the caked blood from his eyelid.

'Not much. You can do it harder than that if you like.' He inclined his head, with both eyes trustfully closed. She knew that she must be hurting him a good deal; the eyelid was so swollen already that she had to force it open to examine the eye, which seemed uninjured. The cut, when she had cleaned it, turned out to be worse than she had thought.

'You know,' she said, 'this ought to have a stitch in it. I think we'll have to go to the surgery after all.'

'It's stopped bleeding,' he said easily. 'I shouldn't think it would start again.'

'It's not that. If it's not pulled together I think it will leave a scar.'

'Oh, is that all? Don't bother, then; it isn't worth it. It can't leave anything that greasepaint wouldn't cover, surely?'

'Julian,' she said sharply, 'do be realistic. We're not discussing a stage property; I'm talking about your *face*.'

'I am being realistic.' His mouth had hardened. 'There's no need to bother, thanks very much.'

'But, my dear, you . . . ' No, she thought, why should I? He'll only think me a fool. 'Oh, very well, if you want to go about decorated like a Prussian junker, it's your affair. You'll be sorry, in a few years. Besides, I don't like being responsible for botched work.'

'Don't be cross,' he said, with unexpected gentleness.

'I'm more than cross.' She tried to infuse conviction into this, but found that she had to look away. He opened an immaculately tidy drawer, produced a clean folded glass-cloth, dried himself with it, and threw it into a corner. She felt concerned about this, but firmly stopped herself from offering to wash it out for him. He would have a good deal to explain away, in any case.

There was a cracked square of mirror on the window-sill, left there by a maid. He went over to it and peered in.

'Interesting,' he murmured. 'How long will it last?'

'I should say it's hardly started yet. You may be semi-presentable at the end of a week. I hope your friends in London are unconventional.'

'My—? Oh, yes, I see what you mean. Well, I needn't . . . I'll have to think about that later. Look here, if you're really going to stick a bit of something on this, the first-aid kit is in my room. Would you mind coming up? It'll be easier than my running round the house with all the wrong things.'

'Very well,' said Hilary with professional calm. 'I suppose none of them are sterile, anyway.'

He picked up his coat and eased himself into it with an awkwardness which made her realise that he must have strained a shoulder-muscle; he attempted neither the pullover nor the tie. 'As a matter of fact it's all in guaranteed packets put up by Boots. You have to have something handy, if you're producing a show with any kind of sword-play. Funny things can happen, even when people know how to fence.'

He looked, as always when he was on this ground, suddenly adult, responsible, and self-assured. She remembered the voices in the wings that she had heard appealing to him for arbitration.

She gave it up and smiled at him. 'Tell me you're sorry for behaving so badly.'

'I have.' He smiled back at her; his sound eye, with its long lashes and upward-slanting eyebrow as smooth as a black feather, emphasising the grotesqueness of the other which was darkening fast and narrowed to a slit. 'But I will again.'

'It was so undignified to provoke the man like that.'

'How would you have liked me to provoke him?' He dropped his hand on an invisible sword-hilt, his gesture evoking faultlessly a costume and a scene, and declaimed with ringing clarity:

'Two stars hold not their motion in one sphere,
Nor can one England brook a double reign
Of Harry Percy and the Prince of Wales.'

The comic effect was irresistible, and, though she knew he had played for it, she could not keep from laughing. 'I thought that play was a *bête noir* of yours.'

'It seems to have worn off. Well, I think you've been entertained in the scullery long enough. Shall we go?'

They went back into the stone passage, through a baize door, and into the hall. Taken by surprise in its solitude, the place looked different, intimate, and vulnerable, deserted by a protecting power. On a table a flowering pot-plant was standing in a bowl half-filled with water, which looked like a week's reserve. No doubt, she thought, he would be forgetful of such things; but through a half-open door into the drawing-room she could glimpse the red-braided holland dust sheets that covered everything. The house seemed half to stir, at their footsteps, from a composed, respectable sleep like a duenna's afternoon nap, and to murmur displeasure at being taken unprepared; the stairs gave, under them, the tiny creaks that seem to belong only to empty houses. Julian's unsubdued voice and swift, casual footfall seemed defiant and ostentatious. The place could scarcely have proclaimed more clearly that it expected neither of them, if it had found a tongue to say so.

Upstairs a crimson-carpeted passage, with a broad, square-paned Georgian window at each end, ran between cream-painted doors with old hanging handles of pale brass. The last light outside the window looked a dramatic, sapphire blue, on which was traced in black the hard structure of an ash-tree. The last of the cream doors stood half-open; he put on the light, and stepped back.

'Do come in. It's tidy for once, they did it out this morning.'

It was a big square room, panelled like the passage in cream, and furnished uncompromisingly as a bedroom in solid Edwardian mahogany, with dull, correct hunting prints on the walls; a man's room in the best taste of thirty years before. Indefinably, but unmistakably, it had the curious half-empty pathos of a man's room that is occupied by a boy. The few personal things – books in a shelved recess, a couple of foils on a bracket, an empty leather pyjama-case on the dark crimson bed – had that air of apology and incongruity, of being there on sufferance provided that they continued to behave. Like a boy's room well looked after, it was coldly and scentlessly clean; the air, untinged with tobacco or hair cream or hoarded dust-collecting junk, smelt faintly of fresh linen. He drew the heavy red curtains and shut the door.

'Somewhere in here, I think.' He opened a drawer in the dressing-table, and, as he rummaged, her eyes wandered to the room again. On the mantelshelf was a photograph in a wide silver frame. The face, and the fashion, belonged to twenty years ago; but even in the house of a stranger she would have known at once who it was. The shoulders were draped with some softly falling stuff; gauze filters had been used to frame the portrait in a nimbus of mist; the fair hair, wavy and soft, was pressed down over the forehead with a velvet band. The faint drawing of the features belonged to a time when there were two sorts of women, and make-up was only used by the second. The face had the

237

fashionable softness of the time, the rounded edges, the lips half-parted in a dreaming sweetness, the downcast eyes. It was all very gentle, and yet in the gentleness itself there seemed something inflexible; as if the face would always refuse and resist any strong expression – anger, passion, laughter, or violent grief – and would punish their invasion unforgivingly. It was also the face of a contemporary beauty; but so swiftly do fashions in faces change that she realised this fact last of all. What struck her most forcibly was the complete harmony of the picture with its setting; as if it were to this face, not to its tenant, that the room belonged.

'How's this for equipment?' Julian had brought forth two paper packages marked with large red crosses, and the black japanned make-up box; the smell of greasepaint, as he lifted the lid, seemed so out of place as to be a little outrageous. He found the roll of strapping and put it beside the packages. Stooping had made the cut on his forehead begin to bleed again.

'Splendid,' she said. 'Can I wash my hands?'

She had meant the request in its most literal sense, as a preliminary to the dressing; but he apologised profusely, and led her round to a spruce Victorian room with everything encased in mahogany and brass taps polished like gold. He snatched the iodine from a wall-cupboard, muttered, 'Here and next door,' and hastened off.

'There isn't any towel,' Hilary shouted after him.

'Oh. Frightfully sorry.' He came back, visibly confused, and gave her one from an airing cupboard. 'They seem to have made a pretty clean sweep of everything, don't they? And I'm rather afraid there may not be any hot water, either.'

'It doesn't matter about that.' She washed, thoughtfully. The bathroom had removed any lingering doubts she had allowed herself to entertain.

When she came back he had arranged the iodine and a pair of scissors along with the dressings. The effect was made still more workmanlike by the fact that the top of the dressing-chest was, as she had already noted, quite denuded of brushes and such objects of daily use. A strapped-up suit-case stood in a corner.

'You'd better sit down,' she said. 'I can't reach you up there. Here, under the light.'

He pulled forward one of the stiff-backed chairs, and she uncorked the iodine, which was of the concentrated kind.

'This will hurt horribly. Are you sure you haven't anything else? Flavine, or Dettol, or anything?'

'It's all right,' he said. 'I'm not a baby.' He settled himself, his face turned up to her, his hands on his knees.

It was a ragged cut; she had to open it further to make sure that the antiseptic should do its work, before pulling it together with the strapping. He bore it all with great equanimity, and, during the last part of the process, remarked that the Matron had always used iodine at school.

'She would,' said Hilary, fixing the pad of gauze in place.

'She wasn't a bad old bird.'

'I'm sure. And treated appendicitis with castor oil.' She pulled the strapping tight, and pressed her palms against the ends for the warmth to make them sticky.

'Rhubarb and senna, it was as a rule,' said Julian abstractedly. 'We called her Mata Hari, I forget why. She used to buy me ice-cream, though, when I crocked my knee ... Don't go away, I want to tell you something.'

He stood up so suddenly that, poised forward over him, she almost lost her balance and to regain it caught instinctively at his arms. They went firmly round her. There was a smell of iodine near her face. She looked up quickly; his lips

239

brushed her cheek, and, with sudden decision, closed on her mouth.

He had succeeded, in spite of everything, in taking her utterly by surprise. Before her mind had dealt at all with the situation, she had returned his kiss. Next moment she tried to free herself; but, using his height to the best advantage, he simply swayed her off her balance again. She hung there, help-less, clinging instinctively to him for support. He looked down at her face, laughed, and kissed her again.

'Julian . . . ' Her voice was a pale ghost of indignation, mock-ing her. He tightened his arms, so that she was resting on her feet again; but already it was unbearable to let him go.

'I always have,' he said. 'I always shall. You know that. No, be quiet. What's the use; it's happened now.'

'My dear, no, we . . . '

'Be quiet, and kiss me. Properly this time.'

'No, I . . . ' The words died; she felt, with defiant joy, the stoop of his shoulders under her disobedient hands.

'Oh, God,' he said, 'why did you keep pretending all this while?'

'It's impossible. I shouldn't have . . . Dear, let me go.'

'I shall never do that,' he said, 'as long as I live.' In spite of his evident emotion, he looked not unpleased at having got it right.

A strand of black hair was falling down over his bruised eye. His cheekbone and jaw were darkening already; he had the clear thin skin that marks easily. Balanced with all this was half a face that Kneller might have worked on as lovingly as on his dead Monmouth. Even this absurdity could not make him grotesque. She tried to say something, but her breath caught in her throat instead. With tears in her eyes, she reached her arms up round his neck.

She had never realised how strong he was; nor, it was painfully evident, had he. His first embrace had had, in its swift deliberation, something unconsciously theatrical; something learned, like a step in a dance, by sight. Now, suddenly, all this poise had stopped dead. Her physical sensations became a mere protesting consciousness of breathlessness, aching ribs, a crushed mouth, and a crick in the neck. In this moment of acute discomfort, unmixed with pleasure of any kind, a kind of still, radiant tenderness rose in her, quietly, like a certainty of truth.

Loosing her a little at last he said quickly, as if to forestall her before she could speak, 'It's all right. Don't think about anything, it can't matter.'

'Yes, we must.'

'There's nothing to think about ... I came back here for you. Nobody knows. I'm supposed to be in town. The house is shut up; you saw, of course. When I saw you this afternoon I knew I had to.'

'Why did you do it? It – it isn't fair.'

'Fair? I love you; do you love me?'

He had spoken abruptly, roughly almost, holding her away. When she looked at him she knew that whatever she told him, he would accept and believe.

She looked away. She was one of those people who hold that to lie about the truth of a personal relationship is never justified; she had never lied to David, only kept to herself facts for which he had never asked, and which he would not have understood. Now she would have not only to lie, but to do it well. She tried to think what she would say, but could only remember the naked trust in his face: beside it her own thoughts felt suddenly shabby, and she knew that she had not been thinking, as she had believed, only of him, but of her own image of herself, a competent person with a sense of proportion and life in rein; of what her friends would say if they knew; of how David would laugh.

'Do you love me?' said Julian again. He shook her a little, as if he supposed that in this brief interval she had forgotten about him and needed reminding. Who was she, to patronise him with deceit?

'That's a terrifying thing to be asked,' she said, trying to smile.

'I told you,' he said, 'without being asked. And I was terrified too, if you want to know.'

'You're too clever for me. Yes, I do.'

'I don't know why.' He spoke quite quietly. 'But I hoped you might, because if you didn't, nothing would mean anything.' He stood looking at her for a moment or two in silence, then said swiftly, 'Well, that's all right, then. Now kiss me. Really this time.'

He pulled her back into his arms. She became quite frightened, more for him than on her own behalf. She could have controlled the situation better if he had used his strength deliberately, for mastery. One could deal with greed; this was more like offering hospitality to someone not clearly conscious of starvation. He had the brutality of innocence, of a complete lack of sensual technique; he seemed lost in a bewildered attempt to incorporate her substance in his own. When she could bear it no longer she said, 'Darling, you're rather hurting me.'

'I'm sorry.' He let her go and looked at her as if he were half dazed. She saw a fine moisture on his temples. 'I didn't know I . . . I'm sorry.'

She stroked the hair back from his forehead. He stood without touching her, tense and silent, with closed eyes. 'Be still a moment,' she whispered; and, taking his face between her hands, kissed him softly. It was a variation David had taught her; but she did not remember that.

He stayed, as she had asked, quite still till she had done. Then, not so gently, he returned the kiss. She had scarcely reckoned on so ready a learner, or one who would improve so quickly on her instruction. He shifted his grasp on her abruptly; and at first she did not resist, thinking it an accidental clumsiness which he would notice and correct without being told. But this, she found, was an error of judgement.

'Julian,' she said quickly, 'please let me go.'

He obeyed, sooner than she had expected; he even left her and went over to the window, where he opened the curtain and stood looking out into the darkness, now almost complete. He was evidently preparing to say something; she felt ashamed to accept an apology which, she thought, he ought to be receiving.

He dropped the curtain and came back into the room.

'I'm sorry,' he said. 'That was pretty poor. I meant to do it better. I'm glad you told me off, I should have been spoiling things.' He crossed the room to the door; she thought he was about to go out, and opened her mouth to speak; but he was unhooking his dressing-gown that hung there. He threw it over his arm, and said, rather awkwardly but without any uncertainty at all, 'Knock on the wall when you're ready. I'll be next door. Oh, just a minute.' She watched him, speechless, cross to the bed and throw back the red coverlet. 'It's all right. I thought they might have left it without any sheets.'

He was on his way out. She called him back, in a voice she had difficulty in summoning.

'I only thought,' he said diffidently, 'that perhaps you'd rather I went.'

Hilary recovered herself with an effort. Her heart, she discovered, was thudding in her chest as if she were a frightened young girl.

'My dear, I'm sorry if ... But you really can't rush to conclusions quite like that.'

He looked at her inquiringly, then said, without resentment, 'When a thing's going to happen anyway, it ought to happen naturally. Why not?'

Helplessly aware of talking rubbish in a desperate search for time, she said, 'It's not very good manners, for one thing.'

'I'm sorry,' he said, putting down the dressing-gown carefully on a chair. 'I see what you mean. I should have asked you to marry me first, of course. I suppose I thought you'd take that for granted.'

'Oh, Julian, my dear.' She did not know whether to laugh or cry; putting up her hand to her face she felt it burning. 'Don't be absurd, you know that wasn't what I meant.'

'I'm glad,' he said. 'I shouldn't like to think we didn't understand each other. We always have.' He crossed the room and gripped her by the elbows. The bruises stood out more clearly, emphasised by the pallor of his face. 'Look here. I know what you're thinking. I see this is the way a cad would behave. We ought to be engaged and do everything properly; if a man respects a woman he's supposed to wait for her, and all that. Anyone could say, it's got to be to-night but I can't explain why. It's one of the things men do say to women, of course.'

'Is it?' said Hilary gently. In her experience they either refrained from saying anything, or were armed with abundant and logical reasons. 'I don't think you're behaving like a cad, because I know you're not one. I'm just rather frightened of rushing into anything so serious quite so fast; I suppose it's not the way I'm made.'

'I know,' he said, looking down at her gravely. 'Women are different. I'm sorry if I frightened you.' He put his arm round her with studied moderation, as if she were ill. 'Are you angry about it?'

'No,' she said. 'I can't afford to be.'

'It wasn't your fault,' he explained. 'You couldn't know.' He dropped his arm and stood away from her. 'Listen; I'll say this without making love to you at all; that's fair, isn't it? We'll get married as soon as you like. This week, as soon as I can get a licence; it can't be too soon for me. But – don't go away to-night. I'm not asking just because I – I'm in love with you. It isn't just that. It's a thing I have about it, that it's terribly important. It's ... Oh, God, you'll think I do nothing but quote plays, but it's the best way of saying it:

> Which, taken at the flood, leads on to fortune;
> Omitted, all the voyage of their life
> Is bound in shallows and in miseries.
> On such a full sea are we now afloat.

Do you see what I mean?'

'Yes,' she said slowly. 'But what makes you feel that?'

'I wish I could tell you. It's – too complicated, I don't really understand it myself. I just feel absolutely sure. You do believe me? You don't think I'm just faking something up on the spur of the moment to get what I want?'

'No.' She looked up at him. 'I know you're not. I think you're right for both of us; it ought to be to-night, or not at all ... Julian, will you leave me here for about five minutes? No, darling, not for that; I've got to think. I'm sorry, my dear.'

'Oh, God, why must you think? You said you loved me.'

'That is why.'

'You don't know how long five minutes is. If you're only waiting for an entrance cue it seems a year. Can't you think with me here?'

'I've tried, darling, but it hasn't been any good. Please.'

'All right … You're not worried because you think it's immoral, or anything, are you?'

'Not in the way you mean.'

'There – isn't anyone else to think about, is there?'

'No.'

'Can I kiss you before I go?'

'How much help do you think that would be?'

'You always see through me, don't you?' He felt in his pockets. 'I suppose you haven't got a spare cigarette?'

She gave him one, lighting one for herself along with it. As she did so, she admitted to herself that the moment when he had asked her for a cigarette after the play had been the first in which she had known inescapably that she loved him, and she wondered how she had managed to evade this knowledge at the time. He thanked her and went out, softly closing the door.

Hilary sat down on the edge of the bed. When she began to think she knew that she had been over everything already, not once but many times, under various disguises of irony and hypothesis. Impatient of her own hypocrisy, she wasted no time on obvious practical considerations, such as the effect on her private practice if it got about, as sooner or later, in the country, it inevitably would. Even a very small private income, possessed since girlhood, lends a powerful if adventitious fortitude in matters of this kind. To the social aspect she felt indifferent, having had a love-affair in hospital, where such affairs are, within weeks, the property of almost everybody one knows. She dismissed all this, and turned to the essentials. But here, again, there was nothing new to think about, except her own incredible shiftlessness in not having reached, long since, the decision she had left till now.

Absently, following the habits of a life in which thought had generally to be accompanied by action of some kind, she wandered over to the dressing-table and began to tidy it, wiping the iodine bottle on a swab, throwing the trimmings from the dressing into the waste-paper basket, folding in the edges of the clean packet and opening the drawer to put it away. She looked in, incuriously, concerned only to find a corner into which the packet would fit, and not noticing the key-chain, which she had not seen him use to open it, still hanging from the lock. A vague impression of unexpectedness in the contents, the absence of the routine handkerchiefs and ties, made a second glance too spontaneous for proper feeling to catch it up. It was enough to explain the expressionless look of the room; all the personality was here, safely shut away; the technical books, the photographs, the programmes and stage trinkets and unopened spare make-up and false hair. The likeness of a revolting mask leered up at her; the structure of the face, just discernible, made her deduce the First Madman in *Malfi*. Under it was a head-study of the Oberon, with studio lighting this time, which impressed and even a little awed her. At this point it occurred to her that she was not behaving nicely, and she put them back again, only allowing herself a passing glance at the books out of a casual interest in the literature of a trade so unlike her own. Of the top three, one was a famous theatrical autobiography; was it necessary, then, for him to keep even that hidden away? With the other two she found she had made a miscalculation. One was *Married Love* by Dr Stopes. The second, which she was feeling too much ashamed of herself to notice at the time, she remembered only in retrospect after she had shut the drawer. It had been a thin gaudy little pamphlet with a young man in a flying-helmet on the cover, and a title in red, white, and blue: *The Royal Air Force, To-day and To-morrow.*

The ash fell from her cigarette on to the carpet. It was the room, she thought, that oppressed her, its strangeness, its prim order, its secretive reserve. She summoned her will to defy it, and looked round. Something was different; she missed the focal point at which, unconsciously, her defiance had been aimed. Then she remembered. The silver-framed portrait on the mantelpiece, which had last caught her eye when she went out to the bathroom to wash her hands, was gone. She saw that the clock and vase and the candlesticks had been shifted, so that a gap should not appear.

For a moment she stood still, in an attitude which would have been recognised by people who had worked with her; her hands in her pockets, her lower lip caught in. Then she put out her cigarette, and opened the door.

'Julian.'

He was standing at the turn of the passage, by the window which he had opened to lean out. She saw the quick jerk of his hand and the spark of his cigarette going downward into blue darkness. He came back to her, his head and shoulders poised in a deliberate ease of carriage which looked a little larger than life; and something told her that the tension in which he had waited had produced, by unconscious association, the control of movement that would have carried him through a first entrance on the stage. When he got to the doorway he stopped, and stood waiting, with the same unreal naturalness.

'Yes?' he said.

She looked at him, gathering him into her knowledge and understanding, so concerned with her search that she forgot to smile or to speak, till she saw him, as she had seen patients waiting for a verdict, slow his breathing forcibly and moisten his lips. Then she went up to him and took hold of his coat, but he still stood looking down at her, with a set face, as if he were waiting for her to strike him.

'Darling,' she said, 'if you like you can drive me home and ...' She had smiled as she spoke, but he had not understood, and she saw for a moment in his face a half-hidden despair which shocked her, because it was so helpless and final, and because it seemed to her that it had been there before. She caught him into her arms. '... and I'll find you some supper, because it's long past supper-time. You see, you can't be missed; but my telephone rings in the night, sometimes.'

He began, slowly and cautiously, 'You mean you—' and suddenly clipped the last word against her mouth. She caressed him comfortably, murmuring self-reproaches and foolish endearments. She could still feel the stiff, forced steadiness of his breathing, which only defeated his purpose by accelerating his heart. He let her go and went over to the window; she could hear the half-suppressed gasp as he filled his lungs.

'You were only three and a half minutes,' he said at length.

'Was that all? It seemed much longer.' Constraint descended suddenly between them. In another moment, she thought, they would be talking about the weather.

'If we're going out again,' she said, 'you'd better put on a tie.'

He found one and a clean pullover. She saw that he had difficulty in lifting his arm above the shoulder, and helped him put it on.

'Where does it hurt?'

'Never you mind, Doctor,' he said, suddenly grinning at her. 'Surgery's shut.'

They walked back through the wood to the abandoned car. Cool leaves brushed their faces; the earth had the cold vivid tang of new greenness consuming last year's death. Night makes of the smallest wood a wilderness, of the traveller an outlaw, hugged in his small circle of alien solitude while the native community of leaf and fur and feather discuss him softly, and make plans for him in an unknown tongue. The stealthy quiet was cut suddenly by the thin, intolerable shriek of a rabbit's death-cry in the teeth of a stoat. She said, 'That's a terrible sound.'

'Life is terrible.' He spoke with the passionate certainty of the very young, with the freshness of truth alive in the imagination, not dulled by the weary repetition of proof. They clung to one another, straining against the eternal loneliness of the self. 'I love you,' they whispered, unhappily, hopelessly, as if the words were a failure, a kind of frustrated slang. One could not reach, or enter to cherish, only offer for kindness' sake, from one prison to another, the mortal tokens of bread and wine ... The trees lightened. There was a smell of stale beer on the air. They laughed; the saving vulgarity of living became solid again under their feet.

In the car he devoted himself to driving with more, if anything, than his customary precision, and they ceased to talk. She leaned back, watching his big, cleanly articulated hands making their economical movements on the wheel and gears, and let the guards of her mind fall slack in the security of the darkness, for how long she did not know.

With his eyes on the road, Julian said crisply, 'Have you read any good books lately?'

'Why?' She felt as startled, as if something had been thrown at her.

'You'd better start telling me about them. I think I should drive better if you did.'

'You're driving very well.'

'Am I? I haven't known I've been doing it for the last five minutes.'

'We're almost there,' she said.

They left the car in a lane a field away, and came towards the house by the footpath at the back. As it came in sight he said, 'Is this all right? It's rather early. What about Mrs Clare?'

'I live in the old end of the house,' she said. 'The walls are very thick.' Lisa had been on her conscience already; this was presuming on her affectionate toleration much too far. But that was only one of the things that had had to go. 'Besides, her husband's at home.'

'Is he? I thought they were separated or something.'

'Only by circumstances, his work and so on. They're very fond of each other.'

'I'm glad. She's nice, isn't she? Sort of comfortable and warm. Don't they mind? Can't they do something about it?'

'They find it works out better this way.'

'He must be a queer type.' His hand reached out for hers.

'We'll try the french window,' she said. 'I doubt whether Lisa will have done much locking up.' The door gave; she went over to the light-switch, seeing against the uncurtained glass his outline standing questioningly, his arm making an exploring, blind-man's-buff movement among the familiar objects she knew by heart. The light went on, hurting their eyes.

Setting him to stir the fire she found what she could without risking an excursion to the kitchen; some new bread and cream cheese, and half a bottle of sherry, the gift of a grateful patient, which had been opened some days. They took it on the rug by the fire, sharing the same plate and glass, for these would be found in the morning. They both did excellently by the first slice, and stuck, with hopeless finality, half-way through the second.

'Oh, Julian, try. We can't leave two separate half-eaten bits. You must have more room than me. I shall have to, if you don't.'

'You're not very resourceful, are you?' He picked up both pieces, deposited them in the middle of the reviving fire, and raked them over.

'Darling, what an awful thing to do. Burning bread. When I was little, I'd have been beaten for that.'

'Why is it awful? Everybody ought to waste things who can afford to. It keeps down unemployment. It's only a race-memory, or something, that makes people feel it's bad.'

'I suppose so.' But through the after-sound of his careless voice she had heard another, awfully outraged, and armed with power: 'Miss Hilary! The very next time I see you do such a wicked thing, straight to your father you go. With those poor sailors getting torpedoed to bring it here. Helping the Kaiser, that's what you're doing. A big girl like you that can read the papers, I wonder you're not ashamed.' She had been very much ashamed, for she had been big enough to read all the papers, and to be beginning algebra; too big for Nannie's jurisdiction, except that she was the last. There was no need of algebra just now; a little simple subtraction yielded the date quite easily; it was the year in which he must have been born.

'Finish the sherry, anyhow,' she said. 'That glass is yours.'

He lifted it slowly, looking at her across it. In spite of his disfigured face, the look succeeded, in its way, in being a minor masterpiece. It contained, beside what was simple and obvious, all those half-tones most apt to move, or flatteringly disturb; warning, appeal, challenge, forgiving reproach. He was quite unself-conscious, and very much in earnest. It gave her a feeling as if her bones were loosely joined and not quite solid, which David's well-rehearsed addresses had never once achieved. She looked down at her empty plate, feeling that he still looked at her, and thinking, Next time he does that, he'll do it knowing it works.

'Shall we wash up now?' Only a few minutes ago surely he would have been asking this with a certain anxiety to learn her wishes in the matter. But now he had whispered it, with his mouth just touching her ear. She experienced, for a moment, the kind of feeling the Arabian fisherman must have had, when the first cloudy coils of geni began to float from the unstoppered bottle. 'We needn't,' she said.

'Good.' The whisper ended in an eloquent little kiss. He got up and put the things on the sideboard; looking round, she saw him standing there, trying to seem at ease and waiting for her to say or do something.

'Have a cigarette by the fire. I won't be long.' It had not occurred to her till now that the prospect of stage-managing everything herself would be so unnerving, or even that she had never had to do it before.

He took the cigarette, drew on it, and asked, 'About how long?' with careful offhandedness, tipping non-existent ash into the fire.

'Another cigarette after that one.' She had chosen the first decisive-sounding remark that came into her head. To cover an absurd sense of approaching panic, she reached for the bookshelf, said, 'There's a new *Punch* here, have you seen it?' and pushed it into his hand.

'Thank you,' he said blankly. She felt the last props of her self-possession crumbling, and, before it should become hopelessly apparent, turned to switch on the staircase light. A voice behind her, soft and caressingly amused, said, 'I like you when you're silly.'

She paused with her hand on the switch. In addition to the

253

emotions she had accumulated already, she suddenly felt a fool; much as a provincial music-teacher might if a young Menuhin presented himself, respectfully, for introductory violin lessons. She was invaded, without warning or comprehension, by an impulse to hurt; a compound of self-protection, of pride, perhaps of jealousy, feeding on the empty air of the future. It made her begin to go up the stairs without answering; but the flicker of cruelty died in the moment that she became aware of it, and she turned to smile. He was standing with an elbow on the mantelpiece and *Punch* in his hand, an anxious questioning already in his face. The light returned to it as she watched. It was a terrible thing to mix with love, this sense of absolute, yet tremblingly precarious power. She said, 'You won't lose your way. The stairs only lead up to me.'

Upstairs, she prepared for a hasty tidying of her room and was astonished to find it impeccably neat. She herself must have done it, before going out. If it had been a presentiment, she thought, it had been a singularly ineffectual one; it had instructed her in nothing, except to cover a jar and powder-box and put a pair of discarded stockings away. And even about this she was smitten with sudden doubts; perhaps the successful thing would be to have stockings heaped in every corner, cast petticoats, a powder-puff adrift, a mysterious profusion of female impedimenta. Perhaps he would like that. But clutter had always got on her nerves like dust; and she dared not lose hold on herself; she was too uncertain of it already.

Standing before the long glass, and brushing back her hair into its thick waves, she remembered David telling her that he could never make up his mind whether she wore the wrong clothes, or whether she was simply a type who shouldn't wear any. She had a French torso, he had decided, and English legs.

In the acute stage-fright which had descended on her, she found herself turning up his memory simply for reference, so little it had become. With him it had been as easy and, it had seemed, as spontaneous as sliding down a chute. There had not been anything clearly recognisable as a moment of decision. As with other kinds of highly trained performance, it had seemed so simple, so obviously the thing, that it had taught her nothing at all. Now, when he meant no more to her than any other demonstrator in a specialised subject, she felt she was appreciating him for the first time. Left to herself, what a portentous business she had made of it! She imagined Julian below, solemnly regulating his second cigarette to an average rate of combustion; and felt herself shaken by a giggle which she stifled hastily, having caught in it the first vibrations of hysteria.

She was actually shivering all over. Perhaps it was only the chilly air after the fire downstairs. Better get into bed. But she was out again next moment, having decided to put a nightdress on. It had some confused association in her mind with having received a proposal; with trousseaux, perhaps. At all events, it seemed suddenly indispensable. She unearthed from its tissue paper the gift of an extravagant friend (who must, she had thought at the time, have decided to smarten her up), a deep emerald ninon, fine enough to go through a ring. She had never worn it, but remembered thinking that it would help to raise her morale if she were ever ill. Slipping it on she found the filmy warmth of the silk comforting, and decided that it would do. The cold of the sheets made her shiver again. She remembered what Julian had said about waiting for an entrance-call, and decided that it served her right. She could have spared him this business of crisis and declaration and ceremonious surrender. This left her where she had started, still overlooking the simple platitude that a first lover helps very little, if at all, towards dealing with a first beloved.

Through the stillness of the sleeping house a small sound reached her. It was the click of the light-switch in the room below, as Julian turned it off.

She gave a last swift look round the room. The curtains were open, for the house was isolated and screened by trees; an ice-white moon hung outside, so bright that even through the golden pool of the bedside lamp she could see its pale square slanting across the floor. His footsteps, quiet and light and unhesitating, were half-way up the stairs. In a blank impulse she leaned over to the table and put out the light.

The door opened softly. He stood there, finding his bearings, silhouetted blackly against the glimmer on the staircase, his hand on the switch at the top; standing easily and well, a little too well, a little better than life, as if he were gathering himself together for an entrance from the wings. The light went out, and the door closed. She could not see him now, because the moon was in her eyes. For a little while she could not see anything but the moon; she did not know, seeing herself and her surroundings still with the remembering eye of commonplace, how the shadows and straight lines of light had changed it to a dim green cavern, whose walls were broken by slender stalactites of white rock; how dark the red of her hair seemed in the blue light, like the dark-red stains that stripe the walls of the limestone caves; or that her gown had the look of green water flowing in half-transparent streams from her shoulders over her breasts. She had been trained out of fantasies, and the eyes she widened against the silvery dazzle were for her only the instruments of understanding and of sight. She leaned on her elbow and stretched out her other arm to meet him; and he came over to her slowly, and knelt on the floor beside her and looked up into her face. All her anxious anticipations slid from her like a cloud. She bent and took his head in her arms, and knew that she was completing none of to-night's embraces, but another, strange and haunted and brutally cut off, begun with fear and incantation in the dark. She had wasted her forethought and her care, for his dream was stronger than her wisdom. She had nothing to bring him but what he would ask of her, no knowledge that he would not have given her, no aim and no desire except to clothe his lonely imagination in the substance of love.

As she bent to him and saw his face, white and transformed in the moonlight, flung back in an unbreathing stillness for her kiss, she felt the weight of magic and of legend thrown on her so heavily that she dared not speak. This was not like the kisses he had given her, violent and bewildered; this he waited for her to give, and received it as if it had the power to put a soul into his body. She felt as though it were taking the soul from her own, and was afraid; but the power of the dream held her silent; she could only comfort him in her arms, while, rapt and trembling, he contended with his mystery. It was as if in the kiss she had entered it with him; as if she became, even to her-self, an ageless source, a shelter and a benediction. He seemed to her, in the dream, the dear creation of her own pain and love, and she forgot that it was by him she had been created. 'Come in, my dearest,' she said. 'Come in out of the cold.'

So she yielded the gifts of her divinity and was content. Indeed there is much to be said for an apotheosis; for a deity can receive into grace the most unpractised worshipper and lose nothing of her heaven, while for a woman in love, even for a reasonable woman, it is difficult not to expect too much.

13

It was the dead hour before dawn, and black dark, for the moon had set and the stars clouded over. Hilary stretched out a hand to the little luminous alarm clock on the table, and moved the lever over to 'silent'. It would be due to strike in five minutes. To reach it she had to slide from under stray, overlapping parts of Julian, of which there seemed a good many, all rather heavy; she could have deduced by now, without other evidence, that he had been used to the undisputed territory of a large bed. Her movement did not wake him. He had only turned twice all night, each time to sleep more profoundly than before.

Once or twice she had dozed fitfully herself; but the hours had streamed through her consciousness like a mood or a dream, without the sense of time. Her first restlessness had not lasted long; for then, while the moon was up, she had been able to see him, and there had been a peacefulness in his sleep so deeply satisfying to the heart that the rest had ceased to be of consequence. She thought that, even if she had been a raw girl, she would never have taken his inexperience for selfishness. She smiled into the darkness; he had blundered along with so much poetry, with an imagination that had made his passionate and unsuspecting ignorance easy to forgive and hard to endure. But afterwards, and all night till now, she had been happier than ever in her life. Now she must rouse him, for here in the country people were up and working with the first light, and he might be seen to leave. She leaned out farther, turning on the soft shaded light, which seemed a crude brilliance certain at once to wake him; but he slept on.

It was a somewhat dilapidated Eros whom the lamp of Psyche revealed. The colour of his eye had deepened to the classic shade, the true black-purple not so often seen in nature as in farce. It was evident that he would not be able to open it at all. She knew already that the strapping above it had come adrift (as he was falling asleep he had smiled to feel her putting it back again), so it was without much surprise that she found he had shed his young blood not only on the pillow, but on her nightgown, her bare shoulder, and her breast. She looked down at him in loving amusement, recalling a chapter in Malory wherein Launcelot, being entertained by Queen Guinevere after a combat, had behaved with the same lack of tact. She wondered whether Launcelot had ever gone visiting with a black eye. She leaned over and rocked his shoulder.

'Julian.'

He made a protesting little noise, puckered his unswollen eyelid, and wriggled down under the sheet. Feeling very unkind, she pulled it away, gave him a shake, and kissed him. He fetched a deep sigh, turned, enveloped her comfortably with himself, and immediately went to sleep again.

'Darling, wake up. It's morning.'

This time she must have stirred up a stiffened strain, for he winced and woke. His blurred sleepy face looked touchingly youthful; he felt at his eye as if he had forgotten why it was not doing him service, before taking her in his arms and kissing her drowsily. She said, 'Yes, my sweet, but you've got to go.'

'What time is it?' He turned his head to peer at the window. Now that the light was on, the glass might have been backed with jet. She felt very unhappy about it herself.

'You mustn't wait till it's light. Listen, the cocks are crowing.'

'They crow practically all night,' said Julian conclusively, and slid down in bed again. She felt rather, desperate, from distrust of her own resolution as much as anything. He had curled round confidingly: she felt the just-evident morning roughness of his cheek against her shoulder, and his soft hair tickling her neck. With weak procrastination she caressed him, nerving herself for another effort; but he saved her the trouble by starting away suddenly and exclaiming with wide-awake dismay, 'When did this happen? My God, have I hurt you? What did I do?'

It took her a moment or two to realise what he was talking about. Feeling the dressing, she decided that what was left of it would see him home. 'It's your own, darling. Don't you remember?'

'Oh, is it? Thank heaven for that. But it's on that lovely green thing, too. I didn't know it was that colour. No, don't move.'

'Look at the clock. It will start to be light in half an hour. You wouldn't like to compromise me, would you?'

'Of course not, I ought to be shot, I'll get up right away . . . Lord, I do feel stiff.'

'Let me look at you . . . Oh, my dear. Stiff! I should think you do.'

'It's all right. They're only on the surface, I'll walk it off.'

'No wonder I thought you'd broken a rib. Let me feel it a minute.'

'Feel them all,' said Julian generously. He lay down again.

'Oh, darling, don't be such an effort, I haven't the strength.'

'I'm going, I swear I am. Five minutes.'

'What you want is another four hours' sleep.'

'Is it? What time can I come to-morrow – to-night, I mean?'

'My dear, anything might happen. I'll ring you up. I don't know.'

'But I can't not see you to-night. I – we haven't talked about anything. How can I go away just not knowing *when* I'll see you again?'

'Lisa will want me to meet her husband. We may sit talking till all hours. I might have a call. I'll ring you up, whatever happens. Late, sometime after eleven.'

'Let's meet somewhere in the day.'

'I shan't have a minute.' She could imagine how she would be looking, after a white night and a morning's work. 'I promise, dear, if it's a human possibility I won't keep you away.'

'You won't decide it's all been rather a pity?'

'Darling, you're just stalling for time.'

'Aren't you going to kiss me more properly, when I'm going away for all this while?'

'That's properly enough. It's getting so late.'

'What's the matter? Don't you care about me as much as you did before?'

He didn't speak that piece very well, she thought; almost anyone could have worked in more pathos than that. She looked up; he smiled quickly, but not quickly enough. His face had been taut with suppressed disquiet. He had meant it. It was more than she could bear.

Feeling turned upon her – surely the first blackleg of all time – the betrayed and outraged eyes of a million female generations, she whispered, 'Yes, darling; more, much more.'

The single cock, the knocker-up of the farm-yard, was singing solo no longer. A surprising number of others seemed to have joined in. There was a faint uncertain twitter of birds from the trees near by. Julian was kissing her forehead. She put up her hand to his shoulder and touched cloth. Dimly she opened her eyes. He was sitting, dressed, on the edge of the bed.

'Well,' he murmured with tender complacency, 'you're a nice one, aren't you?'

The clock, even when she looked a second time, persistently said half-past five.

'After being so efficient and telling me off.' He stroked her hair, adding cheerfully, not to say a little smugly, 'It was a good job one of us stayed awake.'

She was so sleepy that it was not till three hours later, in the middle of a solitary breakfast, that she started to laugh.

There was plenty to think about that morning, including work; the concentration demanded by the last seemed, to-day, painfully unnatural exercise. On the homeward drive her mind reverted to personal matters, from the fresh and more practical standpoint belonging to the hour. Thus preoccupied, she nearly walked through Rupert Clare in the garden, like a ghost walking through a wall. Later she realised that this was a normal tendency of preoccupied persons, which Rupert had been at no pains to discourage.

If she had had time lately to build up expectations, she would have found this first sight dismally disappointing. He converged on the front door with her, a slight, neutral-tinted, insignificant man of forty-odd, with a narrow head and lines under his eyes, who looked at her with that air of reserving judgement which clings as an unconscious habit to people who have had to live guardedly. Hilary found it a little repelling. They introduced themselves conventionally and made dim, well-meant conversation, during which she had the feeling that he was taking advantage of her less attentive moments to make mental notes; as indeed, out of ingrained training and routine, he was. It affected her like suspicion. Having disinterred his holiday tweeds, he smelt overpoweringly of moth-ball; his Norfolk jacket, which looked anything up to twenty years old, went incongruously with his very urban and unrevealing face. He asked her, with colourless politeness, what work she had been doing before she came here; she told him, thinking about Julian with half her mind.

'I shouldn't think the adjustments were very easy at first?'

He looked no different, except that he had fixed his small dark-brown eyes on hers; but, as if he had unobtrusively turned on an electric switch in himself, it suddenly seemed that she had been asked a considerable question, that her answer and all her views were important, and must be fitly presented to an appreciative but critical eye. When she ran down he was always on the spot with some economical remark just calculated to start her off again. She was in the midst of explaining Sanderson when, for no discoverable reason, she thought: He knows I've got a lover. At which point, as if he had felt a caution she had hardly had time to register, he started to talk himself, about the medical services in Russia. Tired as she was, he held her attention; but what interested her still more was something underlying the pains he was taking, a kind of signal of goodwill made as it were from a distance through a small window, which seemed to be saying, Don't suppose that I don't like or approve of you, simply because I come no nearer; you must excuse me, I don't go out very much. It was not till his attention flagged for the first time from what he was saying, that she saw Lisa in the doorway, come to announce lunch.

He only looked at her for a moment, before standing aside, with one of his rather stiff little gestures, to let Hilary precede him; his undistinguished face underwent no sharp transformation; it was only that in this brief glance she seemed to see, without other information, the texture of his life, seamed together with dirty Continental railways and makeshift hotels: people who must be watched, and made to like or ignore it, insufferable people who must not be antagonised, repugnant people who must be made confidential, pleasant people with whom it would be indiscreet to be seen, rivals likeable or not, with whom in either case he could not relax, editors who rejected unpalatable facts he had sweated for weeks to prove, or who had bullied him to prove palatable fictions, women with access to information who had to be flattered, women who had found a commercial asset in his loneliness.

When she came in at the end of the afternoon they were sitting placidly by the fire, and begged her, with a kind of lazy sincerity, to come and talk. They so evidently meant this, that she stayed for nearly an hour; they accepted her into their private world as people who are a little drunk welcome strangers into the circle of their geniality. Their reaction was complete, the initial fizz had subsided, the surface was still. She could, she thought, have spent most of the evening with them without feeling that her presence was causing them the least embarrassment. In fact, however, she retired to her room, feeling the need of a little sleep.

Going down to dinner she passed the wide-open door of Lisa's empty room. She would scarcely have known it, with the half-unpacked suit-case on the floor, the clothes flung over the chairs, the brief-case with typescript sliding out of it, the smell of Gaulois Jaune. It looked camped-in, like lodgings in which people are not staying long; like a score of rooms they must both have remembered.

Hilary need not have feared for her chances of privacy that evening. By ten-thirty the house was as still as a school after lights-out.

She sat fingering the telephone uncertainly, her mind set free again for her own self-questionings and doubts, and filled with a renewed sense of guilt about Lisa. With whatever conviction she might say she regarded herself as a legalised mistress, the fact remained that she was a respectable married woman with a correct establishment, and Hilary was making what most people would think an inexcusable use of her house. Lisa ought to be told, in general if not in particular. But there had been no opportunity; and Julian had had his promise. Principle, as well as a strange sensation like a warm shiver in her bones, told her that promises must be kept. She picked up the receiver. The promptness of the reply was such that she could only suppose Julian had been sitting with the instrument on his knees.

Half an hour later he was in her room. When she emerged from his arms she was aware of the cool, sharp smell of narcissus, and found he had laid a sheaf on the pillow beside her. She lifted it to her face, looking at him helplessly through its white stars.

'Do you like them?' he asked, slipping his arm round her waist. 'You look as if there were something funny about it.'

'My dearest, they're lovely, but in a way there is. I mean, it's rather arresting to go into someone's room in the morning and find it full of flowers that weren't there the night before. But perhaps they'll only think I walk in my sleep.'

'Oh, Lord, would you think anyone could be so dumb?' He

was completely dashed. His black eye – which was no better, except that the swelling had begun to go down – made his expression rather comic, but Hilary felt no impulse to laugh. She put down the flowers and kissed him.

'It's all right,' he assured her, 'I'll take them back when I go. I'll make a point of remembering.'

'Of course you shan't. I was only being feebly funny, darling. Lisa doesn't notice things. They're my favourite flowers. Let's put them here in the water-jug, so that I can smell them all night.'

'I'd have brought you something better, but I was seeing too lop-sidedly to drive into town.'

'I should think not. How are you? How have you fed yourself, is the cut all right?'

'Oh, fine. I slept all afternoon and half the evening. I feel terrific. And you, my beautiful?'

'Terrific,' murmured Hilary, with such breath as was not being compressed out of her. She tried to remember what it felt like to be so full of surplus energy at the end of a long day.

'What a marvellous dressing-gown. You do have nice things. And always right with the lighting. That green thing would have looked rather immense under strong blues, come to think of it. Is it all right? Let's look.'

'It's not dry enough yet to wear.'

'Oh, too bad. What are you ...' The sentence remained, rather abruptly, incomplete.

'You've given me doubts now,' she murmured, 'about the lighting.'

'They're quite unnecessary,' said Julian softly.

He had pulled off his jacket when he paused, as if remembering something, and rummaged in the pockets. 'Just a minute, before I forget.' He produced a length of twine, which he tied, with careful precision, round the third finger of her left hand. 'To-morrow,' he remarked, 'I shall be able to get around a bit.'

'Darling, what on earth do you . . .' The words trailed away. It was absurd to feel frightened.

'Forget it,' said Julian airily, withdrawing the string and pocketing it. 'Just an experiment of mine.'

She caught at his arm as he was moving away again, and pulled him back to her. He sat down on the edge of the bed, with an indulgent little smile. Behind it she saw a swift gathering of his resources, a resolution hardened by fear. She smiled back, feeling her own pretence as thin as his. 'What have you been up to? You don't move from here until you tell me.'

'I don't have to move.' He grinned at her defiantly, and undid his shoes with his free hand.

'Darling, this isn't funny. What did you mean just now?'

'We'll talk about that in the morning.' He kissed her swiftly. He was doing it, already, alarmingly well.

'We'll talk now,' she said.

She had been sure of her power in the last resort; the obedience with which he let her go made her unhappy, so she smiled at him again. 'Come along,' she said, 'let's have it.'

'You've had it already.' His gaiety had an increasing quality of desperation. 'We had all that out last evening.' She did not reply, but waited, looking at him. 'It's all right. I haven't had it put in *The Times*. I've only written it out to send to-morrow.'

'Darling, could you be serious for a moment?'

'If you're afraid of the padre thinking you beat me into submission, don't worry. I can work over the eye all right; I had to do it once for another chap. He went to a dance and got away with it. How soon? Three days?'

She laughed a little, and patted his cheek. 'You'll go far, my dear, I always said so.'

He caught her wrists in both hands. It became impossible to laugh any longer.

'Stop fooling with me. You know I mean every word I say.'

'See, dear, let's not lose our heads; I could too, but we can't both. Give me a kiss and stop talking nonsense.'

'Nonsense? I asked you if you loved me, you said yes, you – let me come here. I asked you to marry me when I asked you that.'

'I know you offered to, darling, and I know you meant it. It was very sweet of you.'

'I *offered* to? My God, what do you mean, I offered to?' He stared at her; the set of his face made her more frightened than before. 'Would you be kind enough never to say a thing like that to me again?'

'Is it such a dreadful thing to say? So you did.'

'You've no right to talk about yourself like that ... How do you suppose I think about you? You must have known, or you wouldn't ...'

'I knew you loved me. And that I loved you.' She searched her mind desperately for the right words. 'Marriage is just a way of telling the world. It's an arrangement, that's all; but it's a complicated one; you can't—'

'It's only complicated if you make it. Look at the way people did it in the last war ...' His face deadened suddenly, as if his words had just overtaken his mind and deeply shocked him. He jerked himself into speech again. 'I ought to have told you this, of course, I didn't think I'm afraid, but I'd have about eleven hundred a year, clear of – of everything. I'm sorry if that's less than you've been making yourself, it probably is; but after I get started we'll do better, I hope.'

She clutched at the floating pretext he had allowed to drift in her way. 'You're not suggesting I should give up my work? It means as much to me as acting does to you.' As she spoke she realised, with a muffled astonishment, that this statement had become wholly untrue.

'Not if you don't want to. I just wondered whether you thought I was expecting you to keep me. Some of your ideas about me have been taking me rather by surprise.'

'Dear, please.' The fact which she had been trying to suppress from her consciousness, that she was really very tired, became evident to her. The light made her eyes ache; she shut them, to think better.

'Oh, God, I'm sorry. Hilary, look at me. I didn't mean it, I swear ...'

She opened her eyes again; already she had forgotten the almost involuntary gesture. Bewildered, moved, and shocked by his face, she leaned out and embraced him. 'What is it? I was only thinking what to say. Don't look as if I'd killed you. What is it? I don't understand.'

'Will you kiss me?' he said slowly, at last.

'Here ... What *was* the matter with you then?'

'You looked at me the way people do when they're – sort of rubbing you out.'

'Don't be so silly again.'

'You can't know if people will always be the same. Why won't you marry me, then?'

She took a deep breath, ashamed that it should be so difficult. 'You're not being very tactful, are you, my dear? You must know why.'

He said nothing. He simply waited. His face had a dumb dread which was, strangely, as formless as it was poignant. He looked like someone who has cut the ace of spades some long time back and is expecting now to learn its significance.

She went on, 'You're twenty-four, aren't you? How old do you imagine I am? The truth, I mean.'

He sat back with a kind of gasp. She recognised it as a sound of sheer exasperation. He looked as if she had confessed to having tormented him with a thoughtless hoax.

'Oh, really, this is *too* ridiculous. Good Lord, I thought it was ... I don't know what. What is this, one of those games where you win the cake if you guess the number of currants? I've never thought. Did you read medicine at Oxford, or start after?'

'After. But don't sidetrack.'

'I'm not, I'm working out the length of your training. You had a year or two at home, first, and you've practised since, I'm not sure how long. I suppose the answer is somewhere between thirty-two and thirty-five. So what?' He looked at her impatiently and a little crossly. His beautifully inflected voice made the vulgarism at the end sound queer.

'I'm just eleven years older than you are. Think for a minute, Julian. You'll be thirty-five yourself one day, unlikely as it may seem to you now. As men go, still quite a young man. And I shall be forty-six. Use your imagination.'

He smiled a little, rather to himself than at her, and studied her a moment, with his head on one side.

'I have,' he said, 'long before now.'

He put up his hand and she felt his fingers travel, with sureness and great delicacy, over the contours of her face. There was an authority in his touch which impressed her as it might have done in a man of her own calling.

'Yes.' He nodded his head. 'One can't help it,' he said quite simply, 'if one plays about with make-up at all. With a face that interests one, one works it out instinctively. I forgot till you reminded me. If I had the box of tricks handy I could show you within, say, twenty minutes, what you'll look like ten, and twenty, and thirty years from now.'

'Don't,' she said, with an involuntary shiver.

'Why not? I love you, and it's part of you just as your childhood is.'

'It's – rather cold-blooded.'

'You really are a bit unreasonable, aren't you?' he complained with patient perplexity. 'If you'll just tell me what reaction you *would* consider good form, I'll sit down with my head in my hands and try to work it up.'

It was like wandering on a moor, she thought in bewilderment; one felt one's way, precariously, over so much uncertain, quaggy ground, and then, with no warning, felt one's foot on granite.

'I know how you feel,' she said. 'When I was twenty-four I could have staked anything you liked to name that what I wanted and believed then I would for ever. But if I had to be married now to the sort of man I'd have chosen then, I'd jump out of the window. Don't you see, in ten years you'll be literally a different person; all the cells of one's body change in seven. It's like making promises for a son of yours who isn't born.'

'We'll leave my sons out of it, for the moment.' There was something hostile in his voice, which disturbed her.

'What I'm trying to say is that I'm not thinking only about you. You might have grown on me, by the time you grew out of me. I should be getting to the age when habits begin to form.'

'Do you mean that?' he asked slowly.

'Every word.'

'God bless you, darling.' He rolled over on the counterpane beside her, and put his head in her lap. 'What a perfect thing to say.' He sighed luxuriously. 'So comfortable and warm. Say it again.'

'Oh, Julian, I could hit you.' Her courage had somehow to be kept up. 'You haven't listened to a word.'

'I have. How queer it is that after all this you don't know how I feel. It always surprises me, you know, if ever you don't see through me like glass. Of course I shall change. One changes all the time. But not about you. I – I recognised you, from the beginning. Don't ask me what I mean, it's too hard to explain. I knew you, that's all. Like a gipsy who comes to a house and sees the patteran on the door.'

A rather equivocal simile, she thought, finding it safer to think than feel. Why not follow this pointer too; then everything would be said. She could not see his face, only his dark, tumbled hair with which she had abstractedly been playing. 'Darling, do you know what a patteran is? It's a sign left by another gipsy who's been there before.'

Lazily and without moving, he said, 'I didn't mean that.'

'I expect not. But it's true.'

She could tell by the feel of his head and shoulders, which were still quite relaxed, that at least she had not shocked him. Presently he reached up and took her hand. It was the kind of gesture people make who feel they should be saying something. She reproached herself for her clumsiness in underlining what, after all, he had intelligence enough to have guessed. He did not speak for some time, but played aimlessly with her fingers. Presently he said, awkwardly, 'Were you much in love with him?'

'I thought so, of course.'

'Of course. Sorry. Silly thing to ask.'

'Not so silly. I used to ask myself. But I thought it was sentimental and unmodern to want too much.'

'Too much what?' he asked, with a directness that astonished her.

She found herself desperately embarrassed for a reply; a queer little sidelight on her acquired mental habits. If David's shortcomings had been intimately physical, she could have schooled herself to say so sensibly; whereas, now, under the effort of speech she was blushing deeply and could only just manage her voice.

'Well, it's hard to put intelligently. I mean, in a way that doesn't sound like a housemaid just back from the cinema. Imagination, I suppose. Lightheadedness, poetry, if you like . . . Oh, I don't know.'

'In fact,' said Julian, 'love?'

He turned himself over to look at her. There was nothing in his face but a great and tentative hope.

She could not answer him. He put both arms round her waist; his cheek made a gentle coaxing movement against her side.

'Did you ever care about him as much as you do about me?'

She drew him closer. The answer was so easy; and yet, as if remembered from a long time ago, she had a bewildering inhibition against it, a feeling of having once been taught, by example, the right thing to say. Drifting memories came with it; the feeling of recent tears, of a sense of desperate insecurity, which had somehow to be comforted, of warm stiff silk against her face and a little round button that had pressed against her forehead. ' . . . Do you love me? More than Pussy? More than Auntie May?' And then with bated breath, 'More than Pauline?' And the voice of divine justice, quietly rebuking, 'No. Hilary and Pauline are both my dear little girls. I love you both exactly the same.'

She paid no real attention to the memory; it seemed part of the mere flotsam which meanders through the mind; but it left behind it a deep eddy, a sense of awe and wonder. It was as if a voice whispered, 'Command that these stones be made bread,' and one felt the power, but the voice might be from heaven or hell. She closed her eyes, and took the power from its unknown source.

'I never loved him.' With dreamlike certainty, as if they had waited in her for thirty intervening years, she came to the words which, in that already lost remembrance, the divine justice had refused. 'I love you better than anyone, ever. Better than anyone in the world.'

He did not answer. There is no answer, as she had understood.

Presently he pulled her down to him and kissed her. It was a kiss that simulated physical passion, a kind of cipher for what could not be said.

'You had a narrow escape from marrying him, I suppose.'

Not long since she would have taken a pride in not being ashamed to say, 'Hardly, because he never asked me.' She had been very proud of her honesty, and, it now seemed, of a number of other selfish and tiresome things. 'I should never have married him,' she said, 'when it came to the point.'

'Well, now it's come to the point again ... No, listen, please, you must.' In the urgency of the moment he silenced her first half-uttered word by the simple expedient of shoving his hand across her mouth. 'I'm sorry I'm not older if it bothers you, but there it is and here we are, so why keep on about it? Obviously, we have to get married sometime. Let's make it now. Straightaway, this week. It's better we should, I know it is, I was never so sure of anything in my life. If not' – he was sufficiently intent by now to allow Hilary, who felt on the point of suffocation, to get his hand away – 'we shall get tied up and involved in things, or something will happen ... Something ... Let's get it fixed. If I'm sure of you I can do anything, I've always known that. Things I – I used to think before that I couldn't do, I can do them for you. Will you?

Please. There's nothing in the world to stop us, except ourselves.'

'Please, darling, could you not lean on my collar-bone quite so hard? It's rather confusing.'

'Sorry. Will you marry me this week-end?'

'No, dearest.'

'Why not?'

'For one thing, because everyone would say we had to. What else could they think?'

'Oh, God. I never thought of that.'

'For a woman, you know, it is a consideration.'

'Of course. I'm sorry, it just didn't occur to me. Well, then, let's get officially engaged and put the announcement in. And we'll get married in three months. Will that do?'

'Julian, dear, why must we be so violent and drastic? Can't we stay as we are a little longer, and have time to breathe?'

He let go of her, and propping himself on his elbows, stared into her eyes. His unhappiness, which was very real, was turned by the face that expressed it into a tragic effect much too good to be true.

At last he said, 'You've told me you love me; so I think I've a right to know what it is that makes you feel I'm not to be trusted. Would you mind telling me? I've – got a good reason for asking.'

'But of course I trust you.'

'That can't be true. Tell me.'

She stroked the hair back from his forehead. His face was almost in profile to her on its unhurt side; and now, because her mind had been preoccupied, she saw him freshly, and the words she had been about to say deserted her. She felt in his sudden stillness the certainty of communicated desire; but when he moved, it was to put her wrist abruptly aside.

275

'Yes?' he said roughly. 'Well?'

She had never imagined a rebuff from him. She could not remember what it was she had been going to say.

'Do you really think I've so little control that I'd put myself in a situation like this with someone I didn't trust?'

'Trust for what? Not to boast about it in a pub? That doesn't get us very far, does it?' He had propped his chin in his hands and was staring, obstinately, straight in front of him. 'Something about me makes you think I'm not reliable. I want to know what it is.'

'You're certain it's you,' she said softly, 'that I daren't trust?'

He drew a sharp little breath and, turning to her slowly, embraced her, elaborately, at some length, and with unforeseen skill. When he lifted his head from kissing her he said, with a defensive bitterness that made him for a moment look five years older, 'Well, I may as well make the most of what you're willing to give me, I suppose.'

After all, she thought, what else had she asked for? Perhaps her remorse showed in her face, for she saw a new hope in his. She wondered if he knew how successful his essay had been; it took her a little while to collect herself.

'That isn't fair,' she said. 'It's not you I'm afraid of, it's time, and change, and life; the things that we can't control.' He smiled a little shamefacedly, and said without looking at her, 'Isn't it a bit late to be worrying about those, in this year of grace?'

Her heart turned over; not at the words alone, but at the universal, the contemporary inflection, the air of having made an allusion in admittedly doubtful taste. As their grandfathers would have shied at a sexual innuendo, so these, with circumspection and apology and a sense of bad form, touched if they must on their daily shortening expectation of maturity. There

276

seemed very little to say. He seemed suddenly removed across an invisible gulf; even to kiss him now would be tinged with insult, as if he had asked for pity.

She said at last, 'How much do you think yourself that ought to count?'

'Not at all.' He spoke with sudden force. 'Nobody knows that better than I do ... But I'm still asking you to marry me.'

Suddenly she knew what she ought to have said all along.

'Listen, then, my dear. Don't mind this; it isn't personal, it's just the way things are. Try to see it for a moment not as we do, but as everyone else will. The fact that you're so much younger, by itself, we could probably get away with, if you'd had a chance to get about at all, and meet other women, and get started in a career. But if we announce ourselves now, don't you see how it will seem? When you're only just down from Oxford, you come to me as a patient, and I get my claws in you. I'm not even your family doctor, but I take good care you don't slip away. Before you've had time to turn round, I pin you down and marry you. No, be quiet, darling; I've listened to you, haven't I? I know it's not pretty, but I've heard it said with much less excuse than I'd be giving. They'd go on saying it, too, for most of our lives. You may think me a coward; I expect I am one. But it weighs with me.'

'I think you mean,' he said slowly, 'that the remedy's up to me.'

'Yes; that's what I mean.'

He had gone rather white, but he met her eyes squarely.

'How long do you give me?'

'Would a year be fair?'

'Yes, a year's fair enough. Not to get anywhere, of course, but to know whether one will. You don't expect to see me in the West End by then?'

'I don't expect anything, I don't know enough about it. You'll be able to tell.'

'All right. That's settled then.' He sat up and swung himself off the edge of the bed. She felt cold from his absence, and with sudden fear.

'Julian. Where are you going?'

'Nowhere. You don't want me in bed with my clothes on do you?'

He removed them, in silence, and came back. Now, as often before, she felt her mind reaching out to another impenetrably concealed from her by a disguise too splendid to have any relation to the real. When he put out the light she felt only relief, as if some barrier between them had been broken down.

'Darling, are you angry with me?' she whispered.

'No. I knew it was coming. I know you so well.'

'But you hoped it wouldn't.'

'I'm not sure even of that. They say "the good is the enemy of the best", don't they?'

'You think it is the best?'

'Yes.'

'Will you forgive me, afterwards?'

'Tell me what you told me before.'

'I love you.'

'Go on,' he prompted, so low that she could scarcely hear.

'Better than anyone in the world, always.'

Now, in the darkness, he had lost the fear of self-betrayal, and she of her perilous invocation. In the end it was not only his imagination but her own which was stilled by its enchantment, so that she forgot they had talked of everything but what lay closest to the centre of both their thoughts.

14

'It's very medieval, isn't it,' said Julian, 'all this leaving at dawn. We only want someone with a lute under the window, playing an aubade, with one foot on the end of the rope ladder. "Busie old foole, unrulie Sunne . . ."' He stretched, magnificently, before seeking his clothes.

Hilary watched him from the bed. She had almost slept through the alarm, and her eyes felt tight round the edges. He moved about the room already as if he lived there, and, when he was ready, made unerringly for her hair brush. She had found a black strand in it yesterday, luckily before Annie came to dust. His lazy vitality made her feel dim and blurred; at what age, she wondered, did one lose the urge to quote Donne at five in the morning? They had not slept till nearly two. The prospect of a day's work frankly appalled her. She had been loath to let him go chiefly out of reluctance to be disturbed, for he had already acquired the knack of being comfortable in a confined space, and her back, round which he had neatly fitted himself for sleep, felt draughty and unprotected. She pulled down the end of the pillow into the gap, thinking that in a moment or two, when he had gone, she would get off to sleep again. When he came back to the bed to kiss her goodbye she wished he would not make such a business of it, letting in the draught she had just excluded. But she kissed him tenderly; partly because she felt tenderly disposed, partly because he looked in the mood to persist till he got a response that he considered adequate. He was a romantic young man, and was fast developing an opinionated sense of style; in moments of passion he was much more manageable than when he had made up his mind to a suitable gesture. On such occasions one became suddenly aware of latent standards of criticism. She allowed him, without protest, to scoop her out of her warm place and drape her into a beautiful and touching pose of farewell.

'Don't bother to ring me to-night,' he said, 'it's a nuisance for you. I'll just come along about twelve. If there are any lights still on, I'll wait. I won't let anyone see me.'

'Ring you . . . ? Oh, my dear, I *don't* think you can come to-night again.'

'Why not?' asked Julian. He sounded not so much injured as amazed.

She leaned back on his arm and shoulder, still in the tragic attitude in which he had so sincerely arranged her – like Cleopatra on the morning of Actium, remarked her reluctantly waking brain – and tried to think of an answer that would harmonise. No really truthful one did. 'We might be found,' she murmured. 'Someone might come for me. I'm expecting to be sent for to-night.' This was just possible if several chances, all very unlikely, should all happen to coincide.

'Oh, God. You never told me. Two days and a whole night.' He gathered her up into an embrace which was like a sculptural symbol of despair. It made her feel very paltry and inadequate. She kissed him again; in any case, by now she was broad awake. 'I'll tell you what,' he said with new inspiration, 'I'll wait in the garden and watch till you come in.'

'Darling, I could never keep my mind on what I was doing. I should think about you all the time. I might kill somebody.' These picturesque possibilities became quite real to her as she spoke: reflecting on this later, she recalled the hero of *High Barbary* getting hypnotically inside his part. It ended with her promising to meet him at Pascoe's farm to-morrow afternoon, and go riding. By the time this tryst had been plighted in accordance with Julian's sense of fitness, she felt as wide-awake as the birds. She was, in fact, for the first time alert to the sound of his car starting up, twenty minutes later, a quarter of a mile or so away. It seemed to her an alarmingly penetrating noise; she wondered how many other people had heard it too.

In the morning she spurred herself through her work with the promise of an early night; but in the evening, instead of relief, the falling spirits that went with weariness filled her with images of loneliness and transience, till she caught herself thinking, supposing he were to die to-morrow, and I might have seen him to-night. None the less, when night came she slept for nine unbroken hours, not even disturbed by her unat-tempted sounding of Lisa, who had been separable from Rupert only during the intervals when he went to wash his hands.

Saturday was fresh, bright, and blowing. Hilary tried on and pressed her long-neglected riding things, felt satisfied with the result, and went downstairs too full of spirits to anticipate the obvious until the moment when it happened.

'Well!' said Lisa, coming into the hall with Rupert at her heels. 'Of all the dark horses. You've been here all this while and never told me you rode. We could have done some hack-ing; I've only lapsed myself for want of stirring up. Rupert, doesn't she look nice?'

'Very nice,' said Rupert accommodatingly, taking his eyes off Lisa just long enough to convey an air of considered judgement.

'Is anyone mounting you, or are you going to The Chestnuts?'

The Chestnuts was an excellent riding-stable, less than a mile away; not merely the obvious, but the only place to go. Hilary gave her crop a careless little flick; too careless, she felt immediately after.

'How absurd we never thought of going together. I only wanted stirring up, too. In fact, I got it the other day quite by accident. I ran into young Fleming – you remember, I saw him when he was thrown last year – and he was very full of having started to ride again. He's supposed to be finding me something at the place where he keeps his own. I've no idea what they've got; I'll let you know.' For an impromptu, it seemed to her not bad. Someone would certainly turn out, later, to have seen them together.

'You're lucky with weather,' Lisa said. 'I suppose they can't have gone away after all, then. The Flemings, I mean.'

This, from Lisa, was far more reassuring than discreet silence; none the less, it caused a certain inward jolt. 'Were they going?' she asked vaguely. 'I see so little of them.'

'Probably not. I never do retain a very clear impression of anything Mrs Fleming says. She always seems somehow to be on the other side of a pane of glass. I think she disapproves of me.'

Hilary suddenly recalled Julian's voice saying, 'I thought they were separated or something.' She turned to look out of the window; with an anxiety to which the radiant sky gave little support. Like most people of her colouring, she blushed with vivid awareness of the fact.

'It'll keep fine,' said Rupert's non-committal voice. 'Speaking for me, last time I was involved with a horse was in France in '17, and when I say involved . . . ' He reminisced, farcically, for several heaven-sent minutes. It was not till she was driving away that she thought of suspecting his imperturbable ease, and imagined the conversation continuing behind her: 'I felt a change of topic might be indicated.' 'Oh, my dear, you *must* be wrong . . . Well, it happens of course, even to quite sensible women. He's very good looking.'

In anything she had contemplated saying to Lisa she had never had the faintest intention of using Julian's name. For one thing her personal code would have demanded that before doing so she should ask his leave; for another . . . yes, she had to admit a reluctance to let Lisa know. She and Rupert, even in their most cruel divergencies, were so wholly adult and broken in to the world. All Lisa's charity would only soften, not alter the picture at the back of her mind. No, it was not possible, now, to say anything to her yet awhile. Concluding thus, and experiencing a relief which disturbed her conscience but raised her spirits a good deal, Hilary dedicated herself to the moment.

She found Julian in the stable-yard, engaged in a sentimental reunion with Biscuit, who saw her first and appeared to inform him of the fact. He swung round, swept her with a respectful adoring glance, and exclaimed, 'My God, you do make me feel a tramp.'

He was certainly very shabby; and, though privately she thought his ribbed sweater and old corduroys became him very well, insisted on explanations. 'Mother got rid of my riding things – in case I should yield to temptation, I suppose. Sent them off in a parcel to the Missions to Seamen, or the Distressed Gentlewomen's Aid, or something suitable. I had to unearth these from the attic. I do hope you don't mind.'

'Your eye's improving,' she remarked when she had reassured him. From a purely technical point of view, it was; but the fading bruise had taken on a sensational variety of shades from red to yellow and green. It would certainly be some days yet before it got back to normal. The cut had healed, more or less, and he had removed the dressing, making it more than ever apparent that at least one stitch would have improved matters. Half of it would be masked by the eyebrow, but it seemed likely that he would carry the other half-inch for years, if not for life. She did not invite trouble by remarking on this; she felt too pleased to see him. The last thirty-six hours had passed slowly for her.

'This looks a nice animal you've found me. What's his name?'

'Hatter.'

'Don't be silly.'

'Well, he answers to Hi, or any loud cry. I call him Hatter. Don't you know your *Alice*! "You might as well say," said the Hatter, "that 'I see what I eat' is the same as 'I eat what I see'." Trouble is he's been out with learners a lot, I'm afraid, and suffers from a hard mouth and chronic boredom. He's got quite a nice action once you get him interested. Would you like Biscuit instead?'

She declined with thanks, not only because Biscuit was much too big for comfort, but because she would not for worlds have foregone the pleasure of seeing them together. After a short battle of wills, Hatter allowed himself to be interested. They took the shortest way up to the unfenced downs.

There was a great broad trackway there, one of those archaic grass-roads which were formed when forest filled the valleys, and beside which the Roman ruler is modern stuff. There was nearly a mile of it. It was glorious. The gorse and bracken streamed away behind; in the far distance the blue wave of Painswick Beacon seemed to ride beside them. Julian eased Biscuit to a canter – all Hatter's ardent emulation could not make his pace – and looked round to smile as she caught him up again. She thought, this is the best moment of my life, I know it now and I shall know it always.

At the end of the track they stopped, glowing and content, to breathe their horses and take a last look at the prospect which trees would presently enclose. After a moment or two Julian said, 'Lord, I shall miss this. Still, you can't have everything.'

'Miss it?' she asked, forgetting what he meant. Hatter, his recovered wind now permitting, plunged down his head and attacked voraciously some vegetable at his feet. Looking at Julian she forgot to remind him of his manners.

'Oh, of course it was yesterday and I haven't seen you. I've composed a beautiful letter to Finnigan; I meant to bring it out with me and post it, but I forgot.'

'Who's he?'

He gazed at her in tolerant affection. 'He runs the Barchester Rep. Don't you remember, he's the chap who saw me do Oberon and offered me a trial?'

'I might have remembered better if you'd ever told me.'

'I always credit you with omniscience. Sorry. If he falls through I *could* try Liebnitz. He made a vague gesture too. But you don't want me to, do you?'

'I don't know. I thought he was something to do with philosophy.'

He laughed so loudly that Biscuit threw up his head as well. 'You *have* kept yourself unspotted from the world, haven't you? This Liebnitz is a Mogul. Celluloid.'

'Oh.'

'That's what I thought, too.'

'When was this?'

'Oh, after *The Dream*. It wasn't the Emperor in person, of course, some minor spy. He came behind to see me with my make-up off, and wanted me to go for a test or something. Of course, it's all right later, when you've had time to learn to act.'

'What did you tell him?'

'Well, that, more or less.' He added, as an afterthought, 'I didn't care much for his way of talking.'

And to-morrow, she thought, he will astonish me again by his humility. She stole a glance at him, sitting straight and easy with his eyes on a gap of distance between the trees; his face had a look which had taken from it everything immature. She never ceased to wonder, whenever she rediscovered in him, amid so much that was unformed and unsure, this vein of hard integrity. It was a thing that touched on her own world; she knew how to respect it.

'Though, mind you,' he was saying, 'I wouldn't say no to a year in a French studio, doing bit parts and messing about on the technical side. That would be education. But if you once get one of these Hollywood reach-me-down personalities hung round your neck . . . No, thanks.'

Feeling sufficiently secure in the moment to risk it, she said, 'So you don't want to grasp at the fallen mantle of Valentino?'

She was pleased by his calm, till after a moment of blankness he asked, 'Valentino? Who's he?'

'I forgot,' she said. 'You wouldn't remember.'

They rode on.

'I'm starving,' he said, 'aren't you? I hope you can eat an enormous tea. Mrs Pascoe does them.'

They ate it in a parlour adorned with crochet antimacassars on red plush, white china fern-baskets, Marcus Stone infants at play, and mass-produced rayon cushions in hideous designs. Julian held her hand under the cloth, with considerable difficulty, because the table was too large, and chiefly, it seemed, for the pleasure of dropping it and simulating polite formality when Mrs Pascoe came in. Afterwards he produced, with some triumph, a case completely full of fresh cigarettes.

'You're improving,' she told him as they got up to move to the plush arm-chairs. 'I wouldn't even put it past you to have matches as well.'

'You underestimate me. I have a lighter.' He put it with the cigarettes beside a china lion on the mantelpiece. 'All in good time.'

'Someone will come in and ask if we want more hot water.' She lifted her face.

He no longer snatched at a kiss, as though he feared that if he gave her time she would think better of it. He had learned to hold her eyes for a moment before he began. 'I don't think I like you in riding things,' he said presently. 'You look so nice and you feel so inaccessible. What time shall I come to-night?'

'I'll ring you up. It's safer that way.'

'I'm sick of being safe. I want everyone to know. Listen; let's go away somewhere. Now, from here.'

'You're crazy. Dressed like this, with no luggage?'

'I've got some money. You could get things on the way. There's a little pub on the Wye, just above Chepstow, Chris and I put up there once. Nobody goes there, this time of the year. Ring up from here and say you won't be back.'

It was only the concreteness of this last that brought her down to earth. 'I couldn't,' she said. 'I've got some ill people.'

'One of the others would see them. Just twenty-four hours, to go on as we are now. One always remembers having wasted things.'

'Would you?' she said. 'With your understudy not warned? Even if it wasn't a very good play?'

He said at once, 'You've got me there. I shouldn't have asked you.'

'I shall be loving you just as much as if I'd gone.'

He thought this over. 'No, you won't. Not that you aren't right. But one ought to keep things distinct. There's no substitute for living.'

She had nothing to say to this, for she had known it when she spoke. He had, as she perceived in moments like this, a capacity for truth, which would ensure that, for every evasion of it, he would always suffer the full penalty. If circumstances did not exact it, he would exact it from himself. It was as if she saw the pattern of his life beginning to form.

On the way out Mrs Pascoe, who was short-sighted (or perhaps the light had been bad) noticed his eye for the first time, and remarked on it with concern. He laughed cheerfully. 'Oh, this? Just a bit of jay-walking in Cheltenham the other day. I stepped out from behind a parked car – silly thing to do – and ran slap into another. It was in reverse, by a bit of luck, and going fairly slowly. I did this on the edge of the kerb. It's nearly better now.'

Mrs Pascoe was interested, for something very similar had happened once to her husband's sister. She went into details. So did Julian. An entire episode, complete down to the ministrations of a mythical Samaritan who had asked him in and patched up the cut for him, sprang circumstantially into life. Hilary was fascinated by his glibness. She noticed that he had remembered the missing stitch, and made the Samaritan an amateur. She herself would have found the half of it beyond her powers; and, if she had attempted it, her extreme of embarrassment would at once have betrayed her.

288

As they were crossing the yard she said, 'That was a very efficient improvisation.'

'Oh, it wasn't improvised. That was the official version of the incident, constructed with great pains. Do you approve?' He might have been speaking of the plan for an afternoon's outing.

'It was most convincing.' She had not lost sight of the fact that it was her own choice which had made this, and much more of it in the future, necessary. Her shrinking seemed rather hypocritical. 'But if you were too much knocked out to feel like travelling, it would seem reasonable to have seen a doctor.'

'I did consider it. But when I woke in the morning I felt so well. I didn't think I ought to bother a doctor . . . much.'

'Shameless creature.' Her disquiet dissolved, as often before, in laughter. 'Well, I'll book you an appointment, and it's more than you deserve. Be careful where you park the car.'

'I shall be the most private patient you ever had.'

'Night calls are very expensive, for private patients.'

'Whatever it costs,' he said slowly, 'it won't be too dear for me.'

She let in the clutch quickly, afraid that someone might have seen their faces from the farm.

Very late that night, when both of them were sleepy, and there seemed nothing that could not be said, she asked him a question.

'When you said once that you recognised me – what did you mean?'

'Oh – I remembered your voice, and the feel of your hand.'

'From the hospital, you mean?'

'Yes.'

'But when I went to you then, you thought you knew me.'

He whispered quickly, 'What did I say?'

'I can't remember. I think, that you wouldn't have minded if you'd known I was there.'

'You told me I hadn't made a fool of myself.' He turned his head away.

'You didn't, darling. You'd been having a bad dream, I think.'

'Did I talk about that too?'

'No ... You surely don't remember it now, do you?'

'No. No, I shouldn't think so.'

'Never mind. But I've have liked to know who it was I reminded you of. You don't think I'd be angry?'

'It isn't that sort of thing.'

His voice, gruff and embarrassed like a boy's, was half smothered in the pillow. She said, 'Go to sleep. I won't keep on at you any more.'

'I never thought of your thinking anything like that.'

'I didn't think what you mean. It doesn't matter. Good night.'

'Don't go to sleep yet.'

'It's terribly late.'

'I always thought somehow that you knew.'

'Sometimes one just talks for the sake of talking.'

'You know really, don't you. It's just a sort of a thing I had. When you're a kid and you're a good bit on your own ...'

She leaned down; it was her own face she was trying to hide, though the light was out.

' ... but when one reaches years of discretion one ought to pack that sort of thing up.'

'Everybody has things. Of course they do.'

'You're crying.'

'I love you so much.'

It was a little while before either of them spoke again. Then he said, 'I'll tell you something. I was afraid to before.'

'Why?'

'Well, because it's rather done-before. It's a thing people say. I thought you might not believe it, and if you hadn't it would all have seemed so sordid, it would have spoiled things, I thought.'

'You know I'd always have believed you.'

'You say that because you don't know what it is.'

'It can be anything.'

'You see, what I kept thinking was, probably this other man told you the same. Sure to have. He would. I mean, that he'd – never had anyone before you. And then you found out it wasn't true. Well ... this time it is. That's all.'

She thought it was laughter she was holding back, till her eyes ran over again. As soon as she could, she said, 'Darling, you ought to have known I'd have believed anything you told me, even that.'

'I don't think you guessed, did you?'

'How could I have done?'

'I never wanted anyone before. Not enough for it to seem worth doing anything about. I thought one might as well wait, rather than go messing about out of curiosity. That can be pretty dismal, from what people say. It ought to be important, I think.'

She said to herself, It might have been anyone. A combination lock may yield to infinite patience and a delicate burglar's touch; or, on a single day, chance may set the first three letters, and some passing amateur, casually tinkering, stumbles on the word.

'Actually,' he was saying with some hesitation, 'I did have the opportunity offered me once; but that was off-putting, rather than not.'

'Was it?' She recalled, in passing, the glances of Nurse Jones

291

and the Dusky Maiden, and wondered how, precisely, he would define an opportunity. 'What happened?'

'You don't want to hear about it, do you?'

'Don't be silly, of course I do.'

'It's a pretty pointless sort of story. Still, if you like ... It was just a thing that happened one Easter vac, down in Sussex. A man in my year was having a twenty-first, and a bunch of us stayed over for a long week-end. We all did things more or less together, nothing much in the way of pairing off, all quite cheerful and uncomplicated. Then the night before the party was due to break up, this girl came along to my room and said had I got some aspirin, because she couldn't sleep. I was half asleep myself when she arrived and feeling a bit vacant, I suppose; and as everyone had been float-ing about in dressing-gowns and so on quite freely, I didn't think much about it, except to feel slightly affronted at her thinking I was more likely to be stocked up with aspirin than the women were. I said I was sorry I hadn't got any, and she came and sat on the side of my bed, and we talked vaguely about one thing and another. She was good fun and pretty in a way, and after I was properly awake I admit I quite enjoyed having her there. In fact, if things had gone on quietly as they were for a bit longer, I don't know ... well, it's hard to say. But she suddenly got frightfully intense and started talking about self-fulfilment and God knows what, only it was much more embarrassing at the time than I've made it sound. I didn't know how on earth to stop her. And the more she kept on, the more impossible the whole thing seemed. Is that abnor-mal, do you think?'

'I've felt exactly the same myself.'

'Have you really? Still, that's a bit different, isn't it? Well, anyway, after trying for some time to keep the discussion on an abstract plane and not succeeding, I said the trouble was I'd just got engaged, only it couldn't be given out yet because her people were abroad.'

'I hope that settled her.'

'You might have thought so, mightn't you? In actual fact, it only seemed to make things worse. Quite honestly, I don't think even now I could dwell on all the details. I'm afraid in the end I more or less told her to go to hell. And after that I could have done with some aspirin myself.'

'Oh, darling. I'm not really laughing. I mean, not at you. It's the time of night. I never realised there were drawbacks like that to being a man.'

'I see what you mean – well, that's one way of looking at it, I suppose. I mean, it's the sort of situation it's impossible to come out of well, whatever one does, isn't it? If you don't mind, I'll tell you something I'm afraid will really rather shock you. In spite of being completely turned up and revolted by the whole performance, after she'd gone I nearly got up and went after her. I think I might have, except that it struck me she might have gone along to somebody else by then, in which case I'd have felt a bit of a fool ... I never imagined myself telling this story to anyone. Life's queer, isn't it?'

'Yes.'

'It made me wonder whether it wasn't all rather overrated. Men used to come back after the vac and say they'd done this and that, and one rather felt that being able to talk about it was the principal object, though I hardly know why, because when you'd heard one you'd heard the lot. The real people didn't talk, I suppose, but that doesn't occur to you till later ... There was one woman who produced a good deal of effect on me. But that was impossible.'

'Why?'

'I only saw her act. I never got the chance to meet her. I don't think I really wanted to.'

'Tell me. Have I seen her?'

'Ten to one you have.'

'Who is it? Don't be mean.'

'No, if I do you'll only say, 'But my dear, she's over fifty.' Because I happen to know she is. All the same, for quite a while the thing that bothered me most about not getting started on the stage was that I wouldn't get the chance of playing opposite her before she got too old. I didn't want to meet her any other way. I suppose you can hardly call that being in love.'

'I dare say you were quite right not to tell me her name.'

'If I did you'd understand, I think; but I won't. It's queer to think about now, because it seems always to have been you . . . Oh, God, you're a doctor, why don't you invent something people can take instead of sleep?'

'I've got you instead. That's enough for now.'

'It is for me.' But he was half asleep already. Her own eyes were closing when he said, 'Will you do something for me? Or rather, not do?'

'Either. Anything.'

'That first day in the hospital. Don't ever tell me what really happened. Do you mind? I'd rather keep it the way it is.'

'Have I made it true for you?'

'Yes. More than true.'

'I wanted to, even then.'

'God bless you. I mean that, too.'

In the morning she scarcely knew when he went – he was growing quite reliable about looking after his own departure – and woke feeling peacefully happy with the prospect of Sunday ahead, and only a short round of morning visits. In the after-noon Rupert and Lisa went out walking (in order to lose themselves, she surmised, in case anyone should call), and she decided that it was warm enough for a deck-chair in the garden. It was pleasant to lie there, with sun on her face and a rug against the cool wind, and to think about the immediate future and the immediate past, which were more satisfying than excursions, in either direction, of longer range. An hour of this had gone by like ten minutes, when an insistent inter-mittent sound reached her, the voice of the telephone indoors. She sighed, shook herself together, and went in to answer it. A male voice, with a strong Gloucestershire burr, said, 'Can I have a word with the doctor, please?'

'Dr Mansell speaking.'

'Oh, hallo, darling, it's me. Are you alone?'

'Yes, it's all right, the house is empty. You did that rather well. Except that they have a special voice for the telephone, as a rule. How are you, my dear?'

'I'm all right.' His voice was hurried, and so low that she could only hear it with difficulty. 'Listen, I'm most terribly sorry, but I don't think it's going to be possible to-night. Mother's back, she got here this morning.'

'I thought it wasn't till the middle of the week.' Uncon-sciously, in the solitude, she had dropped her voice to match his. Suddenly she felt as if a heavy weight were inside her.

'I know; things wound up sooner than she thought. She wired me at Chris's, and the wire was returned, of course. She got rather worried; it's all been a bit difficult.'

'I'm so sorry, darling. Of course don't come; we'll fix up something later. What about your eye?'

'That was all right. I'm seeing Lowe to-day; I'm rather in trouble for not having gone before, but it's all right really. Listen, suppose I can't let you know when I'm coming, are those glass doors locked every night?'

'They're supposed to be.' The cautious voice was getting on her nerves. 'I'll unlock them last thing. I'd rather you let me know if you can.'

'I'll try to. It's hell about to-night. I don't suppose we shall get to bed till late, talking and so on. You know the way it is.'

'Of course.'

'You're not angry? I couldn't bear you to be.'

'You know I'm not. Don't worry. I still ... It's hard to say things over the 'phone, isn't it?'

'I know. If only ... Well, fine, that's a date for next week, then.'

'What is?' asked Hilary, puzzled not only by the remark, but by the change of tone, which was suddenly quite careless and unconstrained. 'Which day?'

'About the car,' went on the cheerful, friendly young young voice, exactly as if she had not spoken. 'It sounds a bit like plug trouble to me. Try shorting them separately, and listen. If you still can't locate it, let me know and we'll have a session with it if you like. So long, Tony.'

The receiver clicked, with a finality in which, for a few moments, she found it impossible to believe.

Returning to her deck-chair she lit a cigarette and tried to float back into the comfortable torpor of five minutes ago; for, after all, she said to herself, this was inevitable, and would continue to be so, thanks not to him but to herself. It was really very trivial. With David it would have been hardly worth bringing up for a laugh when they met again. None the less, she was acutely miserable, and found no comfort in the thought that David with all his self-possession (which was boundless) would not have carried it off half so well. Hoping that things would look better in the morning she turned in early; but in spite of having the whole night, and the whole

296

bed, to herself, she did not sleep very well. If he were careless and indiscreet, she thought, I might have something to fuss about. She fell asleep at last, her mind unsatisfied, and heard nothing from Julian the next day and night, or the day and night following.

On Wednesday morning she had a letter. She looked at it as it lay unopened beside her plate; she could never quite accustom herself to his unformed hand, the total absence of idiosyncrasy; neatly spaced lines on a blue envelope, in a clear, slanting Oxford script, scarcely modified from the tidiness of a school exercise book. She turned it over (for she was alone) noting absurd trifles, such as the thoroughness with which the flap was licked down, before she opened it.

Darling,

I cannot imagine what you must think I have been doing with myself all this while. I haven't written before because I kept expecting I would see you. But you know the sort of complications that happen in family life. Aunt Laura went off to Scotland, which altered everyone's plans. You can guess how I have been feeling with all this hanging about.

Lowe has seen my eye and takes the view that I shall live. He has secret doubts about the kerbstone, but kept them to a dirty look, which he shot at me privately. I expect you realised why our telephone conversation ended in a rather unsatisfactory manner. The 'phone here is in the hall, I forget whether I mentioned this before.

It seems years already since we met. I hope it will not be long now before I can get over. I am writing this in bed. [The next line was crossed out, so impenetrably that it defeated all her efforts.] I wonder what you are doing now? I shall never forget that ride on Saturday. I should like to say more, if I were better at it. Chris Tranter would be more the man for this, but I shall not co-opt him, as it would be unfortunate if you were gradually to fall for him like Roxane for Cyrano, particularly as he has quite a normal nose. I wonder if you share my view that Rostand is only actable in the original French. Of course one sees that this feeling about ham is a recent thing and may not outlast our generation. But I did not begin this to talk shop.

I have been thinking about you a lot. I wish that we could talk instead of writing. You would understand if you were here. I never knew till now [another deep erasure] that I would miss you so much.

I have been writing this since eleven o'clock and it is now nearly one. But I was wide awake and felt [in the obliteration of the next line and a half the nib had gone twice through the paper] that I would like to spend the time writing to you. I am sorry that this letter is getting to be such a mess and that I put things so badly. But you know how I feel.

Yours ever with my love,

JULIAN.

PS. There is a poem on page 53 of the *Oxford Book of English Verse* beginning 'O western wind'. I wonder if you know it?

Hilary smoothed the sheets, read them again, and again held up the crossed-out portions, vainly, to the light. She and David had spent all their time together under the same roof; so this was the first love-letter she had ever received.

Four more days went by. He did not write again. She began to fall into the state of mind where every remembered straw of uncertainty, every trivial dissatisfaction and doubt, rears up from the past and throws an enormous shadow, as low-growing weeds do in the light of a sinking sun. She began to sleep badly, and at last, disapproving of herself but growing desperate, took a heavy dose of sedative. In the small hours of the ensuing night she was seized by a hideous dream; she was in the post-mortem room, and the subject she was dissecting lifted a dead, cold arm and fondled her face. Half aware that she dreamed, she fought to wake. She woke, and the dank fingers were still on her cheek. Gripped by the dumb paralysis of nightmare, she made a choked indrawn sound, a sleeper's scream.

'Don't be frightened, darling. It's only me.'

Slipping from terror into sheer relief, from relief into con-sciousness of a dulled body and heavy head, from consciousness into protest, from protest into recollection and effort; all this caused her response to be somewhat delayed. The light went on beside her; she covered her eyes with her hand.

'I'm terribly sorry I'm so late.'

She took her hand away. He was kneeling beside her, his black hair straightened and glossed with rain. Rain was still wet on his forehead; a steamy smell was rising from his tweeds. The clock made it ten minutes to three.

'I walked here,' he said.

'*Walked?*' Dimly she tried to reckon the distance by the shortest way. Using all the footpaths, none of them easy in the dark, it must still be a good seven miles. She struggled with her blunted brain. 'But it's raining.'

'Only the last half of the way. You see, the trouble is about getting out the car. It would wake everyone. I never thought, till it came to the time.'

'Your hands are so cold.'

She took them in hers. Night after night at first, she had expected him, even when at last she slept; to-night, careless with dejection, she had bundled her hair into an old stringy ribbon, forgotten the becoming cream which served for night as well as day, and had not retouched her mouth. Even a young girl's face, she thought, would look dull and puffy after such heavy sleep. He, too, pursuing a fixed image with the silliness of youth and desire, must have had his expectation spoiled in the moment when she had failed to awake in instant welcome at his touch. Though she knew this she resented the faint disappointment in his eyes, thinking of the hair ribbon and her neglected face.

'You can't go on doing this,' she said, 'walking about all night. It's ridiculous. You'll get no sleep at all.' His hurt look told her, better than her own ears, that her voice had been fretful and half-awake.

'That doesn't matter.'

'You'll look like it, too. People will notice.' The sense of failure made her continue, obstinately, to fail.

'Why should they notice?' With the swiftness of emotion over-keyed, he was becoming annoyed. 'I've got my strength, I haven't one foot in the grave.'

'If you had a job of work to do, you couldn't spare a night's sleep so easily.'

She had supplied and answered her own implication; she knew it even while she spoke. He had missed it still; but he was staring at her in a flat, aching disenchantment. Sometimes fear is a swifter stimulant than love; she caught him in her arms, explaining, consoling, remorsefully chilling her unprotected warmth against his cold wet hair and sodden shoulders. He brightened at once; but, as with a child who has been slapped when confidently expecting praise, a gain of doubt and distrust remained behind. He had seen it all in the manner of Hero and Leander (indeed, he could not have been much wetter if he had negotiated the Hellespont itself), and she had given the picture a false brush-stroke which could not quite be painted out, though both of them did their best.

The little electric heater, which she had made him turn on to dry his clothes – though it would scarcely have time to do more than warm them – gave the room a strangeness with its dull red glow, and through everything there was an indefinable difference. She was still a little slow and stupid from the sedative she had taken, and though she confessed to this and he forgave her, nothing was quite as it had been at other times. Besides, they dared not fall asleep, for it would take him two hours to get home again, and it was not worth while to set the alarm. At last they talked perfunctorily, to keep awake, with nothing real to say. She remembered, after he had gone, that she had not asked him whether he had had any answer from the producer he had written to, nor how they were to meet again. She woke, in daylight, to find Annie, the morning tea in her hand, gazing with curiosity and disapproval at the forgotten electric fire. Unable to think of any excuse for it, she pretended sleep.

That day Rupert Clare went back to Berlin. She longed, if not to comfort Lisa, whose reserve made comfort a touchy business, at least to distract and entertain her – an office which she knew would be gratefully received. But the feeling of flatness and depression added itself to the torpor of the sleeping tablets which she had inadequately slept off; she felt, wretchedly, that her efforts were perfunctory and mechanical, and, for Lisa, scarcely preferable to being let alone. Besides all this, a patient she had put on a course of M and B developed intolerance through taking insufficient fluids, and she reproached herself with not having made her instructions clear. The course had to be stopped before it could become effective; blaming herself for her want of alertness, at the back of her mind she blamed Julian a little too. It continued to rain, thinly and drearily, for two days.

On the third the rain stopped; but a grey, low-hanging quilt of cloud remained, making everything leaden and wan. She was sitting, tired and dispirited, over a late tea, when there was a knock at the door.

'Mr Fleming, Doctor.'

'Oh, yes. Show him in.'

She ought not to have got so promptly to her feet; had her face given her away? She had not foreseen this panic at the first meeting before other people; the Pascoes had been too remote to count.

Still conscious of Annie, she approved the calm, amounting for him almost to stolidity, with which he greeted her. As the door shut, she felt that he was rather overdoing it; he could have afforded to smile with a little more animation. There was a blurred air about him, which made him seem not much more than passably good-looking. Advancing cautiously, he said, 'I'd better not kiss you.'

'You can, darling. I heard Annie go.'

'I mean ...' An urgent dive for his pocket made his meaning all too clear. He emerged from a huge handkerchief to explain, unnecessarily, 'I've got a bit of a cold.'

He had; as colds go, it was a classic, a monument. Remembering that after two hours in a warm bed he had gone out in the wet, not having slept, in half-dried clothes and with no overcoat (it had been mild that night, before the rain), she reflected that it might quite well have been worse. She fussed over him, making him hot tea and settling him by the fire, and suppressed the sneaking thought that he might have stayed away till he was less violently infectious. It was the kind of cold that can almost be seen radiating around the subject, like an aura.

'Let me take your temperature. You ought not to be out.'

'It's all right; it's below normal. It happened to be rather a good chance this afternoon; it seemed a pity to waste it.'

If only, she thought, he would say crudely, 'Mother was out, and it saved questions about where I was going.' It was these continual indirections which rubbed her nerves raw. All she said was, 'But, dear, you look wretched. We could have talked on the 'phone.'

'I wanted to see you again.' She knew that he too had felt, after last time, unsatisfied and full of the need to be reassured.

'Come and sit by me, here on the rug; it's warmer.'

He came and leaned, heavy-headed, against her lap, scarcely attempting conversation; and yet in this interlude of bathos she found something curiously moving. It called up something in her which his most charming moments of gaiety had left undisturbed. He sneezed and shivered beside her knees (reminding her of a big beautiful dog with distemper, or whatever it was that dogs had when they were a little older) and made painstaking, intermittent attempts at brightness; and she wondered why she did not become irritated, as most women she knew would have been. But it all seemed quite natural and rather endearing; and it occurred to her, in one of the moments when she half listened to what he said, that her past had conditioned her to him not less than his to her. The difference was that he had had the candour to admit the foundations of his love, as far as he understood them, and to leave open to her those of which he was unaware. Perhaps he could afford it better, she thought, and wondered why she had not thought it before.

'What a shame,' she said, 'after you'd caught your death out on the cold hills, that I should have waked up cross.'

'It was worth it. I've unearthed an old bike in the stables, and I'm getting it furbished up. It would look a bit noticeable to buy a new one. I think it will do.'

'These roads aren't safe for cycling after dark. The spring's hardly begun.'

'I know all the bad places. I biked over them for about fifteen years, before I had a car.'

'You're a terrible worry to me. Sometimes I wonder whether you're worth keeping ... Oh, my sweet, don't be silly. Drink that while it's hot enough to be some good.'

'It's lovely to be here.'

'I've missed you terribly ... Tell me, have you heard anything yet from this Finnigan man? I've kept meaning to ask you.'

'Well, no.' The cold had flattened his voice. 'As a matter of fact, I'm not certain if he's in England. I seem to remember something somewhere about his going to New York.'

'But he must have left someone behind who'd have acknowledged your letter.'

He shifted himself a little nearer to the fire. 'The assistant director doesn't know me. Contacts are vital, in this sort of thing. A deputy you haven't met is no good.'

'But I thought ...' She felt her way, slowly, to the fact behind this verbal haze. 'Do you mean you've not written yet at all?'

'I'm watching the papers. As soon as I see he's back I'll post it off.' He sounded so willing, so anxious not to emphasise the fact that he was feeling low, that for a moment she felt quite ashamed of herself for bothering him. Then her common sense reasserted itself, together with a suspicion that he had not been quite unaware of producing this effect.

'But if you want to know whether he's there, why don't you just put a trunk call through to the theatre and find out?'

'It doesn't do to seem in a flap. Puts people off.'

'You needn't ask to speak to him. Or even say who you are. The box-office would tell you, surely?'

'I suppose they would. Yes, that's quite an idea. However, as it turns out it's just as well I left it; if he'd sent for me this week I'd have looked pretty silly. I'll obviously have to wait now till my voice comes back.'

This seemed unanswerable. 'Yes,' she said. 'You'd better, of course. What happens at an audition, by the way?'

He began to tell her, with anecdotes. When he forgot himself and became interested, he seemed better at once. His symptoms were, obviously, quite genuine; but lethargy and lack of resistance had doubled their potency. He must have felt this himself, for he said, 'It's done me a world of good, talking to you. I knew it would.'

'Some quinine would do you more. Wait a minute, I'll see if I've got some.'

'That's very sweet of you ... Oh, by the way, does it matter if you take a double dose?'

'It will make your ears sing, and you don't need it.'

'I mean I might have to have another, when I get back.'

In a sudden flare of exasperation she snapped, 'Then why on earth couldn't you say so?'

'Sorry,' said Julian, looking at the fire. 'It was nice of you to think of it.'

'It was ordinary common sense.' With a reasonableness that seemed the product of some vast muscular effort she added, 'My dear, you don't need to apologise to me for being properly looked after at home. I'm very glad you are.'

For a moment he looked almost shocked; when he spoke

and smiled she sensed an effort something like her own. 'Never mind, you do me more good than quinine. I ought to be going, I'm afraid. I wish I could kiss you good-bye.' The clock struck in the hall. He looked at the one on the mantelpiece, which said ten minutes to the hour, and asked sharply, 'Which of those is right?'

She glanced at her wrist. 'The hall one. I must put this on; I never look at it when I'm wearing my watch.'

'Oh, my God.' In the ensuing pause he seemed searching for words which would excuse, without explaining, the tone he had just used. She could not remember, afterwards, what he did say in the end. In any case he was gone. She found herself wandering round the room, and sat down with a cigarette.

As she lit it, it was as if the flash of the lighter had had an internal counterpart. She knew, suddenly and certainly, the reason for all his trivial reticences which had so confusedly goaded her. She had been over-subtle in her interpretation of him; the truth had been too obvious to see. A vague repression would never have driven him to these circumlocutions; he would have overriden it, and said what appealed to him as the proper thing. Therefore he must have a reason, a conscious one; a staring embarrassment in the foreground of his thoughts. There could be only one. Mrs Fleming had not forgotten her, nor had her opinion softened with time. It must have been driven in on him inescapably, for certainly he would have escaped it if he could; and recently, or he would have persuaded himself to forget it. Inevitably, he would have let it pass in silence, not trusting himself to challenge it without giving himself away.

'What *does* it matter?' said Hilary to herself. To be quite sure, she said it aloud.

15

She might have known (as she told herself a day or two later) that she had not sounded the trough of anti-climax to its bottom yet. The decisions of that last evening had carried with them, at the time, the sense of hauling on a slack rope, which is one of life's quiet intimations of irony. No crisis confronted her. She merely developed Julian's cold.

It was the kind of cold which wet-blankets every activity of body and mind, while never permitting one the indulgence of being really ill. She was merely tired, stupid, miserable, and plain. When she thought of Julian it was with dim goodwill and an earnest wish that he would stay away. Among the symptoms she had caught from him, a craving for company was notably absent.

It was faintly comforting, however, to get one of his rambling inarticulate letters, containing a paragraph, startling in its sudden neatness and point, about *The Ascent of F6*, which he had apparently just read. Having herself seen the play indifferently done, she was seized with a positive eagerness to discuss it with him. She had actually sat down with the pen in her hand before she remembered. Receiving herself, in the course of her work, a constant stream of letters locally post-marked, she had forgotten that he got probably very few, in long-familiar scripts. She had never learned to use a typewriter, and, now that Rupert had gone, there was none in the house. She sat staring at the sheet of paper in front of her, oppressed with sudden frustration and loneliness. To dispel it she picked up his letter and read it again. A final line which she had over-looked, because it had been squeezed in along the side-margin, read, 'How are you? My cold is gone, except that for some reason I have completely lost my voice.'

She wished more than ever that she could write to him; he could not be doing much, and must be feeling lonely and bored. He would be anxious, too, about the audition, and prob-ably making things worse by forcible efforts to improve them; she would have liked to warn him about this.

It was on the following Sunday evening, five days later, during church-time, when he called again. By that time her own cold, an acute one, but of the short-lived variety, was better, and she had developed some respect for her appearance, so it was with unqualified joy that she heard his ring. He entered with his most charming smile, and kissed her warmly as soon as he was safely inside.

'Darling,' she said, 'how have you been? I've missed you so much.'

He kissed her again, and looked down at her half humor-ously like someone who has a little joke for which there is no hurry.

'I've had your cold, you wretch. But it's better now.'

'I'm terribly sorry.'

'What are you whispering for?' she asked, puzzled. 'There's no one to hear.' Then she remembered his letter. 'My dear,' she exclaimed in concern, 'hasn't your voice come back *yet*?'

He smiled apologetically and shook his head. 'I can't think why not. It's never played me up like this before. Lowe says I'm run down or something. I *feel* all right.'

He managed to make the unvocalised sound quite expressive, helped out by his naturally eloquent face.

'You've been straining it. You ought to go to bed and rest it completely. Don't talk at all till it comes back.'

'I tried that, actually, for a day or two. But it didn't make any difference, so I got up again.'

'You shouldn't be out in the evening, anyhow. If I weren't so pleased to see you, I'd be rather cross.'

'There's a kind of theory that I don't go out at all. But I felt all gummed up with stopping indoors, and I wanted to see you. So I slung my hook.'

She made some outwardly cheerful answer; but secretly she was reviewing all the more sinister possibilities. 'You've never had anything the matter with your chest, I suppose?'

'Good heavens, no. I've always been as strong as a horse. It can't be anything. For the Lord's sake don't start worrying about it.'

'But how long have you been like this?'

'Only about a week.'

'It shouldn't last that long. You must see Lowe again – promise – if it goes on.'

'I'll promise what you like,' he whispered, kissing her, 'if you won't get into a flap about it. It's only some sort of freak thing. I'm perfectly well really.' He drew her back to him. 'Well enough for anything.'

She remembered, suddenly, that it was some time since he had made love to her; they both remembered. Speech became unnecessary, and, presently, a whisper so natural as to call for no remark.

'Does the fact that you opened the door to me mean that everybody's out?'

'Annie is. I think Lisa is too.'

Perhaps it was the interval of separation which made him seem, to-day, more charming than her best recollections, more tender and sincere. He had learned the art of persuasion with a most flatteringly personal technique, which was the more disarming, because it was so spontaneous. When they went up, presently, in the clear spring twilight, the blackbird was singing, clearly and fluidly, on a branch so near her open window that the sound seemed within the room, and a soft wind blew in, scented with pine.

'You're to look after yourself,' she said as he was going.

'I don't need to.' He smiled at her; his voice, hoarse but audible, slipped for half the sentence uncertainly on to the vocal tones.

'It's coming back already. But don't force it. Let it alone.'

Whispering obediently, he said, 'It's just the perversity of things, isn't it, that this should happen now?'

'Never mind.' It was still the hour of the angel, and the future – whether days or minutes ahead – was unreal to both of them.

A few nights afterwards he came, late, to her room. The bicycle was in repair, so he arrived a little before one. They were exchanging the inconsequent murmur of talk which passes for conversation on the edge of sleep, when she remembered to say, 'How soon did your voice get right again?'

He turned his head lazily on her shoulder. 'It hasn't, yet. Silly, isn't it?'

'But, my dear . . .' The drowsiness cleared from her mind, like a haze congealed by cold. They had, of course, been talking in undertones, as always when the house was asleep, so she had noticed nothing. A few minutes before, she had put out the lamp; now she turned it on again, and, sliding her shoulder free, leaned on her arm to look at him. He blinked at her with faint protest and cloudy affection, narrowing his eyes.

'Don't worry. Lowe says it's nothing to worry about.'

'But, Julian, it's nearly a fortnight now. Has he gone over you properly?'

'Exhaustively.' He pulled her down, and settled himself back into the place from which she had disturbed him. 'He even had an X-ray done of my chest, heavens knows why, and peered down me with a light. He says it's nothing to matter. It's a nuisance, though; it holds everything up. I'm sorry, darling.'

It was the time of night when thought slips too easily into words. 'Darling,' she said, 'are you *sure* you couldn't if you really tried? You're not just getting worked up about it?'

Moving his head, he looked up at her with the bewilderment which attests innocence more powerfully than anger.

'But of course I've tried. What do you think? You surely don't suppose I'm doing it for fun?'

'Of course I don't. It's only that ... well, it's all too technical. But it's one of those things you can make worse with worry and so on. I think if you were to go away, just for a bit, it might ... Why not stay with this man you know in town?'

'What, like this? When I'm at Chris's we talk till the morning milk. No, it's sure to clear off when the weather's warmer. I'm not getting into a state about it. What a neurotic type you must think I am.'

She murmured some easy reassurance, and put out the light. Soon he was tranquilly asleep. She lay looking at the dim shadow of his hair, and confronting the truth with which he had just presented her.

She was neither shocked nor, she found, even surprised. She

311

seemed to feel, as naturally as the weight of his head on her shoulder, his broken will resting on her heart. Untouched by the contempt she would have felt for a planned deceit, she never doubted the honesty of his conscious mind; she only recognised it for what it was, the mark of the deep flaw that goes to the foundations. The root of it was that he did not know. He had escaped out of the reach of his own self-reproach.

He lay breathing peacefully, like the childhood into whose helplessness he had retreated; innocent, his mind at rest from the conflict his body had refused. She had neither condemnation for him, nor the arrogance to credit herself with generosity, because she had none. After a struggle she rejected too the temptation of condemning where she most longed to condemn. The harm had been done too long ago.

For a little while she wondered whether, if she tried to explain any part of this, she could make him understand. All her experience pointed the other way. The hidden resistance went too deep. He would never see – lay people never did – the distinction which was so clear to her; he would always think, at the bottom of his heart, that she had accused him of a shabby and grotesque trick, and his trust in her would never survive it. What had happened so far was trivial in itself; it had importance only as a sign.

At this point her meditations were broken; he had started in his sleep, so violently that it woke him. She kissed him and said, 'You're dreaming like a dog. I've always wondered what makes them do that.'

'Did I wake you up?'

'No. You've not been asleep very long.'

'I dreamed I was falling off a mountain.'

'Oh, one of those. With me it's tripping when I try to run.'

'It must be a book of Smythe's I was reading. I generally fall when I have this sort of dream.'

'What sort?'

'Oh, I don't know.' He seemed as wide awake as if he had not slept at all. 'Well, for instance, in this one I was in the Alps, and some peak was supposed to be unclimbable; silly sort of thing you get in dreams. So I started out to do it on my own, no tackle or anything, and of course, being a dream, I just did it like going upstairs. It felt marvellous. Bright sunlight, and beautifully warm. Part of the time I just skimmed up it, about ten yards to a stride, half flying you know. And then I got to the summit, and had a feeling it was too good to be true; that there was a law against it or something. It was all snow, not rocky at all, and not cold; you know those clouds in Italian pictures, that have cherubs sprawling about on them, or gods; it felt like that. I was lying up there, feeling very good at having made it, and yet somehow not so good, if you see what I mean. It was a long way up from anywhere, miles and miles. And then I noticed one of those lightning-conductors they often have, and thought it would be awkward if there was a storm. As soon as I'd thought of it, there was a terrific clap of thunder, and a great flash struck the lightning-conductor and knocked it flat; and I could feel the whole side of the mountain collapsing under me. I remember thinking as I started to fall, "Of course, that's why people aren't allowed up here." And then I woke up.'

'What a rotten dream. A nice beginning, though.'

'Oh, they always have nice beginnings. I don't often have them, now. But the ones I do have seem somehow to have got worse.'

'Tell me another.'

'You won't get any sleep.'

313

'I'm not sleepy.'

He reflected, and said, suddenly definite, 'I can't remember any more.'

'I don't mind if it isn't proper.'

'No; I forget ... It was queer, though, to wake up and find you here. I couldn't believe it, for a moment or two.'

'Try and believe it, darling.'

He took her immediately in his arms. It was all very simple and natural; too simple by half. She loosened his hold gently.

'I meant more than that. When you're alone. Never think that – that you can be punished because of me. You've had nothing from me, ever – you can have nothing – that it isn't your right to have.'

'Why do you say that?' he asked slowly.

'Oh, because ... I don't know enough to tell you intelligently. I just think you've put me in your imagination with other things that have been there much longer, since you were a child, and because of that I've probably stirred up feelings you had then about what seemed wrong.'

'But of course I don't think we're wrong.'

'Not think. It's more difficult than that.'

He took this more quickly than she had expected, and said after a little pause, 'Well, I was brought up in the country; I suppose I picked up the facts of life in a pretty average way. Don't you think children are bound to think sex a bit squalid? I mean, only having the instinct can really explain it. It's just a phase everyone has to have and get over, isn't it?'

'Yes, of course. But I think it was harder for you' – she tried to speak as if they were discussing trivialities – 'not having both your parents, and resenting your father because of the way he'd behaved. It makes a difference, they say.'

There was a longer pause. When he spoke it was with the forced flatness people use for the unspeakable. 'Talking of dreams, I dreamed once that I'd killed him.'

She said, lightly, 'Well, that's quite natural; it doesn't mean you're a potential murderer, you know. What was he like?'

'In the dream, you mean? Oh, like the photo we've got at home. Dim and soldierly. Until after I'd killed him, anyhow.'

'And then?'

He gave an unnatural little laugh. 'It was funny, that part. When he was dead, he looked just like me. Only dead, of course.'

She kissed him, and said, 'It's about time you had someone to sleep with you.' He had been resting on one arm, but lay down to hide the fact that he was shaking with reaction. She pretended not to have noticed it.

'I expect,' he said casually, 'you must be thinking me rather a morbid type.'

'No. You've been by yourself too long. Everything's going to be different now.'

'It is different, already.'

'Will you remember something, if I ask you to?'

'I shouldn't wonder.'

'It's only that since I've known you I've been happier than I knew it was possible to be.'

He said, softly and incredulously, '*You?*' and, presently, 'I thought loving me must have been nothing but a nuisance to you – what with everything.'

'Well, you know now. Don't forget about it.'

'I'll tie a knot in my handkerchief.' They talked no more that night.

In the morning, as he was leaving, she said, 'Would you like it if we went riding, one day this week?'

315

He was enthusiastic; though, when it came to fixing a time, she could see that he was involved in some anxious calculations. His final choice was not very convenient for her, but she did not say so. She lay awake, after he had gone, thinking over what she had decided. She was not proud of it; but it was the only resource that seemed to fall within the scope of her limited knowledge, and it would have to do.

The day of the ride turned out grey and cool, but settled enough. They met, as usual, at the farm. He had still not recovered his voice; she had not expected it, and the comfort she had tried to offer had not been given in any such hope. As before, he was cheerful and optimistic about it, and dismissed it lightly, the better to emphasise, in the whisper which practice was making more expressive than ever, his delight at seeing her. It was now possible to conduct a conversation with him at normal distance, even out-of-doors. He assured her that he felt very fit, and that it was sure to clear up in a day or two. Lowe had given him some new stuff for it.

When they were in the stable-yard she said, 'Did you really mean it when you offered to let me try Biscuit? I feel rather tempted to-day. We'll change over to go back.'

With the warm generous smile that never failed to move her, he said, 'Why, of course. All the way if you want to. Get up and I'll fix the leathers.'

As soon as Biscuit ceased to feel his hands she realised how fresh the horse really was, how powerful, and how much bigger than anything she had ridden before. Pride, as well as the resolution she had taken, nerved her; after a few strenuous minutes she was aware of having won a guarded toleration and respect. Julian, for his part, had mounted Pascoe's second best as if nothing could be pleasanter. He looked so naïvely happy at being permitted to spoil his ride for her sake that she felt sickened with herself; but her mind was fixed. He would have taken the lane they had used before, the one that went up to the open downs; but she suggested a detour across the fields.

It was easy country; the fences were good, mostly dry-walled stone topped with grass. She had taken the car out before, to confirm her memories of the terrain, and now she knew exactly where to go; but, without putting anything into words, she affected a little unfamiliarity with the neighbourhood, looking at him questioningly once or twice before taking the direction she had meant to take all along. It was easy not to talk, since he was too far away to answer her. She was reassured to see that he knew every inch of the way; a point on which every-thing depended.

At last they were in the field for which she had been making; a long sloping pasture of coarse grass, contoured so that the fence at its distant end bounded the near horizon; the usual wall, with a hedge, a little higher, on its far side. Towards it the slope was sharper; she had been right in believing that even from saddle-height, one would have to come within yards of it to see beyond.

The sky was clearing; here and there, in the thin sunlight, the gorse burned, its new year's shoots making the old growth look black.

All this while she had not given Biscuit his head; if she had, Julian would have been left far behind. As it was, she was lead-ing; looking back, she saw that already he was turning off towards the gate on the left. He waved, and pointed to it with his crop. She smiled uncomprehendingly. 'Over there,' she called, with a vague cheerful gesture towards the fence; and urged Biscuit into a gallop.

Behind her she heard the hoof-beats change, the sharp slap of a crop brought down, and his horse's startled response; but

317

in a moment the sounds fell away; she was gaining fast. Biscuit had been impatient all along. To Hilary he seemed to go, now, like a charger of the Apocalypse. For the first time she knew how easily he might get away from her. The field seemed, suddenly, not nearly as long as she had believed. The final slope, whose crest was the stone fence, was rising only a little way ahead. It was not steep enough to slow him much. Already, perhaps, she had left it too late. Her hair whipped in the wind. She suddenly ceased to care. Present effort checked imagination; she had a blurred memory of being told by some survivor that it hadn't hurt much, at the time. Biscuit's great shoulders began to breast the foot of the slope.

'Look – out! Hilary! *Stop!*'

The raw, harsh shout behind her might have belonged to a stranger, if she had not heard her name. She had no time to give it much attention. She flung her strength against Biscuit's, to get him round; he pulled angrily, uncertain of her and having begun already to gather himself for the jump. He would rear at the last moment, she thought, and probably roll on her. But he was answering the rein. When she brought him round she was near enough to the fence to see over it, down the twenty-foot embankment into the sunken lane below.

A glove came down over hers on the rein; Biscuit snorted, slowed, and stopped. Julian's face, so set with strain that its lines were like those of anger, stared into hers. Both of them were too breathless to speak. There was a stillness broken only by the breath of the horses, and the sound of a wood-chopper a long way off.

He said, at last, 'Look over there.' His voice was tight and husky, but still quite audible.

'I know. Thanks, Julian. I'm sorry.'

'By God, I should hope you are.'

'I think perhaps you'd better have Biscuit, now.'

'So do I,' said Julian through his teeth. He dismounted and held Biscuit's head.

When she was on her feet he gripped her by the sleeves of her coat, and stood looking down at her. She felt none of the tender and triumphant emotions she had earned; she was, in fact, more frightened, having more leisure to feel it, than when Biscuit had begun to mount the slope. She murmured weakly, 'Dear Julian,' for her own reassurance as much as anything else.

'Don't dear-Julian me. I could beat the life out of you.'

Before she had time to think she had actually braced herself in his hands. She relaxed, shamefacedly. 'I might have killed Biscuit,' she said. 'I don't wonder you're annoyed.'

'Shut up.' His grip shifted from her sleeves to her arms. Quite consciously this time, she braced herself again. Even so, the violent embrace in which he gripped her was more than she had been ready for. Remembering that the horses must make them, even from a distance, conspicuous in this large and empty space, she tried to loosen his hold.

Pausing at last for breath, he said, 'I hope I never live through a minute like that again.'

'I'm sorry.'

'Did you go crazy, or what? Charging a blind fence like a drunken sailor?'

'He got away from me.' She had meant to manage without telling a lie; but the united efforts of Biscuit and Julian had shaken her nerve. 'I was too busy pulling him in to notice.' She had always taken a decent pride in her competence on a horse; later, perhaps, she would have time to reflect on having poured it so lavishly down the drain. At the moment she found that the process gave her a curious and unexplained pleasure.

Julian kept her locked in his arms. One of them was threaded through Biscuit's rein, and he was twitching at it irritably, producing as little effect as Hilary's effort to get free. With equal indifference, Julian ignored both. He was talking into her hair. All she took in was, '. . . all that stuff about one's past life flashing before one's eyes.'

'It didn't before mine. No time.'

'I had time. And the future as well.'

'I'm not worth it.'

'After this I'll be afraid to let you out of my sight.'

She suddenly realised that she had ceased to think about his voice; it had become perfectly normal. It would be better, probably, not to leave him to discover it by himself. She said, as if by an afterthought, 'Did it hurt, shouting like that?'

'Good Lord, do you think I had time to notice? As far as I remember, I just kept on till something gave way.'

His good faith was wholly transparent, if she had ever doubted it. He felt at his throat and said, 'Seems all right now. A bit rough, that's all. Must have shifted something, I suppose.'

'I don't wonder. Well, it was more than I deserved. Darling, if we stand like this much longer the whole neighbourhood will be arriving on bicycles to take a look.'

'Oh, what the hell. I keep seeing you down in that road.' He let her go reluctantly, and caught his own mount, which was half-way across the field.

On the way back she wondered what had ever made her suppose that she would feel self-satisfied with her success. It had worked; oh, yes. But he had put a trust in her which he had never demanded in return; she had not enjoyed deceiving it.

The following day was a Sunday. Opening her paper she turned first to the dramatic column. (Once it had been the book reviews; but at some stage in recent months, how long ago it embarrassed her a little to remember, the routine of years had undergone a change.) The critic, for lack of anything worth notice in town, had concerned himself that week with provincial repertory, giving a longish paragraph to Barchester. Commenting on the enterprise shown by this company, he noted that its director, Mr Padraic Finnigan, had decided to tour the American little theatres in search of new ideas, and would be, the critic understood, outward bound by the time those lines went to press.

Hilary picked up her cigarette in time to save the tablecloth from burning. She almost longed, for the sake of emotional escape, to make the false judgement which it was no longer in her power to form. But long ago the image of Julian, working inward, had passed from the mind into the blood; she could trace almost the processes by which his memory had edited some advance rumour or printed line. He had believed what he had told her. Loving her, and conditioned to lying, he had fought himself to keep truth with her, even while she had entangled him in a whole new course of lies. Something had cracked in the tug-of-war; playing Sancho to the Quixote of his will, his body had taken over, a better liar than he. She might just as well have made a holiday of yesterday's ride, for to-day's news would have cured him. It was a judgement on her, she thought.

He came round to see her a few nights later, full of the news about Finnigan; charming, sincere, apologetic, unable to think how he could have made such a muddle, been such a damned fool. That this should happen, just when his voice was right again, was typical of the perversity of things. He brought her a new book she had been wanting, a new embrace which only lack of imagination had kept her from wanting, and Faustus's invocation to Helen, delivered in a thrilling undertone in the dark. He had had no more bad dreams, he assured her, but rather a good one, which he would tell her if she wouldn't be shocked. He was irresistible; at the top of his form. A sorcerer innocent of his own devices, he offered her forgetfulness like an enchanted cup. She took it, and entered with him his kingdom of escape.

16

It was years, they said in that part of the country, since they had had such a spring. Under its mild suns and tingling, unmalicious breezes, people threw off their winter ills, and Hilary had time on her hands. She read poetry – an occupation she had let lapse for some years – drove about, when her round was done, and left the car often to explore on foot. One such expedition brought her to a little grey church with a dog-toothed Norman arch, and a slanting churchyard beyond whose yew-hedge one looked straight across blue air to five-mile-distant hills. She wandered in, reading the faint lettering on the soft Cotswold headstones, with their reliefs of spread cherubs, fluted urns, wreaths, and skulls; and passed on into the cool porch, where the parish notices hung on cross-cornered baize boards. The oak door stood ajar, and opened to her silently. It was a little church, the chancel hardly bigger than her own room. Here was the six-sided font, carved with the story of the Fall; the red wool curtain to screen the ringers under the tower; there an exuberant eighteenth-century monument, with a periwigged Roman squire and personifications in weeping marble; here the Commandments in tarnished gold on a black board. She walked up the aisle, the stone blocks gritting softly under her feet. The altar, with its frontal of faded purple silk, was flowerless; the window over it, of plain, old glass, showed the blue eastern sky, broken only by the pattern of the leads.

Free of the scrapings and shiftings of a congregation, or the focus of ritual, the thick walls seemed to distil, in quiet self-communion, their nine centuries' saturation of prayer. Their stillness did not reproach her as a stranger and an intruder; it gave her a sense of loneliness in which, half aware, she reproached herself. She thought of the dogma that had driven her away, but as one might think of a petty bickering which has cost one a friend a long while back; there were faults on both sides, perhaps, but one has forgotten the argument, and only remembers the loss.

Let into the wall, beside the chancel arch, was the village war memorial, a square of dressed stone with its double column of names, and a little St George on a ledge, his dragon and a bowl of violets at his feet. It was not unlike the one in the church near her parents' home, which carried her second brother's name. Looking at it, she could almost smell the pink metal-polish with which, proud of the task entrusted her, she had cleaned his buttons on his last leave, breathing heavily in front of the nursery fire. She was still begging everyone to admire them when the car came to take him away; he had been killed at Passchendaele a week later, a day or two short of his nineteenth year.

She was only half conscious of her eye travelling down the repeated local names, or the fact that its course had been arrested at the foot of the first column. Rousing herself, the remembered dust of the metal-paste still on her tongue, she read, 'FLEMING, Richard H., Maj'. Walking across country, and missing the village, she had kept her sense of direction only in the background of her mind. She read the line again; then turned to look back at the font with its stiff-limbed Adam and Eve and the forbidden tree, thinking of the brief meeting that had taken place there, the acquaintance which Major Richard Fleming had been too much occupied to renew. Presently she slipped into the nearest pew and, as naturally as if she had done it any time these last ten years, knelt down to say her prayers.

When she began she felt her lack of practice; but there was a feeling in the place of patience, and time to spare; so that she might have persevered a long while, if some sound in the chancel had not warned her that she was no longer alone. Delivered by her own acquired habit to instant, embarrassed consciousness of herself, she kept her face covered in hope that the new-comer might kneel also, or disappear. Then she reflected that it might be the vicar, preparing to begin some office. The thought of composing a congregation alarmed her; she partly lowered her hands, and looked up.

After all, it was only one of the ladies of the parish, who had come in from the vestry, busy with the altar flowers. She had just put down, on the Gospel side, a brass vase of jonquils, and was making a last adjustment of the stems. The vicar's wife, Hilary guessed, distantly noticing the back view of hat, cardigan, and tweed skirt; good, with that kind of near-dowdiness which conveys an air of well-bred decision. The back looked vaguely familiar; she tried to remember whether they had ever been introduced. The awkwardness of discovering one another's presence would probably be mutual; the church gave her, now, the feeling of having been taken in hand, of being very Church of England. Ashamed to continue, out of social hypocrisy, a gesture whose impulse had been sincere, she leaned on the arm-rest to rise and slip away. Her movement dislodged a hymn-book, which fell with an echoing slap on the floor beside her knees. The woman standing at the altar turned round; it was Mrs Fleming.

Afterwards, Hilary realised that it could not have been for more than a few startled seconds that their eyes had met. But her perceptions recorded them in slow-motion photography; the first instants of neutral surprise and faintly disapproving inquiry; the doubtful, then confirmed recognition, and then – a hair-trigger exposure which seemed to continue endlessly, as if the projector had jammed – the moment of shocked helplessness, confronting an indecency of circumstance beyond all resource. Hilary wondered later whether her own face had expressed with equal clarity her response to the situation; it had been shame, not for the essential fact between them, but for the chance which had given her a protection that seemed, now, as base as if she had sought it. For she was still on her knees, frozen there in the first intention of rising; and already Mrs Fleming was turning away. As she turned, she slightly inclined her head, and with the movement, her faded, finely cut face composed itself. Nothing could have been better adapted to the delicacies of polite requirement; but her grey eyes, as they withdrew their glance, shifted it almost imperceptibly upward. For the first time since she came in Hilary became aware that she was wearing no hat. Intent on the church and her own thoughts, she had completely forgotten.

Mrs Fleming stood back from the vase and raised one of the jonquils a little higher; then, bowing to the altar as impeccably as she had done to Hilary, she disappeared behind the organ into the vestry again.

Hilary got up and went down the aisle to the west door.

Involuntarily, as she walked, she put up her hand to her head; her uncovered, wind-blown hair seemed to concentrate in itself a nakedness which might have sufficed her whole person if her clothing had been removed. The church itself seemed to withdraw from her, recalled from its meditation to a duty of reproof.

Fortunately – for the impress of those minutes had seemed indelible – it was one of her days for an evening surgery. She drove thankfully into the little market town, where she had two rooms on the ground floor of a small Victorian house, just off the High Street, converted by her predecessor. No one ever came in the evening but the working people, whom she liked and got on with. There was the usual rush about six o'clock; it always thinned later, but one could never be sure. The concentration needed to combine thoroughness and courtesy with speed was just what she had been needing. By ten minutes to eight everyone had gone; she relaxed at her desk with a cigarette, thinking she might safely close a few minutes early, and wondering what was for dinner. Precisely at seven fifty-five the bell on the waiting-room door sounded. Feeling too ill-used to get up she called 'Come in' from her chair.

The communicating door opened. Julian came in, his hair streaked across his forehead from the wind. His eyes looked drawn; he gave her a quick, over-bright smile. A handkerchief was wrapped clumsily round his left hand.

'My dear.' She went through, locked the outer door, and came back to him. 'What is it? What's the matter?'

'Nothing. I just looked in.'

'Show me your hand. What have you done to it?'

'Done?' He looked down, took off the handkerchief and put it in his pocket. 'Sorry, I forgot. I thought if there were other people they might wonder why I was here.'

'But, Julian, you can't do that. You can't come to me as a patient. Whatever you do, never try that again.'

He began, impatiently, 'What does it—' and then, his face changing, 'You mean, because we ... Oh, God, I didn't think. Do you mean you could be struck off the register or something? Of course. I must be crazy. It only wanted that.'

'Really, darling!' She laughed: it partly relieved her tension. 'You should read the *News of the World* more carefully. Struck off for what? You're past the age of consent, and single unless you've been deceiving me all this while. What do you suppose they could charge me with? Indecent assault?'

His strained face relaxed in a faint grin. 'That black eye wouldn't have looked too good.'

'About the only advantage a female enjoys in this profession is that she isn't exposed to accusations of rape. But, seriously my dear, seducing patients from another doctor ranks nearly as high. If you'd been seen, it might easily have trickled round to Lowe. What made you do it? Has anything happened?'

'No. I just wanted to see you.' He began wandering round the consulting-room, opening drawers and peering inside. 'You know, I've never been in here before.'

'Everything's put away.' She was used to seeing these things handled by men who knew how to use them: Julian, vaguely picking up objects of unrelated purpose by the wrong ends, looked irritatingly out of keeping. '... No, I shan't tell you what it's for, you'd think it disgustingly sordid ... Don't undo that, it's sterile ... What *have* you got there? There's a throat swab in that, scarlet fever for all I know. For goodness' sake come away, it's worse than having a child about the place.'

He put down the tube with absent obedience. She realised that he had been only dimly aware of what she said. She took his arm. 'Darling, I didn't mean to snap at you. One gets fussy about one's stuff. Here, have a cigarette. And now tell me all about it.'

'There's nothing to tell.' He sat down beside her on the edge of the desk, and put his arm round her waist. 'I just felt like seeing you, that's all.'

'But why here? If you'd rung me up—' She had been about to say, 'You could have come to-night'; but some relics of her old defensiveness had made it a rule with her always to leave the initiative to him. 'You wouldn't do a queer thing like this without some reason.'

He said, with a constrained smile, 'Don't be so cast-iron rational about everything. Why shouldn't I suddenly want to see you? What's queer about it? Let's go out somewhere; this place smells forbidding, it puts me off.'

'Lisa's expecting me in to dinner. Now look, darling, obviously you came here to tell me something . . . ' She felt her nerves tightening; the effort of control hardened her voice. 'I'm not moving from here till I know what it is.'

He slid down from the desk, crossed the room, and suddenly wheeled round on her. 'For God's sake. What's the point of keeping this up? If you don't want me about, say so. I can find something else to do.' She was too much taken aback to answer; he went on, sullenly, 'If you'd told me straightaway I was nothing but a damned nuisance, it'd have saved time. I'd have been gone by now.'

'Don't let me keep you,' said Hilary instinctively. Almost before she realised that she had said it, he was at the door. Her heart jerked; he was opening it without a backward glance. 'Julian. Come here.'

He came back, looking wary and ashamed. She pulled down his head and gave him one of those caresses which are in the nature of a private joke. 'Another time, when you feel in a filthy mood and want something done about it, you can just tell me. That'd save time, too.'

'I'm sorry.' He suddenly strained her to him. 'Kiss me. No, properly. Don't stop, for a minute ... If you'd let me walk out of that door, I'd have gone nuts.'

'You're impossible, aren't you?' But flippancy broke on him unheeded. His love-making was exhausting, because it was the desperate expression of a demand not physical at all. They stood among the hard consulting-room furniture, while he told her, at irregular intervals, that he knew he wasn't fit to be with, that he had had to come, that it was nothing, that he got like this from time to time, he really couldn't say why, that it would be all right now that he had seen her, if she could put up with him a minute or two more.

Worse than the strain of all this was the effort required to keep from questioning him again. She came from a family which had believed strongly in talking everything out. Since they had all had enough in common to find one another's explanations understandable, it had usually worked, and the belief that this remedy would solve all personal problems was ingrained in her. Forcing herself to silence she resented, more than she realised, the denial of an outlet which her nature required. But she was, at the moment, too concerned for him to think about this. It ended with her ringing up Lisa to say, with equivocal truth, that she had had an urgent call, and letting him drive her out to an appalling meal in an obscure country hotel. He had, as a rule, a healthy and unfastidious appetite; to-night he ate almost nothing. Over coffee in the little smoke-room, which fortunately they had to themselves, she asked him whether he had had dinner already at home.

'No. I'm supposed to be over at Tony's. I rang up from a call-box and told him some story. I've just been driving about, waiting till I thought you'd be finished.'

Beginning again to say 'Why?' she changed it to 'Where?'

'Oh, up and down on the earth. Like Satan, you know. Satan walked, though, didn't he?' He began searching his pockets; she gave him another cigarette. 'I went over Mott's Farm way, or thereabouts.'

'Did you ...' She caught sight of his profile, bent over the match, and finished quickly, 'see anything interesting?'

'I contemplated the beauties of nature. The aesthetic type, you know.'

Hilary got up and went over to examine a picture on the opposite wall. It consisted, she found, of a complete set of cig-arette cards depicting British fresh-water fish. Later she could recall several varieties of eel, though at the time she had not been aware of seeing anything at all. She thought, however, as she went back to her chair, that it would make as good a sub-ject of conversation as any other. What she said was, 'Julian, I can't stand much of this, and nor can you. Had we better change our minds?'

He had followed her with his eyes across the room, and, when she turned, looked away at his cigarette smoke. Now he said, 'What do you mean?' He had made his voice blank; his eyes were those of a man who has evaded arrest for a long time, and feels a hand on his shoulder.

'What I say. I won't be a burden on anyone's conscience, least of all on yours. What I think right or wrong doesn't matter; your mind hasn't been at rest since this began. I know why; I don't want you to tell me about it. What matters is that if you come to me with a conviction of sin, we shall never be happy and it can't last. I'm not willing to go through with it on those terms. Tell me now – you've had plenty of time to think – and if that's how it feels to you, we'll say good-bye. Now, to-day.'

He got up, and stood looking at her. There was a moment when she thought he was silent from indecision (it was the moment in which he was still trying to realise what she had said); and in this interval, the cold sinking of her heart told her, with merciless point, how much further she was committed even than she had been aware. But she had trained her face, long ago, not to give her away, and it served her now. Julian was less successful; perhaps it would be truer to say that he had no such concern. He simply stared at her, his whole mind turned outward from himself. There was something in his eyes so single, so careless of defence, that it showed her her impulse for what it had really been. But she had taken a stand from which women of her kind do not easily go back: she waited.

He said, at last, 'I can't blame you. I expected this.'

'Did you?' she found herself saying. 'I didn't.'

In a voice from which all its characteristic vividness had been bleached away he said, 'Oh, yes. You think I've got bad blood in me. I have, of course; you can't say I didn't tell you the truth about it.'

'Julian,' she said, bewildered out of her purpose, 'what *are* you . . . ' She stopped; the waiter had come in for the coffee cups or perhaps with the bill. Julian swung round at him and said, 'Two more coffees, please,' with the grand-seigneur manner he adopted when highly wrought. Looking surprised (understandably, thought Hilary, recalling the chicory essence, tinned milk, and tepid water) the waiter retreated. Evidently not insensitive to atmosphere, he closed the door firmly after him.

'I can't drink it,' she said mechanically. 'Julian, are you out of your mind?'

'Not at the moment. You're trying to put it nicely, of course. But of course I know; I've always known. You can't have a father who's a swine and a brute, as mine was, without wondering where it's going to come out in you. You've been thinking that, too, haven't you?'

She could not believe, at first, that it was not a piece of deliberate theatre, designed to turn the issue. But a look at him was enough to demolish this theory, which at least she could have understood. His sincerity was far more alarming.

Collecting herself, she said, 'How could you suppose such a thing? You must be mad. One would think your father had been a criminal. If you know as little about him as you say, you've no right to speak like that about a man who died as he did.'

'In the war, you mean? That's sheer sentimentality. Every kind of man died in the war.'

'You don't know what kind of man he was. You don't know how people lived then, or what men had to go through. You don't know any of the circumstances at all.'

'I know the only thing that matters. I hope to God I never know anything more.'

Something in his tone, or his face, arrested her. He was like someone who, stumbling blindly, finds he has crossed a forbidden threshold and that it is too late to step back.

'I think it might be better for you to know.'

'*Better?*' There was a discreet tap; the waiter, with two more cups of stagnant coffee. Looking at him with aloof loathing, Julian said, 'And the bill, please. Thank you. No change.' Hilary reckoned the tip at roughly cent per cent, and admired the waiter's restraint in not throwing it at his head. The door shut again.

'You don't know what you're talking about. I'm sorry, I don't mean to be so bloody rude. Perhaps it would be better to know, for you. On the other hand, I suppose it's partly because nothing like this has happened to you that you're the person you are. Not that I'd have you different. But you can't tell what it's like to have lived all your life knowing there's – something, and – and that in any crisis it may suddenly come out.'

Hilary saw light. Anything but daylight; but light of a kind. It illuminated much in the past; it left her, in the present, groping more blindly than before.

'But, my dear, this is ... Hearing things is bound to be painful, at the time. But there can't be anything you could hear that wouldn't be better for you than this. The war was littered with broken marriages between quite average people. They had violent experiences apart from one another, and it made them feel separate. It's part of the general beastliness of war.'

'I'm not talking about average people, I'm ... I don't want to talk about it. Or think about it. Just tell me whether or not you're through with me. If you are, then I shall know.'

'What will you know?'

He was silent; still looking at her, but having ceased to see her. At this moment the door burst open, and a mixed party surged into the smoke-room, banging the ash-trays cheerfully on the table and demanding drinks. Julian picked up Hilary's coat, and in rigid silence helped her into it. They went out.

He stopped the car at random; in an almost pitch-dark field, by a palely weaving stream, they sat on Julian's coat. Somewhere an invisible horse trod and snorted and tore at grass. Still locked in an almost palpable silence, Julian sat with his arms round his knees. Presently she took one of his hands – it was stone-cold – and held it. The stream gurgled secretly, the horse made a chumping noise, and slivers of black flickered stilly across the sky.

'Our cook,' said Julian conversationally, 'has a thing about

334

bats, that they'll get in her hair.' His hand closed on hers, crushed it violently, and slackened again. 'She got me out of bed once at three in the morning, to put one out.'

'They have lice.' She contributed a second hand. 'People say they squeak, but the pitch is too high to hear.'

'Too high? The place is alive with them. Can't you hear them now?'

'Only the horse. You must have very good hearing.'

'I hear them every night, at home. Try again. S-sh, now.'

He took her hands between his. She heard nothing. The grey sky with its flittering shadows was blotted out from her upturned face.

'You're not listening,' he whispered.

'Yes I am.' She drew him down to her.

At last they had been still so long that she began to fancy she could hear faint flaws in the stillness as the bats went over. The chill of the ground began to come up through the coat they were lying on, and the chill of the dew through hers which she had shared with him. She could see no end to it all, only a pendulum swinging, up and down and side to side, in the same rhythm, endless and enclosed. She began to shiver; he gave her the whole of her coat again and held her tightly, trying to warm her lest she should wish to go. She would have stayed, but the shivering once begun would not be controlled. 'You'll take cold,' he said. 'We'd better be getting along.'

'It must be getting late. I ought to go.'

He said, without moving, 'As well now as later, I suppose. I was just thinking it would be less trouble to die.' It was a statement, not a protest; before she could answer, he was getting up.

Lisa was keeping coffee hot for her by the fire. Thankfully, and with an unspoken blessing, Hilary offered her quota of the small talk and petty news which, unbearably tedious when overheard from others, comes to life in the company of those whom one likes. In the midst of it, and without much change of tone, Lisa said, 'Tell me, now, if a woman came to you who'd lost two babies in succession, would you call her a fool to be starting another?'

'Oh, not necessarily at all; it would depend on ...' She looked up. 'My dear, of course not. I always said that. I'm terribly glad. Isn't it a bit soon, though, to be sure?'

'I feel pretty sure. It's just like the other times.' She explained; Hilary agreed that she was probably right. 'I think,' added Lisa lightly, 'that I should feel quite disappointed if anything happened this time.'

Hilary said, with firmness and certainty, 'It won't. We're going to make a job of this.' Seeing the reinforced hope in Lisa's eyes, she thought she must have said it well. It occurred to her that lately she had had practice in reinforcement.

Lisa would have dropped the subject almost at once; she always had difficulty in believing that anything personal to herself could fail to bore other people, perhaps because her intimacy with Rupert was so complete that all others seemed, by comparison, degrees of courtesy. Once Hilary had disposed of this, she was glad to talk. She was severely practical, with the insistence of one who dares not begin to be anything more. Hilary gave her all the advice she knew; she reflected that a necessary part of the treatment would consist in not leaving Lisa too much alone.

Emphasis was not in Lisa's nature at any time; so Hilary was a little while in realising, from one day to another, the eager trust which her trained knack of confidence inspired. The discovery profoundly moved her; she was grateful to Lisa for so much quiet easing of life. She took pains with the arrangement of her work, and once or twice put Julian off, not always with very adequate notice, when she discovered that Lisa had an evening on her hands. The reasons she gave were not very adequate either; she knew herself to be the only person in Lisa's confidence and respected her almost fanatical love of privacy. Now and then she was conscious of an unhappy satisfaction, which was not wholly the fruit of self-sacrifice. With Lisa for a decent reason, she obeyed impulses which she would not openly have entertained; to prove to herself her independence, to revenge on him certain moments of solitary thought; to stir, in a way for which she would not afterwards accuse herself, his sense of insecurity. She caught herself thinking, sometimes, that she had been making things too easy for him, reconciling him too readily to a state of affairs which it was right that he should find intolerable.

In a distant contemplative way, Julian had always approved of Lisa. She was not, therefore, as well prepared as she might have been for the caustic response he gave when, one night in her room, she mentioned Lisa's name. She remembered the night when she had told him about David, and his quiet acceptance of the physical fact. That he might actually become jealous now had never entered her head, and seemed so fantastic that she could not take it seriously.

'She's quite amusing, I dare say,' he pursued, 'but there can't really be much point in your seeing so much of each other. I mean, you obviously haven't much in common. You're so sincere, and anyone can see she's the frigid type.'

'Oh, Julian!' Finding this too much, or perhaps curious to know what he would say next, she lapsed into that helpless silence which is the most goading of retorts. Julian became dogmatic.

'You've only got to look at her. Naturally she wouldn't tell you so. I don't suppose women boast about it, any more than men do. But take it from me, she's the sort of woman who'd tell you all the time not to disarrange her hair.'

'Well, darling, perhaps she was just going out when you tackled her. You shouldn't be put off so easily.'

Julian ignored this as it deserved. 'After all,' he told her, 'a man can generally form a fair idea.'

Hilary peered up at him, from under a protecting fold of sheet. She longed suddenly to call out 'Hold it!' like a producer at a felicitous moment. He looked at her reprovingly; solemn, cocksure, ridiculous, beautiful; she could have wept for tenderness, even while she held herself rigid to keep the laughter in. The rigidity was the only thing he noticed.

'Now I've annoyed you, I suppose. Well, of course I've no right to tell you how to arrange your time.'

'That is a point, isn't it?'

He drew himself away with a gesture which lost nothing in emphasis, if something in effect, from the lack of room.

'At least I never fetched you ten miles on a dark night to tell you how much I like being with other people. Ever since you got thick with this woman you've been different to me. You didn't want to see me the other evening. You keep me like a dog hanging around. That's her idea of how men ought to be treated, I suppose.'

'Darling, stop being such an unmitigated ass.' She reached over for him, but he turned his head aside.

'Her husband didn't stand for it, anyway. I've been a fool, I suppose, to let you know I . . . '

'Yes?'

'Oh, shut up,' he said, 'and let me alone.'

This was not the end of the conversation; but the rest was conducted in a different language.

Afterwards, she realised how deeply comforting this silly episode had been, and why. For jealousy is soothing to jealousy, like a homoeopathic drug; it is only an irritant to untroubled emotions, or those that are expending themselves elsewhere.

When she searched her mind she knew that, always, it was his reticences that she found intolerable. The circumstances themselves, which were partly of her own making, she could have borne. She knew, without the need of explanation, that, all his life, his time had been a blank engagement diary for his mother to fill in, and that it was impossible for him to make any drastic change in this routine without giving a reason. Only too gladly she would have been understanding about this; only too readily she would have commiserated, if he had only asked for commiseration. What worked upon her was the tormented, impregnable loyalty which was eloquent in his silences. She tried to be reasonable about it, reminding herself that the person who makes one an ally in disloyalty will, sooner or later, transfer one to the receiving end of the process. She had always prided herself on not being possessive; sincerely believing, at the time, that her affair with David had presented a crucial test. It came as something of a surprise to her to find that reason could be convinced, while leaving the emotions quite untouched. In his absences she was not only lonely, but solitary in her imagination; seeing him in her mind's eye engrossed in some familiar concern, more than half content without her. If he came later than he had promised, or found it impossible to get away, the disappointment which had belonged to both of them began to seem wholly her own.

All this she was revolving in her mind on an evening when she had expected him for tea and he did not come. She had delayed as long as possible ringing for the tray to be taken away, and at last Annie had come unsummoned to collect it. The evening had been carefully cleared; she had no work left to do. Lisa was out to dinner. There was a book in her lap, which she had looked forward to reading; she turned it over, unopened, thinking how the first five chapters would be spoiled by listening for his car, the next five by trying not to listen; while he, probably, after ten minutes' chagrin, would be making the best of it with a cheerfulness which first he would pretend to, and presently feel. She indulged this thought until in reasonless reaction, she said to herself that he might be ill, he might have crashed his car or been thrown again on one of his stolen rides; all this time when she had been accusing him he might be dead. She saw him lying again on the hospital bed (it was not her week for casualties, no one would tell her), but this time with the change of colour that comes when the blood has stopped. Only his dark hair would be still alive, and warm to the hand; they would brush it smoothly, a little differently from his way of brushing it . . .

There was a tap on the french window. She started as if death itself had knocked. The latch turned.

'Hallo,' said Julian cheerfully. 'You look very surprised to see me. I believe you'd forgotten I was coming to-day.'

He shut the door behind him and pushed back his hair with one hand; it had been windy outside. He had on the grey suit he had worn on the first night she had brought him back here; his eyes, as they often did when he had been driving, looked blue.

'To-day?' said a voice for which she felt no responsibility. 'Yes, do you know, I believe I had.'

'I take a very poor view of that.' He came over; she put up her face with a smile. As if she had expressed everything she felt, she found herself expecting of him some acknowledegment of what she had endured, some compensating violence. He kissed her affectionately, and, deceived by her restraint, let her go. Rumpling her head, he glanced over it at the cleared table.

'Haven't you had tea?' she said. 'I thought you would have, by this time.'

'Well, sort of.' He added, with chastened hope, 'But it was rather dainty and refined.'

A vainer man, she thought, would have noticed the revealing discrepancies in what she had said. Or had he noticed, and taken it for granted? There was a wistful, well-behaved look about him. It occurred to her that his attention had simply wandered to the receding prospect of tea.

'I'll make you some more.' She went to the cupboard where she kept some tea things of her own. 'What a nuisance you are.' She was glad not to look at him; for the first time she knew what went on in women who made emotional scenes.

'You're an unfailing angel. Don't if it's really a bother. Actually, I'm as empty as a drum. I've only had a thimbleful of China tea and a sandwich the size of a bus ticket; women and children first, you know. I got roped in at the last moment, or I'd have been here before.'

It was still cool enough for an evening fire; she filled the kettle upstairs, to avoid collision with Annie, and put the pot to warm. He stood about, going through the motions of being helpful; he was too well trained to sit down while she worked, though there was nothing for him to do. To feel him just behind her, standing aimlessly at her elbow, went through her like electricity. She could have turned round and struck him.

'Have a cigarette,' she said.

'Oh, damn. I bought you a hundred, to make up for my depredations; and then what with this bun-fight, I left it behind. Sure you're not short? It's a curious thing I've noticed, how much better your cigarettes taste than the same brand of anyone else's.'

He smiled at her across his burning match. She said, coolly, 'It's probably the sandalwood in the box.' His affection, his charm, his contented imperviousness reached her distorted like images in a heat haze. He was beginning, already, to make a convenience of her, she thought.

'It's nice to be here.' He let down his length into a chair by the fire, relaxed, his head tilted back. His eyes were half shut; the rising firelight emphasised the slant of his brows – a line that looked dashed-in, with two bold strokes, by a brilliantly assured draughtsman – the finely concave planes of cheek and temple and the lifted line of the jaw. It was the bone-deep beauty which, short of mutilation, is almost indestructible; fifty years hence, if he lived, women would be saying, 'What a noble old man,' and trying, with secret regret, to picture him as she saw him now.

He drew lazily on his cigarette, looking into the fire; she sat back in her chair, stubbornly imitating his ease. Already restless, she would have liked to get up from her chair; she could get a cigarette; but he would light it for her, and she could not endure him so near. She wished that her will had sharp edges, with which to hurt him.

The kettle began to sing, a comfortable homely sound. He stretched himself in his chair with a little sigh and, turning his head towards the fire, stroked his cheek with half-conscious pleasure against the linen cover.

'I don't know what it is,' he said, 'but I feel good to-day.'

She got to her feet and went to the table where the ciga-rettes were. Over her shoulder she said, 'I'm glad, I thought you were perishing of hunger.'

In the fire a silky block of coal was jetting a blue-edged flame. Watching it drowsily, he said, 'What could be nicer than feeling hungry with half a Dundee cake at your elbow?'

'Start on it now, the tea won't be long.' She lit her cigarette quickly, before he looked round.

'No, I'll wait now. God, there was a wind up on the downs to-day. Makes you sleepy, doesn't it, coming indoors? I'll wake up when I have some tea. You look so energetic. Come over here and sit on my knee.'

He had never asked her this before; she knew he only wanted to complete a vague mood of domestic cosiness. She made an irresolute movement towards him, felt a tremor pass over her, and moved away.

'No, it would mean such a sordid scramble if the maid came in. I've got a new record; would you like to hear it?'

'Is it very intellectual?'

'It's Handel; part of the *Water Music*.'

'Just what I feel like.'

She collected this, delicately, into her private irony, and put the record on. Returning to her chair she tried to hear it. Julian had abandoned his cigarette and shut his eyes. Wholly ignorant of musical structure, and without shame about it, he delivered himself up to the vivid dream-pictures which he never pretended not to indulge.

Hilary, for her part, was recalling the ambitions and the indignations which had seemed important to her a year or two ago. It was as if somebody had repeated to her a very old joke, of which she had only just seen the point. How anxious she had been to prove that she could get an appointment over

343

David's head! To do this, it had seemed, would prove something or other about women and men. It was excruciatingly funny to think she might have got it – or the presidency of the College of Surgeons, for that matter – only to find herself exactly where she now was. The hard core for a feminist to bite on had, after all, been something as simple as this. She recalled the times when Julian had arrived to find her sleepy or preoccupied, and the manner in which, quite successfully, he had dealt with the situation. She would have despised him if he had been afraid to try, lest she should think him importunate. Now for the first time it was borne in on her, like a piece of news, that being a woman was a fact about which absolutely nothing could be done. She had spent so long in battle with the non-essentials; the essential had stolen up on her unaware. It had the last word in a long argument. She felt the unshed tears burning her eyelids.

The gramophone clicked; and, almost at the same moment, the boiling kettle hissed into the fire. She got up and made the tea.

Julian blinked, sat up, and said, 'That was quite something. I got some good ideas from that.'

'I'll put on the other side.'

'No, let's talk. You know, it suddenly struck me just now, I wonder why no one's thought of using eighteenth-century Venice as a setting for *Othello*. Canaletto backcloths and peruques and frightfully elaborate manners – you see how the contrast would throw Othello up? Proud and barbaric and dressed like Byron's Corsair. He *is* a bit Byronic, come to think of it. And Iago, of course, would come over perfectly as a man-about-town of the Age of Reason; a sort of Congreve hero's-friend gone bad. I should rather like to do it.'

She said vaguely, 'Because of the blacking?'

'Blacking? Oh, Lord, not Othello. Othellos are born, not

made. Iago, I mean. I'd never get it, though; too tall. Get landed with Cassio, I suppose. But you know, the drunk scene ... '

'Since I've made this tea you might drink it before it's cold.'

'I've got my eye on it; I can't drink it as hot as you can.' He returned to *Othello* where he had left off, punctuating his discourse with absent-minded mouthfuls of cake. She had enjoyed listening to this kind of thing, until to-day. Now she felt like the tea, stood on one side to cool. He scarcely saw her. She was background music. Julian looked up, pausing in a momentary failure of ideas. 'Well, I'll have to think it out in more detail later. Now tell me what *you've* been doing.'

But she saw that, courteous rather than curious, he had still half his mind in *Othello*. Looking past him, she said, 'Mine's not so interesting. I've only been working; not handing cups of tea to old ladies and thinking what sort of doctor I'd be if I could only make the effort to be one.'

Julian put his cup down slowly on the table. He had been so unready for it that nothing had had time to show in his face but a jarred questioning, as if at some unexplained physical blow, which is perhaps an accident. He studied her face. At last he said, carefully, 'You don't seem to like me very much this evening.'

'I'm getting a little tired of these pipe dreams, that's all.'

He began, protestingly, 'But how can one help ... ' then stopped, and looked at her again. In a different voice he said, 'You told me once it didn't bore you. I've rather traded on it, I'm afraid. I'm sorry.'

She felt herself go white with anger. 'Don't try to put me in the wrong. You know it didn't bore me, as long as I believed in it. If it had the slightest reality, it wouldn't bore me now. You're like a child bragging of what it will do when it's grown

345

up. Except that a normal child wants to grow up, and you're afraid to.'

He continued to look at her, attentive, silent. She perceived that he was absorbing not the content of her words, but simply the fact that she had aimed at inflicting pain. The pause lengthened so unendurably that, merely to break it, she began again, 'You must see—'

As if he had not heard, and still looking at her, he said, 'The point is – what is it that you're really angry about? You'll think me rather dim to be asking you. I suppose I ought to know.'

She had not foreseen, when she reproached him with childishness, that he would display so promptly the child's gift for taking an unconscious revenge with an instinctive truth. 'Don't you see,' she said, 'that things pile up, and one suddenly reaches a point when one can't take it any longer?'

'I know,' he said. 'It's partly because I saw that, that I asked you to marry me straightaway.'

'Yes. You asked me to make myself the talk of the county, simply because you hadn't any confidence in yourself to hold out when things got difficult.'

'I suppose it must seem like that to you, now ... I had another reason, too, if you remember.'

She said, impatiently, 'Because you'd slept with me, you mean.'

She saw in his eyes a hurt too deeply felt to be turned outward in reproach. For a moment her anger felt like an enemy external to herself. It was misery that drove her on.

'Yes, very well, you behaved like a gentleman. You made a point of that at the time. But we're living in the twentieth century now; being a gentleman isn't a career any longer.'

He got to his feet, pain darkening slowly to anger in his eyes. Driving too deep, she had defeated herself. A moment or two ago he had looked defensive and ashamed; now, sincerely outraged, and pierced by her desecration, he grew suddenly splendid. He stood, his head up, his mouth closed proudly on his rising anger, his eyes, level and grey, blazing at her; exalted in a passionate sense of wrong. Nothing of it was histrionic, or conscious at all; simply his body was, in the old sense, a maker, gifted with language where another would stammer or be dumb. It retaliated for him, better than he knew.

She faced him, feeling her breath shorten. If she had been a peasant woman and able to feel her own nature, she might have released it by a burst of weeping, or by running at him with the kitchen knife. But a long and expensive education had made her slow at understanding very simple things. She allowed her background to interpret for her in its own devious way.

'It's no use your trying to look ill-used, Julian. Somebody has to tell you this. If you can put up indefinitely with this lap-dog life, I can't put up indefinitely with watching you lead it. You can't afford it, you know. Your looks are against you.'

Everything stopped. It was as if she had spoken the charm that turns men into stone. The change seemed rather one of substance than expression, because not only motion but colour left him. His eyes grew a little lighter, as the iris, opened just now in anger, slowly closed down its grey ring. It was the only thing about him that moved.

Hilary, watching, did not recognise in herself the peasant woman who had struck her blow and whose voice protested within her that she had only meant to show him; that she hadn't known the knife was so sharp or that he would lean on it in her hand; that this would turn out in a moment not to have happened at all. To translate these gestures into the terms of civilisation carries its own penalties; one cannot, for

347

relief, scream to the neighbours to come and help, or snatch up a dishcloth to stop the blood.

A cinder fell into the grate with a light brittle noise, sending a curl of smoke into the room. As if it were this which called for some reply, Julian said, with colourless distinctness, 'Well, good evening,' and moved towards the glass doors.

She stood where she was; as it happened, across his path. The furniture was so disposed that, not to pass her, he must have taken a circuit of half the room. When he found she did not move, as if he had gone already and were delayed on his way by something inanimate, he took her by the arms to put her on one side. Her mind was still in arrears with the situation; but when he touched her, her body, unprompted, made a fierce movement to shake him off. She felt him check in the stride which was to have carried him past her; his hands tightened, pressing her arms against her sides. Furiously she resisted; he shut his teeth and held her motionless. She could feel through her flesh the bones of his fingers against the bone of her arm. Her strength, not inconsiderable for a woman, was reduced to complete impotence. This was probably his only purpose, if he had a conscious purpose at all; but it enraged her. With the evenness of controlled hysteria, she said, 'Let me go, Julian. Do you hear? Let me go.'

Unmoved, or unhearing, he stood with his hands locked round her arms. She pretended submission, and, when she felt his grip beginning to slacken, freed one of her arms with a quick jerk. Seeing her about to escape, he snatched her back by throwing his whole arm round her. She lost her head, and began thrusting at him with her clenched hands; leaning back, she found herself looking into his tautened face.

'I hate you,' whispered the peasant woman, getting through to the surface at last.

'I know that, damn you,' said Julian from the back of his throat. He brought down his mouth on hers, and held it there with his full strength.

She continued to struggle, for some moments of mechanical persistence, while he kissed her furiously, implacably, and at last, when her resistance was finished, with a slow drowsy hunger and closed eyes. She began to feel something drugged and trance-like in him which infected her, so that she ceased the caresses into which, by degrees, her struggles had merged, and held him softly and still. Just as she was feeling, with a cloudy kind of acceptance, that this might go on till they slept on their feet, he lifted his head abruptly.

'And now,' he said, in a voice perfectly hard and steady, 'you'll tell me this thing. I said, now.'

She gazed at him vaguely. Even if she had known what he was talking about, she could not have replied. In some perception of this, he gave her a moment or two; then added, curtly, 'You heard what I said.'

Trying to collect herself, she murmured, 'Yes, but it didn't mean anything.'

'Try again. That cock won't fight.'

'Dear, be quiet a little while. We've been rather ... It will be all right in a minute.'

'All right in a minute. God! Am I supposed to laugh?'

This got her awake. She looked up at him appealingly. 'I swear to you, Julian, I don't know what you mean.'

'Have you really forgotten? I believe you have.' He gave a bitter little smile and suddenly kissed her again. 'Well, think back a minute. This won't be the only time. I've got to know, before it happens again. I've made up my mind; so you may as well.'

'You mean, why we quarrelled? Oh, my dear, don't be silly.'

'Can't you be honest with me? That wasn't a quarrel, and you know it. All that about my getting a job – oh, yes, I dare say, but that wasn't it. It's something about me, myself. Suddenly I'm intolerable. You felt it so that you couldn't keep it in. Without anything happening, you hated me; you said so. This has gone on too long, it's driving me mad. What is it? You'll tell me, or I don't leave this room. It doesn't matter what it is. Tell me. I've got to know.'

His intensity seemed to her so absurd that she would have laughed, if she had trusted herself to begin.

'Oh, be your age, Julian. How can you be such a fool? You've the instincts of a man, and heaven knows you've the strength of one. And you ask me that, now.'

He said, doggedly, 'I don't know what you're driving at; so you may as well say.'

'You must know, of course you do. You're doing this on purpose, and it isn't fair. You're just trying to pay me out.'

'No, I've got over that. You can tell me now.'

'I'm not going to, why should I? Nobody would.' She swallowed quickly; but it was no use, the next sob was quite audible. She tried vainly to smother it in his coat; she had not expected this at all. Nor had she anticipated the words which presently emerged; she tried to smother them too. ' ... sitting there,' she concluded, 'as if I were made of wood, just eating and talking shop.' She snatched the handkerchief out of his breast-pocket, choked, and blew her nose.

There was a short pause. Suddenly he clutched at her arm. It was bruised already; she said, 'Don't *do* that,' and looked up.

'Is that the truth? Is it?' He dragged the handkerchief away from her face.

She cried out, exasperated, 'Couldn't you *tell*?'

'Swear it. Swear by Almighty God.'

'Don't be outrageous. Give me that back, I haven't finished with it.' She wiped her eyes, and was putting the handkerchief back where she had found it, when in silence he caught her violently into his arms. She would have lifted her face, but he pressed it down against his shoulder, and held her so that she could not look up. She could feel his mouth moving blindly over her hair. At last he let out his breath in a long, gasping laugh. They kissed. She said, 'I must look awful, let me get my bag.'

Above the mirror (which confirmed her worst fears) she stole a look at him. His face was transformed; inwardly lighted, and free. Presently he said, 'Here, give it me,' and before she could protest took the powder out of her hand. 'You look all right, but if you must do it, do it properly.' He ladled powder on to her face, and with long, firm strokes began to smooth it in.

'You're dropping it over everything. Why can't you behave like other people?'

'There. And don't start asking for lipstick, because you won't get any, and this is why ... I can't make women out. What was the idea, what were you like that for? If you – if that was it, why in heaven's name didn't you do something about it? Didn't you think I could take it, or what?' There was an interval, while Hilary's compressed feelings sought expression. 'All right,' said Julian hastily. 'God bless you, keep your hair on.' He passed an anxious hand over his own. Suddenly they both began to laugh. Presently Julian said, 'Who's in tonight?'

'Annie is; and she's not been up yet to do my room. It's time you were going, anyway.'

'Fetch your coat,' said Julian briskly. 'We'll go for a drive.'

It was an excursion which she recalled, afterwards, in disjointed sequences, uncertain in place and time. Julian, when some while later she asked him where he had taken her, said that he thought he could find the place somewhere in Shelley; in *Alastor*, he fancied, but not on the map. For her own part, she remembered a rush through blue-white, windy stars; a moment when another car came out of a blind turning, and Julian performed some split-second miracle while continuing to sing; and, more clearly because it lasted much longer, a hollow near the top of a high hill-side, to leeward of the wind, drifted with curled crackling leaves that felt like beech. Below, a valley of unknown depth was filled with a tarn of mist, over which hung a curved and smoky moon. She remembered stroking Julian's hair backwards, and, when he suggested that she should try the other way, explaining that she had thought it would give off sparks. She remembered that they laughed a good deal, became for a short time desperately tragic, and then laughed again.

'I won't come in,' said Julian in the garden, when he brought her home. 'I shall remember all this on my death-bed, if I have a death-bed. I don't want to tail it off.'

They stood a little longer, screened from the house by a deodar, whose sharp aromatic smell came to them on cold ripples of air.

'There's a Victorian song,' said Hilary hazily, 'about being under the deodar.' She was growing sleepy. Julian said 'Yes,' and hummed a bar or two softly. 'Fancy your knowing that,' she murmured. 'My mother was fond of it.'

An owl came winnowing over them, startlingly near. Julian said, 'It was true in a sense, part of what you said. Let's not talk about it now. I could, but let's leave to-night as it is. I'm going to see to-morrow whether Finnigan's back.'

Somewhere in the shadows a little way off the owl had found an ambush, and imitated, cunningly, the mating-noise of a mouse.

'You'll be cold,' he said. 'Let me feel if I brushed the leaves off properly. Look, that would have been a nice thing; here's one in your hair. We'll have to think why we're late for dinner, I suppose. Shouldn't that scarf be tucked in or something? No, I can do it. Funny to think that in two minutes from now this will be over, isn't it? This is good night, then. I shall love you till I die.'

The lamps within the house were like a sudden darkness, which one's eyes paint with the last-seen images of light.

I7

Mrs Theobald tinkled her bedside handbell for the second time. No answer; her suspicions were confirmed. Clive must still be closeted with that woman, somewhere downstairs. She had listened very carefully, and there had been no sound of the car driving away. This happened too often, now; and when, afterwards, she pressed him for an account of what had been said, he was most unsatisfactory. Sprinkling eau de Cologne on her forehead and pillow, Mrs Theobald made up her mind. There must be a change.

Clive was, without encouragement, sufficiently obtuse and self-centred. His own family was coarsely robust; it had taken a long training to make him realise what highly strung, delicate women went through, and lately there had been a definite falling off. Twice in the last week or two he had mislaid, on the day, the note-book in which the date and time of her more important symptoms were jotted down; and sometimes, when the car had driven away and he came upstairs, there was an air of cheerful reassurance about him which was simply soulless. She suspected increasingly that, instead of pointing out how much more acutely she suffered than a less sensitive person with the same complaint, he minimised things, glad of any excuse for a selfish complacency. But one was used to selfishness; the intolerable thing was that he should, in that of all quarters, receive support. As the last unheard tinkle of the handbell died away, Mrs Theobald resolved, finally, to change her doctor.

It had been a great mistake, of course, not to have taken steps when Dr Pierce left; she had thought of it, as soon as she had heard that a woman was taking the practice over. But he had made it awkward by bringing her along for a personal introduction; and, after all, it had been reasonable to expect that a person of the same sex might have sympathy with one's complex, intimate troubles. How mistaken! That callous briskness should have been warning enough.

One could have tolerated crudity, thought Mrs Theobald (searching the bedside table for one of the special chocolates), one could have endured, even, those bracing ineptitudes about its being a long time now since the operation and nothing really organic being wrong, if the woman had even troubled to be socially agreeable. Nobody could say that Mrs Theobald, for her part, had made no effort. She had been only too anxious to make her doctor a real friend, to whom she could bring her confidences, who would explain things nicely to Clive and ensure that he worried a little more. But no; not even that. Today's visit had been the last straw.

It might have been supposed that anyone, the most unimaginative person, would have realised that an invalid relied on her visitors to keep her in touch with things. Naturally, with one's social life so restricted, one liked to know what was going on in the neighbourhood; and, even if it happened to be unpleasant, a benevolent interest was not out of place. It was not as if she had been in the least obvious or intrusive; all she had said – absolutely all – was that Mrs Clare must often feel lonely when her husband could spend so little time with her; that it seemed a pity he could not get something to do in England, as people were apt to drift apart with separation; and with delicate tact, that she seemed to enjoy the company of young people. She had rounded the whole thing off with a harmless little joke, saying she only wished that, while Clive was buried in his eternal books, she could find a handsome young man to sit with *her* in the evenings. Not a single uncharitable word, unless, of course, anyone were determined on a wrong interpretation.

No, one's nerves were quite unequal to dealing with these brusque people. And if she really *was* so friendly with Mrs Clare as to jump up in arms (which Mrs Theobald doubted, for in her experience women were not loyal to their own sex), then either she had no idea what was going on, and ought to be told, or, demonstrably, she was not at all a nice woman herself. Mrs Theobald almost wished, now, that she had come into the open about it; tact was entirely wasted where it was so little appreciated. One had only expected a quite noncommittal answer, just some little intimation that the facts were understood and deplored; but, really! Actually to turn pale with annoyance, and then to say baldly, 'I think you must be thinking of someone else. What young man?' Naturally Mrs Theobald, whose fineness of feeling even in childhood had been a household word, had withdrawn at once into her shell. No person of refinement could have ignored so pointed a hint. And to say in that emphatic manner, so unsuitable in a sick-room – aggressive would be a better word – that to her personal knowledge Mrs Clare was a particularly faithful and devoted wife! She had actually used the word 'faithful'; it was evident that she was not even a lady. A faithful and devoted wife, indeed; it would have been quite laughable, if the affair had been less disgusting. And there was no possible doubt about Mrs Theobald's information; she had had it direct from Mrs Cotter, to whom Nurse Price had been on her way when she had seen him – at *that* hour! – leaving the house.

Well, sooner or later (Mrs Theobald examined the chocolates critically for a soft centre; the last had been, disappointingly, a hard one) everyone would have an eye-opener. It would get to some friend of the husband, who would feel in duty bound to let him know. (She devoted a few minutes to considering how the friend should phrase the letter.) Not that one could feel much sympathy for him; obviously, like Clive, he had been selfish and neglectful, and being so much on the Continent it went without saying ... but that, no doubt, if he took proceedings, couldn't be proved. Nor was it necessary to waste emotion on Mrs Fleming, a stand-offish woman who had thought herself, apparently, above calling on Mrs Theobald when she came to the neighbourhood in search of the health-giving country air. If Mrs Fleming had devoted less thought to her social prestige she might have given more to the morals of her son. Mrs Theobald herself could distinctly remember having remarked to someone, quite a year ago, that he would come to no good. Young men with these film-star looks never did; unscrupulous women turned their heads with flattery, and snapped them up. One had only to look at Mrs Clare to perceive that she knew far too much about sex. (This one was a coffee cream; she noted the shape for future reference.)

There, at last, was the sound of the front door shutting; and, yes, there went the car. Mrs Theobald pushed the chocolate-box unobtrusively under the *Express*, rang the handbell with emphasis, sank down into her pillows, and weakly, patiently, shut her eyes.

*

Hilary felt the hummocks of the village green bump under her wheels, jammed on the hand-brake, and walked over the grass to the telephone booth. As she stared at the scribbled panel over the instrument (numbers, a doodled face, and an obscene word heavily pencilled over) she felt with the back of her neck the attentive eyes in the front windows, speculating about the urgent message that would not wait till she got home. Groping with cold, stumbling fingers for coppers in her bag, she found her mind protesting that, if one side of the structure could be made opaque, why not two, or three? The naked glass squares around her seemed to express, and prove, the essential squalor and indecency of the world.

'Number, please?'

She gave it. Why not an automatic exchange, why this necessity for personal contact at every turn? At least there had been twopence in her purse: she might have had to go into the post office for change.

The wire made a clicking sound; she swallowed, but it was something at the exchange, no ringing followed. One of her gloves fell from the ledge to the floor, disloged by the shaking of her arm. If she could have gone straight from the room, instantly, to a telephone, she could have managed, she thought, quite well. It is one thing to know one has swallowed poison, another to feel it working into the body. But she had allowed herself, from habit, to be ushered into the forlorn, dusty study with the woolwork crested cushions and the moustached college groups, and had doled out to the wretched husband his regular dose of mental tonic; chiefly, she supposed, because it had always been he whom she regarded as the patient. He had seemed to notice nothing. The pennies in her hand, with which she was tapping on the telephone, picked out – for one must peg down one's mind somehow – a Bentley rhythm:

What I like about Clive
Is that he is no longer alive.
There is a great deal to be said . . .

'Two pennies, please.'

She began to search for them, found them between her finger and thumb, and dropped them in. Her fingers, missing the hard edges, went on tapping. 'There is a great deal to be said for being dead.'

The bell began ringing. She knew the sound; it was the right number. She had felt so sure of getting a wrong one that she had allowed her readiness to slacken; the sense of tension returned like a violent shock. The ringing stopped. She imagined she could hear a breath drawn in to answer, and that already she knew the voice; without waiting for it, she said, 'Lynchwick 23? Is Mr Fleming in?'

'I believe so. Who is speaking?'

'Dr Mansell.' Oh, God, let her be offended enough at being taken for the maid; let us not converse.

'Will you hold the line, Dr Mansell? I'll see if I can find him.' The tap of heels receded, faintly, on a polished floor.

From the green outside the ragged rhythmic chanting of children trickled through the glass. 'Bill-y's a sill-y, Bill-y's a sill-y.' It went on and on, tirelessly; her ears began straining for Billy's retort, which never came. 'Bill-y's a . . .'

'Hallo.'

The taut, colourless voice seemed only to deepen a present impression, as if she had heard it, already, before it spoke.

'My dear, I'm sorry about this. I can't explain now, I will when I see you. Can you come this evening? I shan't be free till then.'

'Yes . . . Well, the only thing is . . . About what time?'

'You can't say anything now, I suppose?'

'Not very well.'

'Would the afternoon be better?'

'If possible.'

'Come over to the surgery, then. I'll be there at four.'

'If that's all right? I thought ... ?'

'Yes. That doesn't matter ... Julian, are you there?'

'Yes.'

'You know this is important?'

'Yes, of course ... Well – look here – would you tell him I'll be along about four, and see what I can do about it? And thanks very much for ringing up; I hope it wasn't a nuisance for you. Tell him I'll fix it. And not to worry. Good-bye.'

Hilary went back to the car and continued her round. The remaining visits were in the new housing estate, ancillary to the aircraft works. Most of the people here had moved out recently from the large towns and brought with them a pre-occupation with the affairs of their own street. To them the established local gentry were a species of privileged aboriginal, inhabiting an uncharted world. They were not sufficiently aware of Hilary as an individual to attach her in their minds to this or any other class; she was The Doctor, or, for distinction, The Lady Doctor. They offered, for the next hour, an escape so complete that it was undermining. She experienced, after every call, the sensation one has on awaking from sleep after some disastrous news, that one has perhaps exaggerated the night before, or even invented, that if one can fight off the returning certainty, the facts themselves can be kept at bay. When she arrived at the surgery, and found herself standing, at an hour when she was never ordinarily there, in its neat emptiness, she felt less ready than she had been when she had walked out between the yellow privets of Mrs Theobald's front garden. In the interval her supporting anger had grown cold and the pathogenic energy that follows shock had left her. Unable to bear a passive watching of the clock, she pulled out a drawer of dressings and began to tidy it. She was re-rolling a bandage when the bell on the waiting-room door sounded. She put the half-rolled bandage away; part of her mind registered a protest at not having been given time to finish it.

He walked through the inner door, which she had left ajar, and shut it behind him. It was a sharp, bright day, with a north-east wind; he had on a dark, heavy driving-coat and gauntlets, and his face looked pinched with the cold. He waited in silence. She felt, suddenly, terribly separate and remote. Just as she was about to speak, he said, strain making his voice impersonal and almost formal, 'Are you working here?'

'No. No, I was just doing something till you came.'

'What's happened?' He pulled off his gloves, looked round vaguely for somewhere to put them down, and kept them in his hand.

'I'm sorry I had to ring you up at home; it was awkward, I expect.'

'That's all right. I knew something had happened. What is it?'

'It's been happening for some time, but I've only just found out about it. I had to see you to-day.'

He stuffed the gloves in his pocket, came over and took her by the elbows. The skin looked drawn round his eyes and mouth.

'You should have married me. I told you, didn't I? I said something would happen. If one takes a chance, it always does.'

'Yes.' The known truth obsessed her, so completely that

361

she had not foreseen his thought, and did not recognise it even now. His stricken look seemed to mirror her own mind, and, amid her self-reproaches, she did not find it strange that he should reproach her. 'Yes,' she said, 'I ought to have known.'

'It was my fault, I suppose,' he said dully. 'I'm bad at talking about these things. One thinks one will, and then when it comes to the point, one feels it will spoil things. I thought, being a doctor, you'd probably warn me if ... well, there's no point in going into all that now. If we'd got married we could have gone away somehow and been by ourselves, and ... anyhow, not like this.'

His meaning began to penetrate her concentration. She looked up at him, stupidly.

'I feel I've lost you now,' he said, 'before I've ever really had you. Really, to myself ... I'm sorry. It's rotten of me to talk to you like that, you must be as worried as hell. We'll get married straightaway, of course. How soon—' He stopped and swallowed – 'how soon are you going to have it? Do you know?'

She had not meant, when she found her voice, to exclaim with exasperation; the sound seemed to escape of its own accord. 'Oh, Julian, be sensible. As if I'd have sent for you pell-mell like this about a thing I'd have been suspecting for weeks. Don't you know anything at all?'

'Not a lot,' he said mechanically, 'about that part of it.' As delayed realisation went home to him, his face lightened till ten years seemed to fall away from it. He took her in his arms. His coat was so thick that this seemed to bring him no nearer; she only felt the pressure and the bulk of the cloth. 'Thank God. But didn't you see – I mean, what else would I think? I've been going crazy.' His voice had a crossness sharpened by relief. As if in an afterthought he could not make real to himself, he added, 'But what is it, then? Has someone found out about us?'

'I wish to God they had. That's why I sent for you. Because we're going to have to tell them.'

'Tell them?' A little irritably he drew his brows together. Then she saw his mouth stiffen; his eyes began, warily, to question hers. She went on quickly.

'I've wondered, often, why no one was different to me. I thought it was bound to get about, in a place this size, where everyone talks. I found out to-day. A kind woman let me in on it. It's Lisa you're supposed to be coming to see.'

'Lisa? Mrs Clare?' He spoke in an angry kind of helplessness. 'But – but how absolutely fantastic.'

'What is there fantastic about it? Lisa's no older than I am, and a lot prettier. People gossip about her already; she's supposed not to get on with her husband. We must have been demented not to have thought of it for ourselves.'

'But, Good God, Mrs Clare. Why, she's lived here years and years. Since before I was born.'

'Exactly, and I've lived here for two. I'm a foreigner, I hardly exist yet. But that's only the beginning. Since the last time Rupert was here, Lisa's going to have a baby. I'm the only person yet who knows. Now do you see?'

He said slowly, 'But, if he was here—'

'He stayed about four days. They spent the whole of it avoiding everyone. I don't think he put a foot in the village all the while; they're like that, when they're together. It's quite likely that the man who drove him up from the station is the only person who knows he was here at all. You know village gossip; what chance do you think the truth has of catching up?'

'But – but this is absolute hell. What can we do? I can't go round telling everyone that we – that I—'

'No, darling, it would be a little embarrassing. Have you still got that engagement notice you wrote out for the paper? You were right, you see, and I was a fool. We'd better have it in the social column now, it's more conspicuous than the other. That should be enough to give them a line.'

'Yes,' he said, 'of course.' She could see that his mind was not there in the room at all. She knew him too well not to have followed it home. Made cruel by the unspoken thought between them, she added, 'It doesn't mean you have necessarily to marry me, you know. After a decent interval we can always break it off.'

He looked at her then. What she saw pierced her bitterness and reached her in spite of herself. She said, 'Darling, I know. I didn't mean it. Of course I know.' And, a moment or two later, her confused emotions focusing absurdly, 'For heaven's sake, take off that awful coat.'

He got out of it, mechanically, and threw it over her swivel chair. Suddenly rousing himself, he said, 'God Almighty, what must you think of me? It's all come so quickly, I . . . Listen. Never think, because it's happened like this, that . . . I can't say it, you know what I mean. I love you more than I ever did, more than at the beginning. You must often have thought . . .' He paused; she saw a look in his face that she had seen before, though for a moment she could not remember when; the awkward shyness of one who must find words for what the best people do not say. 'You see, one's always known it would come to the same thing, in a month or two.'

She stared at him, questioningly, her mind entangled with the present; he went on, not looking at her, 'I forget if I told you I was in the University Squadron, and passed the tests and things. I rather got into the way of keeping it under my hat, because of trouble at home, and – oh, well, you know; I mean what's the point? What I mean is, I don't suppose they'll actually wait till the balloon goes up before they get us in. Any time now, I should say.'

Feeling her fingers tighten on his coat, he went on, with an air of deeper apology, 'I kept thinking, the last war brought her a pack of trouble; it seemed a pity to add anything on. But even so, if there'd been time to feel one could get anywhere ... I had a letter from Chris the other day; someone's going to read one of his plays. But, as he says, if they decide now to put it on they probably won't in the end, and if they do, by that time he isn't likely to be there to see it, and the whole thing feels a bit like make-believe. Well, that's no excuse. I oughtn't to have said that. One ought just to go on regardless; only, as Chris says, a bit quicker. He's started another play. I'm sorry; forget it ... Now this has happened, I'm glad it has. One can go on for ever, thinking and getting nowhere. Now it's settled. We can go ahead.'

'I love you,' she said, and then, 'I'm sorry I wouldn't marry you when you wanted. I wasn't only thinking of myself.'

'I know. I knew why it was ... You're too good for me, you know that.'

'Julian, don't.'

'Why not? That's the whole thing about it, really. It always has been.'

Longing for some escape, however brief, from this moment, she searched her mind for something different to speak of, and she thought of asking whether he had heard yet from Padraic Finnigan, for it was more than a week now since he had told her that next day he would send the letter off. But she did not ask; she knew that she had just been told the answer. She said, 'If you feel like coming to see me to-night, do. I'll leave the doors for you. Or not, just as you feel.'

'Thanks ... If I don't turn up, don't think it's because things have hung fire again. That won't happen now.'

'I know.' This was true. She was certain now; not of a lover, of a schoolboy who knew the rules. It was time to own up and take one's beating, when someone else was being put on the mat. Now that it was gone she scarcely felt it, the victory on which it had seemed that everything depended, and its shadow slid from her opened hands. She kissed him, feeling that it was he who grieved for it, who thought she had been cheated of her rights. What she herself was thinking was that if she had not teased him about Lisa he would like her better, and that would have helped. But at school too, she remembered, it was often liable to be someone for whom one didn't much care.

'When we're married,' he said, 'I'll make up to you for all this.'

She smiled at him. 'When we're married, I won't turn you out of bed at four in the morning.'

'That's definitely a thought.' Both of them felt that this was a moment to be seized. He let her go and picked up his coat. 'It must be tea-time. Let me give you some, somewhere, before you go back. Look, I tell you what, let's start being dashingly blatant straightaway, and have it at The Crown. We'll sit at the middle table and exchange flaming glances when everyone's looking. Come on.'

'If you like. I expect we shall find ourselves flaming at a brace of commercial travellers, on the way through from Bristol.'

'Never mind. Dress rehearsal. Oh, and remind me on the way there to buy some cigarettes.'

18

The curtains were still open; the last of the sunset was fading from thin green into pewter. From its source in a city where encircling brick had made it already night, flying through the dusk to be recreated in its little cage of walnut and glass and wire, the voice read on.

'To the beauty of earth that fades in ashes.
The lips of welcome, and the eyes
More beauteous than . . .'

'Another cup of coffee, dear? . . . Oh, were you listening? Never mind, it's still quite hot.'

'Till once again the witch's guile entreat him:
But, worn with wisdom, he
Steadfast and cold, shall choose the dark night's
Inhospitality.'

The cage, for a moment untenanted, purred and crackled softly to itself. Outside, two starlings clashed over a roosting place, swore shrilly, and were abruptly silent.

'That concludes this evening's reading, which was from the poetry of Walter de la Mare. We are now taking you over to the New Rialto Cinema, Hackney, for a . . .'

'Turn it off, dear, will you, before it has time to begin?'

' . . . Song-hits of Yesteryear.'

'Julian. Do please wake up and stop that horrible noise.'

'Oh, sorry.' The heaving tremolo faded to a whimper, and clicked out.

'I thought you were listening, but if you could sit through *that* . . . Are you well, my dear? You've been day-dreaming terribly this evening.'

'Yes, of course, thanks. I was just thinking. Is there any coffee to spare?'

'My dear boy, I offered you some only a moment ago. You're not very good company to-night, are you? I spent such a dull afternoon at the Harpers and now I want to be entertained. Come and sit down here and tell me what you've been doing. Did you get to the bottom of the trouble with Tony's car?'

'You'd never do that. It's beyond everything but first-aid.'

'I must say he seems very incompetent with it himself. It was lucky for him that Dr Mansell happened to pass. I didn't know they knew one another; the family have always gone to Dr Dundas.'

'I suppose they've met somewhere.' He stirred his coffee, bringing the sugar to the surface and letting it sink again. Now, he thought. Now.

She had come to the end of the ball of wool with which she was working, and was splicing it carefully to another; soft, white rabbit wool for the edging of a bed-jacket. The jacket was pale green; her dress, on which it lay, of stiff brown silk, falling composedly to the ground. She moved her hands nearer to the light; fine, narrow hands, with two beautiful old rings,

368

and the wide gold band, lying on them loosely. There was a story about the emerald; when he was cutting his first teeth, he had bitten on the stone which had come away; she had got it out of his mouth just in time. A year or two later she had told him about it, and that he could still remember. 'If I'd swallowed it, Mummy, would I have been valuable too?' She had lifted him up into a smell of lawn and lavender and kissed him. 'If that ring could swallow you, my precious, it would be the most valuable ring in the world.' He had asked her the same question next night at bedtime, to make it happen again; but she had said, 'Conceited little boys are never valuable, whatever they swallow,' so he had not tried it after that, knowing already that to be conceited was worse than other forms of naughtiness, and took much longer to put right.

She had almost finished her business with the wool. There would still be time to change the subject before she could pursue it. But he had vowed to himself to accept the first signal that offered; if he refused one, he would refuse them all. He had had as it was to let one pointer go, for it would have been an impossible start, owning to a lie; besides, she might think he had been put up to it, she would want to think that. But now ... He finished his coffee, framing it in his head: I'd rather you didn't talk about her like that, Mother, because I've been seeing a good deal of her lately, and ...

'Do you know, Julian, what I've been thinking?'

'No?'

'That this year we might turn the path by the south wall into a rock garden. Do you remember one of the college gardens – I forget which?'

'St John's?'

'Yes, of course. We can get the stones sent from the quarry, but I think, don't you, we could arrange them ourselves, with you to manage the heavy ones? We shall enjoy it when it's finished so much more.'

'It should look pretty good. What about the pear-tree?'

'It's getting old; it never bears well now. Mrs Layton says their rock garden's so overgrown that she could spare us quite a number of things, for a beginning. It's not a thing I should care to tackle alone; but then, why have tall sons if one doesn't make use of them?' Her fingers, light and cool, rested for a moment against his cheek. As he leaned his head towards them, they moved away.

'Fetch me my glasses, will you, dear? This wool's so fluffy, it's hard to see.'

He went up and found them, lying on the drawn-thread runner among the silver and cut-glass. She had dropped a little powder on them as she dressed; on the way down he rubbed the lenses with his handkerchief, the faint scent clung to the linen as he put it away. Pausing in the hall, he thought, one could simply walk in at the door and say, 'There's something I want to talk to you about.' But she was waiting for the glasses, he would have to give her those first.

'Here they are. All polished up.'

'Thank you, dear.' She put them down on the walnut table beside her. 'Just take a look at the *Radio Times*, and see if there's anything we might like to hear when this thing is over.'

'A music-hall, on the Regional. I'll try Daventry if you like; there's some Shakespeare, *Taming of the Shrew* ...' He found himself adding, with overpitched, deliberate emphasis, 'Good Lord!'

'Why do you say that?'

'A man's producing it that I know.'

'Someone you knew at Oxford, you mean?'

He felt a kind of giddiness which was not of the senses, a

terrified exhilaration like the moment in his first solo, when he discovered the undercarriage to have left the ground. What had made him do it this way, of all ways? But it was done. In that exclamation over the programme, needless, easy to have suppressed, he had given himself the signal. It had begun.

'Yes. He was assistant producer in *The Dream*. When I was Oberon.'

Silence. He looked up. She was bent over her crochet hook, quietly working. What answer, beyond silence, could he have foreseen? Silence, and the dark night's inhospitality. The solitude enclosed him, familiar, yet strange; for this was the first time he had ever bidden it to him. For a moment, feeling its first chill, his mind flew to the familiar resources, the tricks for redemption and return. But, suddenly, all he could remember was a moment behind the dressing-screens; Toller clowning, stripped to the buff except for the ass's head, and himself coming in with the noise of applause drifting after him. Lest anyone should suppose he was listening, or wished them to listen, he had said, 'Tally-ho!' and prodded with his silver boar-spear at Toller's rump. And now, in the dark night's inhospitality, it was this moment that reproached him and would no longer be betrayed.

'I'm glad,' he said, finding his voice not much different, 'that Johnny's got his foot in somewhere. He was good all round. By the way, he did a quite handy line in photography. Did I ever show you the one he did of me? In the play, I mean?'

The needle jerked evenly on. He began to think she would not speak at all. When she did it was without checking her fingers.

'No, thank you, Julian. If I'm to see a photograph of you, I prefer one as you are, not striking attitudes with a painted face.'

Now he knew the point to which they were moving; to which he had known always that they must first return when the time came. He had forgotten this certainty, but it had directed him. His mouth felt dry, and the palms of his hands wet.

'It was quite well painted. You couldn't see it at all. Would that make you feel better about it?'

'I'm afraid I shouldn't be much interested, in any case. Will you ring for Clara, please, to mend the fire.'

He went over to the coal-box and picked up the tongs.

'What I asked you to do, Julian, was to ring the bell.'

'How do you think a woman feels, being rung for to shovel coal with a man looking on?'

'I don't think you're quite yourself to-night. If you'd rather not stay here, I think I should prefer it too.'

'I'll finish the fire, shall I?' He picked out small lumps and placed them carefully. 'I was just thinking, we haven't discussed my future lately, have we? It struck me, seeing Johnny's name, that perhaps he could get me something. Broadcasting's very decent. Just a bodiless voice.'

'I should rather go into it some other time. I can't feel it would be very helpful this evening.'

'It's always some other time, isn't it?' He took up a thin log and balanced it on top of the fire. He could feel the blood rushing to his face, the remembered sickness, as if it were happening now again. It was strange to discover it was not happening to the same person. There was a streak of coal-dust from the tongs on his cuff, a bent shape. I shall remember that mark, he thought. 'There's something to be said for an announcer's job. I mean, it's safe. Nobody can wait for him to come off the air after his first broadcast and tell him' – he picked up the log by one end and thrust the other into the red of the fire – 'that he's got a cheap effect by exploiting his looks, which may be forgivable in a chorus girl but is revolting in a man. Or that he's given an exhibition of self-conscious charm that made them want to sink through the ground with shame.'

The room looked no different. He had a sudden thought that perhaps he had not said it at all, only prepared it like the other things, and would wake in a moment to find himself silently mending the fire. But the cold sweat on his palms was real.

The ivory hook had stopped. It was only her hands at which he was looking.

'I told you, at the time, we would never refer to that again. Those are my wishes, Julian. Will you please respect them; you seem to have very little respect to-night for yourself.'

'It's taken me – what is it? – seven years, to collect the little I've got, starting from scratch. Didn't it strike you at all that what you were talking about wasn't something that had just happened; it was me; not now of course, there wasn't anything left, I just had to begin again. I don't think you know what that means.'

'I know what it means, Julian, a great deal better than you do. Please don't use these wild exaggerations; it's hysterical, and it doesn't impress me. If something's happened to upset you, tell me about it straightforwardly. I should be sorry to let you go to bed in this state.'

'It shouldn't have upset me, of course, being sliced to nothing after my first proper part. Sort of thing one ought not to notice. But people do mind, in some extraordinary way.'

He looked up; he could manage it now. As always when she shut him out, he could read nothing in her face except exclusion; yet he felt the surface brittle; unknown movements of the will were going on behind it. He was shaking a little, but only felt it vaguely.

'I think I must take you to see Mr Sanderson again. I've noticed, of course, that you've never been the same since that operation. I told Dr Lowe so, but he considered that it was nerves and that it would be better to ignore it, so I said nothing. Try, please, to control yourself, and remember that you're speaking about a little entertainment given by schoolboys, not about some important step in your career.'

'You could hardly call it a step, I suppose; no.'

'Since you've let yourself dwell on it, I'll say this, and then we'll talk of something else. I didn't want to hurt your feelings; you should have known that I've always put your interests first. You know how delighted I was, for instance, when you were made a prefect and when you got your House colours, don't you?' She paused, commanding a reply. He forced himself to withhold it. As if he had answered, she said, 'Well, then, you see. But this was quite different. It was a cheap success of the wrong kind; it brought out traits in you which I'd always feared, and which I knew could bring nothing but misery to you or other people. It would have been mistaken kindness to encourage you, and very wrong. I was sorry to have to speak to you about it at a celebration, but I couldn't let it pass. One can't choose one's own time.'

'I shouldn't worry about the timing,' he said slowly. 'That was one hundred per cent.' In a kind of detached incredulity he heard his voice go on, 'You didn't meet Malcolm Blake, did you? No, of course, I was going to have brought him along afterwards.'

'I may have met him; I met a great many of your friends.' She picked up the crochet again, as though the attention which that would leave would be sufficient.

374

'Not Malcolm, he was finishing in the Sixth, we only got together over the play. He produced it and took Hotspur.'

'Oh, yes. I thought that was one of the younger masters.'

'No, that was Malcolm. He knew his stuff all right. In fact he was the only person whose opinion was worth anything, and he'd been pretty decent to me, so I was rather keen to know what he thought. He came along just before I saw you, while I was changing.' Finding a soiled ball of handkerchief between his hands, he put it in his pocket.

'If he wasn't satisfied with you, I dare say it was very disappointing. But doesn't that bear out what I said?'

'We never quite got around to that. He'd had a better idea in the meantime.'

'Do say what you mean, Julian. I should like to get this discussion over.'

'I was trying to put it delicately. But if you want it in words of one syllable, he just made what's vulgarly known as a dirty pass.'

Her hands sank into her lap. After so much calm, the horror in her face gave him a convulsive impulse to laugh. He said, 'That isn't the point of the story, you know. I hadn't got to it yet.'

'Julian. I can't believe – I simply can't believe you should have kept such a thing from me. When I think that I left you in that horrible place for another two years . . .'

'Well, it isn't usual.'

'Usual! I'm appalled beyond words that it should have happened at all.'

'I mean, it isn't usual to retail it at home along with your batting average. You learn to cope with that sort of thing down in the Fourths. It was a bit of a jar coming from Malcolm, I admit, especially just then, and I suppose I let him see it.

Anyhow, he told me I wasn't worth the trouble he'd taken over me, and he'd always known he was a fool to do it. He was a bit wrought up, of course. I thought he meant it, at the time.'

'He should have been expelled. It was very wrong of you not to tell me. A man like that should be stopped, before he has time to do harm.'

'Who, Malcolm? He wasn't a man like that, he'd gone a bit temperamental over the play. I doubt if the idea had ever occurred to him before that afternoon. However, if it does you good to know, I hit him as hard as I could.'

'I'm very glad to hear it.'

'Yes, I thought you would be. He could have beaten me up one-handed, but he just gave me a look and walked out. It was his last day, I never saw him again. Well, that disposed of Malcolm. After that I had a shower and dressed and came round to see you. Taking one thing with another, you can imagine all that about chorus girls and flashy charm went down pretty big with me.'

He got up from beside the fire, straightened himself, and waited. He had rehearsed it so often, though differently, in his mind, never for a moment believing that he would ever say it. He knew that, even now, a black wall would be split and light would enter, if after all she would take it back.

'I hope it was a lesson to you, Julian.'

He rested his arm on the mantelpiece and looked at her. At last he said carefully, to make sure, 'You mean you're still quite happy about it, you don't regret it at all?'

'"Happy" is a very frivolous and cruel word to use. I scarcely know you this evening; I can't imagine who's been influencing you. I suppose it must be this Communist you know in London, who sent you that play you were ashamed to let me read.'

'If you mean Chris,' he said mechanically, 'he isn't a Communist, he's Labour.'

'Please don't split hairs, this is much too serious.'

'Let's say, then, you'd do the same again?'

'If you'd been open with me and told me what a shocking thing had just happened, naturally I should have dealt with the matter in a different way. But later on, when you were feeling calmer, I should certainly have pointed out to you that displays of that kind do attract these unwholesome people. Besides, I told you how much it upset me that you'd been so secretive about the play, and told me nothing till I arrived at the school. To say you meant it for a surprise was such a weak excuse. You must have known it couldn't possibly please me.'

'In God's name, why should I have known? Why?'

'When you've apologised for swearing at me, I'll listen to what you have to say.'

'I'm sorry, Mother. But—'

'Very well; I hope it will never happen again. What is it you want to tell me?'

'I was asking you – why? Why should I have known? We're not living in the first half of the nineteenth century. How was I to know you felt like that about acting, as if it were like prostitution or something? Sorry, but you know what I mean. I've met some actors, you do in Ouds, they're just human beings doing a job. Why do you feel like this about it? I'm sorry if – if it's something you'd rather not talk about; but you must have known I'd have to ask you sooner or later.'

'I see no reason for discussing it. I'm quite well aware that some people on the stage are quite pleasant and moral; they're fortunate in having strong characters, I suppose. In any case, they're professionals. Why drag in such a side-issue?'

'You don't really believe it's a side-issue, do you?'

'All I understand in that remark is its rudeness.' But she was pulling the white wool through her fingers, so that its pile turned to a thread.

'I could have been a professional for the last couple of years. Don't you believe me? I mean I was offered a job, at money one could live on if one had to. I can't go on like this. Acting's my thing, I've known that since the first time I was inside a theatre. Why do you think I've dragged on since I came down, doing nothing; because I wanted to settle down into a local lad, like Tony? Whatever else I do, I'll only rot.'

He realised, when he came to a stop, that he scarcely wanted all this to end, without knowing that what he feared was the physical reaction afterwards. She was looking down; he glanced at her quickly, to gain an instant's preparation. But all he could perceive was that she seemed to be emptied, to have become leaden and null, so that her face looked, strangely and frighteningly, more a thing of flesh than of mind. Then, just as he had defined this thought to himself, she laughed. It was not emotional laughter; it was, in intention, humorous, forgiving, indulgent. It was like something cold creeping over his skin.

'Really, my dearest child, you're so absurd that I shan't trouble to be cross with you any longer. You'll be telling me next that you want to be an engine driver. Now stop talking like a big baby and getting excited about things that are over and done with. Just kiss me good night and go to bed, and we'll say no more about it. Come along, dear.' She held out her hand with the palm upward and lifted her cheek.

His face must have shown her, almost at once, her own reflection as clearly as a mirror. He felt this as their eyes met, and it was more than ever shocking that she continued to hold, with desperate fixity, the generous consoling look and the winning smile. Not only their falseness was horrible, because she had never in his life held out to him an insincere cajolement; but also their inexpertness, and the fact that she was afraid. While he was thinking what to say, his memory, ambushing him unawares, showed him the comparison which instinct had been thrusting off. His own thought so appalled him that he made a sharp movement of bodily withdrawal from it; but he could still see the woman's face. After he had walked past her it had occurred to him that she was perhaps hungry (she was ageing and shabbily dressed) and he had gone back and given her something; on which, like an automaton, she had begun all over again. I must be going mad, he thought; and tried to black-out the image with a convulsion of will. Then he remembered; she had said 'Come along, dear,' too.

Forcing his voice and feeling it dry in his throat, he said, 'We'd better get this over, Mother. I mean what I said, you know.'

'Nonsense, dear. You're simply havering.' It was a word she had used in his childhood, a nursery joke. 'I think when those doctors opened your head they must have filled in the hole with rubbish, I really think they must.'

The words pointed his mind to a refuge. Pressed out till now by more imminent things, the thought of Hilary possessed him suddenly; but it brought no comfort, for his struggling emotions twisted it to physical desire. He turned away; but this confronted him with his own face in the mantel glass. Hoping she would not see in the reflection that he had shut his eyes, he said, 'I'm sorry you feel that way about it. But if you don't care to give me any reason, I'm afraid I shall just have to use my own judgement, and go ahead.'

'You don't know what you're saying.'

He swung round; at the change in her voice everything in him had sprung on guard. It was as if he saw opening before him the precipice of his dreams, and a kind of vertigo was spinning him towards it. Better to leap than to fall.

'No, I don't. How should I? Why haven't you ever told me? Do you think I haven't the guts to take it? I think it's time I knew what my father did. I mean, besides dying for king and country and being photographed in a Sam Browne. What's the other thing you think I shall take after?' The dead blankness of her face heightened in him the sense of pitching down into vacancy. He gripped the edge of the stone mantelshelf. 'Did he dope, or keep half the Folies Bergère, or die of syphilis, or what? You couldn't tell me anything by now that wouldn't be a relief.'

He saw her turn white, and tried to be sorry; but he was feeling too sick to focus his mind. He did not know whether she was quick or slow in replying; it was all he could do to force himself to attend.

'If I were a man, Julian, grown-up as you are, I should thrash you for that. How dare you? How *dare* you stand here in his house and use this – this filthy language about a man who was better than you'll ever be? Yes, I won't deceive myself, I know it now.' Feeling her voice slipping out of control, she waited to govern it. 'He never did a disgraceful thing in his life. I wish I thought anyone would ever respect you as I respected him. But I've given up hoping for that. Every day of your life I have wished that you had been ... ' She checked herself again, and finished, more evenly, 'I have prayed every night that you might grow up to be something like him.'

He looked past her, into the room. Its properties were meaningless, like the accumulated properties in his mind, of which these few seconds had made so much junk. The outrage in her face and voice could not have been assumed. He could not think about it; he only felt a strangeness in his own absence of relief, in the tension which would not slacken, but increased in him so that he could have cried out with it, having no purpose left by which it could be eased.

He said dully, 'But I didn't.'

'If you had, you wouldn't be making me so ashamed of you now.'

'But then, what has it all been?' He tried to say, 'What is it that makes you hate me?' but, even now, the locks had not been loosened as deeply as that. 'Was acting against his religion or something, did he tell you I wasn't to have anything to do with it?'

'He certainly didn't consider it an occupation for a man.'

'Of course not. I could have told you that. You've only got to look at his face. No, there's something more, there must be. There is, isn't there?'

'Julian, I've put up with a great deal to-night. I really have no more to say. When you've slept, you'll be sorry you made this scene; but you need not tell me so. We'll both agree to forget all about it. Good night.'

Suddenly the thing which he had planned to begin presented itself to his mind as a safe and easy retreat. He did not know why; he simply felt it. There's something different I had to tell you, Mother; I'm getting engaged. Why had it seemed so difficult? It beckoned now like a heaven-sent bolthole. He could hardly believe he had rejected it, till he heard his own voice.

'Very well, Mother. If that really all you want to say, I'm afraid what will happen to-morrow, among other things, is that I get out the car and go after a job. I'd rather know whatever it is you won't tell me. But that's for you to decide.'

He saw her gather herself together; but he could tell, before she began to speak, that she was putting up a last screen, so he let himself relax for a little to be ready when it was over. He felt in the pockets of his dinner-jacket for his cigarette case; but it was empty, he had left the packet in his room. He would have liked to ask her where the silver box was that she kept for guests, but she was beginning now.

'You're my son, Julian, and I only say this because you forced me to it. But if you think, you'll realise that you have all the faults which would make that kind of life absolutely fatal to you. I've tried to train you out of them; but I'm afraid under the surface most of them are still there. You lack balance and self-control. You love admiration, though you cover it over; see how you've brooded over a criticism I made so many years ago. Without some discipline in your life, you'd become hopelessly neurotic. There's another thing I'm sorry to remind you of, since I think we've conquered it; you were very untruthful as a little boy. Such an artificial life would certainly bring that back again. And there's this, too; though you're not personally to blame for it, I'm afraid you must face this. Your looks are – no, perhaps it wouldn't be fair to say effeminate. But they would certainly confine you in a class that . . . well, a few years ago one talked about matinée idols. The type that shop-girls wait for at the stage-door, and no one else takes very seriously. They grow to live for that sort of public; and so, I'm afraid, would you; you lack the character to rise above it. You should have been a woman; I've wished, often, that you had been one.'

He had remembered, while she was talking, where the cigarettes were. Going over to the tallboy, he took one; then, recalling the rule, said, 'Do you mind if I smoke?'

'Since you've begun, it seems hardly worth while to ask me.'

'Sorry, I was listening . . . No, I'm sorry, Mother, I'm afraid it still won't do. I mean, that's an old story, isn't it, one way and another? And it isn't what you're really thinking about.

We'll leave it at that, if you want. But my mind's made up, I'm afraid.'

He looked her in the eyes. The combined effort of exploration and defiance was as racking as some physical ordeal, like holding a weight on the outstretched hands. Just when it seemed about to crack him, she looked down, picked up the work in her lap and turned it over.

'Very well,' she said.

His cigarette, which he had forgotten, had slipped in his fingers and was burning his hand. He glanced at it curiously; it seemed to have only just been lit. The little smart in his palm was the only thing he could feel to be real.

Passing her fingers over the white edging, she said, 'I should have known it would be useless. The evil in the world seems always to be stronger than the good. There's some purpose in it, no doubt. Yes, make your arrangements, Julian. I don't want to be told what they are. Will you go now, please? Good night.'

'Good night, Mother.' He would have bent to give her the kiss which, even when something was wrong and she had turned it into a cold ritual, they had exchanged on every night they had spent under one roof. But she bent over her work, turning away. He crossed the room slowly to the door.

'Julian.'

The door-handle had been in his hand when she spoke. As he turned back he was thinking that, if he had made the fraction more of haste which would have taken him into the hall, she would not have called again.

'Yes?' he said.

'Come back for a moment. I want to speak to you. Sit down, please.'

'I will in a minute.' He could no more have sat than he could have lain down and slept. She glanced at him standing there, and then looked aside; her expression was like a faint shrug of the shoulders.

'I said I'd done everything possible to keep you from ruining your own life; but I realise now that it wasn't strictly true. Facts do influence many people more than principles; I think you're of that type. At least I owe it to you, I suppose, to try.'

His first feeling, as far as he was aware of what he felt, was a kind of weary disgust with himself for not having been able, somehow, to shorten the preliminaries. He felt stretched already in all his bones, and aching; it was like having had to swim a river under fire and the real battle only now to begin. 'Yes?' he said again.

'You know I'm not a person who forms strong opinions without some very good reason. I hoped that might be enough for you. Once it would have been; you've changed very much lately, and not for the better. To show you I don't speak simply from prejudice, I want to tell you about a man I once knew who had most of your weaknesses. He had certain gifts, as you have, and he abused them, as you want to do.'

'You mean he was an actor?' He spoke not because he wished to say anything, but as a substitute for walking about the room.

'Yes, he was an actor. He could never have been anything else.'

'Most actors couldn't, you know.'

'*Will* you be quiet, Julian, and let me speak?'

It was the first sign she had given of snapping control. Curiously it acted on him in some degree as a sedative. He went over to the arm-chair on the other side of the fire and sat down.

'I met this man during the war, when I was working in France as a VAD. You remember my telling you about the base hospital, the Château St Vaux. I was there at the time. There was a French HQ a few miles away, and he was attached there as a liaison officer; he was a Canadian, but with an English commission.'

'French-Canadian?' He was thinking. Suppose this turns out to be some colossal anti-climax? He did not ask himself what he meant.

'On the mother's side, I believe. He was almost bilingual. He came to us as a patient, but I didn't meet him then. He had had some slight accident with a motor-cycle; minor injuries, but his face was quite badly cut. I was working in a different wing. The sisters who dressed him used to make jokes about his face being his fortune and say he was terrified that his looks would be spoiled; that was how I heard he was on the stage. I realise now, of course, that they criticised him to one another because they didn't want it to be thought they were competing; when they were with him I'm sure they behaved quite differently. But I was inexperienced for my age (I was twenty-five) and I imagined he must be getting very unsympathetic treatment. Besides, I was interested in another way. At that age I had a number of very stupid ideas; I think the most foolish was the value I set on good looks. That, I'm afraid, was partly my parents' fault. In most ways they brought me up very strictly, but they were proud of my being considered pretty, and discussed it more than was really wise. When I was twenty they commissioned a portrait of me, which was shown in the Academy that year.' Seeing him look up, she said, 'No, I haven't it now; I destroyed it, after they died. It would have hurt their feelings to do it before.'

'*Destroyed* it?'

'Please don't interrupt, it's quite beside the point. What I was saying was that having been allowed to think looks so

385

important in women (I don't think I ever entered a roomful of people in those days without looking round to be sure that I was the most attractive girl there) I'd developed an even sillier idea that they were equally important in men. Just before the war I refused a young man whom really I liked a good deal; I think simply on those grounds. Not that he was ugly; my own standard was absurdly high. I'd decided that if one had a gift of that kind, one had a duty to ... well, I tell you all this simply to show you how foolish my ideas were. We think people vulgar who are proud of making money; but even that's a personal achievement, of a kind. However, I was telling you about this man.'

'What was he called?' The words, as he spoke them, felt oddly familiar. Then he remembered how, when he was small, she used to tell him stories at bedtime, whose hero was always a boy of his own age; adventures with hunters and Africans, the backgrounds vaguely filled in from Victorian books, which must have been passed down from her parents when she was a child. Soon after the story had begun he had always asked, 'What was he called?' and she would say, always the same words, 'His name was Julian. Isn't that funny?'

She hesitated for a moment, and he recalled that in the stories she had hesitated too, to tease him, so that sometimes he had prompted her when she took too long.

'His name was O'Connell. André O'Connell. We had a very good plastic surgeon at the hospital, who took trouble with him because he was an actor, and the cut left scarcely any trace. He was discharged without my having seen him, but being, I suppose, short of amusement – we were a good way from a town – he was continually coming over on one pretext or another, and eventually there was an evening party, at which I met him for the first time.'

386

She had been talking with her hands in her lap; now she picked up her wool and began to work with it.

'I realised what the sisters had meant; his looks were ... I should say, now, ostentatious. Though he was amusing, I could see at once that he was not much liked by the other men; but I put that down to jealousy, having experienced it myself, there was one sister in particular ... When he left the people he was with and crossed the room to speak to me I was pleased, though I think I regarded it as a right; I was vain, as I say. I thought his manner delightful at first; but shortly after he suggested playing charades, because several of the men had leg wounds and were out of the dancing. That was what he said; of course what he really wanted was to show himself off. It was typical of him. He chose me first for his own team. I told him I had no talent whatever for that kind of thing, but he insisted on my acting a scene with him, giving me a part for which I was quite unsuitable—'

Julian opened his mouth interrogatively, but she forestalled him with a look, and he closed it again.

'And, instead of being helpful, he laughed at me for not having enough animation. I thought him extremely rude, and showed it. He apologised later and asked me to dance. He danced very well, though rather showily, and we attracted notice, which pleased me, I'm sorry to say.' She looked at the crochet critically. 'It was a waltz, from *The Maid of the Mountains*, called ... ' And then, as if reproving him for something, 'You wouldn't know the tune.'

He did, but said nothing. He had managed to reduce himself almost to vacancy, and did not want this state disturbed.

'After that, he discovered the times when I was generally off duty, and managed to see a good deal of me in the next few weeks. No doubt he interested me partly because he was a type of man I should never have been allowed to meet at home. He had, of course, as I realised, no background whatever. His father and grandfather had run what was called a stock company, and his mother had been a music-hall singer, I believe. He himself was much more ambitious, as he often told me. Just before the war he had been in New York, and had had some offer he considered a good one, but by that time he had made arrangements to enlist. It's very probable that he only said it to impress me. He seemed very little perturbed at missing the chance; he said that his looks would be enough to get him started again, and after that he could shift for himself. He spoke as though that were a quite normal thing to say. I didn't allow him to see I thought it bad form. He was very self-assured, and one is nervous at that age of seeming old-fashioned. As he was always ready to talk about himself, I said very little about my own family. He had the usual colonial idea that people of our sort were very arrogant and hidebound, and I was afraid he ... I allowed him to influence me in many ways. In the beginning, I had been interested in him because he belonged to a type I had set up in my own mind, but in time ... What *is* it, Julian; where are you going?'

'Sorry. I'll just get another cigarette. Don't bother about me, I'm listening.' He opened the tallboy, and, though the box was under his hand, went through movements of searching for it.

'In time, as I say, it was different. Then, one evening, he ... he behaved in a way which should have warned me, at once, of the kind of man he really was. Indeed, I think it did; but, shocked and horrified as I was, I made some excuses for him to myself; my own vanity, unfortunately, helped me to make them. However, I told him it was quite impossible for me to meet him again, and that I had no intention whatever of changing my mind. I think you'll find the cigarette box on the second shelf, with the bridge things. You had better bring it with you; when you fidget, it makes it very hard for me to think what I'm saying.'

He came back with the box, and after the cigarette was going, found it was an Egyptian, which he loathed. He continued, however, to smoke it, and to feel its taste and thickness as half-conscious irritants.

'A few days later I had a letter from him. I should, of course, have returned it unopened. However, I was weak enough to read it. He said in it that he was deeply ashamed of what had happened; that he should have known, and in fact had known, that I was not the kind of woman to tolerate it, but that his feeling for me had made him lose his self-control. He didn't put it, of course, quite as I do now ... He wrote that he had intended at the time to ask me to marry him – Julian, don't you realise your cigarette is touching the chair-cover? I can smell it even from here. Do get an ash-tray, please.'

He went over to a table at the other end of the room, where one was generally kept, hearing her voice still directed to the place where he had been sitting.

'He said that when he saw how angry I was, he had been afraid to ask me; but he hoped I would forgive him and marry him as soon as possible, as life was so uncertain at that time. He sent the letter by a French dispatch rider. That was the kind of thing he did.'

The ash-tray was there; silver, and highly polished. It seemed a pity to use it. He put it on the mantelpiece and remained standing beside it and flicking his ash into the fire.

'I was in a great deal of doubt and unhappiness; I don't think I slept at all that night. I had allowed myself, before all this happened, to become very fond of him; and after this letter, which was very persuasive, his conduct didn't make the difference that it should have done. What I thought of far more was how appalled my parents would be. I was afraid even to hint at it in a letter home. My father was in poor health (this was a few years before he died) and I knew they worried a good deal about me already, and exaggerated the danger from shell-fire and so on, which was really very slight. But on the other hand, Andy said ... ' She jerked the crochet hook quickly through its loop. 'Captain O'Connell said there was a chance of his being moved at any time, perhaps to the line ... I never discovered whether that was true.'

She had come to the bottom corner of the bed-jacket, and made the turning carefully, pausing while she did so. Julian occupied the time by closing the curtains. Parting the last again, he looked out. It was quite dark outside. He tried to imagine for a moment that he was there, alone. Soon, he thought, I can get away somewhere. Five minutes, ten; fifteen, surely, at the most; it wouldn't seem very long, if one were sitting with a book. If only, he thought, one could leave one's body in the chair to hear out the rest, dump it there like a ventriloquist's dummy, and from some dark hiding-place manipulate the strings ... With a nerve in the back of his head, he sensed that she was about to look up, and came back to the fireplace.

'One heard a great many excuses, after the war, for what wasn't excusable; that people's nerves were strained, that one was living in the presence of death, and so on. I always detested it. You were a child during the next ten years, you have no idea of the depths people reached in that way. Many of them had put up with very little; and, in any case, what is the use of having standards if they break down at the first test? I don't justify myself, because one can't justify deceit. I said to myself of course that my parents would understand, and that I would make it up to them in every possible way; but even if that had been so, it would have been no excuse at all for continuing to write to them as if nothing were changed. Letters like that are lies in themselves, even if nothing untruthful is actually said. And there was another thing which, although I thought a great deal about it, I knew in my heart could never have been right. Knowing he was a Roman Catholic, I agreed to be married by a Roman priest. In fact, I did more than agree; he would have been willing for a Protestant wedding (he told me he had lapsed, as they say), but I knew that he would be thought by his own Church to be living in a state of sin. It seemed too much to ask of him; I felt that I, who belonged to the less bigoted religion, would suffer less. So, in the end, it was I who insisted ... You wish to ask me, I expect, why I never told you that I had been married before; it will naturally seem very strange to you. You will understand in a moment or two.

'The priest who married us was a military chaplain from a French army rest-camp, not far from the place where he was stationed. He was very pleasant and kind, and I think in his way a good man, though he hoped I should become proselytised, I'm afraid. Still, perhaps that was natural, and one has certainly no right to judge him, for he was killed a few days later, when his detachment went up to the line again. I believe he died very bravely, giving a sacrament in No Man's Land, or something of the kind. It must have been quite irregular for him to marry a British officer, and I don't know how he was persuaded to do it. I expect he must have been deceived in some way.'

She said this as she might have said, 'I expect the maids must have overslept.'

'I forgot to mention that we had both succeeded in getting

leave together. I don't know how he managed; I have an idea he was much more popular with the French officers than he seemed with ours. I, of course, had told no one at all what I was doing. We spent our honeymoon at a small hotel in Paris; not uncomfortable, but the kind of place where only French people would generally stay.' With careful distinctness, she added, 'The Germans had a large gun, which they fired at the town from time to time. One could hear the shell coming from quite a distance; an odd noise, rather like a train. No one paid much attention to it.' She held the line of edging away from her, and, finding some unevenness, pulled and smoothed it into shape.

'The day before we were due to leave, he went out for a short time, I think to get theatre seats for the evening. We had spent the first part of the afternoon resting and talking about these plans he was always making for his career after the war. He had been showing me some photographs and cuttings from Canadian papers – only local papers, of course – about parts he had taken in various touring companies to which he'd belonged; I can't remember now, and it's of no consequence. I had been quite interested in the cuttings, and after he had gone, I took them out again, as we hadn't had time to go through them all. I knew he kept them separately; had they been with private things, I should, naturally, not have touched anything. One or two were quite long notices, the kind of thing that provincial papers print; gossip and description, rather than criticism as we should understand it here. There was an actress in the company with one of these very obvious and affected stage-names; I remember thinking that her real one was probably something very prosaic. Then I came to a paragraph which said that in private life she was Mrs André O'Connell.'

While she had been speaking her ball of wool had rolled from her lap to the carpet, a little way from her feet. She had not let her eyes follow it, unwilling perhaps to seem in need of distraction. Julian had been watching it; the tiny jerks it made, as the pull came from above, had given it an air of associating itself with the story. Now he took an uncertain step forward, and, kneeling, picked it up. He held out his hand to her, open, with the wool in it, his eyes on a level with her lap. She seemed about to turn towards him; but after all took the wool without touching or glancing at him, and dropped it into a secure place on the chair beside her. After a moment or two, in which he drew a little nearer without receiving any acknowledgement of his presence, he sat down where he was on the floor.

'My first thoughts were not of the kind people imagine. One doesn't, in real life, believe in such things happening to oneself or to people one knows. It seemed rather stupid and odd, and I wondered how the mistake could have happened; though provincial papers of course are always making these *faux pas*, one so often sees it in *Punch*. And I thought that if I had been a character in one of these plays of his, I should have taken it seriously and some absurd situation would have arisen. But it gave me, somehow, a restless, unpleasant feeling, and I hoped he would not be out too long.

'He was back within, I think, about five minutes. As soon as he got inside the room he looked at me quickly; and immediately, it was as though he had told me. He had remembered, after he was in the street, what was in the cutting and had come back to put it out of the way. He had not had nearly time to do what he had gone for; I suppose he would have found some explanation. But we both knew, before either of us had spoken a word.

'He told me, at first, that she was dead. I never had an instant's doubt that he was lying; I was recovering my natural instincts, I suppose. He admitted it, almost at once. He said, then, that he knew he was in mortal sin (a Catholic expression) and that it was because he hadn't wished me to have any part in it that he had told me this added lie. I don't think there was anything in the world that he wouldn't have met with some invention. To me, of course, everything he said had become quite meaningless. I think he told me something about his marriage, that they had parted after a few months and that he had had no news of her for years; that it would have taken a long time to trace her and that as they were both Catholics she would probably not have divorced him. I had no means of checking his story; I never had any wish to try. He saw, I think, that he was making no impression on me. When he'd exhausted all these excuses, he said that though he had felt unable to live without me, he had wished to preserve my innocence, even at the price of his own soul; it was the Catholic marriage he meant, I suppose. It was all so melodramatic and horrible that I couldn't realise at first what he was leading up to – he actually thought that he could persuade me to go on living with him, as his wife. It was some little time before I could make it clear to him what my feelings were.'

Slowly and with difficulty Julian lifted his eyes from a study of the carpet, every thread of which he knew, by now, like a part of himself. But she was looking at something in the middle distance, and her words seemed to be directed at it, as if again she must make an intention perfectly clear. Something was touching his forehead; putting up his hand, he found that it was his hair, grown heavy with damp. Very quietly, lest the movement should catch her eye, he drew out his handkerchief and wiped his face.

'I went back to the hospital. I didn't wish to meet people; but I was afraid that if I had nothing to occupy my mind I might give way to some wicked impulse. The Germans had begun to advance. I hoped I might be killed in the ordinary way, which perhaps was even more wrong, for had we been shelled others would have suffered. But it was more than the facts in themselves; it was the feeling that there was no justice in the world. There were women I had seen behaving with complete lack of decency and control, who for that very reason had not been subjected to the same ignominy. The very name. A police-court word. My mother had had a servant, a kitchen-maid, to whom the same thing had happened the year before, the circumstances were almost exactly similar. I remembered my father saying that she had been victimised because she was a respectable girl, and giving her money to help her over her – her difficulties.'

Julian tried to look up again. In the effort to force himself, he dug his nails into the pile of the carpet. When he could see the sweep of her skirt, with the highlights along its fall, he found he could get no further. Stealing out a hand, he drew towards him a fold of the stiff silk, and bent his lips to it.

When it moved, she turned her head and looked down at him. One of her hands, which had been lying on the wool in her lap, half stirred towards him. But even at this moment, when he could not have spoken to answer a threat against his life, his body carried, like a brand, its inbred eloquence. The gesture had finish; it was fatally and damningly right. Her eyes concerned themselves elsewhere; quietly she moved her hand across her knee, and, smoothing the stuff, withdrew it from his fingers. The whisper of its corded surface sounded as clearly as a word.

There was a small piece of fluff on the carpet which he had been noticing for some time. He picked it up.

'Everyone at the hospital took it for granted that I had spent my leave at home. People asked, of course, the usual questions about how I had enjoyed myself. I felt so contaminated with falsehood and deceit that nothing would have induced me to add to it. So I simply said that I had had bad news towards the end of the time. It was assumed, I suppose, that someone I cared for had been killed, and nothing more was said. I was put on night duty. There had been a number of changes in my absence – more casualties had come in, and others had been moved to make room for them – but I found that Richard was still there. Your father.'

It came to him, dimly, that something was being expected of him. 'Yes,' he said. 'Yes, of course.'

'As some of the more senior officers had gone, he had been given a small room to himself; he was one of the patients whom I used to settle for the night. Most of them were glad to talk for a little, and I was thankful for the distraction myself. He told me he had missed me very much while I was away. It made me ashamed of having always been so cool to him, although I knew he cared for me a great deal more than he had ever told me. Your father was always reserved; nothing was on the surface with him.

'One evening the sister-in-charge came in while I was there, and found that I had made some mistake or other. My mind, of course, was not on my work, and she was quite justified in pointing it out to me, though not, I think, in the presence of a patient; she was an ill-bred woman, the staff there was very mixed. I behaved with the proper etiquette and didn't answer her; but when she had gone, your father said something sympathetic. It sometimes has the effect of upsetting one more than unkindness. I had been sleeping badly; night duty never suited me. At all events, I broke down; the only time, I think, that I had allowed myself to do it since I was a child. My parents were very strict about fuss and never took notice of us as long as we cried. Your father showed great kindness and consideration. When I was feeling more myself he said that he hoped I would forgive him for saying something personal, but that he had always felt that O'Connell was not, as he put it, up to my mark, and that sooner or later he would let me down. It was quite beyond me even to begin to speak of it; but when he saw from my manner that he hadn't been mistaken, he said that that was all he ever wished to know, and that if I would marry him he asked nothing better of life than to help me forget any unhappiness I might have had. I realised then that he was everything Andy' – she checked, but seemed now too indifferent to correct herself – 'was not; straightforward and genuine and controlled, the kind of man who respects a woman's reserves and would never ask anything from her which – which afterwards she would be ashamed to remember: the kind of man I was really adapted to care for. It made the last few weeks seem like a kind of nightmare. I knew that, feeling all this, I could grow to – to love him, as indeed I did. So I accepted him. We were married a fortnight later, when he was discharged from the hospital. My parents, who knew his family on the Stanton side quite well, were delighted, and didn't press for a longer engagement, which neither of us wanted. He brought me back here; he didn't wish me to return to France, and I was very glad to leave it.' Her voice took on the note of conclusion. 'Shortly before we were married, he told me again that he thought we should be happier if we decided never, in any circumstances, to refer to the past. I agreed, and we never spoke of it afterwards.'

Julian had been occupied with the piece of carpet fluff, which he had discovered would roll into different shapes. The cessation of her voice took him unprepared. He tried to assemble his mind, searching for words as one might for a lost coin in a heap of rubble.

'I am afraid,' she said, 'that if he had lived, you would have been a great disappointment to him.'

Julian looked up. The coin he had found was not quite what he had been searching for; but he was too weary to seek further. He said, speaking to the bit of carpet fluff, 'Don't you mean that I was a great disappointment to him?'

Her profile was as hard and clear as the head on a cameo. 'It has been my greatest regret that he didn't live to bring you up. I think he might have been more successful than I have.'

'Only after he'd taken a look at me, he – put it off for a bit?'

'Service on the Western Front was a very severe strain. A short time after you were christened – he was on leave then, as you know – he wrote to say that it was beginning to tell on him; that men reached a point when they dared not entirely relax, because the effort of going back was greater in proportion. A number of officers, he told me, felt like that.'

Julian murmured to himself, '*Journey's End.*'

'What did you say?'

'Nothing. Sorry.' Malcolm, an odd thread of his brain remembered, had wanted to put it on at school, but the Head had vetoed it; it had unhealthy undertones, the Head considered. The thread twitched, stirring others. He tried to accustom himself to the thought that this, which had impended all his life (for he could not reach back to a time when his instinct had not felt it, so that now his mind seemed to have defined its expectation) had come, and was over. But not over, for, he remembered, what he had heard was not a curtain-line (how gladly he would have seen the lights go down, and the sheltering darkness come); it was his own cue. He must tell her, now, that he would make the only amends she wanted, the death of the offending part of him, from which, when it knelt to her, she had drawn her skirt aside. Tenacious of life, it prompted him still with its outcast impulses; to lay his head against her breast where once it had been accepted, to kiss her hands. But she would only see an actor's gesture, and would make clear – as clear as she had made it in Paris – what her feelings were. Nothing was required of him but the single act of atonement. In his mind he had already made it, and scarcely knew in what blind impulse of delay he spoke.

'And – this other man – O'Connell? Was he killed, too? Or didn't you ever hear?'

She looked before her, patiently; as if she had hoped, now, to rest, but was ready to finish, even in superfluous detail, the task she had taken up.

'He was discharged dishonourably from the army, of course. I believe it was in Canada that he served his sentence. After that he returned, I imagine, to the kind of life where he belonged.'

He was aware in himself of physical sensations, separate from thought; sickness, or cold, or something of both. His mind, a little dulled by the feeling as in illness, pursued its inquiry.

'How did they get on to it? I thought you said the padre was killed?'

'One has a duty to society. There might have been other women. I informed his commanding officer myself.'

The cold spread in his body. He had felt something similar when he had put out his knee at rugger; not at once, but after he was off the field. If he kept still, it would go off in a minute, he supposed.

She continued, in the voice which implies that one is fore-stalling the weariness of further questions, 'I knew where the headquarters was, because – I had once been told. After some trouble in getting there, I had no difficulty in seeing him alone. He knew my name at once, and it turned out that he had been at school with my father, and at Sandhurst as well. He was so distressed, when he knew, that for a moment he couldn't trust himself to speak. Then he told me that he had always thought O'Connell the worst kind of Temporary Gentleman (that was a term the Regular Army had for people they thought outsiders). If it had been in his power, he said, he would have had him shot. I assured him that all I wanted was ordinary justice, and to protect other people. He said I must leave it all in his hands and that I could be sure my privacy would be respected. A little later he called at the hospital (I believe he let the Matron think he had a message from my father, he handled everything with great tact) and he told me then what was being done. He would have dealt with him, he said, even more quickly, but there had been some delay in tracing him; he was found eventually in the French forward line, where he had no business whatever to be. That was typical of him, the colonel said, and he looked forward to getting a dependable officer in his place. I hope he did; he was a very courteous and charming man. Some years later I met him in town at a dinner-party, and he gave no sign of having remembered me at all.'

Suddenly, as she finished speaking, Julian found that the heavy nausea had left him. He was still very cold, but differently – a light empty cold, as if he had been hollowed. Out of this emptiness, which was filled with a vague turning like the movement of smoke, anything might come. While one waited it was a little like being newly dead.

He said, his voice suddenly light and clear, 'And you never heard of him – O'Connell, I mean – again?'

'I saw him once; in a sense. You may have seen him, too; but I don't suppose you were attending.'

'I saw him? Where?' It was quite easy to speak now; one waited, and it came of its own accord.

'A year or two ago. In a film, at Cheltenham. There was a thing about Chinese peasants you were anxious to see; you may know the title, I thought it rather depressing. It rained, if you remember, and we had to go in early and sit through part of the supporting picture. It was rubbish, as they generally are; a kind of farce, about an American night club. He was one of the waiters. I knew him at once, although he was very much altered.'

'I don't remember the film at all. Did he have any lines?'

'He had the usual make-up, I suppose. He had aged a good deal.'

'I mean, did he say anything?'

'Oh, no. He was just moving about in the background.'

He said, half aloud, 'An extra, in a quota film.'

'I'm afraid those terms mean very little to me.'

Softly, under his breath, he added, '"And it's of no consequence."' She did not hear it.

'He had probably never had talent,' she said, 'except in his own opinion.'

'It would be hard to know. I mean, he'd find it a little difficult to get started, when the agencies asked him where he'd been. And if he got started, he could never star.'

'Do you think a man of that kind would have made any good use of success?'

He lifted his eyes, because he felt, now, strangely protected, as if he himself were a long way behind them.

'He was a rotter, of course. But I should think he loved you.'

She looked at him as though he were a stranger whom she only now realised to be distasteful to her.

'*Loved* me? You don't know the meaning of the words you use.' She turned the emerald slowly on her finger. 'You must always remember that the harm such people do doesn't always stop short with one generation.'

In the lightness and the emptiness, he said, 'No, I don't forget that. I see why you felt that both of us ought to die for it.'

She closed her eyes. But, even now, he could see in her face what it was that her first instinct had flinched from; not the thing he had felt, but the fact that he had expressed it. Suddenly he wondered what he was doing, sitting here on the floor. A bad position to speak from. It felt wrong. He got up; the box of cigarettes was where he had left it, on the arm of the chair. He took one and lit it, neatly and decisively, in the manner whose naturalness convinces from the right distance away.

'Well, Mother, thank you for telling me all this.' In a recess of his mind something stored away the sense of timing which the cigarette gave. 'I'm sorry. It must have been a pretty depressing job for you all these years, trying to lick me into a gentleman. I wish I could have done more about it. But I'm afraid what's come out, in the end, is just another cad of an actor.'

She sat upright in her chair, with the unforced straightness which, like a good seat on a horse, must be acquired in childhood.

'Yes,' she said. 'Unfortunately, you seem to be right.'

He looked towards the curtains which had beckoned him some time ago, and, through them, reached for the handle of the garden door. When he set it ajar he felt on his forehead a cool drift of rain. Out there the air was sweet and cold, and almost entirely dark. In a moment, he thought. He paused, holding the brown velvet open with one hand.

'Canadian-Irish. And French you said, didn't you. Not one of the old Quebec families, I take it. If you should happen to know at all, had he got the Indian strain?'

The heavy curtains framed him, as if he were taking a curtain-call. She pressed her pale, fine-edged lips together, and lifted her head.

'I have no idea, and I feel sure he had none either.' Her eyes travelled, in what seemed a detached surmise, over the tall young man holding, between the curtains, the easy-seeming, perfectly effective pose. Presently she added, 'He was very dark.'

Julian considered this, holding the curtain steady in its folds. 'I see. Well, never mind. It wouldn't really matter, apart from getting married. One feels one should give people some idea ... Oh, of course, that was what I started out to tell you. I'm going to marry Hilary Mansell. But you won't mind about that, now.'

The little heap of green slid from her lap as she rose to her feet; a soft trail of white led down to it from the ball in the chair.

'I think you must be mad. We know nobody of that name.'

'That's all right, Mother. I mean who you think I do.' He was about to go, but stopped to add, 'Of course, now, I shall have to ask her again. I'd rather, for one thing, be living on money that's really mine, as soon as I can make any. The great thing, I suppose, is to stay out of jail. Well, that seems to be everything. I think I'll just go out for a bit. Good night.'

He hesitated, still, for a moment, with the dark at his back, before he turned to enter it; and she was reminded (not realising it, among her other concerns) that his eyes were grey, like her father's and her own. What was in them did not belong to his words, or to his unconscious skill with the curtain; she had seen it, and felt it sometimes without seeing, many times in many years. But her imagination was with other matters; the curtains fell together, and the latch clicked home. In the silence the silky sound of her skirt filled the room as she ran to the still-swinging velvet and caught its edges in her hands. But she did not open them. She stood there, with her cold fingers in the stuff, hearing the light sound of his thin-soled shoes cross the paving of the terrace and fall to silence in the wet grass.

19

'Yes,' said Hilary into the telephone. 'Yes, nurse. Quite right. Carry on as you are doing. I'll be there in ten minutes.'

She hung up and went for her bag. This, she thought with a misery too deep for bitterness, was the first night call she had had for a fortnight. Even so, it might have been something that would have let her be back here in half an hour. But it was an obstructed labour. She might be gone half the night. Half-past eleven. After all, he had said that he might not come. Of all human selfishness, she thought, the wish to be depended on is the most insidious; one sets out on Olympus and ends in the Cannibal Isles. Going out to the garage she said to herself for the third time that if he were coming, by now he would be here. It was raining, beside.

She was on the road when the thought she had been trying to shut out broke through her resistance; all the other times when his resolution had been fixed, the nights when it was to have been to-morrow. They rose up like a procession of ghosts against the flow of the road into the headlamps. In the end the only exorcism strong enough to lay them was the thought of the woman to whom she was going, to whom already her mind ought to belong.

From the sloping lamplit room three children had been expelled, along with the man who was trying forlornly to make them comfortable on the kitchen floor and to invent for them explanations of why they were there. Two small ones were almost asleep, but the eldest, a boy of five, was sitting bolt upright, listening with wide, nightmare eyes to the noises from the room above. Trying to make her reassurance of the husband sufficiently obscure, she thought, That child will remember every word I'm saying till the day of his death. I used not to let my mind wander like this. She went upstairs, where the nurse was craning after her from the door.

She was there two hours, and in the end lost neither the mother nor the child. One part of her mind was directing her hands through a matter of anatomy and mechanics; another part was with the unknown creature she was trying to free, which seemed to resist life more passionately than many she had known had resisted death. We ought to thank God, she said to herself, that none of us remember.

It was a boy. When at last she had brought it forth, it would not breathe; she had to go through the whole routine, the slapping, the swinging, the alternate hot and cold, before with a despairing wail it submitted to existence. Downstairs, the husband had made a pot of black, stewed tea; he hoped she would take a cup, if she would excuse its being served up a bit rough. She drank and commended it; but a sudden sense of urgency made her finish it so quickly that it scalded her throat, and when she was away, she almost ran through the dark drizzle to her car.

When she got back there was a light in the hall.

It was foolish that her heart should stop and pound at the sight of it. It was late, but Lisa, who slept uncertainly, sometimes went down for something hot to drink. It will only be that, thought Hilary as she walked from the garage to the door, and felt her hands and feet chilling.

Yes, she thought, it's all right after all, Lisa couldn't sleep. For there was Lisa to prove it, sitting in a dressing-gown by the warm ashes of the fire, with a cup beside her. Her heart settled again.

'My dear, are you having a bad night? Let me give you something.'

Lisa got up. Hilary thought, If it were anything to do with herself she would smile.

'No, I'm all right. But I thought I'd better see you before you went to bed.' She seemed to hesitate. 'Someone came. It might not be urgent. But I didn't quite know how to put it in a note.'

'You shouldn't have stayed up,' said Hilary mechanically. Her fingers tightened on the handle of her bag. 'I hope it's been nothing to worry you.'

'I don't know if it should have.' She smiled uncertainly. 'But Julian Fleming was here. About twenty minutes after you left. I rather thought that perhaps he wasn't well again.'

Hilary put down her bag.

'Don't worry, my dear,' said Lisa quickly. 'I mean, not about me. Please. It was no trouble. I hadn't gone to bed.'

In a dreamlike numbness Hilary comprehended all that the words and the voice contained. There was no time, now, to wonder how long Lisa had known, and how much forgiven, or felt not to need forgiveness. She only said, 'Lisa, I'm terribly sorry. Did he leave any message?'

'No. That was really what worried me.' She spoke without embarrassment, only with concern, as if about something that had long been taken for granted between them. 'I was just starting to undress when I heard something. I thought it might be

407

you coming in, and that I'd see if you'd have some Ovaltine, or anything, because of the rain. So I went into your sitting-room, and he was standing there. He was wearing a dinner-jacket and no coat, and I think he must have walked here like that. He looked like it, and I hadn't heard the car. When I came in he looked round vaguely and said, 'Oh, excuse me,' as if he'd never seen me before. I asked him if he wouldn't like a drink, or to dry his jacket while he was waiting, but I don't think he took it in. He said something about having just looked in and that he was sorry, and simply went, before I could stop him. I wish I'd let him alone. It's been worrying me ever since.' She looked at Hilary, and added quickly, 'It was just that I thought perhaps he wanted something for his head, because of having hurt it last year. If so, of course he'd have come to you.'

'Lisa, I ought to have told you—'

'My dear, of course you oughtn't. Whatever you mean. Let's not bother with all that now. All I've been wondering was whether you knew anywhere he might have gone. I just had the feeling it might be better if he had somebody with him.'

'He might have gone anywhere, and it's pitch dark.' She was distressed for him, but Lisa was engaging half her concern. Afterwards she thought that she might have done nothing, for she was slow with fatigue, if Lisa's words had not jogged her memory into play. 'At least, there is somewhere, I suppose. Perhaps I'd better try.'

'I rather think I should,' said Lisa, 'if I were you. I'd offer you something for the road, only it might be a pity to waste the time.'

Her mind, weary with the day's stresses and the night's work, still tried to refuse all this, reminding her that Lisa had never seen him, till now, except in moments of restraint and calm.

'He'll probably have gone home to bed by now. There's so

much I ought to be saying to you. You know, Lisa, this isn't the first time he's been here. I ought—'

'My dear, please. If it's that . . . I've thought so often, since I met Rupert, suppose I'd been married to someone else when he came. It gives one a point of view . . . Hilary, if I were you, I think I'd go.'

'He has moods, sometimes.'

'I don't think,' said Lisa, 'that he ought to be alone.'

'I'll go.' It was not till after she had spoken that the fear which had been accumulating under the surface of her mind drenched coldly over her. 'Yes,' she said. 'I'll go now.'

As she went she heard Lisa's voice behind her saying, 'If you find him, of course bring him back here. I'll keep Annie away.' She answered something as she shut the door, and began to run.

When she was driving she had a few moments' panic, uncertain whether she could remember the way. The concentration needed, the use of the map, were a kind of comfort while they lasted, pinning down her mind. After that was settled she tried to think of Lisa again; but her thought took colour from her own formless dread, so that Lisa too seemed to carry some shadow of fatality, and she imagined the coming child destroying her, as the child she had delivered to-night had nearly destroyed the mother to whom it had clung. She rid herself quickly of the thought, rating herself for hysteria. Two years later she was to remember the half-prescience which had sprung from the memory of Lisa's exalted face. Lisa, in the end, was to accomplish both her wishes; the child, and the reconciliation of her own and Rupert's irreconcilable lives. After no foothold was left in Europe even for the war reporters, Rupert came home to London, and Lisa to Rupert. No more decisions confronted them. In one of those hotel rooms, about whose recurrence in their story Lisa used to laugh, everything was settled for them while they slept. The little girl, kept in the country for safety (Lisa had rightly guessed the way her own choice would go) was left, to resolve in herself two elements so perversely formed to attract but never to combine.

Hilary thrust from her mind the finger-tips of the future – for it was important to be practical – and drove on. By now, if he had walked back, he had had time to be home, and, worn out, was probably fast asleep. She would be ashamed, when they met, to tell him about this wild-goose chase, which even he would think absurd. One was impressed by Lisa, because of her habit of understatement; but pregnant women were unstable – Lisa herself had confessed to nerve-storms in the past. Julian had looked, as sometimes before, disturbed and wretched; Lisa had been tired and imagined the rest. Another and more concrete thought came when she was half-way. By the time he could have reached the place – and, walking, he could barely be there yet – everyone would have been in bed for hours. The door was padlocked, he could not get in. This seemed so conclusive that she was easing the accelerator, and looking for a place to turn back, when stray memories came to her of other small country show-places, and the procedure when one went for the key. Four times out of five its custodian unhooked it from somewhere in the front porch. She cast her mind back to the day when he had brought her there and had talked to the woman at the door. There had been no moment of the time when he had been left waiting alone. Her foot went down on the pedal again.

She had forgotten that, unless the farm was to be roused, she must walk the last part of the way, and was already almost too near for safety when it occurred to her. She parked on a grass verge, and was thankful for the big garage torch which after her last call she had left in the car. Shading it carefully and walking softly, she crossed the yard. She was tempted to look in the porch, for, if the key were hanging there, she could save herself the rest; but she was thankful not to have risked it when, as she was climbing the gate, a dog barked and leaped on its chain. Her skirt had torn on a nail. She hurried on into the field; the track frayed into ruts and faded away. All she would have to guide her now was the outline of the hill; and she could see nothing beyond the circle of her torch. Putting it out, she stood still, sensitising her eyes to the darkness, and at last something was visible against the thick starless sky. She had her direction, and was about to switch on the torch again, when she was aware of something more: a fine flaw in the blackness, the shape of an inverted L. Then she knew what it was; the edge of a door ajar, thrown up by a light beyond.

She ran towards it, not daring to use the torch again lest its dazzle should blind her; stumbling through muck and puddles and half tripped by coarse grass; once a sheep started up, out of dead silence, almost under her feet, and her gasp seemed as loud to her as a cry. But after all this haste, when at last she reached the door she stood still; breathless already, she was almost choked with fear. Even with Julian, in full day, the cave had frightened her; she had had no time to think what it would be to enter it now alone. Suddenly she thought that it might not be he; anyone might be there, for any purpose, crime, or some obscene assignation. Nothing that happened here, at this hour, could fail to be horrible. Quieting her breath, she listened, but there was only the silence she remembered, more powerful than any sound. She was beginning to feel sick and could trust herself to delay no longer. Flattening herself to leave the rusty hinges unstirred, she went in.

As she squeezed through the narrow fissure at the ladder's foot, she told herself, This is the worst, it will be better beyond.

It was longer than she had thought; her head and chest felt compressed and there was a bursting in her throat. The passage bent; she was through, she drew breath and looked. But the first chamber of the cave was empty; and, beyond the pillar, all that was visible was empty too. She had put on the torch again, to give her courage through the crack; now, as she moved it, the shadows of the stalagmites moved too, stealthily, like things bending and crouching to spring.

She would look for a moment at the floor and think of nothing. For a focus she shone the torch there too. In the centre of its circle something dark stood out on a surface of naked rock; the print of a man's wet shoe, a nailless sole, with a fresh cake of mud.

Snapping off the torch she walked forward. The prints petered out quickly, dried in the dust; but she went steadily on towards the dividing arch, her own feet silent, for she had on the shoes wedged with thick sponge crêpe that she kept for wet days. She could not bring herself to call or even to speak. It was fear of the echo, partly; but much more it was the fear that only the echo would answer.

Reaching the arch she paused again. When she could look she felt a confused mingling of relief and fear; fear of the solitude, and relief because this part too was empty. He must have come and gone, leaving the lights forgotten. She could see everything, now, except the few feet still hidden from her by the screen of stalactites and the rock beyond them, which Julian called the chair. She was about to turn and face the journey back to the passage; but she did not move. She was not conscious of hearing any sound, except the thud of lime-laden water. She simply knew that she was not alone.

Still she could not make herself go forward, but stood with one hand pressed on the pillar where the light-switches were.

It was he who moved, rising to his feet out of the hidden space where, since first she entered, he must have been. He did not see her; and when she would have spoken, her voice was held, for the thought had visited her that if she called to him he still would not see. In the yellow downward glimmer he looked like the dead. He was mud-splashed to the knees, his hair and clothes sodden, his collar pulped to a rag and open; he must just have loosened it, for she could see the tie he had taken off dangling from his hand. As she looked he let it fall, then, seeming to reflect, picked it up again and stuffed it in a pocket. He walked on, away from her, till he was stopped by the edge of the pool, and stood there, looking down.

She was still gathering herself to speak, for his face made her more afraid than the cave had done, when he stepped back a few paces from the water, and she saw his arm move. She thought he was taking something from his breast-pocket, a handkerchief perhaps; he was half turned from her, so that she could not clearly see; but now she realised that he had made the sign of the cross. When he knelt she thought that it was to pray, and that she would wait, now, till he rose, and pretend she had not seen and had only that moment come. But his prayers were said, it seemed; he was taking off his shoes.

It had needed this to make her understand. Even now that she saw, she stood helplessly frozen; for he was far enough away to be, perhaps, already beyond her reach. If she startled him he might not wait for her, so near to the promise of the last darkness which had become for him the promise of the first. After the final rejection, the final return.

There would be no time to overtake him, either on his way, or after, when a running dive had carried him into the covered water under the rock. He stood for a moment with his shoes in his hand, then pushed them deliberately into the pockets of his jacket, and began to strip it off. Suddenly she knew the only thing that was left to do, with any certainty of checking him. Reaching up to the switches just above her head, and hesitating for a second to get the right one, she put out the light.

She heard the wet thud of his weighted coat on the ground, then stillness. It was all clear to her now, as if it had been solved for her while she was somewhere away. She crossed quickly to the throne of rock, while she still remembered distance and direction; groped, felt it under her hand, and sat down.

'Julian,' she called softly. 'Julian.'

She heard him move; but so slightly, his shoes being off, that she could not tell which way he was going, and a terror seized her that, in his familiarity with the place, the darkness might be no hindrance to him. Forcing her voice into control, she said again, 'Julian. Come here to me.'

As she ended the last word one of his hands brushed her. She reached out for him and would have risen; but already his head and arms were on her knees.

The cold of his body horrified her; he might have been already drowned. As once before, she gathered the edge of her coat round him; but when it touched him, he began to tremble so violently that it slid away. She took him in her arms, and lifted his head. He began to speak; she could hardly hear, because his teeth were chattering. 'I didn't know I'd done it.'

'Darling, you're here with me.'

He put up a hand to touch her face and dress; then clung to her, silently. After a few moments he whispered, 'Oh, God. I'm so cold.'

'Dear, I know.' She covered him with the coat again. 'You must come home now,' she said softly. 'You've been out too long. You're tired. You must have a hot bath and a drink, and come to bed.'

He shook his head. His voice muffled in her breast, he was trying to tell her something. She could hear less than half he said. It told her, however, as much as for the present she needed to know. She held him closer, thinking not so much of what she had learned as of what she must do for him; that there was a rug in the car, and the flask of coffee which she had not had to-night, that she must put on the bedroom fire, or perhaps Lisa, being what she was, would have done it already. While her mind ran on these things she murmured over him without much thought of what she said, the kind of foolishness she had indulged sometimes while he slept. 'My dearest boy,' she whispered, 'my beloved, my beautiful.'

He made a sudden violent sound; it was like something tearing in him. Pulling his face away from her, he pressed it into his arm. The sound came again, muffled; she could tell that he had shut his teeth on the flesh. She felt painfully helpless. The nurses used to say to women, 'Have a good cry, dear; it will make you feel better.' But though she had heard men groan often, and had once heard a man scream, she had never heard one cry, and found that she did not know whether it made them feel better or not. Judging by what she had just heard it seemed unlikely. 'There, my darling,' she said uncertainly, 'you're tired and cold. You're not well. I'll take you home.'

'No.' His breath caught; he stopped till he was ready. 'I'm no good.'

'I love you; what about me?'

'I'm no good to anyone.'

She stopped thinking; there seemed suddenly no occasion to think. She loosened her dress to make a warmer place for his head, and took him into it. The words seemed not to come from her mind, but from some deep place in her body, as blindly and certainly as a caress in the night.

'You're the best of all. You're what I wanted always. Before you were born I wanted you, and all your life. I always wanted him to be just like you.'

She was a fool, she decided next moment; she had only made things worse. But it came to him more easily now. He was starved with cold, she thought; it was draining the life out of him, he would be comforted if he were warm. So she slipped down beside him, on to the step of rock below the throne, where she could be nearer. At first he grew tense as if he were afraid, and began to shiver again; he had gone a long way, to-night, into his private world. She made him as comfortable as she could, leaning against the cold stone; and after a while he lay half relaxed and still; cautiously still, like a child who expects, if he gets himself too much noticed, to be sent away. But through his wet shirt he began to seem a little more like the living; and at last she felt against her breast the faint movement of a kiss. It was guarded, almost stealthy; not like a caress, like a half-hearted worthless claim that will be seen through and rejected, hardly worth making. It filled her with impotent anger; but all that was done with, and had never been of use. She said, 'I love you. Better than anyone,' and kissed him.

Soon they must go, but with his head in her arm she stayed for a little longer. He was quiet and, it seemed, at rest, and she could not bring herself yet to stir him into effort again, though sleep, his first need, would be at the end of it. Weary herself, she let her mind drift, and found it wander to the hours before she had gone in search of him; strangely, it seemed now as if all that while she had been seeking him still. It was true, she thought; for the second time that night she had listened to the resisting cry of birth. But this time it would cost her more. This time she was completing it not with her hands but in herself,

416

it was she who had it still before her to suffer and be torn. What she had now was not for her possessing. She was only the Madonna of the Cave, Demeter who fashions living things and sends them out into the light. All she had done, and had still to do, must work to accomplish her own loss; to separate and free him, to make him less a part of her, and more his own. Already the new claimants were waiting to receive him from her; the dangers of the coming years; death, perhaps, not this that he would have chosen but alien and lonely; if he lived, the work which would be his most demanding love; the men who would be his friends; the women who would be beautiful when the last of her youth was gone. Lisa had found an answer, but that was not for her. She would never bear a child to him. It would be too long before she could spare for its needs the love of which his own need had never been satisfied; before his mind was ready, her body would be too old.

He stirred in her arms. 'Now you're getting cold, too.'

It was true that she had shivered a little. She had not thought that he would notice it.

'This is a cold place, darling. Let's go home.' She tried to remember where she had put down her torch.

He got to his knees beside her and took her in his arms. It was the first kiss, to-night, that he had taken for himself.

'You were frightened,' he said, 'when we came here before. Aren't you frightened now, so late in the night?'

She had forgotten; but she felt what was needed of her.

'Yes, I am a little. I'm always afraid of the dark.'

He stood, and lifted her to her feet, taking her weight on his arm. Drawing her face to his damp shoulder, he patted her hair.

'It's all right, beloved. See, I've got you. There's nothing to be afraid of, if you just keep a tight hold on me.'

417